MJ Summers currently resides in Canada, not far from the Rocky Mountains, with her husband, three young children and their goofy dog. When she's not writing romance novels, she loves reading (obviously), snuggling up on the couch with her family for movie night (which would not be complete without lots of popcorn and milkshakes), hiking, Zumba and yoga (to make up for the milkshakes), swimming and camping (with lots of gooey s'mores and hard ciders). She also loves shutting down restaurants once a month with her girlfriends. Well, not literally shutting them down, like calling the health inspector or something. More like just staying until they shut the lights off. MJ is a member of the Romance Writers of America, as well as the International Women's Writing Guild.

Visit MJ Summers online:
www.mjsummersbooks.com
www.facebook.com/mj.summersbooks
www.twitter.com/MJSummersBooks

BREAKING LOVE

MJ SUMMERS

piatkus

PIATKUS

First published in the US in 2014 by HarperCollins Publishers Ltd
First published in Great Britain in 2014 by Piatkus

3 5 7 9 10 8 6 4

A CIP catalogue record for this book
is available from the British Library.

ISBN 978-0-349-40708-1

Printed and bound in Great Britain by CPI Group (UK) Ltd, Croydon, CR0 4YY

Papers used by Piatkus are from well managed forests and other responsible sources.

MIX
Paper from
responsible sources
FSC® C104740

*For my mom, who taught me that love is something
you do every day, and my dad, who taught
me to work hard and dream big.*

Neither of you should ever, ever read this.

Dear Reader,

Thank you so much for purchasing this book. It is an honour to have people willing to take a chance on me with both their valuable time and their hard-earned money. It is my sincerest hope that in exchange I will provide you with a true escape from the everyday pressures of life. *Breaking Love* (Book 2 of the Full Hearts series) is a romantic, sexy journey about starting over, taking a leap of faith and finding a family.

Those of you who read my debut novel, *Break in Two* (Book 1 of the Full Hearts series), have already met Luc, the leading man in this new story. This is not a sequel as such, but rather picks up where Luc left off in *Break in Two*. All of my novels are stand-alone stories with characters that are featured in the other Full Hearts books.

I hope that you will find yourself lost in Luc and Megan's story and that you will fall in love with them as much as I have. On the following page is a list of the songs that inspired me as I wrote. I am sharing them with you in the hope that they will enhance your experience of *Breaking Love*.

Happy reading,

MJ

Breaking Love Playlist

"These Arms of Mine" by Otis Redding
"Skyscraper" by Demi Lovato
"One Thing" by Finger Eleven
"Stay" by Lisa Loeb
"Fade Into You" by Mazzy Star
"Flowers in December" by Mazzy Star
"Come Away with Me" by Norah Jones
"I Will Be" by Leona Lewis

ONE

London—New Year's Eve

Rain nightclub exploded with the sounds of champagne corks popping all around as the crowd finished their countdown. As off-key strains of "Auld Lang Syne" filled the room, Luc Chevalier stood silently looking out the window to the balcony, where Claire Hatley and the love of her life, Cole Mitchell, held each other and kissed passionately. It was obvious Cole had just proposed as they embraced and when she stared down at her now-adorned ring finger. Luc felt a little like a voyeur, watching their tender exchange, but he couldn't look away. Why would anyone ever want to do such a thing? What would it be like to love someone so much that you lost all sense of good judgment and tied yourself down for the rest of your days? He had heard that being in love created the same chemical reaction in one's brain as heroin, which was the only thing that made sense to him about the whole affair.

His thoughts were interrupted by Simone Pelletier, his long-time friend and assistant, as she handed him a flute of champagne.

"*Tiens* . . ." she said. "You look lost in thought." She had noticed him staring at the romantic scene unfolding on the balcony outside.

Luc shook his head as if to clear his thoughts. "I was just think-ing we should put tables out there for the warmer months."

Simone gave him a skeptical look. "Are you sure you aren't watching the happy couple out there? It looks more like you're start-ing to regret not settling down to domestic boredom."

"You know me much better than that, Simone. I should go check on the kitchen. I want them to bring around more hors d'oeuvres." Luc gave Simone a quick peck on the cheek and moved briskly away.

Simone's heart fluttered at his kiss, as it did each time she saw him. She had fallen for him at her job interview six years ago, but the feeling wasn't reciprocated by her boss. Simone exhaled sharply as she watched his powerful frame make its way through the crowd. In her time as his assistant, she had felt like she had one foot in heaven and one in hell at all times. She was closer to him than any other woman ever would be; he shared his days, dreams and plans with her, but never his bed. She had watched helplessly as he courted other women, falling in and out of lust with them, each time wishing she would be next.

Two years earlier, Simone had gotten extremely drunk at a staff Christmas party and made her move, but Luc had turned her down, saying he would never take advantage of a drunken woman. When they came back to work three days later, she had slunk into the office, fully mortified. Luc had done his best to ease her mind while also managing to make it clear that she was far too important as his assist-ant and friend to ruin things by becoming lovers. Simone's heart had cracked at his words, although she managed to laugh it off, making it seem like the other night had been a momentary lapse in judgment brought on by too much wine. She tried to tell herself eventually he would realize they were meant for each other and they would be together forever. But after so many years of pretending she also was anti-marriage, nothing had changed between them. She was starting to lose hope anything ever would.

A few minutes later as he exited the kitchen, Luc saw Claire and Cole walking to the front door, arms wrapped around each other. Luc was surprised by an unfamiliar feeling creeping over him. He couldn't quite place it, but he realized it had something to do with not getting what he wanted. This was a new experience for him and not a welcome one at that. Luc knew Claire only slightly, having first met her on a flight from New York to London two months earlier. He had gone out with her only once, and she had left after only a few minutes, having been highly offended by his views on her previous relationship with Cole. Now that relationship was whisking her out the door. As much as he regretted not sleeping with her, he hoped for Claire's sake things would work out between them.

He needed to distract himself from this unsettling feeling. He was a man who was used to being in control of everything, including his emotions. He was used to feeling one of two ways: satisfied or restless. Most of the time, he was exceedingly gratified by his choices and his success, but there was always an undercurrent of restlessness which he attributed his wealth to. He was always ready for the next challenge, the next conquest, never one to sit back and enjoy his accomplishments but rather ever spurred on to the next challenge.

Luc quickly shifted his thinking to the successful nightclub empire he was building, with Rain as the crown jewel. Of the eight clubs he owned, this one was by far the most profitable. Everything had come together beautifully to create this enormous success. Rain had the right location and the right decor, and he had hired the right people to run it for him. He had learned the hard way, through trial and error, how to make a business thrive. Between his clubs and his real estate holdings, his fortune at age forty-one was large enough for him to have shed any concerns about price tags years ago. He had almost forgotten what it was like to grow up poor.

His lifestyle was fast-paced—full of travel, sex, parties and very little sleep; it was a life he never intended to give up. Luc was always going somewhere and rarely stayed more than two weeks at a time at home in Paris. His was not exactly a lifestyle that would allow a long-term relationship to thrive. He had been with a succession of beautiful women but it always ended the same way. Eventually they wanted more than he could give. He wasn't home enough, he wasn't attentive enough and once they realized he really *didn't* want to get married and have children, they would leave to go find their dreams. He wasn't a man who was ever going to become transformed into husband material. Luc Chevalier was going to remain unattached; he had yet to meet his match and he doubted her existence. When he *did* find a woman he admired enough to see on a regular basis, she would inevitably become jealous of all the women he was surrounded by at work, and they would start fighting. It had all grown so predictable that it bored him to tears at times.

* * *

Three hours later, Luc sat alone in his office, sipping a Scotch and regretting that he had given up smoking over a decade ago. He could use a cigarette right now as he pondered his reaction to seeing Claire again. He chalked it up to being tired and having not slept enough recently. Deciding to give up on his attempts at getting paperwork done, he finished his Scotch in one unceremonious gulp and grabbed his long wool coat. He shut his office door behind him and walked across the nightclub to the front door. It now looked like a typhoon had hit—party favours, confetti, napkins and glasses strewn everywhere. A few balloons floated along the floor as he strode past them, creating a breeze. Luc had let the staff go home without cleaning up; they had worked hard and deserved the time off. The considerable mess could be handled the next day. As he stepped into the cold night air and locked up the club, he became aware of how quiet the world seemed. It was the start of a new year and Luc couldn't shake the uncomfortable feeling that something was about to change.

Boulder, Colorado

Megan Sullivan, having just added another log to the coals, flopped down onto the couch in front of her fireplace. Elliott was now asleep in his bed. He had been fighting to stay awake until midnight but had finally lost the battle and nodded off on the couch. She had carried him up the stairs to his room and tucked him in with his favourite blue teddy bear. Now back in the living room, Megan picked up the bowl of popcorn she had made earlier in the evening and flipped the TV on, looking for something to distract her.

This was the worst time of the day for her—right after Elliott went to sleep. It was when the loneliness would wash over her like a wave during high tide. In the past five and a half years since she had left Ian, this time of day hadn't gotten easier, and there were times when she was surprised by just how empty she still felt. She and Elliott were better off without him, a fact Ian himself would agree with. His addiction to OxyContin and alcohol had ended not only his marriage but his baseball career as well. What had started as relief for a painful shoulder injury and subsequent surgery had taken over his life, changing it forever. Megan had tried desperately to get him help, but he had spiralled out of control in spite of her best efforts. She had been horrified to discover that no amount of love would fix him. Unless Ian wanted to get better, he never would—and until he did, he wasn't fit to be a father to their son.

Megan had pushed forward with her life without Ian, raising their son with the help of her mother, Helen. She picked up the phone to call her mother, who was visiting Megan's older brother, Mark, in Portland.

Her mother answered the phone on the third ring. "Hi, sweetie! Happy new year!"

"Happy new year, Mom. How is Portland?"

"It's been terrific, except that I miss you and Elliott terribly. I sure wish you had come with me."

"I know, Mom. I would have loved to have been there, but Mark and Lenna and the kids need to have you all to themselves for a while. We get you all the time."

"It probably sounds silly, but a week just feels like so long not to see you both. How's Elliott?"

"He's fine. I took him tobogganing with a few of the boys from his class today, so that was fun."

"Any of those boys have single dads?"

Megan groaned. "No, Mom. They are all married, and even if they weren't, I'm not looking, remember? I'm really, *really* not looking for a man. I'm starting to worry about your memory because you keep asking me that. We might need to take you in to the doctor to have you checked."

"Okay, I get it. You want me to back off. A mother can hope, can't she? I just want to see you happy."

"Oh, please! You just want more grandkids."

"Is there anything wrong with that?"

"Yes, and I seriously need you to drop it. Bug Mark and Lenna if you want more grandkids. I'm done. I've been burned once and I'm not going to let it happen again."

"You act like it isn't even *possible* for you to find the right man. It's ridiculous. You are letting one bad apple spoil the bunch. There are plenty of wonderful men out there who would be happy to be with a beautiful girl like you."

Megan let out a loud sigh. "Mom, can you just let it go already? I'm *so* sick of this conversation. We've been having it for years and you haven't been able to convince me yet."

"Is it so wrong for a mother to want to see her daughter happy?"

"I *am* happy, Mom. Trust me. I have a very full life."

"Oh, really? Then why are you in your flannel pyjamas already and sitting there alone, watching TV on New Year's Eve?" Helen asked, not willing to give up yet.

Megan looked down at her plaid PJs. *Damn it.* "Because I *want* to be at home watching TV rather than out on some blind date with a guy who is going to text me a photo of his penis while we're having appetizers."

"That happened once, Megan, and you need to let it go. That guy was an idiot but that doesn't mean they all are."

"You know, Mom, I didn't call to hear the 'you need a man' speech. I called to wish you a happy new year."

"Alright, I'm sorry. Happy new year, my girl."

"Love you, even though you make me nuts."

"I love you, even though you won't give me more grandkids."

"I'm hanging up now, Helen."

"See you in two days."

"Safe journey, Mom."

"Good night, sweetie," Helen said as she hung up.

Megan sighed as she got up and wandered over to the kitchen. She opened a box of Turtles that was sitting on the counter and shoved one into her mouth, followed quickly by another, filling each cheek with gooey chocolate. *I couldn't do that with a man standing in front of me.*

Staring out the window at the falling snow, Megan was suddenly overcome with a deep sense of frustration. The snow meant she would have to shovel her large driveway and long sidewalk again the next morning, a chore she hated. It was one thing that always made her feel so *single*, and not in the independently sexy way her best friend Harper was. Megan was single as the result of a tragedy. Her dream of raising a family and growing old with her husband had been stolen out from under her before she had gotten little more than a taste of it. For the most part, she had managed to forget how she got where she was and instead made the best of the life she had now.

However, the snow piling up outside reminded her of that tragedy. It was just one of the small ways that having a husband would have made her life easier. There were lots of things she had learned to manage on her own over the years. Jobs she had no interest in learning but had to do anyway. She had taught herself how to change the oil in her lawn mower and the battery in her car. Each autumn found her shakily climbing a ladder to clean out the gutters. But it was more than that. She no longer had that person with whom to share everything. All of her hopes, dreams, failures and successes were handled alone, as were the joys and burdens of parenthood. She had no one to share her financial worries with, either. Ian worked sporadically as a baseball coach for various minor league teams. He sent some money when he could, but it was never much. They had taken a huge fall—from living the dreams a major league baseball player's salary afforded them to living a much more humble existence. When Ian did manage to convince someone he could work, his drug addiction ate up much of what he earned, leaving little for him to send to Megan and Elliott.

As she stared out the window, she made a resolution. She would find a way to make enough money in the coming year to hire out some of the jobs she hated doing. Shovelling was first on her list. She had long ago stopped wishing for the companionship of a man, but she could sure as hell pay someone to do all the minor things she couldn't stand doing anymore. Yes, that would help take the sting out of it a little.

As she bit down into another chocolate, causing caramel to drip over her bottom lip and onto her chin, her mind wandered back to her conversation with her mother. She was completely fed up with everyone she knew trying to set her up or talk her into dating again. If it wasn't her mom or a friend, it was an insecure married acquaintance who wanted her husband nowhere near Megan, even though Megan was certainly never going to be a threat to anyone's marriage. She wasn't interested in dating a single man, let alone starting up with a married one and adding an incredible mound of complications to her already overburdened existence.

On nights like tonight she was still furious at Ian for needing the drugs more than he had needed her and their son. She was sick to death of her mom pressuring her to get married again and have more kids. As much as Megan loved her, it was a conversation she would happily never have again.

Her mom was one to talk, anyway, having had virtually no dating experience herself. She had married Megan's dad straight out of high school, and they had quickly had three kids. He worked for the post office, and she stayed at home. He had retired at fifty-five and they had spent four years travelling until he died suddenly of a heart attack. In the three years since his death, Helen had made no moves of her own to find love. She busied herself helping Meg with Elliott and volunteering as a literacy coach, insisting that she was too old to start over with a new man.

Megan reached for another chocolate in the now-empty top tray. She had polished it off without noticing.

"Shit," she muttered as she put the lid back on the box. She decided to leave the bottom tray intact until tomorrow.

She poured herself a glass of red wine and checked to make sure the back door was locked before making her way up to her bedroom, turning off lights as she went. She decided a nice, long hot bath was the way to ring in the new year. Setting the wine glass down on the edge of the tub, she ran the water and added some lavender bath oil, then lit a few candles and switched off the light before getting undressed.

She caught her reflection in the mirror as she walked over to the tub. At thirty-five, she still looked much closer to thirty than forty. She was tall and slender, with angel-blond hair cut just above her shoulders in a classic bob. Her skin was ivory, her face heart-shaped, lending a fullness to her otherwise slender frame. Her body showed hardly any signs of her having had a child, other than a now-faded line across her lower abdomen from the C-section incision. She had been lucky enough not to gain much weight when she was pregnant with Elliott, and her breasts had remained relatively perky. She knew that she was attractive, having received her fair share of male attention since she was a teenager. None of that mattered to her anymore, however. Whatever currency her beauty had earned her as a younger woman was now irrelevant. Megan would just as soon be utterly plain in order to avoid advances from the opposite sex.

Her looks had gotten her into the arms of a major league baseball player; her fun-loving and caring nature had secured her there. In the end, relying on a man to take care of her had ended in disaster. If the experience with Ian had taught her anything, it was to stand on her own two feet, to support herself and to never again rely on someone else to look after her. There was no trace of the carefree, quick-to-laugh woman she once had been. Megan had replaced her with someone strong, independent and hardened.

She had books, wine, baths and BOB, her battery-operated boyfriend, to keep her company. None of them would ever leave the toilet seat up, forget to call when they were out of town or develop a serious drug problem. She had already gone years without a man, and she preferred to keep it that way. As she slid into the soothingly hot water, she felt her frustrations start to dissolve and her body begin to relax. She would find a way to pay for what she wanted from a husband—help around the house. The rest she would leave for women who still believed in fairy tales.

TWO

"What do you think? Does it look a little bit like a cat?"

"Nope. I think you made Mickey Mouse again, Mom," answered Elliott, who was standing on a stool beside the stove.

Megan stared down at the large pancake in the pan. "I think you're right, buddy. You know, if you would just ask for Mickey every time, I'd have an almost one-hundred-percent accuracy rate."

Elliott grinned at his mother. "What would be the fun in that?"

"The fun would be in the feeling of victory I would have at getting it right every time. Now, go rinse the raspberries, already. They've been sitting in the sink calling your name for ten minutes now."

"Okey-dokey. But I get extra syrup because it's a new year," Elliott proclaimed as he climbed down and moved his stool to the kitchen sink.

"Since when is that a tradition? Besides, I decided your New Year's resolution should be to give up sugar."

"What?! No way! Sugar is my favourite food group. I can't live without it." His eyes were wide, showing his distress at the thought.

Megan smiled at him. "That's because you are exactly like your mother. Alright, extra syrup, but only because you're going to help me shovel us out of here today."

The phone rang before Elliott could start complaining. "I'll get it!"

Each time the phone rang, it broke Megan's heart a little. She knew Elliott was secretly hoping it was his dad, even though he would deny it if she asked. They hadn't heard from Ian over Christmas, even though he had promised to come up from Florida to see Elliott during the holiday. Megan could tell it wasn't him as soon as Elliott heard the voice on the other end. She watched as his face fell a little, wishing she hadn't allowed her son to hold out so much hope that his father would ever be a bigger part of his life.

"Hi, Auntie Harper," he said, trying to sound enthusiastic. "Where are you today?"

There was a pause, and then Elliott said, "Good. Santa brought me a new toboggan and Lego Hobbit stuff."

"Thank her for the Wii game," Megan whispered to her son.

"Oh, my mom said I have to thank you for the Wii game." He paused again. "Yeah, she is bossy. She says that's how moms are supposed to be."

Megan took the phone from him. "Go wash the berries," she whispered to him. "Hello, Harper! How was your New Year's Eve extravaganza?"

Harper Young, who had been Megan's best friend since high school, spoke in her usual lively tone. "It was great until some total asshat lawyer got a little too handsy. Other than that, New Year's Eve in New York is amazing. How was yours?"

"Pretty quiet, just the way I like it."

"Liar. You're trying to convince yourself that you like it quiet. I know better. I saw you as a teenager."

"Well, I grew up—unlike some people," Megan replied, cradling the phone against her neck so she could pour another scoop of batter into the pan.

"You didn't grow up. You got old. You're like an eighty-year-old in a hot, young body. Which brings me to my New Year's resolution—to get you laid."

"Oh, for . . ." Megan wanted to swear but had to censor herself with Elliott in the room. "Seriously, not necessary. Thank you for the offer, though."

"Oh, it's happening, lady! You are coming with me to Paris! I'm running a photo shoot there in three weeks and you're coming with me. Anita Wolfe is shooting. I told her about you and she said to bring you along and she'd be happy to give you a few pointers! Seriously, Megs, you'll learn a *ton* watching her!"

"Okay, first of all, you seem to be forgetting I have a child, so I can't just up and leave for Paris whenever the whim strikes me. Second, I don't exactly have a lot of money to spend on trips. Third, I'm not a fashion photographer; I do weddings and family stuff, which is completely different."

"You're coming. I already talked to your mom. She's going to stay at your place. It's only four days. Elliott will be just fine without you. As far as money is concerned, you're staying in my suite and your flight will be covered because I told the magazine I'm trialling you as my new assistant, so the trip is virtually free. I've taken away all of your excuses."

"You talked to my mom? Harper . . . I really can't."

"Meg, you haven't gone anywhere with me in, like, forever! You always say you will and then you never do. The only time we see each other is when I come to your place. I miss my best friend. Please come. Please, please, please . . ."

Despite Megan's slight annoyance with her friend, she couldn't help but smile a little at her perseverance. "Harper, you're making me feel guilty. I just can't. Three weeks from now Elliott has a class field trip I volunteered for, and he needs me here."

"Grandma can come," Elliott interjected. "You should go have fun, Mom."

Megan gave her son an exasperated look.

Harper could hear his loud voice and chimed in. "See, even *your son* has more sense than you. He knows you need a break. Four days and then I promise to deposit you right back into Dullsville."

"How long of a reprieve will I get from the guilt trips if I agree to come?"

"A year."

"Two."

"One and a half, no guilting or trying to get you laid. Pinky swear."

"No deal. Four days and then you stay off my back about both things for two full years."

"Oh my God! I can't believe you agreed to it!" Harper shrieked into the phone.

Elliott heard and started dancing around the kitchen, yelling, "Four days of TV and junk food and staying up late!"

Megan held the phone away from her ear and rolled her eyes at the pair of them.

THREE

Paris—Two Weeks Later

Luc walked into his apartment and tossed his car keys onto the table in the entranceway. He had just gotten home from a long dinner with friends and even though it was late, he was wide awake. He wandered from room to room in his expansive penthouse, trying to find something to do. He was restless in a way that he hadn't been in years. Somehow, lately his business ventures weren't holding his interest like they used to. He walked over to the bar in the living room and poured himself a Scotch. Standing by the window, staring out at one of the best views in Paris, he sipped his drink.

He wandered over to his bedroom, taking off his tie and shirt as he walked. He finished undressing and took a long, hot shower, letting the water rush over his muscular body. There was no reason for him to feel dissatisfied with his life. He had everything a man could want—money, power, excitement, women. So why was he feeling so edgy? He towelled off and made his way over to the bed, slipping under the covers completely nude. He decided that the next morning he would schedule a kickboxing session. It had been a few days since he had been to the gym. Exercising always made him feel better.

Maybe he needed to find another woman to be with. It had been a while since he had shared his bed with anyone, and it felt large and empty to him as he tossed and turned. He lay awake for another hour, reminding himself of all the reasons he intended to remain single.

Boulder

Megan rushed to her son's school to pick him up. She had been at a client's house, photographing their new baby all afternoon. The baby girl was tiny, having been born three weeks early. Megan had felt a stab of yearning as she picked her up and positioned her in different poses. She would have liked to have had more children, especially a little girl of her own. As she drove, she thought about what her life would have been like if Ian hadn't gotten injured. Would they still be together? Maybe with more children?

One thing was for certain—they would have more money. As it was, Megan got by, but there wasn't enough for any extras. As soon as she had realized the extent of Ian's addiction, she had convinced him to put their large home in Atlanta up for sale. They had split the proceeds and she had moved back to Colorado to be with her family, purchasing a modest home for herself and Elliott. Ian had stayed in Atlanta and ridden out the remainder of his contract before being let go by the ball club.

She knew it was pointless to think about what could have been. Nothing was going to change what had happened. Ian had been a hard drinker before his injury and it was possible they wouldn't have made it anyway. As she stopped in front of the school, she saw her little boy's face light up. He waved enthusiastically at her, not seeming to be at all upset that she was a few minutes late. She grinned back at him and all her self-pity dissolved in an instant.

* * *

That night as she stared into her closet, a sudden sense of dread came over Megan. She realized she had nothing to wear that would allow her to fit in with the fashion-conscious Parisians. She was going to stick out like a sore thumb—or rather, a frumpy one. There was no way she could justify new clothes for just a short trip. Her entire wardrobe had been purchased to be comfortable and functional. She had a classic style, but it was on a tight budget and was far too casual for Paris. Her closet consisted mainly of black shirts and jeans. She definitely didn't have the right shoes, boots or coats to wear, and her only purse looked tattered to her as she stared down at it on her bed. She normally didn't give much thought to what she wore, but now that she was going to the fashion capital of the world, her heart sank at the thought of how out of place she was going to feel.

Shit, she thought, *I do not want to do this.*

She was second-guessing her decision to even go to France in the first place. In the week before her trip, in addition to packing, she needed to stock up on food for her mom and Elliott, clean the house and make sure the laundry was done, and find a neighbour to shovel the driveway. It was a week's worth of work just to go on a trip for four nights. At the moment, it seemed like a bit too much. She decided to go to bed early and tackle the wardrobe issue after a good night's sleep.

Megan walked down the long hall to the arrivals area at Charles de Gaulle Airport, pulling her suitcase behind her, finally allowing a little flicker of excitement to start building inside her. She knew that Harper would be here to greet her, having insisted on taking time away from her meetings at the Paris office. Even though Harper had tried to brush it off as no big deal, Megan knew that as a fashion director stationed at *Style*'s head office in New York, her friend's time when she was here was precious. As she scanned the waiting crowd, she spotted Harper rushing over with her arms open. Megan broke into a huge grin at seeing her best friend, and the two gave each other a long hug.

"Oh, I missed my friend," Harper said as she pulled back from Megan. She was the picture of sophistication in her black riding boots and fitted tan pants. She wore a short black-velvet riding jacket and her auburn hair fell in curls down her back. She was as tall as Megan but with generous curves accented by her choice of clothing.

Megan felt horribly underdressed in her best jeans, scuffed low-heeled boots and old wool coat. "I missed you too. God, look at you. You are so fashion-forward compared to my fashion-flawed. I am not going to fit in here very well, am I?"

Harper grabbed Megan's arm with both hands and squealed in delight. "Oh, yes you are! Our first stop is the *Style* office. I have to go pick up the wardrobe for the shoot. We're going shopping in *Style*'s closet, only it is *so* much better because it's free and the world's best will be there to dress you."

"I'm size eight, Harper, not size zero. Nothing there is going to fit me."

"You're a six, not an eight—none of your clothes fit you properly. It doesn't matter anyway. They have lots of sizes for celebrity shoots. This is going to be the most fun ever!" Harper linked arms with Megan and they started walking to the exit.

* * *

Four hours later, they arrived at the hotel. Megan was too exhilarated by her new wardrobe to feel any exhaustion from the long trip. Harper had managed to sneak her five new outfits, complete with coats, purses, jewellery and footwear. As they stepped out of the cab, Megan felt like a new woman in a full-length, dark red wool coat; black, wide-leg pants; and a sexy pair of pointed-toe, high-heeled black boots. She wore a chunky gold necklace and her hands were cozy in long, ruched black lambskin gloves.

Everyone at *Style* had been incredibly kind to Megan. Harper had even managed to find a new set of hard-sided luggage for her, left over from a shoot several weeks earlier. They had managed to cram it with Megan's new clothes as well as most of what she had brought from home. Harper had given Megan's well-worn purse, suitcase and carry-on to an intern to dispose of. She had practically screamed with disgust when she saw the ratty white cotton briefs and beige bra Megan had packed.

"What. The. Fuck. Are. These?" she asked, holding up a pair of panties with one finger, as if they were diseased.

"Put those back!" Megan hissed. "They're very comfortable."

"And they're garbage. Our next stop is to get you some good lingerie, my friend. Matching, lacy, underwire, push-up, sexy stuff. You're going to feel like a whole new woman."

After a stop at an upscale lingerie shop, they made their way to the hotel. As Megan looked up at the tall old hotel, she realized Harper had been right. It was as though the world was full of possibilities again. Today, Megan was no longer just an ordinary single mom with another average day to look forward to. She was a young, sexy woman in Paris, of all places! For once in her life, she had the right wardrobe and she had four luxurious days to be whoever she wanted to be—four days without any responsibilities whatsoever, and she intended to make them count.

Once they were inside, the hotel manager met them at the elevator. He turned to Harper. "Bonjour, Mademoiselle Young. You will let me know if you need anything."

"As always. Thank you." She smiled.

When they got into the elevator, Megan turned to her friend. "He knows you by name. Did you ever imagine you'd have this life when we were in Mr. Dumphrey's math class?"

"Honey, that's all I did in his class. That's why I barely passed tenth grade." Harper laughed.

"Well, my friend, you have arrived and I can tell you that this whole life is a world apart from mine. We aren't even on the same planet, as far as I can tell," Megan replied with a smile.

As they walked down the long hall to Harper's suite, Megan couldn't help but savour the feeling of the incredibly plush carpet that lined the corridor. Excitement built in her, anticipation at what the room would be like if the hall had such a sense of grandeur. "So, what's on the agenda tonight?"

"We're going to hit a club tonight for a work thing I have to go to. Should be fun. Loads of hot guys. I thought you might want to rest first. Maybe we can order some room service for dinner and chill for a while?" Harper unlocked the double doors to the suite and pulled one of Megan's suitcases inside.

Megan grinned. "I'm up for the party but I have no intention of resting. Now that I'm here, I think I should make the most of it. *Really* have some fun."

"Well, look at you! Ms. Responsibility has done a one-eighty to

Party Girl! I love it! Come on, let's put your things in your room."

Megan was too busy gawking at the incredible room to respond to what her friend was saying. "Wow! Do you get this suite each time you come to Paris?"

"I used to, but not anymore. Budgets have tightened up big time. I had to pull a few strings for this. I wanted to give you the full glamour experience."

The suite was bright and airy, with an expansive living room in the centre and French doors leading out to a large balcony. Classic French furnishings, including a white couch, loveseat and chairs, were scattered throughout the room, creating several seating areas. A round dining table sat in the corner with a huge bouquet of flowers on top. Two hallways flanked the entrance, each leading to a bedroom with its own ensuite. Oversized bouquets of white flowers could be found in each room.

"Oh my God, Harper! This is too much. I mean, I love it—it is complete luxury—but you really didn't have to go to such trouble, seriously," Megan exclaimed as they deposited her bags in what was to be her bedroom.

"Honestly, it was no big deal. Just a little sweet talking when I checked in last night and a couple of tiny favours for the hotel manager."

When they reached the living room again, Megan wandered over to the balcony doors to admire the view. "Ack! You can see the Eiffel Tower from here! I'm really here! In friggin' Paris! With you!"

"I know! I've been as giddy as a schoolgirl for days, knowing you were coming," Harper replied, matching her friend's enthusiasm. Grabbing a bottle of champagne from the mini-bar, Harper held it up. "Shall we?"

"I believe we shall," Megan answered, clapping her hands with delight.

Two hours later, the pair were sitting at the dining table, eating supper and giggling hysterically.

"God, I've missed you, Megan," Harper said, after she finally recovered from their latest bout of laughter.

"I've missed you too," Megan answered. "I can't remember the last time I laughed this hard. I bet it was when you came to visit in the summer."

"Me too. I just never get this silly with my new friends. They just aren't the same, somehow," Harper said. As she spoke, her cellphone buzzed. "Speaking of new friends, I think we should start getting ready. I wish we could hang out here, but I have to put in an appearance tonight."

Megan wrinkled her nose. "Should I really go with you? I could just stay here and hit the sack early."

"Are you kidding me? No way! It'll be fun, I promise."

"It's just that it's a work function for you and I don't want you to feel like you have to babysit me all night."

"I will be happy to have you with me! Besides, I could never live with myself if I let you miss out on all the men!" Harper gave her a wide-eyed grin.

"I am NOT interested in the guys, so give it up already," Megan responded.

"Oh, fuuucck! Don't go all dull on me now."

"Hey, I'm here to dance and drink and laugh and fully enjoy not being responsible for anyone, but I *really* don't need to bone some stranger while I'm here."

"Yeah, you do!"

"Oh, fuck off!" Megan exclaimed, pushing Harper playfully on the arm as they stood to get ready.

"Oh, you're *so* going to get laid while you are here. That's a promise!" Harper laughed as she walked down the hall to her room.

"Am not! So forget about it already!" Megan called back to her.

Megan opened the new suitcases and selected a sleeveless, black, jersey-knit minidress with an asymmetrical neckline that showed off her shoulders and willowy arms. She tossed it on the bed and quickly took a shower, then dried her hair. She put it up in a twist at the back, leaving a few pieces framing her face. A minute later, Harper walked in, fully dressed and ready to go.

"You're fast!" Megan exclaimed.

"You learn to be when you're in my line of work. Let me do your makeup," Harper said, holding up her cosmetics case.

"Okay, thanks." Megan smiled at her friend.

She sat on the bed while Harper worked on her quietly, paying careful attention to every detail.

"You really are beautiful, Meg," she commented. "You totally could have been a model if you had wanted."

Megan rolled her eyes. "Sure, sure."

"I'm serious. I know what I'm talking about. You're gorgeous and you have a smokin' hot bod too."

Megan shrugged. "I know. I'm the shit." The pair giggled at her tongue-in-cheek response.

"Okay, time for the big reveal. Go look in the mirror!" Harper watched excitedly as her friend turned to see herself.

"Wow! How did you *do* that? I look hot!" Megan turned back to her friend, her face shining with pride. "I never knew I could wear red lipstick. I thought I'd look like a clown."

Harper handed her the lipstick, then started to pack up her makeup case. "You just need the right shade. Keep it."

"Well, I'll use it for tonight, anyway." Megan dropped it into the clutch she had been given earlier in the day, then looked up at her friend. "Harper, thank you *so much* for this trip and the clothes and the luggage. I hate to admit you were right, but I really did need this.

It's been a long time since I've treated myself to more than a good book and some cheap wine," Megan said as she put her cellphone into her clutch.

Harper put her arm around her friend and gave her a squeeze. "I know, sweetie. If anyone needs to be spoiled, it's you. You've worked so hard being everything for Elliott for the past seven years. You need to find Megan the woman again, not just Megan the mom."

"I do," she agreed. "Now let's see if she's at whatever club we're going to!"

FOUR

They breezed past the line of chilly hopefuls waiting outside the door of Cloud, one of the hottest clubs in Paris. The doorman smiled at Harper. "Mademoiselle Young, lovely to see you again. I believe you will find your friends in the VIP room."

"Perfect! Thanks!" She flashed him a killer smile as they walked in the front door.

"Even the bouncers know you?" Megan inquired under her breath as they shrugged off their coats and gave them to the coat-check girl.

"Only here. The owner is an old friend," Harper answered. Leaning closer, she spoke into Megan's ear. "Now remember, no male models, okay? They make horrible lovers. They never stop posing."

"What? Oh my God, that's hilarious!" Megan put her hand to her mouth to cover her loud laugh.

When she had recovered from the mental image, she touched Harper on the arm. "Listen, I might flirt a little just to see if I've still got it, but I'm really not going to sleep with anyone."

"Oh, you will. And I just figured out who," Harper replied firmly.

Megan's gaze followed Harper's eyes. Across the room at the bar stood the most impossibly handsome, impeccably dressed man she had ever seen. He had dark, medium-length textured hair that had a sexy just-out-of-bed look, chiselled cheekbones and a strong jaw. Megan couldn't help but stare as he laughed at something the petite, sophisticated-looking woman beside him was saying in his ear. He had a wide smile with perfect teeth and lips that would make a woman want to feel them all over her body.

"That's Luc Chevalier. He is *perfect* for you. Come on," Harper said, dragging Megan by the arm in his direction.

Megan found herself wanting to protest but was unable to. Her common sense was being overridden at the moment by her need to see Luc up close. Part of her had to see if a man so good-looking could actually exist. A remix of "Royals" by Lorde was playing as they pushed their way through the crowd to him. Megan's heart was suddenly racing and she realized she had no idea even what to say to a man anymore.

As they got near, Megan noticed the short, black-haired woman beside him stiffen as she took in the sight of Harper heading for them. Megan managed to wriggle her arm free so she could approach them on her own. As soon as she did, she realized it was a mistake. They were walking far too quickly for Megan's limited skills with heels as high as she was wearing. She tripped, flinging her arms out to stop herself. Her hands, then her face, landed squarely on Luc's chest.

He looked down in surprise, reacting quickly and grabbing her elbows to pull her up.

"Oh shit! I'm so sorry about that," Megan muttered, her face burning with humiliation. "Did anyone else see that cat run in front of me just then?"

Luc laughed, surprised at her quick wit, still holding her up. "I saw it, yes. It was very fast. I don't know how all these damn cats keep getting in here," he replied as he locked eyes with her. He was immediately struck by her beauty. Her eyes were a brilliant green, light in the centre with dark green rims. Her light blond hair was done up with a few pieces framing her flawless ivory face; her full lips were painted the perfect shade of red. Her skin felt buttery and smooth and a little bit cool to the touch. He held her arms for much longer than he had intended to. She blushed as she looked back at him.

"Are you alright?" he asked, trying to recover from her awe-inspiring smile.

Megan nodded as her smile faded a bit. *Sweet Jesus, this man could peel off my panties with just his voice.* "I'm fine. Just a little embarrassed. Thank you for breaking my fall."

Her hands were still resting on his hard chest, refusing to move, even though she kept telling them to. She took in the sight of his broad shoulders and muscular build up close. He hadn't even budged when her full weight hit him. He was rock solid under that suit. This man was not just swoon-worthy, he was who every Hollywood producer tried to recreate in any romantic film ever made about a Frenchman. Up close he was even hotter than from across the room, and he smelled like all kinds of sexy.

"Anytime," he replied, giving Megan a smile that made her mouth come very close to dropping open.

The moment was interrupted by Harper. "Luc Chevalier, meet Megan Sullivan, my best friend in the whole world."

Luc reluctantly let go of Megan's arms and turned. "Harper, my dear, it's wonderful to see you." He kissed Harper lightly on both cheeks.

He turned to face Megan, locking eyes with her but speaking to Harper again. "Harper, I must admit I'm more than a little annoyed with you for keeping Megan a secret from me for so long."

"That's completely on her, Luc," Harper replied distractedly, looking down as she adjusted her boobs in her low-cut dress. "I've tried to get her to Paris many times before but this is the first time she's taken me up on it."

"We will have to make sure it isn't the last," Luc replied, tilting his head a little as he appraised Megan's expression.

Finally the petite woman beside him spoke up. "Oh, Luc! There's lipstick on your shirt."

They all looked down and noticed a crimson stain on his shirt.

Megan's face turned bright red again. "Oh, I am *so* sorry about that. If we could get some club soda on that right away, I could scrub it out."

Luc gave her a devilish grin. 'Well now, Megan Sullivan, I've never had a woman try that line to get me out of my clothes. I'm tempted to go along with this to see where it will go."

Megan's cheeks flushed a deeper red and she gave an embarrassed laugh. The woman beside him rolled her eyes and excused herself, walking away.

"That was Simone. She doesn't like me very much," Harper said to Megan.

"I don't think she'll be my biggest fan either," Megan replied into Harper's ear.

Luc ignored their comments and grinned at them. "Ladies, what are you drinking this evening?"

"Surprise us!" Harper replied, then turned to Megan. "I trust Luc's opinion completely. He always seems to know what I want better than I do."

Luc turned to the bartender behind him, speaking in French. When he turned back a moment later, he was holding three glasses of champagne.

"We are celebrating Megan's arrival, no?"

"Yes, we are!" Harper exclaimed.

Megan took a glass from him, letting her finger graze over his for a second as she did. A tingling feeling went through her entire body at the touch of his skin. *Fucking Harper*, she thought. *I want to rip this guy's clothes off and I've only been in France for seven hours.*

She downed the entire glass, trying to extinguish the lust that was heating her up. All the champagne did was make things worse as she looked up into Luc's deep brown eyes. He was taller than she was with her heels on, which would put him at just over six feet. Other than the lipstick on his chest, he was dressed to perfection in a black European-cut suit and a crisp white dress shirt, unbuttoned at the top to give him a slightly casual look. Megan could see that he was older than she was, but not by much.

Luc wore an amused expression as he watched her, almost as though he could read her mind. Turning, he grabbed the bottle of champagne the bartender had left on the bar and filled her glass again without asking if she wanted more.

Megan took a sip, then said, "Luc, I missed your last name when Harper introduced us."

"Chevalier. It is French for *knight*."

Something about his response made Megan laugh far too loudly in spite of herself.

Luc looked taken aback for a moment. "Why is that funny to you?"

"I'm sorry. It's a great name. Really. And it must work on the ladies."

"But not you?"

"Nothing works on me," she responded, taking another swig of champagne.

Luc was about to say something when Harper decided to make her exit. "I haven't made it over to the VIP room. I better go check in with everyone."

"Sure, let's go," Megan replied, realizing she would be smart to get away from this man immediately.

She turned to Luc. "Thank you for the drinks, Monsieur Chevalier. It was lovely to meet you."

Luc gave her a slight nod and smiled at her as the pair turned away. He watched her make her way through the crowd; she moved with a surprising amount of grace for someone who was so clearly inexperienced in heels. He gazed at her ass and her long, lean legs as she disappeared around the corner, forcing himself not to follow her. How could a woman like that insist she was through with men? She was absolutely beautiful and utterly unconcerned with impressing him. She had even laughed at him. Luc was not a man who was used to such a reaction from women. He was used to standing back and letting women try to impress him. Megan had turned the tables on him and he wasn't entirely sure he liked it.

An hour later, Luc stood on the second level of the club, leaning on the railing, staring down at the dance floor. He watched Megan as she moved to the beat of "Neon Lights" with Harper and some of her colleagues. They ignored the several men trying to dance with them; these attentions caused Luc's blood to heat up with a sense of urgency. His gaze fell onto Megan's hands as she moved them slowly down over her hips and let them glide over her outer thighs. Her short black dress skimmed her form perfectly, showing off her figure without being tawdry. She laughed with Harper, the two of them affecting the sexy moves of music videos, but the effect was the same as if Megan had meant them seriously. Luc could feel his body responding as he watched her. He ran a finger along his lips absentmindedly as he thought about what was under that dress of hers. He had a sudden urge to clear the club of everyone but her.

Luc didn't notice a pair of eyes narrowing as they fixed on him from the main floor of the club. Simone grabbed the arm of a waitress who was passing by, asking her to tell Luc that he was needed in his office.

* * *

Two hours later, Megan and Harper left the dance floor to go get more drinks. By now, Megan was far past tipsy. She realized she was drunk as she walked purposefully toward the bar. Each drink had allowed the carefree, wild Megan to emerge a little more. It was safe for her tonight to give the ever-vigilant, unyieldingly responsible woman a much-needed rest.

"Let's get a rum and Coke for old time's sake!" she called into her friend's ear. "I am *hammered*!"

"Good! I'm glad I'm not the only one!" Harper hollered back, teetering a bit in her heels.

When they reached the bar, Harper ordered. The bartender started to get their drinks, then looked up. He made eye contact with someone behind them for a moment and then looked back at Harper. "I'm going to get you water instead. Boss's orders."

"What?" Harper asked indignantly. "Who? Luc? Where is that fucker?"

The bartender just shrugged and pushed the glasses of water in her direction, then stepped over to help the next patron. Harper looked around wildly, trying to spot Luc. Just then, Megan felt a hand rest gently on her waist, causing her to jerk in surprise. There was that delicious smell again. Luc was standing dangerously close behind her, with his head leaning toward hers.

"I'm glad to see you're having fun. Be careful, though. There are a lot of men here who would like to take you home tonight." He held his mouth to her ear so she could hear him in spite of his low tone.

"Oh yeah? Are you one of them?" She turned, her body brushing against his as she gave him a hard stare. She had completely lost all inhibitions after her last drink.

"Of course I am, but not like this. You are too drunk now. When I have you, you will be sober."

"*When* you have me? That's *incredibly* presumptuous!" Megan tried to level him with an annoyed look. It had no effect on him.

"I don't think so," he replied, gazing down at her lips.

Harper looked over, spotted Luc and pointed her finger at him. Her words slurred together. "Hey, you asshole! You don't get to decide when we've had enough to drink. We are independent, grown-up women!"

Luc smiled at her. "I do get to decide. This is my bar. Besides, I would hate to see you vomit on those beautiful heels of yours."

Harper looked down at her shoes, completely distracted for a moment. "They are lovely, aren't they?"

Suddenly realizing what Luc had just done, Harper turned her face back to him. "Hey! That is not going to work, Luc. Now quit acting like my dad and let them serve us another drink, already."

She looked over at Megan. "He's all bossy and parental, just like you. I told you he was perfect for you!" She wagged her finger in her friend's face as she wrinkled her nose and laughed.

Megan pursed her lips and gave Harper the wide-eyed look that was the silent version of "shut the hell up."

"You did, did you?" Luc asked, looking amused.

Megan interjected. "What *she* thinks is really irrelevant. You are not *at all* perfect for me."

"Why is that?" he asked, looking surprised.

Megan over-pronounced her words, trying to appear sober. "It's not personal. You smell incredible, and I know you're hiding a rock-hard body under all those expensive clothes, and you're probably some type of sex god, but there really is no perfect man *for me* out there."

"This is confusing. You're obviously attracted to me—which is, of course, how it should be—but you don't want to be with me? How is that possible?" he asked with a teasing grin.

Harper broke into the conversation, wagging a finger at him. "Because she's too fucking picky, that's why. No man will *ever* be good enough for her."

Megan gave Harper a dirty look, then turned back to Luc and held up her finger as she spoke. "That's not true. I'm *done* with men. It's completely different. You're perfect, Luc." She touched his jaw with one outstretched finger. "If I ever did want to fuck someone, you'd be in the running. But I don't. Nothing personal."

Just then, Harper, who was attempting to sit down at the bar, miscalculated the distance from her ass to the stool, ending up on the floor. Luc rushed over and picked her up before someone in the crowded club stepped on her.

"Oopsy daisy!" Harper laughed, her eyes closing.

Luc turned to Megan. "I think we should get her back to her hotel. Come this way." He started to walk toward the back of the club, keeping Harper propped up as he went. As Megan followed them, she felt a stab of jealousy at the sight of her best friend in Luc's arms. Through her foggy thinking, she realized how ridiculous it was for her to feel jealous about a man she wasn't interested in. *But what would it feel like to have those arms wrapped around me right now?*

They went through a door marked PRIVATE and found themselves in a brightly lit hallway. Luc led them into his office and helped Harper to the brown leather couch opposite his desk. He got the coat-check stubs from Megan and called a waitress to get their coats. As they waited, he put on his long wool overcoat and grabbed his cellphone and keys off of his desk.

"I'll bring my car around back and come get you. Keep her here. I don't think she'll want her colleagues to see her this way."

Harper's eyes were closed but she spoke up after Luc left the room. "For a bossy prick, he's pretty awesome, isn't he?"

"Yeah, he seems very thoughtful and he's totally hot. Why haven't you gone out with him?"

"You know me, I like my men under thirty. Get 'em young, break 'em in . . . But you two would work . . ." she said, drifting off again.

Megan sat on the couch next to her friend, trying to focus her thoughts through her drunken haze. She knew when she sobered up she would be shocked at how turned on she was by Luc. She hadn't reacted like this to a man since she met Ian years ago.

Her thoughts were interrupted by Luc coming back into the office. He smiled warmly at her. "I've parked out back. Let's get our friend home, yes?"

Megan stood up. "Yes. Do you have a bag in case she gets sick?"

"Oh, right. I'll get one."

A few minutes later, Megan and Harper were cozy and warm in the heated back seat of Luc's Mercedes CLS as he smoothly navigated his way through the busy streets of Paris. The contrast of the quiet car to the loud club was a welcome change for the now-tired friends.

"How is she doing?" Luc asked.

"I think she'll be alright. She might be feeling rough tomorrow morning, though."

"I expect she will." Luc watched Megan in the rear-view mirror as he waited at a set of lights. "How did you two meet? You seem so different from each other."

Megan looked out the window to avoid eye contact with him. "We met when we were thirteen. Her family moved to town and she ended up at the same school as me. We hit it off right away. At the time, we were both wildly unpopular girls who towered over everyone in the class. We've been best friends ever since, even though our lives have gone in completely different directions."

"That is very rare—to have a childhood friend with whom you remain close throughout the years."

"It is. She has really been there for me through all my ups and downs. I'd be lost without her."

"She's a special woman, for sure." They rode along in silence for a few moments before Luc spoke up again. "Megan, I don't know anything about you, but I would like to."

"Oh, um, well, there's not much to tell." Megan smoothed her dress with her hands, watching him in the rear-view mirror. "I live in Colorado and work as a photographer, mostly weddings and family portraits. I'm a single mom. I have a son, Elliott, who is six. Pretty typical story, I suppose."

"It must be a recent change for you, to be single. I can't imagine you would have to go long without men tripping over themselves to meet you."

"Ha! It's not exactly like that when you have a child. I've been on my own for five years. My ex developed a rather unfortunate drug problem when Elliott was a baby. It became clear he wasn't going to be able to kick it, so I had to leave him. He's not really part of Elliott's life."

"That's tough for a little boy." Something about his tone told Megan he was speaking from experience.

"It is indeed. He tries to pretend he's fine, but every time the phone rings he gets this hopeful look in his eyes. His face always falls a little when he answers it because it's never his dad. It's hard to watch him be let down by the man who is supposed to love him the most." Megan wasn't sure why she was telling Luc this. It was something she never talked about.

"That must break your heart a little, no?"

Megan felt her eyes welling up as she gazed out the window. "It does."

"Men can be such assholes. Please pardon my language. It's just that you don't see women abandoning their children like that. But so many men do it easily."

"I wouldn't say it was anything close to easy for him. He's just been so lost to his addiction for so long now."

"So this is why you said you are done with men, yes?" Luc asked as he pulled into the hotel parking lot.

"Pretty much, yes. I just can't risk letting another man into Elliott's life and then having him get hurt again. We're better off on our own."

Luc stared at her in the mirror as he took the keys out of the ignition. "You can't risk *him* getting hurt, or you?"

Megan felt immediately irritated by his question. "Him," she answered firmly. "I'm an adult. If I ever rolled the dice again, I could live with the consequences. It's not fair to do that to a child, though."

"Have you considered that what you are doing might, in fact, be *unfair* to your little boy? You are removing all possibility of finding a dad for him when the one he's got is a dud."

Megan gave him a hard look in the mirror. "Wow. That might be the most arrogant thing I've ever heard. I've known you for . . . what? Five minutes? You might not want to start telling me I'm doing a crappy job raising my son, whom you've never met."

She woke Harper to get her moving and got out of the car. Luc got out and tried to help but Megan blocked him by positioning herself between them.

"I can take it from here. Thank you for the ride." Megan's voice was icy as Harper tried to steady herself. She almost took Megan down with her as she teetered.

"I have offended you. I'm sorry," he said, propping Harper up over his shoulder. "I have a bad habit of speaking my mind when I shouldn't."

"That is a bad habit." Megan's reply was curt.

She got her key card out of her clutch as they passed through the doors of the hotel lobby. Megan walked ahead of Luc and Harper, taking small but hurried steps that caused her bottom to shift quickly under the clingy fabric of her dress. Luc's eyes were trained on her rear as he all but carried Harper, easily keeping up with Megan in spite of the extra weight. The elevator doors opened and Megan stepped inside, holding the door open for her companions.

Luc glanced over at her as they ascended, seeing her jaw set and her eyes focus intently on the numbers changing above the elevator doors. She was somehow even more attractive to him when she was angry. He opened his mouth to speak and then, thinking better of it, he pressed his lips together.

When they entered the suite, Megan walked down the hallway to the right. "Harper's room is this way."

Luc carefully put Harper down on the bed and Megan took off her friend's shoes and hoop earrings. Luc walked over to the ensuite and brought back a garbage can.

"Harper, there's a garbage can here if you need it, okay?" Megan spoke loudly into her ear.

Harper grunted an acknowledgement without opening her eyes. Megan tucked her under the covers as Luc walked around to the other side of the bed. Leaning one knee on the bed, he picked up two pillows and tucked them in right beside Harper, then turned her onto her side.

"These will hopefully keep her from turning onto her back, in case she gets sick but doesn't wake up."

Megan's eyes followed him as he cared for her friend, some of her icy indignation starting to melt at his kindness. He didn't have to bring them to the hotel. He could have just as easily called a cab for them. He didn't need to help put Harper to bed either. But none of those acts took the sting out of his words in the car.

Megan turned the light on in the ensuite and left the door open partway so that Harper wouldn't be left in the dark. Luc followed her out into the hall.

"So, now that we've gotten her all snuggled into bed, maybe we can have some quality grown-up time together?" he asked with a teasing expression on his face.

Megan gave him a wry look as they walked to the door. "Not tonight. I suddenly have a headache."

Luc's lips curled up in a grin at her quick response, but his smile faded quickly. "Brought on by what I said. I've let my big mouth get me into trouble again."

"Don't take it too hard. I wasn't going to sleep with you anyway," Megan informed him as she opened the front door.

Luc ignored the open door and stood facing her. "Did you forget I don't take advantage of women who have been drinking? I just thought we could talk a little more. I would like to know more about you."

Megan glared at him. "The only thing you need to know about me is that I don't like getting parenting advice from virtual strangers."

"You're right, of course. I don't even have children, so I really shouldn't have said what I did. I'm sorry. I hope this doesn't mean I've lost the chance to get to know you."

Megan gave him a confused look. "Why would you even want to? I highly doubt that you and I have anything in common. I'm just a boring small-town soccer mom."

Luc squinted a little, considering what she was saying. "I think that is what you want people to see, but there is so much more to you. I see the passionate woman you've hidden away, and I can tell she is incredible."

"That's a great line, Luc. But really, I'm no more than what you see. Less, even. Tonight I'm dressed like someone else. If you saw me at home, you wouldn't even give me a second look."

"I find that hard to believe. You might be able to fool everyone else—yourself, even—but you'll never convince me." His gaze fell on her lips as he spoke.

"Look, I'm sure you're used to women lining up to hop into bed with you, and maybe I seem like a conquest to you, but believe me when I say I'm *not* looking for this. I promise I'm not playing hard to get. I don't like those games."

"I believe that is true. And I believe you are determined not to sleep with me even though you very badly want to."

Megan rolled her eyes. "You might have to at least *consider* the possibility that I really don't *want* to sleep with you."

Luc leaned down toward her with a bit of a smirk. "I don't think I *do* have to consider that. You already told me at the bar that you want me."

"I was drunk. I didn't know what I was saying." Megan looked away, trying to avoid his gaze.

Luc gently lifted her chin with his hand so she was facing him. "You are *still* drunk and you said exactly what you would otherwise never allow yourself to say."

Megan looked into his dark eyes, willing herself not to take in how unbelievably sexy he was. She had never felt so confused by any man. Luc was thoughtful and caring and arrogant and insulting all at the same time. She was irritated and grateful and inexplicably drawn to him.

"I'm leaving here in three days," was all she could think to say.

"Then you should make the most of your time in Paris," he replied, giving her a hint of a smile.

"You should stop telling me what to do. As a general rule, women don't like that." She had been unable to tear her eyes away from his the entire time.

Luc lowered his voice. "I don't care what other women like. If it bothers you, though, I will stop." His fingers were still holding her chin up as they spoke and there was no part of her that wanted him to remove them. The sexual energy surged between them so strongly she was sure that if someone happened upon them, they would be able to see it.

"Good," Megan replied in a slightly breathy voice.

Luc took this as an invitation. He leaned down a little farther and kissed her gently on the lips, allowing his mouth to linger over hers, savouring the taste and feel of her as though this kiss were meant to hold him over for the rest of his life. When he pulled back, Megan's eyes were still closed. He smiled, knowing he was right about her.

"I will see you tomorrow, Megan."

She opened her eyes and let out a puff of air. "Okay, but it won't do any good. I'm not going to change my mind."

"You already have."

With that, he turned and walked out, leaving her standing at the door, feeling dizzy with lust.

"Wow," she whispered to herself as she shut the door and leaned against it for a moment, not entirely sure her wobbly legs would hold her up. She had completely forgotten what really being kissed felt like.

FIVE

The next morning came far too early for Harper. She woke up to her cellphone alarm buzzing beside her. It was already eight o'clock and she should have been on her way to the photo shoot by now. She sat up, feeling her brain slam against her skull as she did. Turning to the window, she sighed inwardly, seeing rain pour down outside. In an instant, her brilliant vision for October's feature article had dissolved.

"Oh, son of a bitch," she groaned, realizing they would need to do the shoot indoors at their alternate location.

Dialing the office, she got through to Eddie, the photo editor, almost immediately. Her voice came out as little more than a croaking sound as she spoke. "Eddie, we're going to have to save the Musée Rodin grounds for another shoot. Let's just set up at the *Style* studio and do what we can to make it work."

"You're going to hate me, Harper, but I have to give you some bad news. I just found out now that the studio is not an option. It flooded this morning. Some type of storm drain backed up and the entire first floor is under water."

"What? This better not be a joke, Eddie, because it is *not* funny."

"Believe me, there is *nothing* funny about any of this." Eddie's words spilled quickly out of his mouth, conveying the panic he felt. "Joelle came down here to my desk about twenty minutes ago, absolutely spitting venom. And believe me, when she found out you weren't here, I thought she was about to snap my neck. I told her you already knew and that you were out trying to find another location. If we can't get one, it means we're going to lose Anita. She's leaving for Peru in two days and won't be back for five weeks. And Joelle wants Anita on this."

Harper's already pounding headache moved from awful to "put the covers over my head, I don't care if I die" with the weight of the crisis. "Shit. Thank you for covering my ass, Eddie. You bought us some time, but where the hell are we going to come up with an empty, well-lit building in the next hour?"

As she spoke, Harper's eyes fell on the shoes she had worn the night before. The heels reminded her of her hangover, which reminded her of where the hangover came from. Which gave her the perfect solution to her dilemma.

"Eddie, I just had an idea, and if we're really lucky, it might be brilliant. Give me a few minutes and I'll call you back, okay?"

* * *

One hour later, a cab pulled up in front of Cloud, carrying Harper and a very confused-looking Megan.

"What are we doing here? Please don't tell me this is where the photo shoot is!" She gave Harper a pleading look.

"Sorry, Megs, but I'm afraid there were no other options. Luc agreed to let us use the club for the day."

"Oh my God!" Megan hissed. "I *cannot* go in there. What if *he's* here? I seriously can't see Luc again, Harper. I'm going to go back to the hotel."

"He won't be here, I promise. He's over at his main office, so don't worry about it. He sent Simone over to let us in," she answered, rolling her eyes and opening the back door to get out of the cab.

"You're positive he won't show up, right?" Megan asked as she slid across the seat and stepped out into the rain, and the two hurried up the steps.

"Promise. He's a busy man. What happened between you two, anyway?"

"Nothing, really. He's just a little bit much for me."

"I'd say it's been far too long since you've had a 'bit much'. You might want to give it a try while you're here." Harper raised her eyebrows and grinned at her friend.

They reached the door and knocked. It was opened immediately by Eddie, a short young man in tight black jeans and a fitted, black deep V-neck T-shirt. "Harper! This place is perfect! Anita is thrilled *beyond* with the two-storey windows." His eyes darted to Megan. "Who is this lovely lady?"

"Megan, my best friend. Megan, this is Eddie. He's the best photo editor I've ever worked with."

"Hi, Eddie. Nice to meet you. I hope it's okay that I'm tagging along."

Harper answered for him. "Of course it is. I already told you that, silly!" She turned to Eddie. "Meg's an up-and-coming photographer and I brought her to watch so she can get some tips. Anita already knows, so it won't be an issue."

Eddie looked impressed. "Oh, maybe I'll be working for you someday!"

Megan shook her head. "She's exaggerating. I do weddings and family portraits."

Eddie smiled. "That's important too, you know. Okay Harper, let's get this going."

Harper turned to Megan. "Do you want to make yourself comfortable somewhere while we get set up?"

"I'm going to sit over there. Let me know if you need anything." Megan wandered over to a couch near the window. She sat, watching the organized chaos. The team was a flurry of movement as the lights were unpacked and assembled, the camera equipment was prepared and a team of stylists, hairdressers and makeup artists worked furiously on the models, who sat in directors' chairs, looking bored. Caterers set up a craft table with various trays of food, coffee, water and other drinks. Harper had her eye trained on every aspect of what was happening in the room. Megan sat in awe of her friend, who had gone from a hungover mess to an organized, calm leader within seconds of entering the building.

Pulling out her camera, Megan started adjusting the settings to take a few shots of a candle on the table in front of her for practice. The light was very good; Harper clearly knew what she was doing bringing them here.

Two hours later, the photo session was still in progress. Megan was shocked at how long and hard they had to work to get the right look. Harper continued to call out directions as the shots were set up and made final adjustments to accessories and clothing, with only the briefest pause to take a breath. No detail escaped her keen eye. The only sign of the effects of the night before was when Eddie put on some loud dance music and Harper requested something slower and softer.

Megan stood quietly at the back, watching Anita, hoping to learn what she could from one of the fashion world's most prominent photographers. Finally it seemed as though the entire crew breathed a collective sigh of relief, having reached some milestone in the shoot that Megan was completely unaware of. They all seemed to relax, including Anita, who had appeared quite tense at the beginning. She turned to Megan and called to her in a British accent, "Harper's friend! Come here!"

Megan walked forward. "Yes?"

"I understand you want to learn some tricks of the trade. Come. I'll show you everything you need to know to do what I do. It's really quite easy."

Megan laughed. "I think you're being very modest! You're amazing to watch. You move so quickly."

"Years of experience. We're always racing against the sun in this job. Let me see your camera . . ."

* * *

After an hour of working with Anita, Megan's head was swirling with everything she was learning. Luc walked quietly through the front door and stood, silently taking in the sight of his nightclub, which now looked like a studio. Immediately, Harper saw him and was about to address him. He put a finger to his lips with a wink and continued to observe Megan. She looked gorgeous in a pair of dark boot-cut jeans, black heels and a fitted, long-sleeved black shirt. Her hair was down and she had tucked one side behind her ear as she worked. She looked very much like a professional as she moved with Anita. She was eager in her attempts to learn and she laughed easily when she made mistakes. Luc loved hearing the sound of her laugh; it was so full and genuine. He wanted to make that happy sound escape her mouth. The day before, he had sensed a sadness in her. As Luc watched Megan, he decided to send her home smiling.

Megan suddenly had a feeling that someone was watching her. She turned to see Luc standing at the back of the room, leaning casually against a pillar, smiling at her. She felt her face heat up as the memory of his kiss flooded her brain. He looked incredible as he ran a hand through his hair. He was dressed casually in jeans, a slim-fitting grey sweater and a fitted black leather jacket with a mandarin collar. Poking out from under the jacket was a silk scarf in grey and burgundy tones.

"Don't let me interrupt," he said.

Anita looked at him and snapped a set of photos of him as he gazed at Megan. "I take it that's your man?" she said quietly from behind the camera.

"No, no. He owns this club. He's a friend of Harper's. I barely know him."

Anita held the camera out to Megan and displayed one of the shots she had taken of him. "Well, that is the look of a man who would like to know you much better." She grinned as Megan blushed again.

Anita turned back to Harper. "Okay, Harper, I think we've got what we need. Should we clear out so this kind man here can have his nightclub back?"

All eyes were on Harper as she made her decision. One quick nod of her head had the entire crew whipping into action again. Luc sauntered over to Megan as she busied herself putting her camera and lenses into her bag.

She gave him a brief smile, trying to look nonchalant. "Hi, Luc."

"Bonjour, Megan," he answered, taking her by the elbow with one hand and kissing her on both cheeks. There was that smell again, and the way he said her name made her toes curl up. She felt completely flustered around him now that she was sober. Megan wished Harper had done her makeup again; she was suddenly feeling very plain with only her own amateur attempt at making herself up that morning.

"How is your day going?" she asked, looking back down at her camera bag so she could avoid eye contact with him. She felt he could see right through her, and she couldn't stand that he probably knew exactly what she wanted to do to him with that silk scarf of his. An image flashed through her brain, making her squirm.

"It's better now that I'm here. Did you learn a lot? You looked like you were having fun."

"Oh yes, Anita is a wonderful teacher. Surprisingly patient and full of amazing ideas. She could turn anyone into a pro if they had enough time with her."

"What a great opportunity for you, then," Luc said. He paused for a moment, then asked, "What are you doing now?"

"Um, I don't know, actually. I'm sure Harper has something in mind," Megan answered, picking up her bag and putting it over her arm.

"I'm sure she does. What do *you* want to do? You have such a short time in Paris," Luc replied, leaning over to her and taking her bag from her. He slung it over his shoulder as though it, and she, belonged to him.

Megan wasn't sure what to say. Should she just let him claim her like that? It seemed so forward to her. He was nothing like the men she knew back home. She found herself wishing Harper would come out already.

"I haven't really thought about what I want to do, actually. I'm just happy to be here and go along with Harper."

"Well, is she going to take you to see the sights while you're here? The Louvre, the Eiffel Tower?"

Just then Harper made her way across the room to them.

Megan smiled at her friend. "Harper, you were amazing! Seriously, I don't know how you do that for so many hours. You manage to just stay on the whole time. I'm a little bit in awe of you, especially because you must not be feeling well."

Harper grinned at Megan. "It's not that hard, really. I would never complain about doing what I love for a living when there are millions of people out of work right now."

Luc spoke up. "That is a most admirable perspective. Are you two hungry? I know a great place near here to grab a late lunch."

"Starving! Thank you, Luc," Harper answered quickly before Megan had a chance to turn him down.

Nervous knots twisted inside Megan's stomach. She didn't want to go for lunch with Luc. She was completely in over her head, and she just wanted to put a safe distance between them.

"I'm a bit of a mess for going out," Megan interjected. "I hardly even had time to put makeup on before we left."

"You look wonderful, Megan. Believe me. You will still be the most beautiful woman in the restaurant, even without makeup." The look on Luc's face was so sincere, it was hard not to believe him.

"Oh please," Megan replied sarcastically. "I won't even be the most beautiful woman at our table."

Luc looked from Harper to Megan as though considering her comment. "I think Harper will agree with me that you have a very rare and elegant beauty."

Harper grinned. "That I would."

* * *

A few minutes later, the three were seated at a round table in a small bistro, looking over menus. Harper was pleased to see that her strategy was working.

"So, Harper, what are your plans for Megan while she's here?"

"I don't know, really. I have a meeting tomorrow morning at *Style*, but otherwise I thought she might like to see the sights and eat delicious cuisine and drink really good wine."

Megan smiled at her. "That sounds terrific. Let's do that."

The waiter brought their soup and the trio began to eat. After a few minutes, Harper looked down at her phone, pretending to have received an urgent text.

"Oh Megan, I'm so sorry. I've been called back to the office. I'm going to have to leave right now. I'm afraid our afternoon is ruined!"

Megan saw right through her friend's obvious lie. "Well, maybe you can drop me off at a museum or a department store near your office? I'm sure I'll find lots to do on my own while you're busy."

Harper smiled sweetly. "Oh no, Megan, it won't work. From the sounds of this text, I'm probably going to be tied up for the rest of the day. I'm so sorry. You stay and finish your lunch. We can't both run out on Luc."

Luc smiled at Harper, knowing full well what she was up to. "Yes, I would be horribly offended if you just left me here alone to finish eating. I propose that you have lunch with me and I'll take you to see whatever your heart desires."

Megan looked from Luc to Harper, fully irritated by their satisfied smiles.

"Perfect!" Harper exclaimed. She leaned down to kiss Megan's cheek. "Don't be mad; this is for your own good," she whispered in her ear. She discreetly dropped a condom into Meg's open purse and gave her a little wink.

Megan grabbed Harper's arm and pulled her in close. "I hate you, you bitch," she whispered back, then gave her a big, fake smile as she released her.

Harper said her goodbyes and rushed out, leaving Megan alone with Luc again. She looked down at her soup, suddenly feeling too nervous to eat.

"We have clearly been set up," Luc said with an amused grin as he tore off a piece of his bun and popped it in his mouth.

"Looks that way," Megan answered. "Listen, you don't need to play tourist with me, Luc. I'm sure you have many other things you would rather do."

"Why are you sure of that? I thought I was clear last night that I wanted to get to know you."

"Yes, and I was clear that there isn't any point, remember?"

"Not everything has to lead somewhere, Megan. Not even to bed. In France, we take the time to pursue pleasure. It would bring me pleasure to show you around my city, so that is what I intend to spend the rest of the day doing."

Megan bit her bottom lip, not sure what to say. She looked out the window, seeing that the rain had stopped and the sky was clear again. Nothing about this was a good idea. Megan didn't know if she could control herself around him. She had never met a man who had this effect on her before. Everything about him—from his sexy hair to his hard body to his accent—stirred up feelings she hadn't had in years.

Luc signalled for the bill as he spoke. "Megan, I'm not going to leave you alone in a bistro in the middle of Paris. Come with me. I promise, I will make sure you enjoy yourself." *That's the problem*, she thought. *I'm going to enjoy this too much.*

Megan smiled reluctantly at him. "Thank you, Luc. That is very kind of you."

"Excellent. I need to make one phone call and then we can be on our way. Please excuse me for a moment."

Luc got up and walked outside to place his call. Megan used the time to run to the ladies' room. She stared at herself in the mirror while she washed her hands. She realized she looked fine—not overdone but good enough. She put on some rose-coloured lip gloss and ran a comb through her hair. When she walked back over to their table to get her coat, Luc was standing there already. He helped her into the new cream-coloured peplum jacket. Megan fastened the buttons and picked up her purse. Luc already had her camera bag slung over his shoulder.

"Ready?" He smiled warmly.

Taking a deep breath, Megan smiled. "I am. Where to?"

"I thought I would take you over to the Louvre first. We can wander around there for a while."

"That sounds wonderful."

* * *

For the next three hours, Luc and Megan explored the Louvre, lingering at Megan's favourite exhibits. As they strolled along the expansive halls, Megan was surprised to find that Luc had a considerable knowledge of the museum as well as of art in general. He had many interesting stories about the various artists exhibited.

"How do you know so much about art, Luc?" Megan tilted her head so she could look at him as they walked side by side.

"My mother was a guide here for English-speaking tourists. She used to bring me along sometimes," Luc answered.

"Did you enjoy it?"

"Sometimes, if there was a pretty girl with the group." He laughed.

Megan grinned and rolled her eyes. "Why doesn't that surprise me?" Turning to him, she wore a thoughtful expression. "Was your mom American?"

"Yes, actually, she was. She grew up in Vermont, of all places. She came over to Paris to study art as a young woman and spent the rest of her life here."

"Really? So you're half American, then."

"Yes, I am, but only the good half," he responded with a little wink.

Megan smiled at him. "Were you close to your mom?"

"I was. She passed away a long time ago now. Cancer." He had a matter-of-fact tone but there was a hint of sadness under it.

"I'm sorry to hear that. I lost my dad a few years ago to a heart attack. I don't think you ever stop needing your parents."

"We have to though, don't we?"

"Yes, I suppose. My mom is a big part of my life. She's with my son while I'm here. I don't know what I would do without her."

"It's nice that you have a good mother. Especially since you're on your own with your son."

"Yes, I'm very lucky," Megan agreed. "Is your dad still alive?"

"Maybe. It doesn't matter to me either way." Luc shrugged dismissively and looked down at the floor. There was something in his tone that told Megan not to ask anything more.

Luc checked his watch and then turned to Megan. "It's almost five thirty; they'll start closing the exhibits soon. I have two more places I want to take you if you'd like to come with me. How are your feet?"

"They're fine, actually. These boots are surprisingly comfortable. How about your feet?" Megan smiled at him.

"My feet are fine too. Let's go. I have the perfect place to watch the sunset."

* * *

They made it to the Eiffel Tower surprisingly quickly. Luc parked and then hurried around to open Megan's door for her. He held out his hand gallantly to help her out of the car. *"Mademoiselle, bienvenue à la Tour Eiffel."*

Megan grinned at him. *"Merci beaucoup,* Monsieur Chevalier," she replied with a formal nod.

As they walked toward the tower, they observed a young couple clearly having a fight. The girl turned her back on the boy, folded her arms across her chest, then turned her head in his direction to display a world-class pout. The young man pleaded with her to forgive him.

Luc leaned into Megan's ear. "He must have told her what to do."

Megan let out a loud laugh, looking up him. "No, no. Nothing that serious. He probably just cheated on her."

They tried to stifle their laughter as they passed by the pair. Strolling to the tower, Luc took Megan's hand in his as though it were the most natural thing to do. The feeling of his strong hand covering hers somehow spread warmth through Megan's entire body. She knew she should pull her hand away, but she just couldn't. It was the most innocent form of connection and yet it awoke a deep sense of desire in her, a feeling that had long since been forgotten.

"Are you disappointed we didn't see more of the museum?" he asked, looking over at her.

"Not even a bit. I'm just grateful I got to see it at all. And I can't imagine a more knowledgeable tour guide. Thank you, Luc." She smiled up at him.

"Thank *you* for letting me bring you. I'm having a wonderful time. I enjoy watching your expression when you see something you like. You are like a girl on Christmas morning."

"Oh, no need to thank me. Honestly, I haven't minded letting you show me around nearly as much as you might think," Megan teased.

"What a relief. All afternoon, I've been trying very hard to think of a way to make this up to you."

The pair laughed at his joke, their bodies moving closer to each other, shoulders touching now. Megan tilted her head back to look all the way up at the tower. She stood staring for a moment before speaking in a quiet voice. "I feel so small all of a sudden. I'm always baffled by man's ability to create something of this magnitude."

"It is incredible what we can do when we dream big and work hard, no?" Luc remarked as they reached the ticket counter.

"It is, isn't it?" Megan agreed, surprised at this insight. She hadn't thought of Luc as someone who had dreams. He seemed more the type to set goals and pursue them relentlessly. She took her wallet out of her purse. "I'm going to pay for the tickets. I don't want you to start thinking this is a date, which it definitely isn't."

"You are mistaken," he said, as they walked to the elevators, stepping through the open doors. "This is most definitely a date."

"No, it isn't," Megan answered as she shook her head. "For it to be a date, both people need to have some type of agreement that they are trying each other on to see if they want a relationship. We're not doing that."

"You're wrong. A date is just two people who are attracted to each other doing something they enjoy."

"Who says I'm attracted to you?" Megan asked with a raised eyebrow.

Luc shook his head and gave her a teasing grin. "You did. Last night. Now, what was it again?" he asked, tapping his lip as if trying to remember. "That I have an incredible body and am some kind of sex god?" His eyes wore a playful expression as he looked back down at her. "Yes. That is what you said."

Megan blushed, remembering her words. "Yeah, well, I was drunk, so it doesn't count."

Luc looked over at her and laughed. "In my experience, women are always more truthful when they've been drinking. It's when they are sober that they hide their true feelings."

"Well, not this woman," Megan began. "She's a *huge* liar when she's been drinking. Huge."

Luc laughed again as they stepped out onto the lower level and crossed to the next set of elevators, which would take them to the top.

He found himself surprised by her answer. "You know, you are really fun when you relax."

"Did your mom ever teach you about what Americans call a backhanded compliment? You say something nice at the same time you say something a little insulting?"

"If she did, I don't remember it. But here in France, we call it the truth. You *are* more fun when you let your guard down a little. Some people are not fun even then. It's a sincere compliment."

Megan gave him a skeptical look. They crossed over to the next set of elevators and Luc pressed the button. He turned his face to her. "You don't know how to take me. Just remember that I am exceedingly charming and kind," he replied, gently bumping her shoulder with his.

"Right. And you remember that I'm smart and I'm onto your game."

"And what game is that?"

"You're a player, Monsieur Chevalier. You probably have different women in every city."

"I don't, but if I did it wouldn't matter to you anyway. This is not a date, remember?" he replied, taking her hand in his again.

The elevator doors opened and a tour group got off, leaving the car open for Luc and Megan. They were alone as they began their ascent.

"You know, when I was a boy, this elevator ride took eight minutes. It felt like an eternity to me; I was always in such a hurry to get to the top. Now it takes just over a minute and I think it's too fast. Part of the fun—the anticipation—has been lost."

Megan gazed at him as he spoke. It was hard to picture him as an excited little boy; he was just such a *man*, so confident and purposeful in everything he did. She looked into his eyes.

"Is the anticipation the best part for you now?" The words came out of her mouth of their own accord. She knew how they sounded, but there was a part of her that wanted to be suggestive.

Luc raised his eyebrow at her and leaned down a little to let his mouth hover over hers. "Not the best part, but it makes it all so much better, don't you think?"

Megan swallowed hard, looking at his mouth, her lips begging her to let them brush up against his again. She felt a little weak in the knees at the thought. She was saved by the elevator doors opening to reveal a view more incredible than she could have imagined. Luc pressed his fingers to the small of her back to steer her through the small crowd on the top deck.

"Come this way," he told her, taking her hand and leading her to the north side of the tower.

"Wow!" Megan exclaimed, slightly breathless from both the view and his touch. "This is stunning. It's hard for me to even believe I'm here."

"I'm glad I could be here for your first time. One forgets how wonderful it is." The sun was just starting to go down, creating the most spectacular scene. The sky was lit with oranges, pinks and purples, giving the entire city a soft glow.

Luc stood behind her and leaned his face close to hers as he pointed out what they were looking at. "The building with the large garden in front is the Palais de Chaillot. Much of it is a museum now, like half of Paris itself. The gardens in front are called the Jardins du Trocadéro. Beyond the city, to the left of the sunset, is Mont Valérien. Can you see it?"

"Yes, I can." Megan could smell his intoxicating scent again and was having trouble concentrating on his words as he moved his body closer to her back. She shivered a little, feeling both cold and overwhelmed with desire. Luc wrapped his powerful arms around her and pressed his body to hers.

"Valérien is an important memorial of the French Resistance. A lot of history there. I wish there was time for me to take you to see it."

They silently watched the sun sink in the sky behind the far-off hills. Megan was in awe of where she was and what she was experiencing. She felt like she was light years away from her normal life. Here she was, in Paris, allowing this sexy-as-sin man to hold her as though they were a couple, when at home this type of thing would have sent her running.

As Luc held her, he realized she had awakened something in him that he hadn't known existed. Her slender frame felt so perfect in his arms, as though she had always belonged there. She was as beautiful as she was strong, as funny as she was smart. He breathed in the scent of her subtle perfume, knowing that once the sky had repainted itself in darkness he would have to let her go. He stood behind her, silently willing the sun to slow its descent so that he could stay in this tender moment as long as possible.

"I can see why it's called the City of Light," Megan said quietly.

"It is a place for love, no?"

"Yes, it is," she sighed. She could feel his face so close to hers. If she just turned ever so slightly, her lips would meet his. Her heart thumped, terrified at the thought. She closed her eyes to allow herself to fully take in the moment.

Luc waited for her to turn to him, but she didn't. He was surprised she could resist what was happening between them. He knew she felt it too, and he was filled with both frustration and admiration for her resolve. He had an almost overwhelming need to kiss her. But he didn't. He would wait for her to come to him.

He finally spoke up, his voice low. "I have one more place to take you tonight. Are you hungry?"

"I could eat."

"Good. Let's go."

* * *

Simone watched the sunset from the window in her small kitchen. She knew Luc was with the American and that they would be on their way to dinner soon. Hours ago, he had called her to cancel his meetings for the afternoon and book dinner for him. Pouring herself more wine, she tipped the bottle upside down to allow the last drops to fall into her glass. The alcohol numbed the pain of knowing he was out with yet another woman who wasn't her. She should have been with him tonight, in his arms, feeling his touch. She was the one who had loved him and cared for his every need for so long now. Simone took solace in the fact that this one would be gone in a matter of days, while she would still be here, waiting and hoping. She was starting to lose hope, however, after years of loving Luc from arms' length.

SIX

Soon after the sun set, Megan was surprised to find that the restaurant they were going to was aboard a 1950s-style luxury yacht on the Seine. She felt suddenly very uncomfortable in her jeans as they were welcomed by crew members. "Luc, we are not dressed for this," she whispered.

"We can wear whatever we like. There will be no other patrons tonight. Just us and the crew," he answered.

"What? You booked this for us? But how could you? When?"

"It was nothing. One phone call." He shrugged. "Come on, let's go inside and warm up." He opened the door to the restaurant. It was decorated with the same classic look as the outside of the yacht. The top half of the restaurant's walls were clear glass on all sides and provided a perfect view. The bottom half of the walls were rich mahogany. Off to one side, leather couches, armchairs and coffee tables created intimate seating areas. The rest of the space held small tables covered with white linens. Opulent lighting gave it a relaxed and utterly romantic atmosphere, with soft music helping to set the mood.

Megan stood at the entrance, unsure of how to react. Walking into this place was like getting a glimpse of a completely different life— one with both romance and lavishness she had never known. In all her years with Ian, he had never taken her on a date like this. He had never really *romanced* her. They had met, they had fallen in love and they had gotten married. Dates had normally involved going out with their friends to movies or parties. They had gone on several wonderful vacations together, but those were always something Megan had planned and Ian had come along for. He had never once arranged a day like this—one that was meant solely for her enjoyment. Megan looked over at Luc, her eyes smiling as she allowed her feet to bring her into the restaurant. Her cheeks were immediately caressed by the gentle warmth of the room.

"I can't believe you did all this for *me*," she exclaimed softly. "We don't even really know each other."

Luc touched her cheek with his fingertips. "I know you deserve to have someone who will treat you like this, Megan. Someone who wants to see you smile."

Megan shook her head. "You're maybe the most romantic man I've ever met."

"So, will you admit that this is a date, then?"

Megan laughed. "Do you always get what you want?"

"Almost always. I can count one or two times that I didn't," he teased.

"Somehow I believe that."

They could feel the boat move as it set off from the pier, quietly cutting through the water. Megan knew her chance to flee was now gone and she was shocked at how happy that made her. Suddenly, her cellphone rang, interrupting the moment. Megan dug around in her purse to find it.

"It's my son. Will you excuse me?" Megan asked, wondering how Luc would react to the reality of her life.

"Of course." He smiled, seemingly unfazed.

Megan walked over to a far corner of the room as she answered the phone and sat on a couch.

"Hello?"

"Hi, Mom! How's Paris?"

"It's great, honey. How are you?"

"Good. Grandma let me stay up an hour after bedtime and I got to eat chips on the couch last night and right now we're on our way to a movie!"

"Wow! Sweetie, it sounds like you're having a terrific time! I'm so glad."

"Yup, turns out I love it when you go on a holiday. You can stay longer if you want, but that doesn't mean I don't love you. I do."

"I love you too, little man."

"Bye, Mom!"

"Wait, Elliott! Can I talk to Grandma?"

"Nope, she's driving."

"Alright, tell her I love her too and I hope things are going well."

"Will do. See you soon! Love you. Bye!"

"Bye-bye."

Megan ended the call and smiled down at her phone; a picture of Elliott smiled back at her. As much as she loved her little boy, she was far overdue for a break. She looked up at Luc, who was sitting at a table near the window, talking to the server. Elliott was fine and there was no reason for her to feel guilty for being here. She *did* deserve some romance, and if Luc wanted to give this to her, why shouldn't she let that happen? She was an adult. She could enjoy herself and then go home without expecting it to turn into forever, couldn't she?

She got up and walked over to the table, seeing Luc gaze at her as she moved toward him. He stood as she approached him, then reached out and began undoing the buttons of her coat. "Everything okay back home?"

Megan was yet again shocked at herself, as she had been most of the day. This time it was for allowing him to unbutton her coat. "Yes. Elliott is having such a wonderful time that he wants me to stay longer."

"He sounds like a smart boy. Maybe you could," he said, sliding the coat off her shoulders and staring into her emerald eyes.

Megan blinked slowly, completely turned on. "I can't. I need to be home for the weekend. I have a photo shoot I've already postponed to be here."

"That's a shame. I don't think I'll be ready to let you go in two days." Luc hung her coat on the back of her chair and pulled it out for her to sit down.

"So, this will be the third time in your life you didn't get your way, then?" Megan smiled as she sat.

Luc took his seat and was about to say something when they were interrupted by the server bringing a bottle of champagne and two glasses. He uncorked the bottle and poured it for Luc to taste. Luc gave a quick nod and the server poured a glass for each of them.

"*Je reviens tout de suite avec les entrées*," he said.

"*Merci*," Luc said.

He turned back to her, explaining that the waiter would return with appetizers. Then he commented, "You know, neither of us is getting what we want here. You claim you don't want to be on a date, and I will have to let you go sooner than I want."

"True. It seems like we're both destined to be miserable."

"I can't think of anyone I would rather be miserable with."

"To misery!" Megan held up her glass in a toast.

"To the pleasure of torment."

Megan quickly scanned the menu on the table. Dinner was pre-selected and was to be four courses, starting with scallops, then lobster with pumpkin and chestnuts in a seafood emulsion, followed by veal with butternut-squash gnocchi and roasted vegetables. Dessert would be chocolate mousse with a raspberry sauce.

"This looks wonderful."

"I hear it is. The menu was designed by one of the most well-known chefs in Paris and the wine has been selected by one of the world's premier sommeliers. This should be a thoroughly enjoyable meal for me. For you, it will be pure torture because you would rather be alone in your hotel room watching television."

"I'll try to make the best of it." Megan rolled her eyes, pretending to be bored.

"You're such a good sport." Luc refilled her champagne glass for her.

"I see you've decided not to sleep with me." Megan said, picking up her glass.

"What makes you think that?" Luc looked confused.

"You said you wouldn't want me unless I was sober and yet here you are, trying to get me tipsy."

"Oh no, I will give you only enough to help you shed your inhibitions, but no more. I have every intention of sleeping with you."

"Well then, Monsieur Chevalier, by the time I'm done with you, you will have much more experience being disappointed."

Luc gave a little smirk. "You know, I'm torn between admiring your resolve and finding it amusing. Either way, you are one of the sexiest women I've ever met."

Megan felt her face betray her. It was impossible to play it cool when her cheeks kept turning red like this. She was rescued by the server bringing the scallops.

"*Bon appétit*," he said as he put the plates down and left the room.

Megan put her napkin on her lap and picked up her fork. She was feeling a bit tipsy already, having not eaten enough during the day. She took her first bite of the appetizer. "Mmm, my God! That's good."

Luc raised his eyebrows. "If that's your response to a scallop, I can't wait to see how you'll react to what I have planned for later." He grinned as he took his first bite.

As the meal progressed, a warm feeling came over Megan. She felt completely blissful watching the sights of Paris go by as the boat moved down the river. She was indulging in the most delicious cuisine she had ever tasted. It was turning out to be the most romantic meal she had ever had, from the setting to the view to the ambience to the man across from her. Luc seemed to always know what to say. He was always in control not only of himself but of the conversation as well. Her earlier feelings of panic had dissolved into desire. She wanted to be here with Luc in this moment and there was nothing she wanted more than to sleep with him.

Luc pointed out various sites along the way and told Megan about them as they ate. He liked how interested she seemed in learning about his city. She asked a lot of questions and listened carefully to his answers. He could see there was a real depth to her personality. She was full of appreciation and seemed to take nothing for granted. As the evening wore on, Luc's desire for Megan grew into an intense heat, one he had never experienced before. He watched her as she ate and dabbed delicately at her mouth with her napkin. He wanted to feel those lips on his body, he wanted to feel his tongue exploring that perfect mouth. He wanted to feel those long legs of hers wrapped around his waist. It took every bit of self-restraint for him not to sweep everything from the table and take her right there.

When the meal was finished, the server cleared their plates and left. Otis Redding's "These Arms of Mine" started playing. Megan smiled over at Luc. "I've always loved this song."

Luc stood and held out his hand. "If you love it, it would be a shame to let the moment pass by. Come and dance with me."

Megan stood and took his hand. Luc pulled her near, wrapping one hand behind her back and holding her other hand tucked in between them. The side of his face was touching the side of her head. Megan felt herself relax into his arms as he led her to the music. She rested her head on his shoulder, smelling his cologne and feeling his hard body against hers.

Their bodies moved together, their need for each other growing thick as the song played on. It felt to Megan as though she was in a haze. It was like the best dream she'd ever had, except it was some-how, amazingly, real. She shifted her face up near his. Their mouths were almost touching now. Luc moved his face down so that his lips were hovering over hers. He wouldn't kiss her, though. He waited for her to make that final connection, needing to know this was what she wanted. Megan swallowed hard, feeling butterflies in her stomach as she reached her lips up to just barely brush against his. The memory of his kiss from the night before came flooding back into Megan's mind and she wanted to feel that again. He held steady, waiting for her.

Megan parted her lips and gave him a slow, sweet kiss, tasting the wine and chocolate on his mouth. There was no turning back for her now. She had made up her mind to allow herself this one night of pure romance and indulgence, to be with Luc in a way she had thought she never would be with a man again.

It was as though Luc sensed the shift in her; he knew now that she needed to be with him as much as he needed to be with her. He kissed her back softly at first, then harder, with more urgency, accepting the invitation of her parted lips to enter her mouth with his tongue. He explored her with the skill a man who knew exactly what he was doing. Megan's nerves were overtaken by her desire now. Neither she nor Luc noticed the server at the door, bringing coffee. When he saw how intimate the couple was, he turned around, heading back to the kitchen.

They indulged in the most passionate kisses until long after the song ended and the one after it had played out. Luc held Megan's jaw with his fingertips, then lowered his hands down to her shoulders and her back, letting his fingers glide ever so slowly over her. When he reached her bottom, he slid his hands into her back pockets. Megan let her hands rest on his chest and abs, thoroughly turned on by how hard he was.

He took his hands out of her pockets and backed over to a couch in the corner, leading her by her hands. He dropped onto the couch, pulling her down with him onto his lap. They sat together, bodies entangled, kissing and exploring each other's bodies overtop of their clothes.

Megan pulled back from him. "What if someone comes in?"

"This is France. The crew would be surprised if we *didn't* take advantage of the moment." He gave her a knowing grin as he pulled her to him again.

They continued like this for a long time. Megan let her fingers wander under his sweater, touching his smooth skin. She could feel herself becoming wet as she moved her fingers toward his jeans. His kisses were like none she had known before, each one waking up a tiny part of her that had been long dormant until she was finally fully alive again for the first time in years. He had a way of moving his tongue and his lips that made her putty in his hands. It had been so long since she had allowed a man to touch her like this that it felt like the first time again. Luc slid his hand up her shirt to her breasts. He let his fingertips graze the outline of her lacy bra, feeling goosebumps form on her flesh as he touched her. He gently squeezed her breasts, savouring their perkiness. He took his hand out and pulled her onto his lap so that she was straddling him now. Megan could feel his erection through the fabric of their clothes as she kissed him.

"I want you, Luc," she whispered.

"Then come home with me," he replied, kissing her hard on the mouth.

Megan nodded, her voice thick with lust as she spoke. "Yes."

"Stay the night."

"I will."

They were completely unaware that the boat was slowing to a stop as it neared the pier. It was only as it gently bumped against the dock that they remembered where they were. Megan reluctantly got up off his lap and stood, feeling as though she were in the most beautiful dream.

Luc stood, kissing her again before striding across the restaurant to get their coats. He left a large tip on the table and helped Megan into her coat, spinning her to him so he could do up the buttons for her. He kissed her neck, sending shivers through her entire body, before grabbing his coat and sliding it on.

They strolled off the boat hand in hand and thanked those of the crew who were on deck to say good night. Once they reached Luc's car, he unlocked it and opened Megan's door for her. As she got in, her head swirled, her desire and her nerves now at war over what she was about to do.

As they drove along to Luc's apartment, Megan texted Harper to tell her she was spending the night with Luc. A moment later she got an answer back.

YAY! I'm already in bed. My hangover seems to have caught up with me this evening and I have an early meeting tomorrow morning. Ugh. You have fun, you vixen! Fill me in on all the details tomorrow afternoon.

Megan smiled at her friend's reply as she put her cellphone away. Luc reached over and covered her hand with his as he drove, an intimate gesture, its comfort not lost on Megan.

"It's hard to believe I'm doing this. Whose life is this?" Megan asked, leaning her head back against the seat.

"Mine, only much better, because you're in it," he replied as he drove into the parking garage under his building.

They parked and strolled hand in hand to the elevator. Inside, Luc inserted a key and the button for ten, the top floor, lit up. Making the most of the ride up, he pinned her body to the wall with his, kissing her long and hard and deep, a prelude of what was to come. When the elevator stopped, the doors opened onto the foyer to his apartment. Luc tossed his keys on a small table and took off his coat. Unbuttoning her own coat this time, Megan smiled up at Luc as he took it from her and hung it on a coat rack near the elevator door.

He opened a set of double doors leading into the main living space of the apartment. It was an enormous, beautifully furnished home, with a definite warmth and charm that was all French, and Megan's mouth hung open for a second as she took it all in.

"You have the entire floor?"

Luc shrugged. "Yes. I like my privacy and I don't want to be bothered by the sounds of other people when I am home. I hear enough noise at work every day."

Megan glanced at him before continuing to look around his home. He had the most amazing view of Paris through the windows that lined the walls on two sides of the room. A large living room led into a beautiful kitchen with a breakfast nook. A formal dining room was to the left, with seating for eight.

Luc walked across the living room and put on some soft music, then went to the bar. "May I bring you a glass of wine?"

"Please," Megan answered, realizing she might need a drink to keep up her nerve.

Luc poured her half a glass and walked over to her, kissing her on the lips. "Not too much, though," he said with a little grin.

Megan gave him just a hint of a smile as she took the glass.

Luc sipped his own drink and put it down. "Are you tired?"

Megan shook her head. "No."

"Good. Because what I have in mind will take most of the night."

Megan's eyebrows went up. She gulped down the rest of her wine before setting the glass on the table, her nerves suddenly winning the war.

It was as though Luc had read her thoughts. "I want you to relax," he said as he wrapped his arms around her. "I'm assuming that it's been a long time for you, no?"

Megan nodded slightly, biting her lip.

Luc kissed her. "I will take care of you, Megan, like you have never been taken care of before. But first, you must promise not to fall in love with me."

Megan rolled her eyes at his arrogance. "Oh please. You seem to think a little too highly of yourself."

"I want to be with you so much I can taste it. But we can do this only if I know you won't leave here broken-hearted."

"Luc, I want to spend the night with you and then go home to my life. That is it. One night and then it's over. I just need to know that *you* won't fall in love with *me*. I can't bear the thought of leaving you heartbroken." She grinned.

"You are mocking me?"

"Yes, I am. I'm an adult, Luc. I'm here to have sex with you. Nothing more."

"Agreed. *Une nuit.* But let's bring a lifetime of passion to this one night before we part ways." He held her face in his hands and kissed her again. Taking her hand, he led her down the hall to an enormous ensuite.

Megan watched as he crossed the room and turned on the water to fill the bathtub. Pouring some oils into the tub, Luc lit a few candles before returning to her, his eyes full of adoration as he looked at her.

Luc leaned down, running his nose along Megan's neck and up to her ear. He carefully sucked on her earlobe, sending tingles through her entire body. She moaned a little at the feeling of it, a sound Luc had been waiting for. He unfastened the button on her jeans, then lifted her shirt over her head, revealing her red lace bra. Megan reached for Luc's sweater, pulling it over his head. Their eyes moved over each other's bodies, taking in the first thrilling sights. Megan blew out a little puff of air as she gazed at his lean muscles, her hands moving to his abs of their own accord. She needed to touch every inch of his sculpted body, starting right there.

Luc reached out, gripping her waist, feeling her soft ivory skin with his fingertips as he pulled her to him. As he moved his body around behind Megan, he planted slow kisses along the nape of her neck to her shoulder. She shuddered as he let his hands move up to her breasts, then down the front of her body, fingers splayed to take in as much of her skin as possible with each movement. Luc's lips grazed her shoulder as he unzipped her pants and slid them off, along with her French-cut lacy red panties. He lowered his body as he removed her pants. Megan turned her head to see him kneeling behind her in nothing but his jeans. He moved his hands over her legs, exploring her slowly, methodically. His touch was so passionate, so tender that it pleased her to her very core.

Placing his hands on the front of her body, he kissed her all the way up along her spine as he stood. He spun her to face him and smiled at her as he undid her bra with one quick flick of his fingers. Megan gasped a little; this man clearly knew what he was doing. She smiled back at him, now completely certain this was what she wanted, what she had needed for so long. She held his gaze as she slid her bra off her shoulders and to the floor, leaving herself completely nude in front of him. Luc lowered his mouth over her breasts, taking his time with each one, gently sucking on her nipples. Megan felt dizzy with the intensity of her desire as she reached for his jeans. She tried, rather ineffectively, to remove his pants, but found herself powerless to concentrate long enough to manage it. His mouth on her skin did things to her she had only read about. Her hand found its way up and alongside her face as she wrapped her fingers around a lock of her blond hair.

Luc lifted his mouth back up to hers, kissing her urgently now. Taking both of her hands, he backed up, pulling her toward the oversized bathtub. Silence filled the air as he turned off the water. "Here, I filled the tub for us, but only if you want to. I wouldn't want to tell you what to do."

Megan took in the sight of his sexy smile and the dimples it created on his cheeks. "You're a fast learner."

She stepped into the tub and let her body slide into the hot water, feeling herself relax. Luc unabashedly removed what was left of his clothing, giving Megan the first sight of him nude. He was more than she had expected and she felt a little bit intimidated as she stared at his erection. *BOB is SO much smaller than that*, she thought.

He climbed into the tub, facing her, before running his hands over her legs. Holding her thighs, he spread them, then pulled her body toward his so that her legs were wrapped around him.

"It's been a long time for you, and I'm afraid I will hurt you if we don't go slowly," he murmured as he slid his hand between her thighs, letting his fingers glide over her sex.

Megan took a deep breath, her breasts, now full with desire, lifting out of the water as she did. She ached for him to slide his fingers inside her. She could feel herself throbbing as he moved his hand slowly over her. Closing her eyes, she let her lips fall away from each other as he lowered his mouth over hers again. He slid his tongue into her mouth as he pressed the palm of his hand to her clitoris, moving it in slow, light circles over her. The feeling of it was completely exquisite to Megan.

Luc put his thumb along the front of her as he continued to caress the outer edge of her sex with his palm. His other hand massaged her inner thigh masterfully. No part of him had entered her yet, but Megan felt she was already close to coming. A sudden desperation washed over her. She needed to feel him inside her like she had never needed anything before.

She pulled her body closer to his, hoping he would lift her onto his lap. Instead, Luc pulled back a little. "Not yet, Megan. You're not ready for me yet."

He smirked as she sighed in frustration. "Did you forget that anticipation is not to be rushed?"

Something about his arrogant smirk ignited an angry passion in Megan. She was not some terrified virgin. She knew how to take control too. Grabbing the back of his head with her hand, she kissed him hard, sliding her tongue into his mouth. Luc wasn't the only one who knew how to turn someone on. She reached down below the surface of the water with one hand and ran her fingertips along the length of him, feeling how hard and thick he was. Taking his cock in her hand, she gripped him firmly and moved her hand up and down in the most deliberately slow movements.

It quickly became a game of who would break first. Luc allowed the tip of his middle finger to slide into her pussy. He felt her press herself against his hand greedily, and there was that smirk again. Megan took her other hand down between her legs and pushed his finger in further, along with his index finger. She gave him a steady stare as she moved his fingers deep inside her, feeling the water lap against them with her movements. Luc's surprised expression gave her a feeling of power. It was her turn to smirk as she pleasured them both.

"I decide what I'm ready for," she said, biting him on his bottom lip. She pulled herself up onto his lap and rubbed herself over his hard cock. She could feel him respond to her as she teased him, rubbing back and forth slowly. She gave him a little half smile, seeing how badly he wanted her right then.

Luc put his hands on Megan's ass and started moving her over himself roughly, the feeling of it almost too much for either of them as water splashed around them and onto the tiled floor.

"Let's take this to bed," Luc whispered, lifting her up off his lap.

Megan stepped out of the bath, Luc following. He watched her backside as she walked through the open door to his bedroom. She had a perfectly curved bottom and her long, lean legs carried her gracefully as she moved. He caught up with her just as she reached the side of the bed, and spun her to him, kissing her possessively now. Megan wrapped her arms around his neck and pressed her wet body to his as he gripped her ass with both hands. She could feel his huge erection pressed up against her stomach.

His hold on her was firm and he intended to regain control of himself and the moment. He pushed her onto the bed with his mouth still on hers, then moved his lips down along her body, kissing and touching her everywhere as he knelt down beside the bed. He parted her legs and held her inner thighs as he took his first taste of her. Gently sucking on her, then letting his tongue slide into her warmth, he caused Megan to gasp. She tightened her muscles around his tongue as he skilfully explored her. He moved with the perfect amount of pressure, at just the right pace and to all the places she needed to be touched. Megan's breathing became ragged; she caressed her breasts and tugged on her nipples with her fingers. She felt the first delicious wave of climax overtake her, causing her to cry out with the force of it. When it was over, Luc lifted his head and gazed at her hungrily. He crawled up her body and Megan lifted her head off the bed to find his mouth with hers.

"Mmm. I'm glad you liked that," he murmured as he kissed her back. "As much as I hate to, I need to go get something for us. Give me one minute." He lifted himself off her. "This is only a suggestion, but you might want to get under the covers to warm up."

"I'll think about it." She grinned.

Luc walked into the ensuite, returning with a bottle of massage oil and a package containing a condom. He paused for a moment to turn on the fireplace on the far side of the room.

"I see you decided to take my suggestion," he said as he took in the sight of her lying in his bed, looking so beautiful. The ends of her blond hair were still wet and her cheeks were flushed. Something about the sight of her there stirred a yearning deep within Luc that he hadn't known existed.

Her head was propped up on one arm as she watched him come toward her. He ran his hand through his damp hair as he watched her. He was completely impressive as he moved his sculpted body toward her, every inch of him rock hard. As he came nearer, a part of Megan started to worry again that he might be too much for her.

Luc noticed the sudden look of panic cross over her face. "Ah, yes. I'm told that I'm big. That's why I was telling you we need to take it slow."

Megan nodded her agreement.

Placing the bottle and condom package on the night table, Luc took one of her hands, brought his lips down to her wrist and kissed it slowly, carefully. He kept his mouth there for a moment, then let his lips glide up to the bend in her arm. He very gently sucked on her skin for a moment, causing Megan's eyes to shut as she took in the delectable sensation of it. Pouring oil into his palm, he warmed the liquid in his hands before massaging her arm all the way from her fingertips to her shoulder. He slowly repeated this methodical treatment on the rest of her body, kissing every bit of her exposed skin and gazing at her as he went. Megan had never had a man who was so thorough before, and it made her ache for more.

"Turn over, please," he said.

Megan happily complied, rewarded by his large, warm hands caressing her back, her legs and finally making their way to her bottom. The air was now warm from the fireplace and the flames gave the room a sensual glow. Luc poured the oil onto her ass, causing her to squirm a little with the cool feeling of it. Bringing his hand between her legs, he rubbed the oil over her and into her centre with his thumbs. He flipped her over onto her back again and continued to move his thumbs slowly in and out of her as he lowered his body over hers. Megan knew she was ready. She needed to feel him inside her, all of him. She reached out and took the condom package off the night table and opened it, unrolling the condom over his length.

"You are ready?" Luc asked

"Yes, Luc, now."

He gripped her hips with both hands and rolled both of their bodies so that he was lying on his back and she was on top of him. Megan moved herself over him, rubbing ever so slowly along his erection for a few torturous moments before she guided the head of his cock into herself with her hand. She moved her body very deliberately over his, bringing him in all the way, inch by inch. He was almost too much for her and she was grateful that she was on top so she could set the pace.

Luc sat up so his mouth could find hers. Megan wrapped her arms around him as she slowly lifted and lowered herself on his lap. He moaned with the feeling of it; she was so wet and warm and tight. Her skin felt like silk to Luc and as she gazed into his eyes, he found her the most gorgeous woman he had ever seen. He watched her as she moved over him harder and more easily with each thrust of her hips. He couldn't remember being with a woman by whom he was so enthralled.

Their eyes locked as she rocked herself over him in slow drags. It was no longer just their bodies connecting, it was as though their very souls had reached each other. Swirls of complete and transformative passion overtook them as they kissed and touched and moved together. Somehow, what had started out as a one-night stand had become the most intimate experience either had known.

"You are so beautiful like this, Megan. You have no idea."

There was that accent again and with just the words she needed to hear. She kissed his mouth, then closed her eyes and parted her lips as she let go. Everything about this moment felt magnificent to her as she moved her body back and forth on his. For so long she had forced herself to forget how incredible sex could be, but after this, she would never be able to lie to herself about it again. Luc was so tender, so passionate, and he knew exactly how she wanted him to touch her. He moved his hands up to her breasts, taking each one in his mouth, sucking on her nipples more forcefully now. He ran his hands along her body, wanting to feel every part of her as she lowered and lifted herself over him. Megan grabbed his face with both hands and lifted it up to hers, pressing her forehead to his as her breath caught and she started to come. Her body jolted with the first wave of her orgasm.

"Yes! Oh fuck, yes, Luc!" she breathed, squeezing his cock as she came, bringing him over the edge. She bit his bottom lip and pushed her body down hard, feeling him pulsing inside her.

"Ah oui! Je suis là! Oui!" he groaned, as he emptied himself in long, powerful surges.

They collapsed into each other's arms, kissing and holding each other tightly as they basked in the all-encompassing after-effects of this most intimate act. As she recovered, Megan suddenly felt her eyes stung by tears. She tried to fight them, but they started to pour down her cheeks in spite of her best efforts. Embarrassed, she quickly lifted herself off Luc and stood, turning toward the ensuite. As she started to hurry away, she could feel Luc's hand on her wrist, holding her in place.

"Excuse me," she whispered, "I just need to run to the washroom."

Luc stood behind her, wrapping his arms around her chest and waist, pulling her close to him. "Stop, Megan. Don't run from me."

Megan pressed her palms to her cheeks, trying to wipe away the tears. It was as though a dam had burst and now a river of emotions poured from her. A small sob escaped her mouth.

"It's okay, Megan. It's okay to cry. I will take care of you." Luc turned her slowly around to face him and held her firmly to his chest.

Megan let him hold her for a long time as she cried, now feeling overcome with both emotion and humiliation for having this reaction in front of him. She felt suddenly pathetic and weak. He lifted her face to his, trying to kiss away the tears.

"You are upset because I'm the best lover you have ever known, and we agreed it was only for one night. Don't worry. I will sleep with you again. You don't have to cry," he teased.

Megan laughed through her tears, now ready to talk. "I don't know why I'm crying. I feel so stupid right now. I can't believe I'm acting like this."

"You have denied yourself for so long, Megan. The tears are part of the release you just allowed yourself. It's natural."

"I'm sorry. I've ruined our night. I should go," she replied quietly, slipping out of his arms and hurrying to the bathroom. She started to pick up her clothes, which had been strewn on the floor. As she straightened up, she felt a warm, soft fabric cover her back. Luc stood behind her, wrapping her in his long white bathrobe.

"You have ruined nothing. Come with me. We will have a drink together and talk."

When Megan turned to him, he gave her that look that made her feel like she was the only woman on the planet. "Come," he said, tying the sash of the bathrobe around her waist.

He strode across the room and plucked a pair of black silk pyjama bottoms off a hook on the door, then pulled them on. Taking her hand, he brought her to the living room and over to one of the couches. She sank into it, curling her knees up to her chest and wrapping the robe around her legs as he poured them each a glass of port. He handed her one and sat down beside her, touching her cheek lightly with his fingertips. She had stopped crying now but knew she must look red and blotchy. She didn't want him to look at her.

"You must think I'm a complete mess," she said into her glass.

"Why must I think that? You are a complex and very genuine woman, Megan. There is nothing fake about you and I like that."

"But to start crying after sex? It isn't exactly sophisticated," she replied with an unmistakable tone of disdain in her voice.

"It wasn't what I was expecting, but with you, I don't know what to expect. You are both powerful and vulnerable at the same time. It's irresistible to me, actually. Your tears make me want to protect you and take care of you, even if it's just for a short time." He pressed his lips to her forehead and held them there for a moment.

"I can't let you do that, Luc. Not even for one night. I shouldn't even be here. What good is it for me to allow myself to feel this . . . this . . . much and then go back to my life?"

Luc held her cheek in one hand. "Why can't you allow yourself to have a full and rich life? You are a sexy, gorgeous young woman. It seems horrible that you sequester yourself like a nun because of your ex-husband's mistakes. You need to live, Megan. *Really live.* Enjoy life in all of its beauty. Like we just did. You are incredible in bed, and I can tell you love it. Why would you refuse yourself that?"

Megan looked down at her hands, speaking quietly. "I told you. My life is complicated. I have a son who needs me and a business to run. I've spent the past five years just holding it all together to give him the best life I can, Luc. I can't afford to be trying to find a man while I am everything for him."

Megan looked into his eyes, feeling her strength return and her protective wall rebuilding itself. "And the truth is, I stopped believing in fairy tales years ago. They don't happen, Luc. They just don't. There isn't going to be some perfect man who is going to sweep me off my feet and love me and love my son forever."

Luc tilted his head. "I agree with you about the fairy tales—they are full of shit. Finding *that* man is not likely. But what if you could find a man to just be with? To just be with but nothing else?"

"Like you, Luc?" Her eyes bored into his.

"I would love for it to be me, but I meant someone who lives near you. Someone you could see more often than almost never."

"I'm just not interested in that, Luc. It really doesn't appeal to me. I'm going home in two days, back to my life, and it's okay. I don't need all of this to be happy. I have my little boy and my family to love me, and good friends. That's enough for me."

"You might believe that, but I don't. You're lying to yourself."

"Don't tell me what I know and don't know about myself. You've known me for exactly one day." Megan was feeling angry and suddenly wanted to be alone.

"I do know you. I was just as close to you as two people can be. I saw your face and felt every part of your body while we made love. You are a passionate woman; you should not hide from that. You need to find someone to be with."

Megan stood up and started walking to Luc's ensuite to collect her things. "What I need right now is to be alone, Luc. I don't even know what I'm doing here. I'm going back to the hotel."

Feeling emotionally and physically exhausted, Megan slowly started picking up her clothes. Jet lag and confusion were clouding her brain now. She heard Luc approaching and turned. He stood leaning against the door jamb, folding his arms across his bare chest as he watched her. Megan couldn't help but stare at him for a moment— there was no denying that he was unbelievably sexy.

He spoke in a low voice as he gazed back at her. "You're breaking your word. We agreed to one night together."

"I'm tired, Luc. I need to go."

He crossed the room and took her clothes out of her hand, placed them on a stool, then wrapped his arms around her. "You're tired and you need to stay."

He lowered his mouth down to hers and kissed her gently. His touch made her knees go weak. Megan was too exhausted to resist his offer. The thought of his warm bed was so much more appealing than going out into the chilly night again. He picked her up and carried her to the bed, setting her down and getting in beside her. He pulled the covers over them both and lay on his side. Wrapping his arm over her, he kissed her on the cheek.

"Let's just sleep now. Let yourself have one night sleeping in someone's arms. You can go back to your normal life again soon."

Megan closed her eyes, feeling warm and safe. Giving in to her exhaustion, she fell immediately asleep.

Luc lay awake, thinking about their day and night together. What was it about her that drew him to her so fiercely? Yes, she was beautiful, but he had been with many beautiful women. There was no doubt that she was strong to have held it together for her son for so long. When she allowed herself to be vulnerable though, she almost broke his heart. She was gorgeous and smart and warm, and if he wasn't careful, he was going to fall in love with her. He would need to work hard to put a stop to these feelings. Luc wasn't going to be the man who would rescue her from her loneliness. He wasn't ever going to be a good father to her son or a husband to her, which was what she needed. He would always be what he was—rich and single and looking for the next challenge, the next adventure.

SEVEN

The next morning when he woke, Luc felt content and well rested. He had finally had a good sleep for the first time in weeks. He reached for Megan but she was no longer in his bed. He got up and made his way to the bathroom. Her clothes were gone. Luc walked through his apartment, hoping to find her in the kitchen. Even though he knew he had to let her go, he wasn't ready just yet.

His heart sank. A note was waiting for him on the kitchen counter.

Luc,

Thank you for a beautiful day and night. You are a thoughtful and romantic man, and I'm glad to have met you. I will always remember my time with you fondly.

All the best,
Megan

Luc sighed heavily as he read it. The realization of how badly he wanted her to be there hit him hard. He had been counting on one more morning together—to talk, eat and make love again. He had wanted to send her off feeling sexy and alive. But after her reaction last night, he was worried she would go home feeling sad instead.

* * *

Megan had snuck into the hotel room as the sun was coming up. She was glad she hadn't woken Harper as she walked to her bedroom and carefully shut the door. She couldn't face her friend just yet. She needed to sleep and get her emotions under control again. For so many years, she had fought to keep her feelings in check, at a distance, even. Within twenty-four hours, Luc had managed to cause those walls she had built around her heart to crumble into dust. She felt like she had been cut wide open, exposed to him, and she couldn't have that. It simply wouldn't do for her to be in love. Period.

She crawled back into bed and lay there, trying to fall asleep. A couple of hours later, she heard Harper leave for her meeting. Megan waited until she was gone and then got up and took a long, hot shower, trying to wash away her memories along with the scent of Luc. There would be no evidence of their night together now, other than a slight tenderness in areas of her body that had been long forgotten.

When she got out of the shower, she walked over to her purse to grab her cellphone. She hadn't checked for messages since the evening before. She dug around frantically for a minute, not finding it.

"Oh no, no, no. Don't tell me I left it at Luc's!" Megan muttered to herself as she walked over to check her coat pockets.

Thinking back, she remembered she had had it in his car when they were on the way to his apartment because she had texted Harper. It was either in his car or at his place, which would make her graceful exit from his life impossible. Now Megan would have to go back there right away in case her mom was trying to reach her.

"Shit," she sighed to herself as she got dressed and ready to leave. She wasn't sure what time Harper would be back from her meeting, so she decided to take a cab over to Luc's.

Megan's heart was in her throat as she paid the driver and got out of the cab in front of Luc's building. She walked up the steps and buzzed, then waited for a moment. She still wasn't sure what she was going to say.

"*Âllo?*" A woman's voice came over the speaker.

"Oh, um, hi. I'm looking for Luc."

"He's not here right now." The voice now sounded bored.

"Okay. This is Megan, a friend of his. I think I left my cellphone there. Is it possible for me to come up and check?"

"Oh, yes, the American. It is Simone. I found your phone. I will send the elevator down for you," Simone responded tersely before buzzing her into the building.

When Megan reached Luc's floor, she found Simone standing in the foyer, lighting a cigarette.

"Come in. Your phone is in the kitchen. I found it earlier on the floor near the couch."

Megan smiled and followed Simone inside. "Thank you. That's a relief."

"Would you like a coffee? Luc's washing machine broke and I am here waiting for the repairman to finish." Simone poured two coffees and pointed Megan to a chair.

"Um, I should just get my phone and go, but thank you," Megan replied, hoping to leave before Luc got back.

"Sit for a minute," Simone said, bringing the mugs over to the table. "That is an old trick, no? To leave something behind so you can see the man again." She gave Megan a knowing smile.

"No, it honestly was just a careless mistake. I should go."

"So, you stayed here last night? His plan worked, then."

Megan gave her a confused look as she slid into the chair opposite her. "Plan?"

"Luc loves American women. All French men do, actually. Well, mostly the boys love the college girls who come over here. But he hasn't outgrown it yet," she said, taking a drag on her cigarette and blowing the smoke out. She continued. "You are known for being, what is that term, an 'easy thing'?"

"A sure thing," Megan answered quietly.

"Yes. That's it. Luc has an expression to describe it—'they hear the accent and then spread their legs.' Megan, you seem nice. I only tell you this so you will not expect more from Luc. He is not going to be anyone's knight in shining armour."

"Right," Megan agreed, wishing she were anywhere but here listening to this. Her eyes searched the room for her phone unsuccessfully.

"He took you to the Louvre, then the Eiffel Tower, no?"

"Yes." Megan flinched in surprise.

"I'm guessing he took you for a private dinner on a yacht, on the Seine?"

"Yes," Megan replied, suddenly feeling nauseous.

"That is what he does. Always the same. The Louvre, the tower and, if the woman is a real challenge, the yacht. You must have been the toughest of challenges to end up back here. Most women give in on the boat."

Simone sucked on her cigarette before continuing. "He is both a romantic and a predator—like most men, maybe, but smarter about it. He sees something he wants and knows exactly how to get it. Don't think too poorly of him, though. He really believes he is doing women a service. Taking them out of their dull lives and into something exciting and romantic for a short time. He likes to send them home feeling sexy."

Megan felt numb as she listened to Simone talk. Her voice came out as almost a whisper. "I should go, Simone. Where's my phone?"

"I have upset you. I only tell you this to help you. I hope you can see that?" Simone tried to look concerned as she got up to get Megan's phone.

"Yes, of course. Thank you," Megan said, feeling confused and unsure if she should be thanking Simone or slapping her smug face. She stood up and took her phone back.

"I'll tell him you were here," Simone said as they walked to the elevator together.

"No, please don't. I didn't intend to see him again anyway." Megan managed a weak smile as she looked at Simone, trying to gage her reaction. She pushed the button to call the elevator.

"I'll keep it our little secret. No point in him knowing you came back for more. He's out with another woman today, anyway. She is French, so he'll have to use a different game."

Her words dug into Megan like talons. Megan willed the elevator to arrive before she had to hear any more. Finally the doors opened and she could escape. She pushed the button and gave Simone a little nod and a weak smile.

"Enjoy the rest of your trip, Megan. I will be here waiting for the repairman to finish." She rolled her eyes as the doors closed.

Megan tried to blink back tears as she rode down. Her worst nightmare at that moment would be for Luc to be there when she got to the main floor. *Please don't be here, please don't be here*, she begged silently.

As the doors opened onto the main floor, she was filled with a temporary relief at finding the lobby empty. She quickly rushed out of the building and into the cold rain that had started to fall. She walked briskly down the street, not thinking about where she was going.

She had been used, and that awful woman had just delighted in filling her in on what an idiot she was. Simone's words burned a hole through Megan's heart: *an easy thing . . . he is a predator . . . most women give in on the boat . . .*

Everything he had said was a lie. This was just a game he played to fuck as many women as he could. He didn't want to take care of her or show her his city. Her mind raced through the day before and all the time they had spent together at the museum and the Eiffel Tower and dinner. He had seemed so sincere and tender. All that stuff about art and his mother. How could all of that have just been a regular routine for him? How was that possible? Maybe Simone was lying to her. But if that was the case, how could Simone know where Luc had taken her? Was that why he had brought Harper and her back to the hotel two nights earlier? Was it all just to get her into bed? Was it all really that calculated?

She walked for several blocks before realizing she had no idea where she was. Stopping to look around, she tried to find a cab. She was no longer on a main street, so she would have to find her way back to a main road to get a cab. She suddenly felt completely alone. She was lost in Paris, it was freezing and raining, and she had been used. Luc was with another woman before the sheets had even gotten cold.

She found her cellphone and started to send a text to Harper, but her phone died before she could hit Send. "Motherfucker!" she exclaimed under her breath. A passerby clearly understood, giving her a dirty look for her foul language. She shoved her phone back into her purse and continued walking, trying to wipe the tears away with her hands. They were streaming down her cheeks now, mixing with the rain. Megan shivered, feeling chilled right to the bone.

Finding herself back on Luc's street, Megan's heart pounded in her chest with rage and, now, urgency. She needed to get out of here before Luc got home and saw her. She would lose all sense of dignity if he saw her here now.

She rushed along away from his building as quickly as her legs could carry her. Suddenly, a sleek black car pulled alongside her. She looked at it out of the corner of her eye, her heart feeling like it had jumped into her throat as she heard his voice.

"Megan!" Luc called, sounding happy to see her.

She refused to look and kept walking quickly.

"Megan? What's wrong? Get in the car before you freeze," Luc ordered as he drove slowly beside her.

"Fuck off," Megan snapped, without looking at him.

"Would you stop walking and tell me what's wrong?" Luc called firmly.

"Nothing will be wrong as soon as I get away from you. Now seriously, fuck off!" she spat as she turned in the opposite direction.

He couldn't turn around because of the other cars on the road, but he could pull over. Luc hit the brakes hard, swerving the car to the side of the road. Several cars behind him honked. He grabbed the keys and got out, jogging up the street to catch her.

Megan felt a hand on her arm, pulling her to a stop. She froze in place and tried to shake his arm away. "Let go of me," she said firmly, through her teeth.

"Not until you tell me what has made you so angry with me," Luc said, spinning her to face him.

Megan looked up at him. He took no notice of the rain pouring down as he gave her a hard stare.

"I found out about your little game. Simone filled me in. I guess I was just another woman to hear your accent and spread her legs, right?" she shouted.

"What?" Luc's head snapped back in surprise. "There is no game, Megan. I don't know what she told you, but I really like you."

Megan scoffed. "I'm sure you liked all of us, for a few minutes." She tugged her arm out of his grip and started to move away.

Luc easily matched her pace, staying right beside her. "Megan, stop. Let me give you a ride to the hotel. I want to get you out of the rain so you can warm up and I can find out what Simone said. There must be some misunderstanding."

Megan quickened her step, ignoring him and craning her neck in search of a cab.

"Megan, stop! This is silly. How can I defend myself if I don't know what she told you?"

Megan stepped out onto the street to flag down a passing cab, but it continued on. "That's hardly my problem, Luc. If you want to know what Simone said, go ask her. As far as I'm concerned, you're just another bad memory. Now fuck off!"

Luc grabbed her arms and pulled her back onto the sidewalk as another car barrelled toward her. The driver of the car let out a long honk as he passed. Luc spun her to him. "Megan, stop this! You are acting like an insane person. Come with me to the car so we can sort this out!"

"Sort what out, exactly?" Megan spat out, her face wrinkling up in disgust. "How you like American women because we're so easy? You won the game, Luc! You knew exactly what to do and say to get me into bed, just like you've done with countless other women! It's my own damn fault for trusting you in the first place."

"Megan, there is no game. I really like you and I wanted to be with you." Luc's voice was a mixture of annoyance and pleading.

Megan rolled her eyes and sighed. "You know what? It doesn't fucking matter! We agreed to one night. No more. We had it. Whether or not you've done the same routine with a thousand women or not makes no difference. It's clearly over. Now just get away from me."

"Megan, I have not done that a thousand times. Just come with me out of this rain. I don't want to end things like this." He pushed his now-drenched hair off his forehead with his hand.

"It doesn't really matter how it ends. It's done, which is how we both wanted it."

Luc took hold of her upper arms with both hands. "It *does* matter. I don't want you to go home so upset. Let me take you to the hotel. Get in the car."

Megan shook him off. "You don't get it, do you?! I told you before—I don't *need* you. I don't fucking *need* a man! I am *not* getting into your car!"

Seeing a cab, Megan stepped off the sidewalk and held her hand up. The cab stopped and she got in without looking back.

EIGHT

Megan's mind was swirling as she fumbled through her purse to find her room key. She was shivering violently and her hands felt like ice, making it hard to unlock the door. When she finally got in, she found the suite empty; Harper was still at her meeting. Glad to find herself alone, she walked directly to her bathroom. She turned the shower on to heat up the water and stripped down, feeling cold and tired. She stayed under the spray of the hot water for a long time, letting the heat rid the chill from her bones.

When Megan got out, she realized she was starving, having not eaten since the night before. She could hear Harper on the phone as she opened the bathroom door, dressed in a hotel robe and slippers.

Harper grinned and waved enthusiastically when she saw Megan. The expression on her face changed as she watched her best friend dissolve into tears and collapse onto the loveseat.

"I have to go. My friend Megan just came in." She paused. "*Au revoir.*"

Harper tossed her cell onto the coffee table and rushed over to Megan. "Oh my God, what happened, honey?"

Megan told her the entire story from the beginning. Her head was pounding by the time she had let it all out. "It's just so humiliating, you know? To find out I am just one of many."

"Meg, do you think you can trust Simone? She's a total bitch. What if she was just screwing with you?"

"I ran into him when I left, Harper. He didn't exactly deny it."

"Oh, Meg, I am so sorry. If I had known that this was what he did to amuse himself, I never would have set you up with him. I just feel so responsible," Harper said, pulling Megan's head onto her shoulder.

"It's not your fault. How could you have known? He seems so sincere and thoughtful. Besides, I knew what I was doing. I made my own choices."

"But Meg, I practically pushed you into his bed. I *literally* dragged you to meet him, and then I left you at the restaurant with him yesterday, like an asshole. I feel just horrible. What kind of friend am I, to push you into the arms of a total creep?"

"Harper, it's not your fault. You were just trying to give me a good time. How could you have known?"

"I really thought I knew him better than that. I never should have done this."

"I chose to go with him, Harper. I chose to get into bed with him. That was all me. I wanted to."

"But you never would have if you had known the truth about him."

"Oh, I don't know why I'm so upset about it anyway. It was only ever going to be one night. What difference does it make if I was the first woman he seduced this way or the hundredth?"

"It makes all the difference," Harper said, giving her a peck on the head.

"It does, doesn't it?"

They sat for a minute and then Megan straightened up suddenly. "You know what? I'm in Paris for only one more night, and I'll be damned if I'm going to let that prick ruin it. Enough tears. What are we going to do?"

"Are you hungry?" Harper asked.

"Famished."

"I say we spend the afternoon eating and shopping and drinking too much wine, then we see where the day takes us."

"Deal."

* * *

Luc arrived back at his apartment thoroughly pissed off. He was freezing and drenched, and the driver's seat of his car had become soaked on the way home. He stormed through his front door, looking for Simone. As he crossed through to the kitchen he could smell her cigarettes, which caused his anger to build. He hated that she insisted on smoking in his home. She had been his assistant for years, but he was furious enough to fire her right then.

He found her reading a magazine at his table, drinking his wine. "Simone, are you feeling especially bitchy today? Is that why you had to upset an innocent woman?"

Simone gave him a slightly bored look, blowing smoke toward him. "So, you heard from the American? I did you both a favour. You can be rid of her now, and she will get over you quickly."

"You forget yourself, Simone. I am your boss. Not the other way around. I never gave you permission to interfere in my personal life! And put out that fucking cigarette! I've told you before, I don't like that in my home."

He stalked down the hall to the laundry room. Finding the

repairman gone, he turned back to the kitchen. When he got there, he found Simone putting on her coat to leave. He crossed his arms and glared at her.

Simone glared back as she picked her purse up off the counter. "I'm going, so you can finish your temper tantrum alone. I don't get paid to be yelled at."

"You also don't get paid to be cruel."

"Why does it matter to you what this woman thinks? She means nothing to you."

"How could you possibly know that?"

"Because no one means anything to you, Luc. Not even me, and I have been the only woman in your life who has lasted more than a few weeks," she declared as she walked out the front door.

Luc let her go without saying anything. He was pissed off and cold and was in no mood for any drama from Simone. He had just finished a long, boring meeting with his accountant, in which he had found himself unable to concentrate. He hadn't been able to get Megan out of his mind since he woke up and found that she was gone. Pouring himself a brandy, he took a long gulp, feeling the warmth slide down his throat. He undressed as he walked down the hall to shower.

As the afternoon wore on, Luc sat at his desk in his home office, unable to get any work done. His mind would not let him think of anything other than Megan. When he first saw her walking in the rain, soaked, he had been excited. He was sure she would be happy to see him and that maybe he could bring her home and spend the night with her again. He had been rushing home to get changed so he could go find her.

As much as he didn't want to admit it, something had changed inside him when he was with her. For the first time in a long time, maybe ever, he had felt completely happy to be with a woman. He had had a taste of what it would be like to be with her and he craved more. Megan was beautiful and caring and strong and fun. But there was more. Something about the way she looked at him when they were alone, and the way she touched him, was irresistible to him. They had agreed to one night, but he knew that would never be enough for him.

Luc grabbed his keys and his coat. He needed to find her. He couldn't live with himself if she left France thinking she meant nothing to him.

He tried calling Harper's cellphone when he got to his car. No answer. Before he left the parking garage, he sent her a text. Harper, I need to find Megan. She's got the wrong idea about me. Please tell me where she is.

He drove over to the hotel and went straight up to their floor. He knocked, waited and then knocked again, louder. Checking his cellphone, he found no response from Harper. He went down to the lobby and used the hotel phone to leave a message on their room voice mail. Not sure where to go next, he took a seat at the hotel bar and ordered a coffee, deciding to wait.

* * *

Harper and Megan had just finished a leisurely lunch at the BHV department store and were wandering around the shops picking out gifts for Megan to take home when Harper's cellphone rang.

She checked to see who was calling and then looked up at Megan. "It's him!"

Megan rolled her eyes. "Why would he even bother? I was very clear that I wanted him to leave me alone."

Harper put her phone back into her purse. "Well, that's that, then."

"Exactly," Megan muttered as she flipped through some skirts on a sale rack.

They browsed around for a while longer. Megan selected a beautiful hat and scarf for her mom and some hand-painted toy soldiers for Elliott. Harper's phone kept buzzing in her purse, indicating she had a text message. She swiped the screen on her phone and read the message from Luc, deciding to show it to Megan.

"He really seems to want to talk to you, Meg. I'm starting to think Simone was messing with you. She's seriously a bitch, and I wouldn't put it past her to try to upset you just for her own amusement."

"Harper, please don't start going soft on me here. He's a total womanizer. He probably just wants to see if he can get me to sleep with him again before I go. That would be a real conquest for him."

"Maybe, Meg, but I don't know. I've known Luc for a long time and the more I think about it, I really don't think he's like that."

"Well, even so, he got what he wanted and it's over. He's just another dick I have to forget."

* * *

Two hours later, Megan and Harper walked through the front door of the hotel, arms loaded with purchases. Megan was finally feeling better as the pair made their way across the lobby, chatting about what they were going to do that night.

Megan glanced over toward the bar. "Oh, fuck me," she said under her breath.

Harper turned quickly to her friend to see what was wrong. She looked over in time to see Luc striding over to them, appearing very uncomfortable. He had his hands shoved into the pockets of his slacks and a concerned expression on his face.

Megan rushed to push the elevator button, dropping some of her packages on the ground. One of the toy soldiers rolled across the floor, landing in front of Luc. He picked it up and looked at it for a moment, then glanced up at Megan. She was doing her best to ignore him, scrambling to get her things gathered up as quickly as possible. He walked over and picked up a couple of her bags, then stood waiting for her to look at him. Megan sighed and gave him a cold stare.

"I've been waiting for you, Megan. I need to talk to you," Luc said quietly.

"There's really nothing you have to say that I want to hear," Megan replied curtly, snatching the toy back from Luc and dropping it into the bag.

"I know you don't, but I'm asking you to listen anyway."

The elevator doors opened and Harper and Megan stepped in. Luc followed them before the door could close.

He stood beside Megan and took a deep breath before he started to speak. "I don't know exactly what Simone told you, but she spoke out of turn. She was in the mood to cause trouble today. You need to give me a chance to explain."

Megan scoffed. "Why do I need to do that, Luc? I already *spread my legs* like you knew I would. I don't think I owe you any more than that!" The doors opened again and they started down the hall to the suite.

"Why do you keep saying that? About legs spreading?"

"Isn't that your charming saying about American women? We hear the accent and then spread our legs?" Megan hissed at him.

"*C'est quoi ce bordel?* Fucking Simone," Luc muttered, shaking his head.

"Have you said that or not, Luc?" Megan snapped.

He winced. "Yes, I'm ashamed to admit that I did say it once, but not in reference to anyone I was with. I was referring to some women at the club one night."

Harper dropped her bags and fished around her purse for her

room key. She looked up and glared at Luc. "Nice," she muttered, her voice dripping with sarcasm.

"Okay," Megan replied, nodding her head, "I think I've heard all I need to, Luc. You can go now."

"I admit it was a horrible thing to say. It was crass, and I've hurt your feelings. I'm sorry, Megan. I never thought of you that way. I promise. Please don't go home so angry with me."

"Why does it even matter to you, Luc? Honestly—why? I am *leaving* in the morning. We are never going to cross paths again. It's over. Goodbye. *Au revoir*. I just want to enjoy the rest of my trip with my friend." Megan gave him an exasperated look.

Harper managed to get the door open and push her bags into the suite, using her feet as she held the door. Neither Luc nor Megan noticed her struggling or the door shutting behind her. They stood in the hall staring at each other, each one waiting for the other to give in.

Luc looked up at the ceiling and rubbed his face, sighing before he spoke. "Megan, I don't know why it matters to me, but it just does. For some reason, I just can't live with the idea that you will go home hating me. I care about you, Megan. I want you to be happy. Everything I said yesterday was true. All of the things we felt together were real. None of it was a lie. I meant everything I said. I *wanted* to show you those places, to take care of you, to take you away from your life, even if just for a little while." Luc touched her cheek with his fingertips.

Megan moved her head away from his touch and glared at him. "Is that whole plan yesterday a thing you do? You take women to the Louvre and the Eiffel Tower and then book a yacht for dinner?"

Luc looked genuinely surprised at her question. "No! I have gone to these places with other women before, but it is not some *regular* thing I do. I just took you where I thought *you* would want to go."

Luc stared at her as she turned and pulled her key card out of her purse. She inserted it in the door and opened it. He picked up her bags and put them inside for her, then blocked the door with his arm, keeping her in the hall with him.

She finally looked up at him, hurt in her eyes. "It just all seems so . . . *targeted*, you know? So calculated. You knew if you did certain things I would end up in your bed. I am ashamed that I'm so predictable and gullible." She grimaced, displaying her disdain.

"Oh, Megan, please don't think that. Of course I wanted you, but is that so wrong? You are a remarkable woman. Since you fell into my arms the other night, I haven't stopped thinking about you. Even when I was with my accountant this morning. She had to ask me at least twenty times if I was listening. It was embarrassing, actually. I haven't felt this turned upside down . . . maybe ever."

"So, the woman you were with this morning was your accountant?" Megan gave him a hard look.

"Yes. Why?" He looked temporarily confused and then his jaw set tightly as he put the pieces together. "Did Simone tell you I was with another woman?"

"She did," Megan answered.

"I don't know what her fucking problem is. I might have to fire her," he said.

"Isn't it obvious? She must be in love with you, Luc."

"No, she isn't." He dismissed the idea. "And even if she were, there is no excuse that I will accept for her upsetting you like this. I'm sorry for her rudeness. Can we please start over?"

Megan shook her head sadly. "No, we can't. I'm going home."

"I know, but I can't let you leave here hating me. Please don't let Simone ruin our time together. Everything was real, Megan. All of it." Unable to help himself, Luc lifted his hand and held her cheek in his palm. The door shut quietly behind him, leaving the pair standing alone in the hall again.

Megan made no effort to remove his hand, softening at the tenderness of his touch. "I believe you, Luc, but I'm also disappointed with some of the things I've learned about you today."

Luc sighed heavily. "I will always regret that I disappointed you, Megan. When I woke up this morning, I reached for you but you were gone. I decided I would come find you as soon as I got out of my meeting. I hoped I could have just one more day with you and maybe, if I was really lucky, one more night as well. I was fooling myself last night to think that one night would be enough with you. It would take a thousand nights for me to even begin to get my fill."

"Those are sweet words, Luc, and I appreciate that you came to find me. I'll go home feeling less of a fool than I did this morning. But it doesn't change the fact that whatever this was, it's over. I'm going to go pack now and spend the evening with my friend. Take care of yourself, Luc."

Luc sighed, realizing he had gotten as far as he could with her at the moment. "I will go, but I'm walking away from you with many regrets. I will regret the things I said and did that upset you. I will regret that I never got the chance to wake up with you in my arms. Most of all, I will regret that you are not with me."

He pulled her to him, wrapping his arms around her one last time. "You *are* a beautiful woman, and I hope you will let yourself have the life you deserve."

Megan's hands were pressed against his chest. She could feel her body respond to his touch and her anger melt away. "I hope you'll do the same. Goodbye, Luc."

He kissed her lips slowly and carefully, both of them taking in the feel of each other one last time before he walked away. Megan felt a sense of heartache settle over her as the door closed behind her. She was confused. Part of her wanted to believe it all was real, part of her still felt used, but most of her knew it really didn't matter. They were done. He would now be just another memory for her.

NINE

The next day, Megan felt completely drained as she waited for her connecting flight in New York. The flight was delayed a couple of hours due to bad weather. She had called her mom to let her know about the delay and then wandered around the shops in JFK for a while. She desperately wanted to get home to her cozy house on her quiet street and return to her very predictable life with Elliott and her mom.

Try as she might, she couldn't help feeling overcome by swells of emotion throughout the day. Luc had occupied her thoughts for most of her flight from Paris and she had finally decided to allow herself the day to get over him. It had come as no surprise how much this was affecting her. It was as though being with him had opened up a floodgate of feelings she had managed to hold back for half a decade. She had allowed herself to be truly vulnerable and intimate with him, and it had been a mistake. Leaving Paris with a sense of humiliation and sadness was not at all what she had wanted.

Megan knew she needed to find a way to put this behind her—and soon. She couldn't afford to spend time wallowing. She had a son who needed her, a home to take care of and a business to run. Once she was back home again, she would be so busy she'd be able to settle back into her routine and forget.

As she waited at the boarding gate, she got a text from Harper.

Missing my friend SO much already. I'm so sorry about how things turned out, Megan. I hope this won't stop you from taking another trip with me someday. I promise not to push a man on you again. XOXO.

Megan thought for a moment before she replied.

Two years, no more asking me to go on a trip with you. We made a deal. Don't worry about the whole Luc thing. I'm over it. I got what I wanted from him, plus he is huge, which was a real bonus. XOXO, Love 'em and leave 'em Meg.

She hoped her attempt at humour would help Harper feel better about the whole thing. Harper had been visibly upset by what had happened and the role she had played in it. Megan had tried to reassure Harper that it was her choice alone, but her friend would not be consoled.

Paris

Luc passed through the door to his apartment, covered in sweat. He had been absolutely vicious at his kickboxing session that evening. His instructor, François, had had a tough time keeping the upper hand. Luc had been trying to work out the intense frustration he felt about Megan. He was angry. He hated that she'd left thinking he was little more than a womanizer. He hated that he couldn't get her off his mind. But most of all, he hated that he would never have her again. That thought was the worst of all. He was going to have to do whatever it took to forget her. He didn't believe in happily-ever-afters. He wasn't ever going to be good for her or her son. He could never give her the life she deserved. As much as he hoped she would find someone good enough for her, the thought of another man touching her enraged him. This thought had made him kick François hard enough to send him flying across the mat.

When he got up, François glared at him. "That's enough for tonight. Go home and come back when you want to learn skills, not take your rage out on me."

The two men glared at each other for a long moment, adrenalin pumping, breathing heavily, both ready to fight before Luc realized he *was* taking it out on François. He apologized quietly and left.

Now that he was alone in his apartment, the expansive space he had always relished felt exceedingly empty. Luc had hoped that going to kickboxing would exhaust him enough to shake off his restlessness and sleep tonight, but it had only served to get him more agitated. He showered before pouring himself a double bourbon. Trying to prevent himself from thinking about Megan had proved futile. Luc needed to get out of there, away from the memory of her. He flipped on his computer and booked a trip to Aspen to go check on his club there. It had been close to six months since he had been there and he was due for a visit. He would go next week.

TEN

Boulder

"Come little man! We're going to be late!" Megan called up the stairs to Elliott's room. She could hear that he had gotten caught up playing with his toys instead of getting dressed like he was supposed to be doing.

She was rushing around, making his lunch and stuffing his snow pants into his backpack. Megan had hit the snooze button twice on her alarm, and now they were running late.

"Let's go! Elliott! The roads are bad today, so we have to leave early!"

He came running down the stairs a minute later. "Sorry, Mom! Lex Luthor was going to take over the world and Superman needed Iron Man's help to stop him."

Megan gave him an exasperated smile as she held his coat out for him. She pulled her new cream-coloured coat out of the closet and put in on. The memory of Luc undoing its buttons for her flashed in her mind. She could see the tender expression on his face as he smiled down at her. For a second, her heart felt like it was being squeezed. *No! Stop that*, she told herself.

"Nice coat, Mom. Is that new too?" Elliott asked.

"Yes, it's one of the things Auntie Harper got for me from the magazine."

"You look really pretty. You're just as pretty as Auntie Harper."

Megan kissed him on the top of his head. "You're a sweetheart. Now, let's get going!"

She dropped him off at school, a few minutes late but in time with most of the parents. Traffic crawled along due to the heavy snowfall that had come overnight. Megan made her way over to the supermarket and did her big shop for the week, struggling to push the cart through the snow-filled parking lot to her car. She was sweating by the time she unloaded the bags into her trunk.

Back at home, she put everything away and started a load of laundry. She didn't have a photo session booked that day, which would give her a chance to catch up on her housework and shovelling, even though every part of her just wanted to curl up in bed, pull the covers over her head and go to sleep for a week. After lunch, she changed into an old coat to shovel. She sighed as she stepped out the door, seeing the mound of snow she needed to move. Picking up the shovel, she got started. She wondered what Luc would think seeing her like this—dressed in an old ski jacket, a hat and mitts, and her big, hideously ugly but warm winter boots. He wouldn't have been even the least bit interested in a woman like that. This was who she really was—not that done-up woman with the red lipstick whom he had met last week. She tried to imagine him out here shovelling, but the image was completely absurd. Her thoughts were interrupted by her neighbour, Charlie, calling to her.

"Megan! I see you're back in time for the big blizzard!"

"Hi, Charlie. Yes, I am! Good thing, or you would have been stuck shovelling all of this for me."

"I wouldn't mind a bit. A man my age needs to stay in shape!"

"Thank you so much for taking care of things while I was gone. I wouldn't have felt right asking my mom to do it." She smiled at Charlie. He was a kind man in his early seventies. His wife had passed away a few years earlier.

"It was my pleasure. Glad I could help."

"One second! I have a little thank-you gift for you in the house." Megan put down her shovel and trudged back inside, coming out a moment later with a bottle of very nice red wine. She walked over to Charlie's driveway, where he was shovelling, to give it to him.

"Here. Thank you, Charlie. I really appreciate it."

"Oh, Megan, thank you. This is a Mâconnais! That's a very good wine. That's too much, really."

"No, it's not so expensive there. I want you to have it."

"Thank you. You're a nice lady." He paused, looking awkward for a moment. Swallowing hard, he looked up from the bottle of wine to Megan's face. "Speaking of nice ladies, is your mom seeing anyone these days?"

Megan's mouth dropped and she smiled at her neighbour. "Why, Charlie, you sly dog! No, my mom is most definitely not seeing anyone."

"Would she be interested in an old codger like me, you think?"

"I don't know, but I could do some recon for you if you'd like."

"Would you?" His eyes lit up.

"Yes. I think you two would make a lovely couple. Besides, it would be good for her to get back into the dating scene."

"My kids have been on me to do the same. I'm finally feeling like I'm ready to spend time with a lady again. Life is for living, right?"

"That it is, Charlie," she agreed. "I better get back to clearing this snow so I can shower before it's time to pick up Elliott."

"Okay, thank you for the wine, Megan. I hope I can share it with your mom."

"I hope so too. I'll let you know as soon as I can."

* * *

That night while she was doing the dishes, Megan called her mom. They chatted for a few minutes before she approached the subject of Charlie.

"So, Mom, it looks like you have an admirer. Charlie Peterson from next door asked about you today. He wanted to know if you are seeing anyone."

Her mom sounded flustered when she spoke. "Charlie? He asked about me? Really? Well, I thought for sure some woman had already snagged him up. What did you tell him?"

"I told him you had lots of men on the go, but that I thought you had said you were free this Friday night," Megan teased.

"What? You did not! You better call him right back and tell him none of that is true. He's going to think I'm a floozy!"

"I didn't tell him that. I'm just kidding. But it's interesting that you care what he thinks. It sounds like you might be fond of him!"

"Megan, I see what you did there, but I am not going to start dating. I'm an old lady and I like doing old-lady things. Looking after my grandkids, gardening, knitting—"

"Knitting? You've never picked up a ball of yarn in your entire life! And you're not an old lady, either. You're young and beautiful, and he's a nice man, Mom. You should go out with him. Just for a coffee. If it's not awful, maybe let him take you for dinner," Megan answered.

"Tell you what. I'll start dating when you do."

"Oh, well in that case, I'll call him and tell him there's no chance."

"Exactly. Now do you still need me to come on Friday evening and Saturday?"

"Yes, they haven't called off the wedding yet. Friday, we have the rehearsal at 6 p.m. Saturday, I have to be at the salon at 8 a.m. to get pictures of the bride getting her hair done."

"Oh my, so that's going to be a long day for you. Is she a bridezilla?"

"The worst one yet, and I get to follow her around from the crack of dawn until they cut the cake. It's okay, though. For what they're paying me, she can be as bitchy as she wants." Megan looked up from the pot she was scrubbing to see Elliott walk into the kitchen. "Oh, Mom. Elliott's out of bed. I better run."

"Okay, my girl. Give him a kiss from Grandma."

"Will do. Love you."

"Love you too."

Megan hung up and dried her hands on a towel. "What's up, sweetie? I thought you'd be asleep already."

"Yeah, sorry, Mom. I was just thinking about my birthday."

"It's not for two months, honey. We can talk about it in the morning," Megan said, gently placing her hand on his blond hair and guiding him back up the stairs.

"I was just thinking, what if we gave Dad enough notice this year? Do you think he could make it then?"

Megan looked down at his little face. He looked so hopeful that it broke her heart. She knew someday that look of hope would be replaced by a cynical expression when they spoke of his father. She always imagined it would happen right around the time he stopped believing in Santa Claus and the tooth fairy. She was not looking forward to that day.

Megan sighed and gave him a weak smile. "We'll see, baby. Florida is pretty far from here. I'll email him after you're in bed to ask."

Elliott smiled up at her as she snuggled him under his covers. "I was thinking maybe he could buy me a ball glove and a bat for my birthday. My old glove that Grandma bought me is kind of babyish and he'll know just what to pick."

Megan kissed him on the forehead. "We'll see, sweetie. For now, you go off to dreamland, okay?"

"Okay. Do you want to meet me there later?" He smiled up at her.

"I do. Where should we go?" Megan gently tapped her index finger on the tip of her son's nose.

"Paris? That sounded like fun."

Megan tried not to wince. "How about Hawaii? I'd like to teach you how to surf."

"But *you* don't know how."

"In a dream, we can be good at anything we want, and I'm going to be a champion surfer tonight. Now, time to sleep, my boy."

"See you at the beach, Mom"

"See you there." She kissed his little cheek before turning off his light.

* * *

An hour later, Megan checked to make sure Elliott was asleep before she picked up the phone to call Ian. Her heart sped up as she dialed his number. She hoped it was early enough in the evening that he would be sober.

She waited for three rings and then a woman answered. "Hello?"

Megan was surprised. "Oh, hi. I'm looking for Ian."

"Sure. He's just in the shower. Can I tell him who called?" She sounded friendly and rather young.

"I'm his ex-wife, Megan. I was just calling him about our son's birthday."

"Oh hi, Megan. I'll tell him to call you right back, okay?"

"Thank you . . . um. Sorry, I don't know your name."

"I'm Georgie."

"Georgie, are you two together now?"

"Yeah, I moved in with him a couple of weeks ago."

Megan felt a stab of pain at the idea of Ian being able to hold it together for some other woman. But maybe he wasn't. Maybe she was an addict too, or was willing to put up with one.

"Good. We'll, I'm glad he's happy," she said quietly.

"Thanks. We both are. I'll get him to call you."

"Perfect. Bye."

Megan hung up. As much as she knew she didn't want Ian back, it was hard for her to think of him with someone else. He had promised to love her forever and he hadn't even made it three years. Maybe Georgie could straighten him out in a way she couldn't. Megan tried to busy herself folding laundry and tidying up the house while she waited for a call that never came.

She thought about a time two years earlier, when Ian had been sober for several months. They had met at their friends' guest ranch outside Colorado Springs and spent two lovely weeks together as summer wound down. She and Elliott had stayed in one of the cabins while Ian had stayed at his friend Ben's home on the property. Ian and Elliott grew close during that time, while Megan kept a manageable distance, observing Ian carefully. Ian had spent every waking minute with their son, trying to make up for lost time. They played catch, swam in the pool and ended each day with Elliott sitting on his dad's lap while Ian read to him. Elliott had fallen in love with having a dad during that trip and a horrible void was created when Ian relapsed shortly afterward, disappearing from their lives again. A pang of guilt accompanied each memory of that trip for Megan. If only she had known then what she knew now—that it was better to let Elliott remain ignorant of what he was missing than to give him a taste of it, only to have it taken away.

By the time she turned her bedside lamp off that night, she was seething with that all-too-familiar rage at her ex-husband. She could try to convince herself that maybe he hadn't been given the message, but she doubted it. He hadn't called or sent Elliott a gift for Christmas. Megan had bought a train set and wrapped it, pretending Ian had sent it. So far, her son seemed to be fooled by her efforts on her ex-husband's behalf for each special occasion, but Megan knew it was only a matter of time before he figured it out. Maybe she should just tell Elliott the truth: that his dad wasn't well and would never be a part of Elliott's life.

* * *

The next morning, after she got Elliott off to school, Megan tried Ian's number again. This time he picked up.

"Hello?"

"Hi Ian, it's Meg."

"Meg, hi. Sorry I didn't get back to you last night. We had to head out for a dinner and I figured it would be too late to call you when we got home."

Megan paused for a moment, trying to push down her frustration before she spoke. "That's okay, Ian. I was calling because Elliott was talking about his birthday last night. He thought maybe if we invited you early enough, you could make it to his party this year."

"Oh, well, I don't know, Meg. I'll have to see, okay? It looks like I might get a chance as a third-base coach for the Suns this year. His birthday is right during spring training camp."

"The Suns? Good for you, Ian. I hope that works out. Maybe you could come up before it starts or something. Bring Georgie. Elliott really wants a new ball glove and a bat this year, and he wants an expert to pick them out for him."

"He still likes baseball? That's nice to hear. I'll see what I can do. How is he doing?"

"He's good. He's growing like a weed and he's doing so well in school this year. He's actually starting to read. It's amazing to watch."

"That's great, Meg. You haven't emailed me any pictures for a while. I miss seeing what he's up to."

"Right. Well, I didn't hear from you, so I wasn't sure if you were interested."

"He's my son, Meg. Of course I'm interested!" She could picture his face screwed up into a scowl. "What? Is that some type of punishment for everything? To stop sending pictures?"

Megan closed her eyes, trying to keep her temper in check. It would do no good to pick a fight. A fight would mean there was no chance that Ian would acknowledge Elliott's birthday.

She took a deep breath and then spoke quietly. "Of course not, Ian. I would never do that. I want you to be a part of Elliott's life, no matter how things turned out between us. He needs his dad. Maybe we could arrange a Skype call this weekend?"

Her placating words seemed to have the desired effect. "Yeah? Okay. I'd like that."

"Good. When would be a good time for us to get a hold of you?"

"I'm not sure right now. I'll email you to let you know, okay?"

"Okay, Ian. We'll wait to hear from you."

"Good. Talk to you soon, Meg."

"Bye, Ian."

"Meg?"

"Yes?"

"How are you doing?" he asked cautiously.

"I'm fine," Megan replied, trying to sound like she meant it.

Ian's voice was quiet as he spoke. "I think about you a lot, you know. Sometimes I worry about you driving around on those icy roads. Did you put snow tires on this year?"

"Um, no. They're pretty pricey. I have good enough tires, though, and I'm careful. Don't worry."

"Listen, if I get this job with the Suns, I'll be able to start sending you more money. You can get yourself some snow tires for next year," he offered, sounding hopeful for the first time in years.

"That would be nice, Ian. But just take care of yourself, okay? I hope you're healthy."

"I've been doing really good lately. I feel like I might be able to kick this thing, finally."

Megan felt a lump in her throat. She had heard that line maybe a thousand times before from him. "I'm rooting for you, Ian."

There was a pause for a moment while Ian let her words sink in. "I don't know how you can be so kind after everything I've put you through."

Megan blinked back tears that Ian would never see. "You're the father of my son, Ian. I'll always want the best for you."

"You too, you know? I keep thinking maybe you'll meet some guy who actually deserves you."

"Oh, I don't think that's in the cards for me. Georgie sounds nice, though. Be good to her, okay? And to yourself."

"I'll do my best."

"I know you will. I should go. Take care, Ian."

"Take care, Meg."

Jacksonville, Florida

Ian sat at the patio table, under an umbrella, in his small backyard. Even though it was early, the sun was beating down already and it was going to be another hot day. He was dressed only in shorts and flip-flops. He sipped his coffee, thinking about Megan and Elliott so far from him, in the cold winter. He hated how he felt each time he spoke with his ex-wife. The guilt was almost unbearable. Part of him wished she would let him have it just once—really scream at him for every shitty thing he had done: every birthday he had missed, every disappointment he had caused her and their little boy. He could imagine her punching his chest with her small hands, and how much better it would feel to take that pain from her, to just stand in front of her and let her unleash her hurt and rage on him. Carrying that burden would be a pleasure compared to knowing he had caused her so much hurt that she had as good as shut down. Ian knew she hadn't dated in the years since they had separated. He knew she was remaining completely on her own and he knew why: she would never trust a man again.

He was a complete fuck-up as a father and a husband. The regret and shame he carried weighed on him heavily every day, making it almost impossible to contact them. But with each day that went by, he gave Megan another reason to hate him and had another reason to hate himself. Ian drained his coffee, deciding to go for a jog before it got too hot.

He had been clean for a month, but now the desire to use was almost undeniable. He knew getting high would put a safe distance between himself and the feelings he didn't want to face. Georgie would be at work until suppertime, so he would have to find a way to get through the day on his own. He checked his phone and found the schedule for the Narcotics Anonymous meeting. He had time for a run and a shower before the next session. He would go and hope it would be enough to keep him clean just for this one day.

* * *

When Megan got off the phone with Ian, she took a large gulp of air, trying to blink back her tears. Things had gotten much easier between them, but she wondered if she would always wish things had turned out differently. She had loved Ian—really loved him—and part of her heart would always belong to him. He had loved her too, for a time, and she could hear in his voice the guilt each time they spoke. Maybe that was part of why he stayed away. It was still so painful for him.

She poured herself a cup of coffee and stared out the window for a minute. She saw Charlie walking along his sidewalk, sprinkling salt around to melt the ice. She threw her coat and boots on and walked outside to see him.

"Hi, Charlie!"

"Good morning, Megan. How are you this frosty morning?"

"Fine. How are you?"

"Good. Keeping busy." He smiled.

"I talked to my mom about you. I think you might have a shot, but she's definitely going to play hard to get. She's claiming that she's too old to start dating."

"Well, that makes two of us, then, but what the hell else are we going to do with our evenings?"

"Tell you what. She'll be here all day Saturday with Elliott. Maybe you could pop by to borrow a cup of sugar or something?" Megan smiled at him. He was a kind person and she knew he would be good to her mom. Why not give things a little nudge?

"A cup of sugar . . ." He considered it for a moment. "Okay. Sounds good, Megan. Thank you."

"Alright, I better get to work. I have some photos to edit this morning, and they aren't going to edit themselves!"

Charlie chuckled and got back to work. "See you later, Megan. Thank you."

"You bet, Charlie! Have a great day."

ELEVEN

Paris

It had been five days since he had seen Megan, and Luc was becoming increasingly unsettled. He had never had a hangover from a woman last this long before. He wanted to get back to feeling like himself—confident, satisfied and ready for his next business endeavour. Instead, he felt more like a cat in a cage—bored, frustrated and needing to get out. He still had two days until his trip to Aspen. It was late at night as he drove home to his empty apartment. He had stayed at Cloud until it closed up for the night, wanting to be with other people. There were dozens of beautiful women he could have taken home, but he had no interest in any of them. This fact alone bothered him.

The two things that normally quashed any feelings of restlessness—kickboxing and women—were doing nothing to help him now. He felt like a pathetic schoolboy, mooning over someone he had known for only two days. *Ne fais pas le con*, he told himself. *Shake it off, you idiot.*

Later in bed that night, he decided to relieve some of his tension, sliding his hand under the covers. Pulling on his now hardening length, his mind allowed him to see only Megan. Her face, her breasts, the touch of her skin, the smell of her were all there for him as he climaxed. He sighed when it was over, feeling fed up with himself for this foolishness.

* * *

Friday morning arrived and Luc hummed to himself as he finished packing. He would be in Aspen in time for dinner and would be meeting Clarissa, a woman he knew well. She was always up for whatever Luc had in mind, whether he needed someone to accompany him to an event or just come by his hotel room for sex. If anyone could stop him from thinking of Megan, it was Clarissa.

Boulder

Megan woke early again for the fourth day in a row. She had been going to bed right after getting Elliott off to sleep all week, telling herself she needed to catch up on her rest after her trip. The truth was that she just couldn't face the evenings alone right now. Not after her night with Luc. She had been reminded of what it felt like to be touched and held and adored. Now that she had had a taste of romance, the loneliness had become unbearable again. It was almost as bad as it had been when she left Ian. Now waking at 4:30 a.m., her body felt well rested, but she wished she could just go back to sleep for a few more hours until Elliott woke up.

She decided to get her equipment ready for the wedding the next day. She put all her batteries into their chargers, then backed up her memory cards onto her computer. Pulling out her cleaning kit, she carefully inspected and cleaned her lenses, then replaced them in their bag.

Megan sat down at her computer to check that the files had backed up, then opened the photos she had taken in Paris. Slowly clicking through them, she found the ones she had taken at the Louvre. The memories of her day with Luc came flooding back to her. She stopped at a photo of him in front of the museum. The light was perfect and she had asked him if he would mind posing so she could practise something Anita had taught her earlier that morning. Now as she looked at him, staring back at her, she felt a surge of desire mixed with grief. He looked so incredibly handsome, with his strong jaw, his eyes—the colour of worn leather—and his sexy grin. She remembered that just before she had taken the shot, he had run his hand through his hair in that way he did when he was feeling a bit uncomfortable. Part of her wished he would show up at her door right at that moment, just so she could see his face again, hear his voice, feel his touch on her skin.

She quickly closed the file and switched off her computer. There was no way she was going to torture herself like that. He was a one-night stand, a womanizer and nothing more. Even though he had seemed to genuinely believe they had had something more, she knew it was nothing of any substance. She needed to shake him off. Looking over at the clock, she realized it was time to wake Elliott for school.

Aspen

"Clarissa, you look beautiful, as always." Luc stood to greet her as she made her entrance into the restaurant at his hotel. He had been seated at a table for twenty minutes already, waiting for her. This was normal with Clarissa. She was always running late, and he suspected it was solely for the purpose of making him watch as she crossed the room.

He kissed her on both cheeks and held her chair out for her. Clarissa was a gorgeous, curvy brunette with full lips. She had on a tight black minidress that was low cut enough to give anyone who wanted it an eyeful of her ample breasts. She owned an upscale lingerie shop that catered to the rich. Luc and Clarissa saw each other from time to time and it always ended well for them both.

"So, Luc, what brings you to town?" she purred, giving him an opening to say something provocative.

"I'm here on business. To check on the club and take a look at a few properties I might purchase," he answered, pouring her a glass of red wine.

Clarissa was surprised at his dull response. He normally said something that made her blush. "That's nice. How long will you be in town?"

"A few days. Until Thursday," he answered, smiling politely.

Luc looked across at her. She was certainly beautiful, but he wasn't getting the feeling of pure lust he normally did when he saw her. His cock hadn't reacted in the least when she sat down and leaned toward him, exposing the top half of her breasts in the process. Usually that was good for at least a semi.

They ordered their meals and ate in awkward silence. Finally Clarissa looked up from her dessert. "Luc, what's wrong tonight? Something's different with you."

Luc shrugged. "No, everything's fine. I am maybe a little preoccupied with these real estate deals. That's all."

Clarissa reached her hand across the table, tracing his hand with her fingertip. "Luc, you can tell me. We're friends, remember? I've known you for a long time."

"It's nothing. Really. Would you like to go upstairs with me?"

She gave him a skeptical look. "Are you sure you want to?"

"Of course I am. Nothing would please me more."

Luc signed the bill to his room and the pair went upstairs to his suite. When they got there, he walked directly over to the bar and poured them each a Scotch. He gave her one of the drinks and sculled his back in one gulp, quickly pouring himself another. Clarissa stood observing him. She knew him well enough to know something was seriously off. The evening had been completely devoid of their normal sexual banter, and now that he had her in his room, he hadn't even laid a finger on her. Usually he would have his hand up her skirt by the time the elevator doors closed. She decided to up the ante and make him talk.

She sauntered over to him, letting her hips sway from side to side like a pendulum. When she reached him, she pressed her breasts against him, running her finger down along his stomach to the front of his pants. Giving him a "come and get me" look, she let her finger slide lower.

He quickly pulled his hips away from her. "Whoa, let's take it one step at a time."

"Okay, that's it!" Clarissa snapped. "Who are you and what happened to Luc Chevalier?"

"Nothing. *Merde*! I don't know anymore." Luc dropped onto the couch, resting his elbows on his thighs and his face on his hands. "I'm a fucking mess right now and I was hoping that seeing you would get me out of it."

"You finally met the one, didn't you?"

"The one what?"

"*The* one. Your soulmate, of course."

"Bah, there is no such thing." He scoffed.

Clarissa sat down on the couch and curled up her legs, placing a pillow on her lap. "Why not?"

Luc glanced over at her. "Look, you and I are not built that way, believing in fairy tales, thinking there will be a forever with someone. That is all bullshit. Lies made up to sell diamonds."

"No, it's not. And speak for yourself, Luc. I happen to believe in fairy tales. I'm going to find my someone, and it *is* going to be forever. It just hasn't happened yet."

"What?" he pulled his head back in surprise. "I thought you and I were alike in this way. We know that life is better lived freely rather than tied down, no?"

"No. That's what *you* think. I don't agree with you. I never have. I just never really told you that before."

"Why not?"

Clarissa shrugged. "What would be the point, Luc? I'm just here for a little fun with you until the right guy shows up. I don't need to argue with you about things."

Luc considered this for a moment.

Clarissa spoke up again, reaching over and patting him on the knee. "Listen, why don't you tell me about her? I'm your friend, Luc, and I'm a hell of a good listener. I think you need to talk more than you need to fuck right now."

Luc sighed and reluctantly gave in. "It's all so stupid, really. It's just this woman I met. She was in Paris visiting a mutual friend. As soon as I saw her, I just had to have her, you know? She is different— very beautiful, yes, but not at all like the women I normally see. She has a son—a little boy—and a shithead addict for an ex-husband. We spent one very wonderful day together and she stayed at my place for the night. When I woke up in the morning, she was gone. I went to see her again. She got the wrong idea about me. She thinks I'm in the habit of using women. Anyway, I tried to clear it up, but it's over. It never would have lasted anyway. I can't be with a woman who lives in the middle of nowhere and has a child. I'm just having trouble getting her off my mind for some reason. I was hoping you would help with that."

"Is that why you came all the way to Aspen? To get her off your mind?"

"A little bit, yes. I needed to come for work as well," he said, rolling his eyes at himself.

"For someone so brilliant, you can be a fucking idiot sometimes." She laughed.

"That's a mean thing to say."

"I'm just trying to help," Clarissa replied plainly. "Listen, if you would fly to another continent just to have sex with someone so you could *forget* a woman, it means you're most likely in love. It's not the way most men react when they're in love, but you aren't most men. You've got yourself so convinced with your bullshit 'pleasure is for the moment, there is no such thing as love' mantra that you don't know it when it's happening to you. No man goes to such lengths to forget a woman he *isn't* in love with."

Luc shook his head. "Well, I'm fucked then. I can't be with her and I'm fucking miserable without her. I have never been this distracted and restless in my life." He raked his hair with his fingers in frustration. "What do I do about that?"

Clarissa looked thoughtfully at Luc for a moment before answering. "You know, Luc, maybe you have to just *be* with her. I mean, what is the point of all your money and power if you won't let yourself have the one thing that would make life worth living?"

"No. That's not possible. She has a son. She lives in Boulder, for Christ's sake. I would be horrible for her. I could never live there, never be a father to her son. I doubt I could even be faithful for more than a short time. I don't want any of it. And I don't want to hurt her. I will have to stay away."

"You want to hear something, Luc? I've never met a man like

you before. I've never seen anyone so driven. When you get an idea in your head, you go for it full on and make it happen. You started with nothing and look at you—you are insanely rich and you did it yourself because you wanted it. If *anyone* can make something work if he sets his mind to it, it's you. If you want to be with this woman, you can. It's really pretty simple, my friend." She patted him on the knee and stood up.

"But I *wanted* to be rich. I don't want this."

"So, you got everything you wanted in life, Luc. But you don't have anything that you really *need*. I know it's scary for you, but most things in life worth having require a leap of faith." She paused for a minute to let her words sink in. Clarissa looked at her friend as she put on her coat. "I'm going to go. I didn't squeeze into this dress just to talk."

Luc stood and walked her to the door. "Good night, Clarissa. I'm sorry about all of this. Thank you for listening to me. And for your advice. I won't take it, but thank you all the same."

She gave him a light kiss on the cheek. "Goodbye, dummy. Call me from Boulder."

TWELVE

Luc tossed and turned most of the night, unable to get comfortable. Clarissa's words haunted him. What *was* the point of his life? He was forty-one and was utterly alone in the world. He had friends and money—and friends who were only interested in his money— but at the end of each day, he was alone. He had felt sorry for Megan and, until this moment, it had never occurred to him that he was every bit as alone as she was. Much more, in fact. She had her mom and her son.

He finally drifted off to sleep around 2 a.m., waking late in the morning with that awful feeling in the pit of his stomach again. Getting up, Luc took a shower and made himself a coffee. He had nothing pressing that day. He had planned to go over to the nightclub in the late afternoon but had thought he would be spending the morning in bed with Clarissa. Wandering over to the desk, he turned on his laptop and googled the distance from Aspen to Boulder. He could make the drive in a little under four hours. Without thinking about it, he threw a few things into an overnight bag and grabbed his coat, stuffing his cellphone and wallet into the pocket, then hurried out of his suite. For the first time in his adult life, he was going to act on impulse without having a carefully thought-out plan.

An hour later, he was sitting in the driver's seat of a rented Durango, hooking up his cellphone to the hands-free. He set the navigation system to guide him to Boulder, not sure where he would find her. How big could that city be? He'd figure out where she was.

Boulder

Megan was up long before the sun to shower and get dressed for the day. She quickly had a bite of breakfast and poured coffee into her travel mug as she watched her mom's car pull up in front of her house. Elliott would still be sleeping when she left. Megan and her mom chatted for a few minutes before Megan picked up her equipment. She stood in the doorway and looked at her mom for a moment, trying to decide whether or not to tell her about Charlie coming by.

"Hey, Mom. Have a really great day. And don't be afraid to try something new today, okay?"

Helen gave her a confused look. "What? What do you mean?"

"Just that. Have a terrific day, alright?"

"I will. You too, honey."

* * *

The day with the wedding party started out rough. The bride, Quinn, was both very nervous and very bitchy at the salon. She had a definite idea of what she wanted her hair and makeup to look like and nothing seemed to please her. Her mom and sisters rushed around, trying to placate her, bringing her some champagne and orange juice to help her relax. Megan tried to stay out of the way and get a few shots as directed by Quinn herself. Megan was dreading the rest of the day as she got into her car to drive to the groom's parents' house.

When she arrived there, the groom, Rodney, looked pale and a little bit green. He was still in a bathrobe, sitting on the couch, trying to choke down some cereal when his dad let Meg in. The groomsmen didn't look much better.

Rodney's mom, Diana, came down the stairs to greet her. "Look at these idiots. Quinn is going to be furious when she sees the shape they're in."

Megan bit her lip, thinking about the mood the bride was already in. "Right. I just saw her and she was a little . . . stressed. We're going to have to work fast to perk them up and get them dressed. I have to be over at Quinn's mom's place in an hour. Do you have some champagne and orange juice, by any chance?"

"In the kitchen. I'll be right back with it."

The men stared vacantly at Megan as Diana walked out of the room.

* * *

"Elliott, when that cartoon is done, come into the kitchen, okay? Lunch is ready," Helen called to her grandson.

Just then, there was a knock at the door. She wiped her hands on a dishtowel and answered it. Charlie was standing on the other side with an empty measuring cup in his hand.

"Hi, Helen. I came to borrow a cup of sugar." He smiled at her. His hair had been carefully combed and she could smell a hint of cologne.

"Oh, sure. Come on in. Megan's not home but she won't mind." Helen turned and led him into the kitchen.

"What are you making?" she asked.

"What?" Charlie replied.

"What are you making that you need sugar?"

Shit. He realized he hadn't thought the lie through. "Coffee."

"Coffee? And you need an entire cup of sugar for that?" Helen raised one eyebrow at him. She knew what he was up to.

"I like it sweet?" He looked a little panicked.

To his relief, Helen laughed and shook her head. "Megan put you up to this, didn't she? Before she left the house today, she told me not to be afraid to try something new. I take it you're what she was referring to."

Charlie lowered his head and then raised his eyes up to her. She was so lovely, with her sparkling green eyes and her shoulder-length blond hair with grey mixed in. She was giving him a hard look, but there was a hint of amusement there as well.

"Yes. I'm afraid my kids have been on me to find someone to spend time with. I finally realized maybe they're right. I mean, what's the point of being so handsome if you don't have a nice lady to admire you?"

Helen laughed. "That would certainly be a waste, wouldn't it? You're barking up the wrong tree, though. I'm not in the market for a man."

"Well, what about someone to go for coffee with? If it goes alright we could try lunch, then maybe by summer we could progress to dinner."

Helen stared at him as she considered it. Charlie was a kind man. He had always been so good to Megan. His wife had been gone for years now and he hadn't rushed out to find someone new to take care of him, like so many men did.

"One coffee. That's all I can commit to," she replied, trying to look serious.

He smiled in relief. "One coffee."

"Now, do you want the sugar or not?"

"Not. But if I could get your phone number, that would be equally sweet."

Helen laughed a little and shook her head. Part of her was annoyed at what she was doing as she wrote the number on a piece of paper for him. The other part of her was extremely flattered.

* * *

As Luc drove, he knew what he was doing was ridiculous, laughable even, but he felt compelled to do it anyway. He needed to see her again and that was all there was to it.

He suddenly realized this could be the beginning of a perfect arrangement for both Megan and him. They could have a long distance relationship. That might suit Megan because they could work it around *her* life and make sure Elliott would not be involved. They could speak on the phone and meet whenever they could, but they would both still have their own lives.

He checked the distance on the navigation system. He still had another hour to go until he reached Boulder. The roads had become icy and it began snowing hard as he got farther north. He'd have to drive quite slowly now, meaning the trip would be well over seven hours instead of four. It reminded of him of drives to the Swiss Alps to ski in the winter. He'd been too busy to do that for a few years, although it was something he had once loved. His mind wandered back to when he had learned to ski. It was one of the first things he had done when he had enough money. Luc had always wanted to go skiing as a boy but his mom couldn't afford to take him. He knew his father took his wife and other children to the Alps each Christmas. That was one of the reasons Luc never saw him over the holidays.

His father, Jean-Paul Chevalier, had been a well-known politician in France, and Luc's mother, Stephanie, had been his mistress for many years. They had Luc, and from time to time, his father would come by to see Stephanie, always bringing a toy for Luc to play with. He would stay the night and leave shortly after breakfast, not to return again for weeks.

As a small boy, Luc always yearned for his father's attention. He wished Jean-Paul would come by to see him and would sometimes ask why his father had never taken him to the mountains. His mother would explain that Luc's father had his other family and that wasn't how this worked for people in their situation. As Luc grew up, he began to understand that as a mistress, his mother would never receive the devotion reserved for a wife. Luc's heart began to harden as his disappointment in his father grew. Luc watched Stephanie pathetically accept whatever pittance she got from Jean-Paul and saw how depressed she became when he left, knowing he wouldn't return for a long time. His father would get what he wanted and then go back home to his real family. Jean-Paul's wife knew about Stephanie and Luc—it was almost expected that a man in her husband's position would have at least one mistress. She looked the other way.

Luc had decided that when he grew up, he would do the one thing it seemed all the very rich did—ski in the Alps. He would show his father and the rest of his father's upper-class friends that he was every bit as good as they were. He picked up the sport very quickly. It had become an obsession, and for several years he skied every chance he got until he was one of the best on the slopes each time he went.

Now as he drove along, memories of his mother's sadness haunted him. Maybe that was why he was drawn to Megan. She had that same air of sadness about her when she spoke of her ex and her son. She was strong in ways that his mother never had been, however. Megan was never going to be taken advantage of. She had gotten away from her ex as soon she realized she had to. Sometimes Luc had wished his mother would move back to the United States with him, taking both of them away from the destruction and disappointment his father caused every time he left them again.

THIRTEEN

Boulder

"Okay, everyone! I know we're all cold, but I promise we have only a few more group shots before you can go warm up in the limo!"

Megan's feet and hands felt like ice as she took shots of the wedding party on a footbridge. She was grateful that she had worn her long red coat, but her dressy black boots were not nearly warm enough, and she needed bare hands to work the camera. The groomsmen had started with the one mimosa that morning and kept on going. All five of them were drunk and unruly by now, making bunny ears or doing the shocker hand gesture each time Megan tried to get a picture.

Megan moved the camera away from her face. "Alright fellas, you've had your funny poses. Now, these ladies here have bare shoulders, and they are freezing. Be chivalrous and help us get through this fast, okay?"

Quinn spun to face her husband's friends, her face now full of rage. "Stop it! STOP IT! You fucking idiots are *ruining* my day!"

Rodney, who was not in the least bit drunk but had a wicked headache, flinched as his new wife screamed. At the moment, this felt like the worst day of his life. He put his hands up, palms out, at his friends. "Okay, guys, seriously. Pull it together here."

The guys rolled their eyes but managed to stand still for a few minutes. Megan took shots as fast as she could and then sent the bridal party back to the limo, leaving only Quinn and Rodney to contend with.

Quinn hissed at him. "You look like a fucking mess. Your face is totally green." Turning her sights on Meg, she snapped, "Megan, are you going to be able to fix this?"

"I can fix anything. It's not that bad, really, through the lens," she lied as she adjusted the zoom. "Well, here you are, just the two of you. And you did it. You got married!"

Megan held the camera back up to her face. "Okay, can you turn your bodies to face each other, look into each other's eyes and hold it?" She clicked away. "Tilt your head up a bit, Quinn. That's it. Perfect! You make such a beautiful couple. How did you meet anyway?"

Quinn spoke up, her voice still a little angry. "I had a flat tire on the freeway and he stopped to help me." Quinn looked over at Megan.

"Oh, keep looking at Rodney," she said. "So he changed your tire for you?"

Quinn started to laugh. "No, he didn't have a clue how. He didn't have the jack on properly, so when he took the tire off, the whole car fell, which caused major damage to it. We had to call a tow truck."

Rodney smiled at the memory. "I was just winging it. I stopped because she was so beautiful, and I figured, how hard could it be? I'm sorry I'm such a knucklehead. We shouldn't have gone partying last night, Quinn."

"That's okay. You're *my* knucklehead."

Finally the couple seemed to relax as they gazed into each other's eyes. Rodney lowered his mouth to Quinn's and they shared a long kiss. Megan breathed a sigh of relief. The day was about to get much easier.

* * *

Luc dialed Harper's number and hit the hands-free button on his cellphone.

"Hello?"

"Harper, it's Luc. How are you?"

Harper's voice was flat as she replied, "Fine. What's up?"

"I need your help, actually. I'm on my way to Boulder to see Megan, and I don't know how to reach her."

"What do you mean? You're going to fly there today?"

"Oh, no. I was in Aspen and I rented a ridiculously huge vehicle and started driving. I want to ask her out for dinner."

"Are you serious? Have you lost your fucking mind? That's an insanely long drive just to ask someone out for dinner. She can't go, anyway; she's working at a wedding all day. I don't even know if she'll want to see you, Luc. She felt pretty upset about what happened."

"I know. I feel terrible about it and I can't stop thinking about her. I was hoping we could start over."

"Start over? With what? It was a one-night thing, Luc, and she made it pretty clear that it's over. I think you should turn around and go back to Aspen."

Luc sighed. "Listen, Harper, I can't. I'm about one hour out of town. I just have to find out if she'll see me, okay? I've been fucking miserable since she left."

"It's not really about you, Luc. *Megan* doesn't want you in her life, or anyone else, for that matter. I don't think you've thought this through. It's not going to go anywhere. You don't even live on the same continent."

"I haven't thought it through at all, to be honest. But it might actually work very well. I could come and see her whenever I'm in the country and treat her the way she deserves to be treated, but I wouldn't interfere with her life otherwise. It might be the perfect arrangement for her."

Harper considered this for a moment. "I don't know, Luc. If you just show up at her house, she is going to be exceedingly pissed at you. The last thing she would want would be to expose Elliott to whatever is going on between you."

"Shit. I didn't consider that. I just started driving. Maybe I should forget trying to see her."

"I think that's a good idea, Luc," she said softly. "Tell you what— I'll call her and tell her what you did and that I told you to turn back, okay? That way the ball will be in her court."

Luc sighed, hating to give up when he was so close, but Harper was right. Megan would be angry if he just showed up at her house. "Alright. I won't try to see her, but I can't drive back right now. I'm in the middle of a blizzard. I'll have to stay at a hotel in Boulder for the night. Maybe if you get in touch with her, you can give her my number and she can call me. I'll be in town until ten o'clock tomorrow morning."

"Listen, I'm going to call Megan for you. But so help me God, if you fuck her around, I will hunt you down and chop you to pieces with a butcher knife, starting with that huge cock of yours. You got it?"

"She told you that about me?" He grinned.

"Dead, Luc. I will kill you dead. The last thing Meg needs is someone who is going to screw her over. She's a good person and she's had her share of disappointments."

"I know that, Harper. I would never hurt her."

"Okay, Luc. I'll try."

"Thank you. Goodbye, Harper."

"Bye, Luc."

An hour later, Megan was sitting at the back of the ballroom, changing camera lenses, when she noticed the light on her cellphone was flashing. She saw that she had missed calls from her mom and Harper. She walked down the hall toward the hotel lobby so she could get away from the noise of the music. She called home and Helen picked up.

"Sorry I missed your call, Mom. How are things going?"

"Great. Elliott's just getting his jammies on and then we're going to read in his room for a while before bed."

"Oh, good. I'm glad."

"Remember this morning when you told me not to be afraid to try something new? I figured out what you meant, you little monkey."

Megan laughed. "So, did Charlie come by?"

"Yes. I agreed to go for a coffee with him. Now listen, I know you're busy. I just wanted to tell *you* to be ready to try something new. If it's good for me, it's good for you. If you meet a nice man tonight, be open to it, okay?"

"No."

"Well then, I'll call Charlie and tell him I can't go out with him."

"Oh, nice, Mom. You're blackmailing me using my kind widowed neighbour's emotions as collateral?"

"Yes. It's called hardball."

"Grr. Okay, I promise that if the right guy shows up, I'll hop straight into bed with him. Does that make you feel better?"

Helen laughed. "That's my girl. Listen, I think I might stay here tonight, okay? The roads are getting much worse and I'm tuckered out. I might just go to bed after I get Elliott to sleep. That way, you can sleep in tomorrow morning and I'll get up with him."

"Thanks, Mom! You really are the best, even if you drive me nuts most of the time."

"Good night, sweetie. Get home safely!"

"Will do. Bye." Megan ended the call and smiled to herself. She wanted her mom to be happy, and even though she had no intention of following through with her own promise, it wasn't a lie. *You never know, Ryan Gosling might be in town for some reason.*

A voice interrupted her thoughts. "Megan, it's been a while. You look hot."

She looked up to see Brad, the appetizer-penis-photo guy, standing beside her with a slimy smile on his face. Megan tried not to shudder as she looked back at him.

"Oh Brad, hi. You know someone in the wedding party?"

"Rodney's my cousin. Great wedding, especially when I realized you were here."

"Yes, a very nice day. Well, I better get back in there. I think they're going to cut the cake pretty soon."

Megan started to walk away. Brad touched her arm. "Hang on. You've got a minute for me, I'm sure. You never called after our dinner. I just wanted to know why. I thought we had a real connection."

Megan turned to him, pulling her arm away from him in the process. "Really? You couldn't figure that one out yourself? You sent me a picture of your penis—such as it is—during dinner."

"I thought it would be sexy. You know, a little taste of what was coming?" He raised his eyebrows at her.

"A 'little' taste is an accurate description, actually. Maybe some woman somewhere would like that, but I don't know who she might be. And on a first date, it's just plain creepy."

Brad looked embarrassed for a second. "Damn it. I'm sorry. I wish I could take that back. My buddy told me it was a good idea."

"Let me guess—he's been single a long time too, right?"

Brad laughed at her observation. Moving in a little closer, he gave her his best attempt at a sexy grin. "Listen, do you think we could go out again? Maybe start over with a clean slate? I promise not to do anything like that again."

Megan backed away from him. "I really don't think so. I'm actually with someone now and it's pretty serious."

Just then, she felt a hand on her waist and lips brush up against her cheek. She flinched and turned, only to see Luc standing behind her. He gave her a firm kiss when she turned and said, "*Mon ange*, I'm sorry that I'm late. The roads were awful getting here. Who's your friend?" Luc narrowed his eyes and clenched his jaw at the man as he wrapped his arms around Megan. Brad had backed up slightly already.

"Luc, this is Brad," she managed to say as she stared at Luc in disbelief. How could he possibly be here at this very moment, looking so gorgeous and holding her so casually?

"We're old friends. I better get back to my table," Brad said as he walked off.

"Yes, you should," Luc called after him.

Megan turned to Luc. "How did you . . . ? What are you doing here?"

Luc smiled down at her. "I came to get rid of that guy. He seems like a slimeball."

"He is." Megan laughed. "But seriously, how are you here?"

"I was in Aspen and I wanted to see if you would have dinner with me." Luc looked into her huge green eyes, feeling that overwhelming yearning come over him again.

Megan put her hands up in front of her, palms out. "Wait—you flew here to ask me out for dinner?"

"I drove, actually, but that's beside the point. I spoke to Harper on my way here, and she helped me realize I couldn't just show up at your house. I asked her to get a hold of you and give you my number so you could contact me if you wanted to. She told me you were working at a wedding today, but I can't believe it's at this hotel! I just picked this place randomly. If I believed in fate, I would say that it had taken a hand in this."

"I was just about to call Harper back," Megan answered, feeling completely shocked to have Luc standing right in front of her. She had been one hundred per cent sure they would never see each other again. "You drove all this way, in this storm, to go out for dinner?" She stared at him in disbelief.

"Not for tonight. I would never expect you to go out on such short notice. I can come back. I will be in Colorado until Thursday. I was hoping we could go out one night this week, if you have time."

Megan gave him a hint of a smile and shook her head. "You're a little bit nuts, you know that?"

"So I'm discovering. In every other area of my life, I assure you that I'm in full control. For some reason, you can make me do stupid things like renting an enormous vehicle and driving for seven hours in a blizzard just to see you for a few minutes. I can promise you I've never done this before for anyone."

Megan stared up at him. He was standing close enough for her to kiss him if she wanted to. And she wanted to. He looked amazing as he smiled down at her with that slightly unsure look, waiting to see what she would do next. But she couldn't let this happen. This was her real life now and she had no room in it for a man like him.

"I don't think it's a good idea, Luc," she said quietly. "I have to go. They're going to cut the cake soon and the bride is going to lose her mind if I'm not there."

"I don't want to interfere with your work. I'll leave my cellphone number in an envelope at the front desk for you in case you change your mind."

"I won't, Luc. I'm sorry you came all this way."

"I'm not. I got to see you again." He smiled at her, but his eyes were sad as he reached up to tuck a strand of hair behind her ear. "You know, Megan, sometimes we have to take a chance on something that isn't logical but feels right. Everything about being with you feels right to me."

"I have to go. Goodbye, Luc." Megan reached up and gave him a peck on the cheek then turned back to the ballroom. Luc leaned against the wall and watched as she walked away.

FOURTEEN

Megan's heart pounded in her chest as she hurried back to the ballroom. She was completely overwhelmed by what had just happened. She still couldn't believe Luc was really there, in the same building as she was, at that exact moment. She thought of his hand on her waist, his kiss on her cheek and lips as he rescued her from Brad, his sad smile as he said goodbye. He had just driven all day in a horrible blizzard to get to see her for a minute and ask her out. How could she *not* give him another chance?

He is no good for you, Megan. One night with him and you were a wreck. Forget him now before you get hurt worse, she told herself.

As she walked through the ballroom doors, she caught Quinn's eye. The bride pointed impatiently over toward the cake, obviously annoyed that Megan had been missing in action. Meg immediately got back to work, trying to clear her mind of all thoughts of Luc.

Two hours later, she finally packed up her equipment to go home. She had taken dozens of shots of the guests dancing and visiting as the evening progressed. It was close to 11 p.m. as she walked out of the ballroom, her feet aching.

She put on her coat and checked her cellphone. There was a text from Harper. I need to talk to you ASAP! Call me.

She ignored it, knowing what was so urgent, and shoved her phone into the pocket of her coat. She walked through the lobby, passing the front desk without stopping. When she reached the revolving door, she stepped into it and made a full circle, then walked purposefully over to the front desk.

The woman behind the counter had been watching her with a slightly amused expression.

"I think there might be an envelope here for me? Megan Sullivan?"

"Oh yes. Right here," the woman said, smiling as she handed it to her. "I had the luck of being here when he left it. I could have just listened to that accent all day."

"Yes. He has that effect on women. Thank you." Megan gave her a smile and walked back over to the doors, deciding to read the note when she got home. That would be the safer choice.

She waded through the now-deep snow covering the parking lot, cursing her dressy boots as she opened the trunk and gently put her camera bags in. Slamming the trunk closed, she hurried over to the driver's side, getting in and closing the door to get out of the biting wind. Megan started the car to warm it up, then rubbed her frozen hands together and glanced over at the envelope poking out of her purse. What could be the harm in just opening it and seeing what he had written? It was probably just his cellphone number anyway.

"Damn it," she said to herself as she tore open the envelope.

Dear Megan,

As much as I've tried, I cannot get you out of my mind. I hope you'll decide to give me another chance. Please know that everything I said to you was true and that everything we did together was meaningful to me. You have a hold on me that I can neither explain nor deny.

I think I have come up with a perfect arrangement so that we can see each other without it interfering with your life with Elliott. I hope you'll agree to meet me for dinner so we can discuss it. I'm in room 637 if you would like to come up, or you can call me on my cell number below.

Yours,
Luc

"Oh, fucking hell," she muttered, jamming her hands back into her gloves and pulling the key out of the ignition. She slammed the car door behind her as she trudged back to the hotel lobby and stamped the snow off her boots and pant legs, then made a beeline for the elevators. She glanced over at the woman behind the counter, who smiled knowingly at her.

"I'd go too," the woman said, nodding. "I'm impressed you even made it outside in the first place."

Megan laughed a little at herself as she rode up to the sixth floor. Taking a deep breath, she walked down the hall and knocked very quietly on the door to room 637. It was late and she realized he might be asleep already. She waited for a moment and then heard the door being unlocked.

Luc smiled warmly at her as he opened the door. He was dressed only in a white towel and held another in his hand as he rubbed it over his wet hair. The room was almost dark, lit only by a single bed-side lamp and the glow from the TV.

Megan could feel her body react to the sight of his almost nude, muscular form. She stepped inside and spoke quickly, before he could get a chance to make her knees go weak with his sexy voice. Her manner was brisk as she began. "So, listen, I appreciate that you drove all this way. It was really sweet. If I were going to get involved with someone, I would pick you, but it just won't work out, Luc."

He just nodded at her as she spoke. Even though he looked like he was sincerely listening to her, he tossed the towel in his hand back into the bathroom and took her purse off her shoulder, placing it on the console table beside them. He then pulled her gloves slowly off her hands, one finger at a time, never breaking eye contact, even as he put the gloves on top of her purse. Megan swallowed hard and kept talking, her words coming out a little slower, less convincing. How could the simple act of having her gloves taken off awaken her body like this?

"There is no way this can happen. We don't even live on the same continent. I won't be coming back to Paris anytime soon—maybe not ever. Nothing in my life has changed since I met you. We just have to accept that this is over, okay?" Megan said, gazing into Luc's eyes.

"You're completely right," he answered finally. "It's a horrible idea." Luc took her chilly hands and warmed them in his.

"It really is. I came up here to tell you that," she agreed, trying not to notice the muscles in his arms and chest flex as he rubbed her hands.

"You could have called, you know," he said, with a trace of that smirk.

"I thought it would be more polite to tell you in person, especially since you came all this way," Megan replied matter-of-factly.

There was nothing remotely believable about what she was saying. She had come up to his room because she needed to see him, and they both knew it. Her mind flashed to what was under that towel, causing her cheeks to grow hot. She could just hook one finger over it and pull, and he would be completely naked in front of her. She tried not to look down as she continued. "I also wanted to thank you for getting rid of that creep for me earlier."

"You're welcome. I wish I could always be there to get other men away from you. The thought of another man touching you makes me unreasonably angry." He was still holding her hands in his.

Megan tugged her hands away from him and walked further into the room to get away from him before she did something she would regret. She took a deep breath and turned back to face him. "So, anyway, thank you, and I hope you find happiness, but it won't be here."

Luc cocked his head to the side and gave her a questioning look. "Are you in a hurry right now?"

"Yes, I should get home. It's late."

"You have to relieve your babysitter? She is waiting up to go home?"

"No, my mom is with Elliott. She's staying over because of the storm." *Why didn't I lie just now?*

Luc tilted his head thoughtfully. "Can you sit for a minute, maybe have a drink with me?" He gestured over to the loveseat on the far side of the room, near the windows.

Megan looked over at the furniture, her feet begging her to take her weight off them. "Just water for me, please. I need to drive home," she replied, choosing the armchair beside the loveseat. There was no way she was going to sit close to him.

"Of course," he answered, opening the mini-bar. He opened a bottle of water and poured it into two tumblers. Crossing the room, he gave her an appreciative look as he handed her a glass and sat on the loveseat. Megan took a sip, feeling the cool liquid flow down her throat. She suddenly realized that she was uncomfortably hot with her long coat and boots on, but she refused to remove them. Removing them meant she might stay. And she definitely wasn't going to stay.

"You must be exhausted," Luc said, propping his elbow on the arm of the loveseat and resting his chin on his fingers.

How can a man in nothing but a towel still exude power? "I am. I cannot wait to crawl into bed right now," Megan replied, then, realizing how that sounded, she quickly backtracked. "At home. I need to go home and go to sleep." Why was she so nervous? They had already slept together and she was just here to end whatever this was.

Luc chuckled softly. "Of course. I didn't drive here expecting you to get into bed with me. I came just to ask you out, remember? In fact, I wouldn't sleep with you tonight even if you wanted to."

Megan rolled her eyes. "Sure," she said sarcastically.

"I wouldn't. It would defeat the purpose of my trip. I wanted to show you that I want something more than just sex with you. This is not—what is that phrase?—a booty call?"

"Yeah, that's the phrase."

"I am here because I want *more* with you than that, and I know this could work. We could see each other around your schedule. Whenever I come to Colorado, I could come here for a day or two. We could spend some time with each other when your son is at school, or if you want to see me in the evening, you could get a babysitter. We could have a romantic relationship that leaves your life otherwise intact. Completely free from worry about Elliott getting hurt."

Megan took another sip of her water. "So, I would be your sure thing when you travel to the US. I'm sorry, but that just isn't all that appetizing to me."

Luc shook his head. "No, you would be the person who I am with. Period. It would be a long distance relationship but real nonetheless. Exclusive. No other women for me. No other men for you."

"This is the strangest conversation I've ever had, Luc. We aren't even *dating* and you want me to commit to an exclusive relationship?"

"Yes, I do. I can't stop thinking about you, Megan. Since you left Paris, I have been restless and frustrated and completely unsatisfied. Last night, I made a point of meeting a woman I know, to try to get you off my mind. I thought if I slept with her, I would be able to forget you . . ."

Megan shifted uncomfortably in her seat as she listened. The thought of him trying to sleep with another woman stung, even though she had no right to be bothered by it. She stared down at her glass of water to avoid eye contact with him.

Luc continued. "But there was one big problem: I had no reaction to her in the usual way. Nothing was there, where there had always been something before. Do you know what we did? We ended up talking about you. I bored her to tears before she finally left."

"I think you might be a little *too* honest, Luc. I'm not as comforted by your story as you might have hoped."

"Ah, of course. Because I tried to . . ." His voice trailed off as he nodded in understanding. "I can see how that wouldn't make you feel better. But I saw her only because I couldn't stop thinking about you, and I needed to do something, anything, to get you off my mind. Last night, I realized there is no point in trying—I cannot. For some reason, I need to be with you and I have to figure out why. What I am proposing could be the perfect arrangement for you. Romance, sex, friendship, but none of the worries of a typical relationship. No pressure for things to go further than what you want. We give it a try and if it makes you unhappy, we stop and I never bother you again."

Megan looked around the room, trying to digest what he had just said. For some reason, her attention fell on the television. He had been watching Formula One racing. Something about that irritated her. She never would have thought he was a racing fan. She hated racing. It didn't matter in the least, but somehow it highlighted the fact that they were virtual strangers. She shook her head. "This is nuts. I don't know *anything* about you! Anything at all, really, and you want me to commit to a relationship with you? That's not how things work in the dating world."

Luc gave her a serious look. His voice was soft as he spoke. "But you don't want to be in the dating world, and what I am offering is so much better. What you do know is that we are attracted to each other, that we have fun together and that the sex is incredible. The rest we'll learn as we go."

Megan just stared at him, refusing to say anything.

"I am offering you romance, a little fun, something to look forward to. I won't ever expect you to move to France or to want to get married or even to introduce me to your son. Your life can continue as it is for the most part, only it will be more satisfying because you and I will have this to look forward to. Something beautiful and uncomplicated."

Megan watched him as he spoke—his kissable mouth, his dark, smouldering eyes, his broad shoulders shifting as he turned his body toward her a little more. His offer was beyond tempting. It was exactly what she had craved for years without letting herself think about it. Here was an unbelievably sexy man who wanted to be with her on her own terms—or what her terms would be if she had allowed herself to have any.

"Can I think about it?"

"Yes, of course. I wouldn't expect you to make a decision so quickly. What if I come back on Wednesday night? I'll stay all day Thursday. If you'll see me then, we can talk more. Have another chance at a day together. You can give me an answer after that."

"Alright. I can meet your for brunch on Thursday."

Luc smiled, relief showing on his face. His eyes locked on hers as though they were trying to say a whole lot of things he never could.

"Excellent," he replied in a low, satisfied tone. "Can I pick you up or would you like to meet me somewhere?"

"I'll meet you here, at the restaurant downstairs. Nine o'clock." Megan couldn't tear her eyes away from his. Her words came out slowly as she started to lose focus on what they were talking about. Her desire to wrap her legs around his waist was building.

"I'll be waiting for you."

"Well," she said, standing up, "I'll see you then."

Luc stood and followed her across the room. Megan picked up her purse and gloves, then turned, not realizing he was standing so close behind her, and her hand grazed his arm. The feeling of his skin against her fingers sent a pulse of electricity through her body. Luc gave her that look she had been missing since she saw him last, the one that told her exactly how beautiful he found her. Megan tugged him to her by the front of his towel and kissed him hard on the mouth, dropping her purse onto the table beside her.

She pulled her face back from his for a moment and grinned. "Oh, what the hell. You came all this way . . ."

Luc cradled her face in his hands as he let his tongue find its way in between her parted lips, and Megan slid her hands up his chest and around his neck. She could feel his erection lifting his towel. She was suddenly transported back to the edge of the world of ecstasy they had created in Paris, and she felt an urgent desire to immerse her entire being in it again. She lowered her hands, exploring his almost naked body with her fingertips, their mouths never parting.

Luc unbuttoned her coat quickly, then yanked it roughly off her shoulders, letting it drop to the floor. Their kisses became almost frantic as he pulled her shirt up out of her pants and over her head. She was wearing a pink, lacy push-up bra and Luc gave a low moan at the sight of it. Megan undid her pants, letting them drop. She stepped out of them, now standing in her bra and matching panties, with her tall black leather boots still on. Luc squeezed her ass with both hands and turned both of their bodies, pinning her against the door. Megan lifted one leg, wrapping it around his waist to rub herself against him. With the extra height of the boots, she was able to reach him exactly where she needed to. She brought both hands down and tugged at the towel, freeing his thick, hard cock with one move.

Luc pulled her panties to the side, letting his fingers explore her core. He could feel how wet and ready she was and he wanted to bury himself inside her at that moment more than he had ever wanted anything in his life. She was beyond sexy. She was irresistible, this woman he had thought he would never see again.

Megan closed her eyes, letting her head rest against the door. She moaned at the feel of his fingers inside her panties, leaning her back against the door, giving herself leverage to press herself hard against his hand. She needed to feel him inside her. Megan used her hand to bring the head of his cock to her pussy, pressing it against her. She could feel his smooth skin against hers and a wave of desperation swept over her. She wriggled her hips from side to side, willing him to thrust himself all the way in.

Luc pulled back, suddenly remembering that he wasn't wearing a condom. "No," he breathed.

"It's okay, Luc. I won't think you're here just for a booty call. Please don't stop," she begged, biting his bottom lip.

"Wait, beautiful, I don't have a condom on," he said.

"Right . . ." she sighed. "Do you have one?"

"I could check my bag but I'm pretty sure I don't," he said, grazing her neck with his lips.

"I need to feel you inside me, now, Luc. I can't wait until Thursday." Megan could hardly think with him sucking on her earlobe. She didn't care about the condom or why he had come or when she needed to be home. She just wanted him to fuck her right then. "Oh! I have some in my bag!" Megan exclaimed, turning her back to him and rummaging through her purse. *Thank you, Harper*.

Luc stared lustfully at this new view of her in only her bra, panties and boots, feeling his cock twitch with desire. He pressed his naked body to her back, pinning her against the table as she searched her bag. He sucked gently on her neck as he let one hand roam down her front and into her panties. Megan drew a sharp breath at the feeling of his fingers sliding into her sex. She ripped open the package and turned to roll the condom onto him.

Giving him a sultry smile, she reached behind her back and unclasped her bra, lowering her arms to let it slide off. Luc's mouth hung open for a moment and he could feel himself harden even more at the sight. She had transformed before his eyes, becoming completely seductive; she was here to get what she wanted and she wouldn't be denied. Hooking her thumbs into her panties, she pulled the waistband out and down, letting them fall to the floor. She lifted her feet out of them, one slow step at a time.

Luc grabbed her waist with both hands, pulling her to him urgently and kissing her hard. He slid his tongue into her mouth as he moved one hand between her thighs, caressing her with his fingers. Steering both of their bodies, he positioned her against the table again, then lifted her onto it, legs spread. Meg wrapped her legs around him and took hold of his cock with her hand, guiding it to her wet sex. Luc stared into her eyes as he slowly pressed his body forward, bringing himself inside her.

"Is this okay?" he breathed, wanting to make sure he wasn't hurting her.

"Yes Luc, I want you. Every inch." She licked her top lip and left her mouth open a little, inviting more. Luc accepted her offer, thrusting his tongue into her mouth in rhythm with the motion of his cock. He was in so far he filled her completely, almost lifting her off the table with each forward motion.

"Yes, like that, just like that," she growled.

Luc continued thrusting himself into her with just the perfect amount of force. He lowered his mouth over her breasts, sucking on her nipples, one at a time. Megan leaned her head back against the wall, closing her eyes and taking in the sensations he was giving her with each touch, each thrust, each kiss. This was pure ecstasy; it was pleasure beyond anything she had known. She could feel herself growing closer to climaxing with every passing second.

Lifting his head, he watched her for a moment as he moved. He could see her legs wrapped around him and her arms holding her up, her fingertips folded around the table for support. He had never seen anything as delectable in his life as Megan in only her black leather boots with her lips parted. Her eyes opened suddenly and she smiled at him, her breathing growing rapid, causing her breasts to heave with each motion. Luc's thrusts became more forceful, quicker and deeper. The look she gave him told him she was close now.

Grabbing the back of Luc's head with one hand, she pulled him to her, kissing him urgently. Pressing her forehead to his, she breathed heavily. "I'm going to come, Luc. Come with me, now."

"*Oh, oui! Oui! Maintenant!*" he breathed.

Megan could feel his body shudder as she felt her orgasm take over her entire body. They were overcome by their need, their desire and the delicious feeling of their bodies intertwined. Luc picked her up, feeling the full weight of her on him as he pulled her body down hard onto his cock. Megan gripped him forcefully with her legs and core muscles as she continued to come. Her orgasm was so powerful that she felt like she had blacked out for a second, resting her head on his shoulder as she finished.

Luc held her there, trying to catch his breath. He gently put her back down onto the table, hugging her tightly to him.

Megan grinned at him. "What did that mean?"

"What?"

"When you came, you said something in French. I want to know what it meant."

"Oh, I don't know what I said. I can't think straight right now, but I'm sure it was highly intelligent." He laughed. "Was that a turn-off for you?"

"Not at all. Everything about that was amazing." She smiled, kissing his cheek and nuzzling into his neck.

"It was, wasn't it? You are a femme fatale when you want to be. Wow. I had no idea."

Megan giggled, feeling oddly proud of her brazen actions. She gave him a teasing grin. "I'm sorry I completely ruined your romantic plan to not fuck me."

"I'm not as disappointed as you might think." He kissed her softly on the lips and pulled back from her a little. Megan groaned, not ready for the moment to be over.

"I should go home." She sighed.

"I want you to stay. Can you stay?" he asked, kissing her softly.

"No. I wish I could. My mom won't know where I am. She might wake up and start to worry."

"You sound like a teenager," he teased.

Megan laughed as she eased herself off the table and walked over to pick up her panties. "I feel like one. Sneaking home late at night, hoping not to get caught."

Luc watched as she bent down and collected her underwear, thoroughly enjoying the view as he removed the condom and wrapped it in some tissue. "I feel like throwing your panties back on the floor so I can watch you pick them up again. *Mon Dieu*, you are fucking gorgeous."

Megan laughed as she walked into the bathroom. He came up behind her as she slid her panties over her hips, wrapping his arms around her, smiling at her in the mirror Letting his fingers glide up her body, he cupped her breasts in both hands and gently sucked on the nape of her neck. "*Je veux te lécher des hanches jusqu'aux pieds.*"

Megan leaned back against him. "I'm almost afraid to ask what that means."

Luc raised his lips to her ear and murmured, "I want to lick you from your hips to your toes."

Megan moaned a little, her desire for him growing from a flicker to a full flame as they watched each other in the mirror. His warm body against her back, his hands skimming over her from her breasts to her hips, the sight of him pressed up behind her, his low voice as he spoke in her ear, was far more than she could resist.

Maybe if she enlisted his help, he would have the strength for both of them to make the choice neither of them wanted to. "I really should go, Luc."

"What's one more hour?" he whispered, gliding one hand over her tummy and into her panties. Rubbing her slowly with his finger-tips, he watched as her eyes followed his hand, her eyelids lowering as she started to give in. His cock twitched with excitement against the lace of her panties.

Her mind reeling, Megan reached into her purse, feeling around for the side pocket where she had stowed the condoms. Pulling one out, she held it up for him. Luc took it from her with his free hand as he continued to pleasure her skilfully with his other. Turning her head, she found his lips with hers, opening her mouth to his to invite him in. She wanted him to take her right there, in front of the mirror so they could see each other.

Putting the condom on the counter, Luc reached for her hand, pulling it down into her panties. He watched as she slid her hand up and down, feeling her fingers meet his. Pulling his own hand out, he ripped open the wrapper, readying himself for her. Megan's other hand reached behind her, guiding him into her panties from behind. "I want to feel you inside me now, Luc. All of you."

Luc pressed her body forward then gripped her hips with both hands and moved himself into the right angle to enter her wet sex. "You are so tight. So wet. So perfect," he murmured, sucking on her neck.

Megan watched him in the mirror as he thrust himself into her. It was all so deliciously naughty. Him behind her, bending her over the counter, his cock in her lacy panties. She could see him, feel him, taste him and hear him as he pulled himself almost completely out before plunging back in. It was deep, it was urgent, it was hot. In and out. Over and over. Lustful gazes. Frantic kisses. Roaming hands. The hard, cold granite against her, giving leverage to his hot, hard body behind her. Bringing him in deeper. Forcefully. Until they both came undone. Waves of unmatched pleasure rolled through them, over them, leaving them both panting and fully satisfied.

"I want to wake up with you. Stay with me tonight." He ran his nose along the length of her neck, wrapping his arms around her tightly.

"Mmm. I wish I could," Megan replied, reaching behind her to touch his cheek with her fingers. "I'll see you Thursday though, right?"

"Yes, you will," he agreed, reluctantly letting her go. Megan made her way out of the bathroom to retrieve her clothes.

Luc pulled on a robe and leaned against the bathroom entrance, giving her that look again. "Is there no way I can convince you to stay? You could call home and say you don't want to risk the drive home."

"Now, don't go getting all attached to me, Monsieur Chevalier. This can't work if you get attached to me." Megan grinned, walking toward him, now fully dressed, and gave him a lingering kiss on the lips.

"Don't worry, I'm a big boy. I can handle this."

"You certainly are a big boy." She smiled coyly, running her hand along the front of his robe. "I hope you're right that you can handle this, though."

Luc laughed a little, then took her face in his hands. "I love to see this side of you. Sexy and fun. You really are worth almost dying in a blizzard to get to."

"Ugh. The blizzard," Megan replied as she shrugged her coat on. "I forgot that when I leave this warm room, I have go out into that cold wind."

"That sounds awful. Maybe we can stay here until spring?"

"Oh, I'd be sick of you well before then, Chevalier," Megan said, then gave him a quick peck on the cheek. "Good night. Text me and let me know when you're coming."

"I will. Can you text me when you get home so I know you made it?"

Megan gave him a funny look. She hadn't figured him for the overprotective type. "What? Are you going to lie awake worrying about me?"

"Yes. The roads are very icy."

"Oh, they're not so bad. You forget I grew up here. I'm used to it."

"Text me anyway," he said as she opened the door. He planted a long kiss on her lips and reluctantly let her go.

"I will."

She sauntered lazily down the hall in her post-sex haze, then pressed the down button to call the elevator. She had been waiting for a few moments when suddenly a door down the hall opened. Luc was striding toward her, fully dressed, pulling on his wool coat as he hurried to catch her. Megan looked at him in surprise.

"What kind of man lets a woman go out to her car alone late at night?" he asked.

"A pretty typical one, I'd guess."

"A complete asshole. What if that slimy guy is down there?"

he asked as the elevator doors opened. He took her hand as they stepped in together. Megan pushed the button to the lobby and the doors closed. Luc spun her to him and kissed her as they rode down together. His kisses melted her, making her dizzy with desire again.

They straightened themselves out as the doors opened, then walked across the lobby. When they got outside, the cold air hit them like a slap of icy water.

"Why do you live here?" Luc asked as they crossed the parking lot. He wrapped an arm around her and pulled her close to block the wind.

"At this moment, I'm not entirely sure. My family is here and my friends—oh, and I love to ski."

"You love to ski?" he asked excitedly.

"I do. Do you?"

"Very much. Can we go together soon?"

"Sure. I'd love that," Megan said as they reached her car. She unlocked it with a press of the button on her key fob and Luc opened the door. The car was covered in snow now and needed to be brushed off. Megan grabbed the brush off the floor of the car and straightened up.

Luc took it gently from her hand. "You get in and start up the car. I'll do this," he said.

Megan happily complied, feeling rather spoiled. *Don't get used to this*, she told herself, *this is only a dream*.

Luc opened the driver's door when he had finished and handed her the brush. "Good night, *mon ange*. Over the next few days, I will enjoy the anticipation of being with you again."

Megan smiled as he kissed her. "*Mon ange*? What does that mean?"

"*My angel*. Is that too much?"

"It's wonderful, actually. Good night, Luc."

"Text me when you get home. I'll wait up."

"I won't forget."

Megan drove slowly home. It was well after midnight and she was beginning to get sleepy now. It had been a long day and she was in a daze from the evening's end. She turned the radio on loud and opened the window a crack to keep her alert for the ride home. When she pulled into her garage, she turned off the car and sent Luc a text. Made it home. See you Thursday morning for round three.

A few minutes later, as she took off her boots and placed them in the back hall closet, she heard her phone chime.

Round three? I thought we would just talk. I'm beginning to think you only want me for my body.

Megan laughed quietly to herself. Smart man. You figured me out already.

For an angel, you are a little bit of a devil.

You don't know the half of it.

I am compelled to find out. Bonsoir, Megan.

Good night, Luc.

Megan smiled as she locked up and made her way to her bedroom. She had a hot shower and then collapsed into bed, grateful her mom would get up with Elliott so she could get some extra sleep.

FIFTEEN

It was almost nine when Megan woke the next morning. She heard the phone ring and then Elliott running up the stairs and bursting into her room. "Mom! Mom! Turn on your computer! It's Dad and he wants to Skype with me!"

Megan rubbed her eyes with her hands. "Okay baby, hang on," she said, smiling at Elliott. She sat up and swung her legs over the side of the bed, trying to steady herself. "Tell your dad it will take about five minutes to log on."

Elliott was already disappearing down the hall, chatting excitedly. "She was still sleeping. She said it will take five minutes, but I know how to start up the computer so I'll do it . . ."

"Shit," Megan muttered under her breath. She was tired and her feet hurt from the day before. She always felt nervous when Elliott spoke to Ian. She knew Elliott would think that maybe Ian would start calling every day or come and see him.

Pulling a sweater over her head, she walked over to her bathroom and took a swig of mouthwash, gargling as she stared into the mirror. Her hair had a wild look to it because she had gone to bed with it wet. She tried for a brief moment to fix it, then gave up, spitting the mouthwash into the sink and padding down the stairs to the kitchen.

Elliott had the computer started and was looking for the Skype icon while Helen looked over his shoulder, trying to help him.

"I got it, Mom." Megan yawned, trying to wake up. She opened the program for Elliott and pressed the video-call button to connect him with his dad.

"It's working, Dad! Can you hear it on your computer?" Elliott grinned up at his mom. The familiar sound of the call connecting could be heard, then Megan looked down to see her ex-husband sitting outside on his patio in Florida in a T-shirt. He was tanned and looked as handsome as ever, if a little bit worn down from hard living.

Ian grinned at his little boy, hanging up his cellphone. "Hey, buddy! Look at you! How'd you get so big?"

Megan walked away from the computer, rolling her eyes at her mom. Helen handed her a mug for her coffee and whispered in her ear, "Time. He got so big while that jackass has been MIA . . ."

Megan stifled a laugh and poured herself a coffee. "Thank you for the sleep-in day. I am wiped."

"So," Helen whispered, "did you meet a man last night?"

"Yes, and I went straight to his hotel room just like I promised you I would," Megan muttered under her breath to her mom.

Helen giggled softly and Megan joined in, but for a completely different reason.

The two moved to the kitchen table, where Megan could casually listen to the call without being seen by Ian. Elliott was chatting away excitedly about the train set he thought was from him. They spoke for about twenty minutes before another call came through on the home phone. Megan was surprised at how sober Ian seemed and marvelled at the fact that he was even awake this early on a Sunday.

The phone ringing interrupted Elliott's happy chatter. He held up a finger to his dad. "Hang on, Dad. It's my friend Jase on the phone."

Elliott answered the call. "Hi, Jase! I'm just Skyping with my dad. He lives near Disney World . . ."

He paused for a moment, then looked over at Megan. "Mom! Can I go to Jase's today? His parents want to take us skiing at Eldora for the day. Can I go? Please, please, please?"

Megan walked over to Elliott. "Tell him I'd like to talk to his parents, okay?"

Elliott did as he was told, then handed the phone to his mom. Elliott, too distracted to talk to his dad at the moment, waited to hear what Megan was going to say.

Ian watched the scene unfold, realizing how far removed he was from even the slightest parenting decision. He didn't know if his son could ski or if this Jase boy's parents were responsible enough to take him along. He saw Megan's torso as she took the phone, then watched as she walked away to the living room. Her gait was so familiar to him, and he could tell she was hiding her slender frame under that big sweater and her plaid pyjama bottoms.

A stab of regret cut Ian hard, an all-too-normal feeling for him. How many Sunday mornings like this had he missed in Elliott's life? All of them, really. He sat quietly, thinking about what it would have been like to be there with them. Would he and Megan go back to bed after seeing Elliott off? Would they still have that heat they used to? Megan had always been so sexy and passionate. There was nothing about *her* that had caused their breakup—it was all Ian and his drugs. If he could take it all back and start over with her, he would.

A minute later, he saw her walk back into the kitchen. She was still beautiful as she smiled at Elliott and gave him a little nod. "Okay, now get back to talking to your dad, silly beans!"

Elliott yelled with excitement, "Yes! I get to go skiing, Dad! Do you like to ski? I love it!"

"I do enjoy it. I don't get a chance to go often living here, though."

"You should come up for a visit and we could go together."

"Maybe I should, Elliott. That sounds like a great idea."

"Mom could come too. She's a great skier."

"I remember."

"Oh yeah, I forgot you kind of know her."

Ian chuckled at his son's perspective. "Yeah, I guess I do kind of know her."

* * *

An hour later, Megan helped Elliott bring his ski helmet and booster seat out to his friend's minivan. Elliott and Jase jumped around in the van, yelling eagerly. Jase's mom, Rebecca, laughed at the pair. "Okay, you two, get buckled in already!"

She turned to Megan. "Can we keep him until after supper? We were planning to eat at the hill."

"Of course." Megan handed her some money, "This should cover his lift ticket, equipment rental and meals."

Jase's dad, Cory, shook his head. "No, no. He's our guest. It's our treat. Really, you're doing us a favour. It's so much more fun for Jase with Elliott around."

"Well, use it to buy everyone lunch, then. I insist."

"Alright." Rebecca smiled. She knew Megan well enough to know that she didn't want to feel like a charity case.

"Thank you," Megan said. "I'm happy for him. He was doomed

to an afternoon of shovelling with his boring old mom before you called."

"Thank *you*!" Rebecca said. "We'll be back around seven, if that's alright."

"That would be perfect." She turned to Elliott. "Have fun, be safe and be on your best behaviour."

"I know, Mom. Love you. Bye!" he said quickly.

"Love you too. Bye, guys." She watched the minivan slowly make its way down the street for a moment before running back into the now empty house to get out of the cold.

Her mom had gone home earlier to get ready for church. Megan wandered over to the kitchen to pour herself another mug of coffee. Looking at the clock, she realized it was close to ten. She wondered if Luc might be in town still. Should she text him? Maybe they could see each other. But would that seem too desperate?

The thought of him made her blush all over—he brought out a wild side in her and she liked it. Sitting there in cozy sweatpants now, she could hardly believe she was the same woman in nothing but leather boots the night before. The memory of his kiss, of his smile and of him inside her filled her mind, bringing a feeling of desire to her entire body.

She grabbed her cellphone off the table and texted him. Hey, you, how did you sleep?

A minute later, her phone chimed. Like only a very satisfied man can. How about you?

Very well. Elliott got invited skiing for the day, so I have the day to myself. Trying to figure out what to do . . .

Really? I know a handsome Frenchman who happens to be nearby. If you ask nicely, I bet he would take you out for the day . . .

Who says I want to go out? I might want to spend the day in bed. I haven't decided yet.

A second later, her cellphone rang. "Is this a handsome Frenchman?" she asked.

Luc laughed a little. "It might be. Is this a sexy American girl with tall leather boots?"

"It might be. Although at the moment, I'm in very alluring blue sweatpants."

"Mmm, if that's all you're wearing, I'll be right over. Sweatpants come off easily."

Megan laughed, feeling turned on by the thought of him taking her pants off. "So, listen, aren't you driving back today?"

"I can't drive back, as it turns out. There's some freezing rain a couple of hours west of here. They had to close the main freeway. I was just trying to get a flight back later today if possible and leave the rental at the airport. The latest flight is at eight tonight. Maybe I can book that one so we can spend the day together?"

"Yes, do that. I'll meet you at your hotel in about an hour, okay?"

"Perfect. Until then," he said before hanging up.

Until then, she thought. Those words coming out of an American man's mouth would sound odd, but from him, wow. Megan hurried up the stairs to shower.

Forty minutes later, dressed in her cream-coloured winter coat, jeans and her new brown suede boots, she locked up the house. She had put on a little extra makeup, including Harper's red lipstick, and put her hair up the same way it had been when she first met Luc. Her heart thumped in her chest as she drove over to the hotel. When she arrived, she was surprised to see Luc waiting for her in the lobby, dressed in his long, black wool coat and jeans, with a sexy grin on his face. He strode over to her.

"You look gorgeous," he said, leaning down to kiss her.

"You look pretty good yourself." She smiled.

"I thought I should meet you down here so we could go have a late breakfast together. If you came up to the room, I was afraid we wouldn't get out of bed all day."

"Why would you be afraid of that?"

"Because we should do *some* talking, don't you think?"

"Talking can be overrated, but I suppose if you're hungry, we should get some food into you."

Luc leaned in to speak quietly into her ear. "Yes, we need to have enough energy for all the fucking we're going to do later."

Megan's eyes popped open and she could feel her body react to his words. "By all means, then, let's go eat."

They made their way along the snowy sidewalk to a little restaurant that served Sunday brunch. Luc held the door for Megan as she stamped the snow off her boots. Inside, the restaurant was warm and busy. A hostess in a white dress shirt and black pants rushed over to seat them.

"Can we sit by the fireplace?" Luc asked her. "My girlfriend is always chilly and I take it upon myself to remedy that whenever possible."

"Of course," she replied, picking up two menus and leading them to a table in front of the fireplace. "Your server will be right with you." She smiled at them.

The pair thanked her and got settled at the table. They ordered their meals and sipped coffee, grinning at each other. Images of the night before and the day to come occupied their thoughts.

"This is a most welcome surprise," Luc said, taking her hands in his. "I did not expect to get the entire day with you."

"Me neither. I thought you might be on your way back already." Megan looked down at his large hands holding hers. The sight and the feel of them removed any trace of chill left over from their walk. "What time is your flight?"

"Seven thirty. I should leave for the airport at six, I think, right?"

"Sounds about right. I should get home around then anyway. Elliott's being dropped off by seven."

"So we have almost seven hours together. We should eat quickly," he said, as their food was placed in front of them.

"Exactly what I was thinking." Megan laughed, picking up a fork and knife to cut a piece off her eggs Benedict.

After the first few tastes of food and sips of coffee, Luc took his phone out of his pocket. "Excuse me. I need to read this email. It's from Simone, about the numbers from last night."

"Of course," Megan replied.

After a moment, Luc put his phone back in his jacket pocket. "I apologize. I try to keep that type of thing to a minimum when I'm out with a woman. I know it's rude."

"No, I understand. I find myself needing to work at unconventional moments and I'm running only one business. You're running a lot of businesses."

Luc smiled. "Thank you. It's nice to be with someone who knows what it's like. It's not a sign of disinterest in you, only necessity."

"I can't see that bothering me, but . . ." Her voice trailed off as Megan reconsidered what she was about to say.

"But? If there's something I'm doing that bothers you, I want to know now, so I can make adjustments," Luc said with a serious expression.

"It's Simone, actually. After what happened in Paris, I'm a little concerned she might try to interfere again. And I'm wondering why someone with such a mean streak still works for you. Surely she must cause problems with the staff at times."

Luc gave a little nod. "Yes, I'm sure it would be hard to understand. Simone has been with me for a long time. She is very loyal and does an excellent job, always putting out fires for me—a lot of them I will never even have to know about. She doesn't have a family—at least, not a very nice one. She is an only child, like me, except instead of a philanderer for a father, hers was abusive. Her mother managed to get away from him only to marry another abuser. Simone has nothing to do with either of them. She and I are both without true families so, in some ways, we have become that for each other. That's why she is so protective of me. Does that make sense?"

Megan's voice was hesitant. "It does . . . but it doesn't really help alleviate my concerns about her possible impact on our relationship."

Luc reached his hand across the table to hold hers. "I know she was awful to you and I am so sorry for that. I will be very vigilant to make sure she doesn't interfere. And if you somehow end up having a conversation with her again that you are troubled by, I need to know right away so I can deal with her accordingly. She will grow used to the fact that we are together and, in time, I hope you two will even become friends. Once she sees what I see in you, I know she'll want to be your friend. How could she not? You are an amazing person. When that happens, you'll see that there is no one as fiercely protective as Simone."

"At this moment, I honestly can't imagine a scenario in which she and I are good friends," Megan replied with a skeptical look.

"I know. It would be unreasonable for me to expect that of you, but I hope you can see why I can't just toss her aside."

Megan picked up her fork and knife again. "I think I get it, but I'm going to hold you to what you said about making sure she doesn't try anything again."

"As you should," Luc answered, giving her hand a little squeeze. "I would never want anyone to hurt you, Megan, not Simone or anyone else. I consider it my job to prevent that from happening."

"Well, I can see how successful you are at work, so that should help me to relax a little about it all."

"Good. And I'm glad you told me rather than worrying about it in silence. Honesty is really the only way to make relationships work."

"Agreed."

On the way back to the hotel, they ducked into a drugstore to buy a package of condoms. Luc also grabbed a small box of chocolates for Megan. They hurried down the street to the hotel, the cold wind rushing them along.

The afternoon was spent in bed. Luc took his time with Megan, exploring every inch of her body with his hands and his mouth. Megan lost count of how many orgasms she had that day; she felt raw in a completely satisfied way. They lay together, bodies glistening with sweat as the sun started to lower in the sky. Megan's head was resting on Luc's chest, her leg slung over his midsection lazily. She looked over at the clock. It read 5 p.m. They would have to leave soon and she was nowhere near ready for him to go.

She lifted her head and selected a chocolate from the almost empty box on the bed beside her. Looking at the legend, she read aloud, "Caramel filled."

"That one is for me, then. Those are my favourites," Luc replied.

Megan held it over his waiting lips and then popped it into her own mouth instead. "Mine too," was her muffled answer as she selected another one. "Here, you can have the orange-centre one."

"Oh, I get the one no one likes? How kind of you, especially since I have spent the afternoon tirelessly giving you orgasm after orgasm."

Megan laughed, dropping the chocolate back into its spot and selecting another. "Here, ganache, but only because you must have a sore jaw by now."

"It will hurt for days but it was totally worth it. It should be fine by Thursday, if you still want to meet."

"Sure, I'm not quite sick of you yet," she teased. "Getting there, but not yet."

Luc laughed and slapped her on the ass lightly. "So, you've stopped enjoying multiple orgasms, then? That seems odd. I thought most women loved them."

Megan laughed, lifting her head to look at him, resting her chin on his chest. "Oh, that part I like. But well-endowed, incredibly handsome sex gods get a bit dull after a while. I can't guarantee how long I'll want to keep fucking you."

Luc gave her a questioning look. "Are you drunk right now? Because you told me you're a huge liar when you're drunk."

Megan laughed out loud, surprised he remembered what she had said in Paris about that. "I am sober, actually, so you'll know it's the truth when I tell you that I haven't had this much fun with a man in years."

"I know. That is a crime."

Megan smiled gratefully at him, resting her chin on his chest. "Thank you, Luc. This has been wonderful."

"It certainly has. There is no part of me that has any interest in going anywhere. There is nothing there that I want as much as you." As the words came out of Luc's mouth, the truth of them struck him with force.

Megan reluctantly got up, sauntering naked across the room to find her clothes. Luc gazed at her lean body as she moved. His cock hardened at the sight, causing him to groan. "Especially when you do that. How is it possible that I am hard again just watching you move?"

Megan turned to him and smiled while she plucked her bra off the lampshade it had spent the last several hours slung over. She gazed at his hard body, not entirely sure how she had ended up spending the day in bed with this incredible man. Only weeks before she had been certain she would never do this again, and now here she was in a hotel room, having just had the best sex of her life. "I'm going to take a quick shower."

"That's funny, I was about to take a shower as well. Maybe we'll have to share."

Half an hour later, Megan stood at the door, pulling on her coat. Luc came to her, hanging her scarf over her shoulders and using it to pull her in for a lingering kiss.

"I have to go and so do you," she said, pulling away from him.

Luc tied the sash on his robe with a heavy sigh. "Thursday seems like an eternity from now, to me."

"I thought you *loved* anticipation?"

Luc grinned. "I usually do, but when it comes to you, *mon ange*, it feels more like torture."

Megan finished dressing and turned to him. "So, skiing on Thursday or another day in bed?"

"Can we go skiing for a few hours and then come back here? Would you have time for that?"

"I should. I'll see if my mom can pick up Elliott from school and feed him supper."

"Sounds perfect." Luc wrapped his arms around Megan and gave her a lingering kiss, one that was meant to hold them over for the next few days but only served to deepen their need for each other. Megan held her eyes shut for a long moment when the kiss was over, trying to prevent the day from ending.

SIXTEEN

"Harper, it's me." Megan drove toward home, using the hands-free to talk to her friend.

"Meg! Oh my God! I've been trying to reach you. You are never going to believe this! Luc went to Boulder. He came looking for you."

"He found me. Turns out he checked into the hotel the wedding was at. I just spent the day in bed with him. Oh, and some of last night too."

"WHAT?" Harper's voice exploded into the phone. "I can't believe it! How was it? Where is this all going?"

"It was unbelievably incredible and it's going into unchartered territory for me. We've agreed to meet when he's in the US and leave it at that."

"Seriously? That doesn't sound very romantic." Harper's voice fell a little.

"I know it doesn't but I don't have time for romance. It's really kind of perfect for me. He wants us to be exclusive, which is fine with me, since it's not like I'd be out looking for other men anyway. I can have a little romance and about a thousand times more sex than I was having, without worrying about it interfering with my real life. Elliott doesn't ever have to know, so I won't have to worry about introducing him to a man who might not stick around."

"Hmm . . . I guess . . . But is that really what you want, Meg?"

"It's what I want for right now, Harper. I know it sounds weird, but in my position, that's really all I can allow myself." Megan's voice was confident.

"But what will happen when it's over? You can't keep things in limbo like that forever."

Megan sighed, not wanting to think about the end. "Listen, Harper, try to be excited for me, okay? Last night and today I had the best sex of my friggin' life and I want to enjoy the afterglow here. I am finally having some fun and I don't want to overthink it. You, of all people, should be excited about it—you've been pushing me to get laid for years now. Luc's so amazing and I think he's exactly what I need."

"Are you referring to his huge dick right now? Because I don't think you should let your vag make your decisions for you."

Megan giggled at her friend's dirty reference. "Okay, I'm not going to lie to you. The cock definitely tips things in his favour. But if he weren't so attentive and thoughtful, I promise it wouldn't make any difference."

"I fucking well hope not. If you end up getting hurt, I'm going to feel very responsible for introducing the two of you."

"I'll be fine, Harper. I'm not a naive young girl. I'm a strong, independent woman and I know what I want. And what I want is in his pants." Megan laughed wickedly at her own joke, trying to divert the conversation.

Harper found herself giggling along. "Alright, I just don't want you to get hurt."

"Trust me, I won't. I know what I'm doing. Now, how are you?"

*   *   *

That night after Megan tucked Elliott into bed, he called her back into the room. "Hey, Mom?"

"Yes?"

"You're really happy tonight. It's nice."

"I *am* happy. I have the best son on the planet. Now get to sleep."

Megan jogged down the steps on her way to the kitchen to prepare Elliott's lunch for the next day. She put her phone in the docking station and selected Katy Perry's latest album. Singing along to "Unconditionally," her whole body felt like it was smiling as she worked. This was the first evening in years she didn't have that empty feeling. All thoughts of her normal state of loneliness were so far from her mind she didn't even notice the empty feeling was gone.

SEVENTEEN

The next two days absolutely dragged for Luc. He kept himself busy with meetings at the club as well as touring a few commercial properties in Aspen he was considering for a new upscale pub he wanted to open. In the evenings, he and Megan talked on the phone late into the night after she got Elliott to sleep. That was by far the best part of his day. He found himself falling asleep quickly, which was a welcome change for him. He told her things he had never shared with anyone before and was surprised how good it felt to have this type of intimacy with a woman.

On Wednesday, he flew to Boulder in the early evening and checked back into the same hotel. After getting settled in, Luc sent a text to Megan to let her know he had arrived. He felt a mixture of excitement and frustration, being so close to her but not being able to see her or touch her until the next day. It suddenly seemed odd to him to feel so close to someone, even though they had spent only a matter of hours together and he had never even seen her house.

Around 9 p.m., Megan called him on Skype so they could see each other. She looked a bit sleepy and her hair was wet from the shower.

"So, this is me with no makeup." She gave him an unsure look. "I hope you aren't scared off."

Luc smiled back affectionately. "You look lovelier than ever. I can't wait for tomorrow."

"Me too. I should be at the hotel around 9:30, so we can go straight to the ski hill. My mom is going to pick Elliott up from school and bring him home. I want to be home in time to put him to bed, so I should be home by 7:30."

"Megan, I want to say thank you," Luc said.

"For what?"

"Thank you for giving me another chance and for making all these arrangements so we can see each other. I know you have very little time in your life, and it means a lot to me that you would give me some of it."

"Oh, you're welcome. Thank *you* for coming all this way twice in one week just to see me. It's really . . . I don't know how to describe it. It's wonderful."

"Yes, I'm a pretty remarkable man, really."

Megan laughed. "That you are. See you tomorrow, Monsieur Wonderful."

"See you then, gorgeous."

* * *

"Hey! You're a really great skier for a French guy!" Megan called to Luc as they neared the bottom of their first run together. He was ahead of her as they carved their way down the hill at top speed.

Luc pivoted and came to a sideways stop, spraying snow behind him. He gave her a hurt look. "Why would you have such low expectations?"

Megan stopped beside him with mischievous look. "I thought you Frenchmen just liked drinking wine and flirting with women. I never would have taken you for the sporty type."

"Oh, that sounds like . . . what did you call it? A back-ended compliment?"

"Backhanded, a backhanded compliment. You catch on fast." She laughed.

Luc gazed at Megan for a moment. She looked beautiful to him, with her rosy cheeks framed by a light pink wool hat and her blond hair flipped out from under it. She had bought the hat and the black fitted ski jacket to go over her grey ski pants earlier in the week, deciding that a little splurge was in order. He leaned on his poles and planted a kiss on her mouth.

"And here I thought you were so kind." He grinned.

"If I were too nice, it would get boring."

"No one could ever accuse you of being boring. Shall we make our way back up the mountain?"

"Yes!"

They sat close together on the chairlift. Luc held his poles in one hand and wrapped his other arm around her shoulder. The sun was shining brightly, warming them as they ascended the mountain. The air was cold but felt refreshing after the exertion of making their way down the hill earlier.

"This feels positively decadent. Skiing on a weekday! I should be at home doing laundry and paying bills." Megan smiled.

"No, you should be here being spoiled. You deserve a day off."

"I do, don't I?"

Luc laughed and gave her a peck on the cheek. "If anyone does, it's you. I'm only glad you're letting yourself do this with me."

"Me too."

"What did your mother think of you coming here with me today?"

Megan looked down at her mitts, feeling embarrassed. "I told her I was going with a few other moms. I know it's completely immature to be sneaking around like this, but she wouldn't approve. She wants me to find a man to settle down with."

"If you were my daughter, I wouldn't approve of me either. I would want you to find a good man who wanted to get married."

"Hmm, I have a feeling you are a good man, and I don't *want* to get married. I did it once and it was a complete disappointment. This will work because neither of us is making promises we can't keep."

"I hope so, Megan, but I want you to tell me if your expectations change. I need to know if this stops working for you. I can't stand the thought of you feeling lonely or sad when I leave. I would never want you to be left unhappy."

Megan bumped him with her shoulder a little. "Listen, I'm a big girl and I can handle this. I think I can go a long time with a fantasy life on the side."

"I hope you can because I don't know when I'll be able to get you out of my system," Luc replied as the chair started to lower.

* * *

A couple of hours later, Megan found herself lounging in a cozy armchair next to a roaring fire in the lodge. She watched Luc as he crossed the room, carrying a tray of food and drinks. Their eyes met as he moved toward her, smiling warmly. Setting the tray down on the table, he passed her a beer and the burger and fries she had ordered.

He chose the chair opposite her and picked up a fry. "I have worked up quite an appetite."

"Me too. There's nothing like fresh air and exercise to make you hungry." Megan slapped the bottom of the glass ketchup bottle, causing a large blob to land on her plate.

Luc took a sip of his beer. "I agree. I haven't skied in years. Thank you for suggesting this. I forgot how much I love it."

"It is wonderful, isn't it?"

"When I was a young man, skiing was the first thing I wanted to do when I could finally afford it. It was more out of a sense of righteous indignation than anything else. I wanted to show my father that I was as good as his other children. It was only after I started to learn how to ski that I realized how enjoyable it was."

Megan tilted her head as she listened to him. In their brief time together, this was the most information he had volunteered about his father. "It sounds like you had a rough childhood where he's concerned."

Luc shrugged. "Well, yes, I suppose. He had another family. My mother was his mistress. We got scraps when it came to his time and affection. But, you know, it's ancient history now."

"Is it?" Megan asked quietly. "I worry a lot about Elliott growing up without his dad. I worry that it will leave a wound too big to heal."

"We all have something that wounds us as children. The important thing is probably more how we are taught to think about life's struggles than the actual problems themselves."

"Is that what your mom taught you?"

"No. That's what I figured out on my own. I learned that life was going to be tough and unfair, so I was going to have to be tough and smart to make my way."

"I didn't learn that until my marriage ended," Megan replied, dipping another fry into some ketchup. "Did you wish your mom had handled things differently?"

"In some ways, I did. She was a loving person and she gave me everything she could. As I grew up, though, I started to realize we would have both been better off if she had sent my father away and made sure he never came back. It would have been easier not to know him at all than to know him a little bit and realize he had other children he shared a home with and loved more than me."

Megan put her hand on Luc's arm, rubbing it consolingly. "That must have been heartbreaking."

Luc nodded his agreement. They sat quietly for a moment before Luc spoke up again. "But we were having a wonderful day and talking about how much we like skiing, weren't we?"

Megan gave him a reassuring smile. "We *are* having a wonderful day. I'm glad you feel like you can share something so personal with me."

"It's funny. I've never spoken about my father like that before. Only with you."

*   *   *

In the middle of the afternoon, the pair found themselves driving back to town along the snowy highway. Megan relaxed into the heated seat of Luc's rental car and closed her eyes as she spoke. "It feels so nice to be a passenger in a car for once. It's positively luxurious."

Luc looked over at her and put his hand on her knee. "You certainly appreciate the simple things in life. It's rather refreshing. Most women I know would never notice something as small as not having to drive."

Megan put her hand over his, and their fingers interlaced. "I guess it's all your frame of reference, right?"

Luc kept his hand on Megan's leg as they drove into town. A pulse of sexual energy flowed through the two of them, and they were both starting to feel the excitement of what was to come. Luc lifted Megan's hand and held it to his lips, running them along her knuckles as they neared the hotel.

When they reached his room, Megan was surprised to see Luc

had booked a large suite this time. He moved over to the fireplace and turned it on as she took off her boots.

"Mind if I take a shower?" Megan asked, feeling the chill from cooling down after skiing.

"Of course not. Help yourself," Luc said, gazing over at her as she removed her coat.

Megan walked into the large bathroom and turned on the shower, letting the water heat up as she stripped down. She stepped in, allowing the glass door to shut softly behind her as the first perfectly warm drops of water hit her shoulders. "Ahhh," she sighed to herself.

A moment later, the shower door opened and Luc stood before her, nude and fully erect. He gave her a seductive look as he stepped inside. "Would it be presumptuous of me to think you might not mind?"

"Yes, but I'll let it go this time," she replied, wrapping her arms around his neck and pulling him to her. Luc lowered his head and gave her a lingering kiss. Megan felt her knees go weak at his embrace. She ran her fingertips down his muscular back, then cupped his firm ass with both hands, giving him a little squeeze.

"That is a solid ass you've got there, Chevalier," she said with a grin.

"I'm glad you like it. It got that way from kickboxing and running."

"Kickboxing? Really? Is that also how these abs got here?" she asked, running her hands along his stomach.

"I draw those on with charcoal every morning. They're not real," he teased.

Megan laughed. "They feel pretty real to me. I better take a closer look," Megan said, kissing his chest, then lowering her body so she was on her knees in front of him. She ran her hands up and then back down as she kissed his lower abdomen and licked his long, thick length. Placing one hand around his cock, she swirled her tongue over the head, then plunged her mouth over him in one long move.

Luc steadied himself with a hand on the shower wall as the water sprayed over him. He gazed down, watching Megan as she moved her mouth over him. This was a welcome surprise for Luc. She continued like this for several mind-blowing moments before he gently pulled himself back and helped her to her feet. As much as he wanted her to stay there, he could see little goosebumps on her skin and knew she was starting to get cold.

"*Viens ici, ma belle.* I need to taste you now," he said. Switching places with her so that she stood under the water, he lowered himself before her, gently parting her with his fingers. Megan gasped at the feeling of his tongue entering her, exploring carefully along her sex. She lifted one leg and propped her foot on the bench beside her, giving him full access to her.

Luc stroked her with his fingers as he thrust his tongue deeper inside her, then wiggled his tongue from side to side, making her moan loudly. Megan closed her eyes and caressed her breasts with her fingers as she allowed the sensation of his mouth on her pussy to overwhelm her. She was amazed at how skilled he was at bringing her so close to climaxing already.

"Oh, Luc, yes, just like that," she breathed.

Luc gently slid one finger along her ass as he continued to slide his tongue in and out of her. He didn't enter her with his finger, but rubbed around the edges, giving her a most exquisite feeling. Megan brought one hand down in front of her and rubbed it along her smooth skin, her fingers feeling his lips where they met her core. She could feel his tongue's slight roughness as he flicked it along her clit with more force now.

He pulled back for a second, and for one moment Megan thought he would stop. Her eyes flew open and she looked down to see Luc staring up at her lustfully. "I will miss this taste when I'm gone."

Megan watched him as he pressed his mouth back between her

parted thighs, slowly sucking on her sex until he finally plunged his tongue into her again. This time his movements were more powerful, as he masterfully urged her to come. She knew he wanted to feel her orgasm, to taste her in the most intimate of acts. His words, his touch, the sight of him there between her legs brought Megan powerful waves of pleasure. Her body rocked over his mouth and she pressed herself closer to him, bringing his tongue in deeper as she came. She cried out with the force of her orgasm, grabbing his hair in her hands.

Luc stayed on his knees before her until she was finished. Megan lowered her hands to guide him up. "Come here," she said. When Luc got to his feet, she kissed him hard, greedily thrusting her tongue into his mouth. She could taste herself on him and the sensation thrilled her. Lowering himself onto the bench, Luc sat facing her, caressing her body with his hands.

Megan straddled him, sitting on his lap and rubbing herself over his thick length. Luc moaned as she rocked her hips back and forth. She was everything he had ever desired in a woman. He lifted his hands to cup her breasts, leaving her already hard nipples exposed for his mouth. Bringing his mouth over her right breast, he sucked on her pink bud, then swirled his tongue around it slowly before moving to her left breast.

Megan pushed her body down firmly onto his lap, squeezing his cock with her sex. The full length of him was just inside her lips, so close and yet not where she needed him. She had to have him inside her. She wriggled her hips until the head of his cock entered her, then pressed herself down, bringing him inside her to the hilt. She moved slowly, allowing herself a delicious moment to feel how hard and thick he was.

Luc gripped her ass and stood, picking her up with him. "No, *mon ange*, we need a condom," he groaned. He wanted nothing more than to feel her riding his bare cock and her coming all over him again, but he knew they couldn't risk it.

Luc pushed the shower door open with his foot, forgetting to shut the water off as he carried her to the bed. Megan carefully moved her hips over him, allowing herself only the tiniest movements as he walked with her. It seemed so effortless for him, as though he could hold her like this in his powerful arms indefinitely.

He gently put her on the bed and pulled out of her, kissing her passionately on the mouth, then along her neck as he stood. Letting his fingers skim over her naked body, he allowed his eyes to follow his hands, taking in the sight of her so open, waiting for him. He could see her breasts lift as she sucked in a deep breath of air and he knew she was more than ready for him again. The look in her eyes as she stared at him showed him that she was burning for him.

Luc walked purposefully to his overnight bag and retrieved a condom, ripping the package open and placing it on his penis before turning back to Megan.

"Now we won't have to stop." He crossed the room to her.

"Mmm, that might be the best thing you've ever said to me." She smiled at him as he lowered himself over her. She was still lying sideways on the bed, her feet resting flat on the mattress, her legs spread. Luc brought his body in line with hers, lying on top of her and slowly working his way inside her wet pussy, causing them both to moan as he filled her completely.

"You are so tight," he said as he moved his hips from side to side then pulled back again. Megan grabbed his ass and pulled him forcefully back into her again. She wanted to feel the full weight of him on her. Luc pulled out again, teasing her with that little smirk of his.

Megan felt the same sense of indignation she had in Paris when he had given her that smirk. She glared at him and then pushed him away, remembering the silk scarf tucked into his wool dress coat, which was slung over a chair. She stood, giving him a serious look, then crossed the room, knowing he was staring at her ass as she moved. She pulled the scarf out of his coat with one swift move, letting it snap as it hit the ground. She turned back and walked over to him, pushing him down onto the bed with one hand.

Luc allowed it, lifting an eyebrow in surprise. "I think I'm going to like this."

"I don't really care if you like it, as long as I get what I want," Megan replied, lifting one of his arms over his head and tying one end of the scarf to his wrist. She pulled the scarf behind the wooden bedpost and tied the loose end to his other wrist, pulling the fabric tight.

"Megan, I had no idea you were such a kinky girl!"

"This isn't meant to be kinky. It's meant to wipe that smirk off your face," she said, straddling him. "Now we go at my pace, and we'll see if you like being teased."

She rocked her body over his, allowing her sex to barely touch him, letting her mouth hover over his but refusing to kiss him. Luc lifted his head but Megan managed to keep her mouth just inches away from him, skirting his every effort.

She straightened her back until she was sitting up on his lap, rubbing herself over him. She could feel his cock react to her and could tell by his expression that he needed to be inside her again. Megan watched him as she slowly caressed herself with her fingertips, pinching her nipples and cupping her breasts for him. She let one had glide down in front of her and slid her fingers inside, making him watch helplessly as she pleasured herself.

Luc's face wore a look of lust and frustration mixed together. All hints of his former cockiness were gone now, and he looked as though he might burst if she didn't fuck him at that very moment.

"Shall I stop torturing you, Luc?" Megan asked with a little smirk of her own.

"Yes, gorgeous, let's fuck," he murmured.

With those words, Megan couldn't wait anymore. She lifted his cock with her hand and pushed her body down hard, bringing them both the relief they needed. Pressing her hands to his chest, she rocked herself from side to side, then back and forth, over and over, harder and harder. She could feel herself becoming more and more wild as she moved. All thoughts of anything outside that room were completely absent as, moving in circles over him, she squeezed his cock. She looked down, seeing the place where their bodies met, feeling his cock rubbing so perfectly in just the right spot as she moved. The sight of him tied to the bed, his chiselled body gleaming with sweat, made her feel powerful and sexy. Megan could feel her orgasm erupting inside her, causing her entire body to jolt as she came. She could feel Luc come with her, his length jerking inside her with each wave of his own climax.

She grinned down at him as they both started to catch their breath again. "I kind of like you this way, Monsieur Chevalier. I might just leave you tied up like that."

Luc laughed at her and shook his head. "If I weren't so concerned with making you happy, I would never have allowed this."

Megan lowered her mouth to his and kissed him hard. "Yes, you would have," she said as she untied his wrists.

"Okay, you're probably right, but only because you're so fucking sexy."

"I suddenly love how honest you are," she teased.

*   *   *

That night as she fell asleep alone in her bed at home, Megan went over the day she had just experienced. She felt giddy at the thought of Luc. His thoughtfulness, his arm around her as they rode on the chairlift, his fingers intertwined with hers as they drove, the feeling of him touching her. Her mind raced along, thinking of all the things she loved about him. The look in his eyes when they met hers was the perfect blend of lust and admiration. His sense of honesty, even when lying a little would be more to his benefit. His thoughtfulness at realizing how difficult it was for a single mom to find the time for a man in her life. He had treated her to another entire day of fun, romance and incredible sex. She didn't think about where this was leading, she thought only about how wonderful it was to have it for now. It was more than she had ever thought she would have, and it was enough for her.

EIGHTEEN

"So, my dear girl, are you going to tell me who you were skiing with yesterday?"

Megan was wandering through the grocery store, pushing the cart with one hand while she talked to her mom on her cellphone. She dropped a box of pasta into her cart and kept moving.

"What?" she asked weakly. She knew her mom wouldn't take long to realize something was up.

"I can tell there's something going on, Megan. Now out with it," Helen said sternly.

Megan, feeling like a child, groaned into her phone. "Mom, it's no big deal. I met a man in Paris—a friend of Harper's, actually—and he came here to see me. He was in Colorado on business so he stopped here on his way home."

"Really? Why didn't you think you could tell me about him? What's wrong with him, is he married or something?" Helen's questions came out like the rapid fire of a semi-automatic rifle.

Megan pulled her cart out of the way of an elderly couple in the cereal aisle and stopped where she was. She gasped. "God no, Mom! Married? Eeew! He's completely single. I just didn't want to say anything because I didn't want a big lecture about it. I already know he lives too far away for this to go anywhere, but we're just having fun."

"Good for you," Helen said supportively. This was not what Megan had thought she would hear.

"What?" she asked.

"I said good for you. You deserve to have a little fun, Megan. I'm happy for you. Is he a hottie?"

Megan cringed hearing her mom say *hottie*. "Yes, Mom. He's very handsome and surprisingly thoughtful too. I really like him, actually."

"Well, I'm glad. Just make sure you use protection."

"Mom," she hissed, "I am *not* an idiot. Of course we're using protection." Just as she finished the sentence, a woman with a toddler in her cart walked past. The woman was trying not to laugh.

"Well, I wouldn't say you have to be an idiot not to use any. It's just easy to get carried away sometimes, especially at the beginning of a relationship."

"Can we change the subject?"

"Sure. Listen, I'm going to dinner with Charlie tonight, so I won't be home if you call."

"Really? That's great. Should I swing over to the condom aisle for you in case you two get carried away?"

Her mom burst out laughing. "You always were a little brat."

* * *

That night, as Megan finished the dishes, she realized she couldn't call Luc. It would be after two in the morning in Paris. She was surprised by how disappointed she felt. She wanted to hear his sexy voice. She looked around the kitchen for a moment, trying to decide what to do, when she heard her cellphone chime.

She had a text from Luc: Are you free to talk?

Yes! Skype?

A moment later, she saw his face on the screen in her hand. She could see his headboard behind him and that he wasn't wearing a shirt. Her heart felt fluttery as she grinned at him. "You're still up? It's so late there!"

"I can't sleep. Jet lag."

"How was your trip home?"

"It was fine, but I'm finding myself missing a beautiful American woman. I was hoping if I could talk to her, I would be able to fall asleep."

"Is she *that* dull?"

Luc laughed. "She is that *soothing*," he corrected.

"Hmm, sounds like another version of dull, but I'll take it as a compliment anyway. So, I told my mom the truth about who I was skiing with. She took it pretty well, actually. She said it was good for me to have some fun."

"So, does this mean you can go to the prom with me?"

It was Megan's turn to laugh. "Maybe. Monsieur Chevalier, what do we do next in your great plan?"

"I was thinking about that on the plane home. Do you think we could figure out a time to talk most days?"

"I think so. I can email you my schedule if that would make it easier." Megan's heart fluttered at the thought of talking with him every day.

"It would, yes." Luc ran his hand through his hair. He had that sexy, sleepy, rumpled look that made Megan long to be curled up in bed with him.

"If I told you I wished you were here right now, would that be breaking any rules? You just look so cozy to me right now."

"I would consider it well within the rules of our agreement. Besides, I already knew it. You just gave me that look that tells me you want to tie me to the bed and have your way with me."

Megan grinned at him, blushing a little at the memory. "I might."

"Maybe next time it will be my turn to tie you up?" he asked.

Meg laughed, feeling both a little shy about talking like this and excited that he was mentioning a next time. "My schedule is pretty full, actually. I'm starting my own business as a dominatrix. I can add you to the list, though."

Megan watched as his face tightened briefly. She could hear his knuckles crack as he stared back at her for a moment. He quickly recovered and asked, "Oh, is that the case? I don't think I like the sound of you with other men. I might have to pre-book all of your openings."

"Why, Luc, are you jealous? Because it sounds like you're jealous," Megan teased.

Luc shook his head. "Certainly not. I just don't want any other men coming within one hundred metres of you. It's perfectly normal."

"Well, that would make it rather difficult for me to run my dominatrix business. I might have to shut it down."

Luc smiled now, feeling foolish for his temporary possessiveness. "Maybe you could be a photographer instead? I hear there's good money in it."

"I suppose I could give it a shot. Hold off on the dominatrix thing until you're back in town."

"Do you have an opening in three weeks? I can be back then."

Megan's heart thumped at the thought of him back so soon just for her. She tried to look casual, as though she had to consider it. "Hmm, three weeks? Let me think . . . You know, I can probably squeeze you in." She used her best sultry voice on the last few words.

Luc raised his eyebrow at her and gave her a little half smile.

"You are very tight, but I know you can squeeze me in if we try."

"This is fun," she replied.

"It is. You're very sexy. Now I don't want to sleep. I want to get on a plane right now so I can run my hands all over every part of that gorgeous body of yours."

"So, this call really wasn't as helpful as you thought it would be."

"Not one of my better ideas, I'm afraid. Apparently, you are only soothing when I've had about five hours in bed with you. Right now, you're waking me up."

"But you should get some sleep." Megan gave him a look of pure adoration.

"I should, I have a long day in the office tomorrow, and I have to be up in four hours. Let's do this again tomorrow night?"

"It's a date. Good night, Monsieur Chevalier."

"*Bonne nuit, mon ange.*"

* * *

As Luc lay in bed, waiting for sleep to come, he thought of Megan. She was fun and sexy and he couldn't wait to hold her in his arms again. Even just to talk with her on the phone again the next day was something to look forward to. Everything about their relationship was a completely fresh experience and thoroughly enticing for him. For the first time, he knew what it was like to live just to see the look in a woman's eyes when she saw him, or to hear her voice as she spoke his name. For the first time, the thought of another man touching the woman he was with was enough to make him lose his mind. For the first time, none of this seemed like nonsense to Luc, even though every now and again, it caused a twinge of fear to build in his chest. Somehow, for the first time, he was able to push that feeling aside, knowing that to fight through it, for Megan, was worth it.

NINETEEN

Paris—Two Weeks Later

"Harper? It's Luc," he said into the phone.

"Hey, Luc! I take it you're calling to talk about my best friend?"

"Yes, as a matter of fact, I am. I'm planning a special date for us and I need your help, if you don't mind . . ."

"I'm intrigued. What do you need?"

"Can you talk to Megan's mom and see if she can stay with Elliott next Saturday night? I want to fly her to San Francisco for the night to see the ballet. I thought she might like that."

"The ballet? She'll love that! Send me the details about when you need her to leave Boulder and when she'll be home, okay? I have to run into a meeting right now. I'll call Helen this evening."

"I will. Thank you, Harper. Oh, and can I ask one more favour?"

"Sure."

"Can you give me her dress and shoe size? I want to buy her something special to wear for our evening."

"Wow, Luc! If I had known you would be like this, I would have slept with you myself."

"I am quite the catch, no?"

"Yes. Yes, you are. I'll send you her sizes and a few wardrobe ideas as well. Talk to you soon," Harper replied. As she walked into her meeting, she grinned to herself at the thought of her best friend being spoiled like this.

Boulder

"An overnight date? In San Francisco?" Helen asked, surprised.

Harper winced. This was not the easiest phone call she'd ever made. "I know. He's quite the romantic. He wants me to get her sizes so he can buy her a dress and shoes for the date."

Helen's voice was full of concern when she replied. "Well, do you think Meg will want to go? It all sounds a little too serious, don't you think?"

"Oh, I don't know. I think she'll like it. He's really putting in a huge effort for her, and I think it will make her feel really special. She could use that for once."

Helen's voice was tentative. "Well, I agree that she deserves to be spoiled, but I don't know about this Luc fellow. He doesn't even live on the same continent. And a bar owner? I can't see this going anywhere."

"Try not to think of him as a bar owner. *Business mogul* would be more accurate. As for your other concerns, I had the same conversation with Meg a few weeks ago. She insisted that this is exactly what she's looking for right now. Nothing serious—just some romance and fun."

"Well, what do you know about this Luc? Is he a decent man?"

"I wouldn't be helping him if I thought otherwise, I promise. I've known him for a lot of years. He's thoughtful and kind. I trust that he wouldn't ever want to hurt her. Having said that, he isn't the type to settle down. If Meg wanted to get married again anytime soon, I'd try to persuade her away from him, but you know, she really doesn't want all of that right now."

"Alright, I'm not sure that I like any of this, but I'll look after Elliott this weekend. I want Meg to have some fun in her life. She's given up everything to pick up the slack for that SOB back in Florida."

"She certainly has, Helen. I'm hoping that maybe being with Luc will remind her of what it's like to let someone into her life. Maybe she'll get back in the game when things fizzle out with him."

"Either that or she'll be put off men for even longer," Helen answered firmly.

"Let's hope not. She's a responsible person. She's not going to do anything stupid or let this go too far. She knows how this will end."

"Maybe, but it's easy to fool yourself into thinking something doesn't mean that much until it's over."

Harper sighed, feeling suddenly worried about her friend. "I know. It's not an ideal situation. Tell you what, I'll call Luc back and tell him that you're willing to babysit, but I'll also scare him a little, okay?"

Helen laughed. "Okay! That sounds more like it. Tell him I know people who can hurt him."

Harper giggled at the thought of Helen as a tough guy. "I will. I'll tell him you'll break his kneecaps if he hurts Megan."

"I'm sure I have a crowbar around here somewhere."

* * *

Megan rode in the back of a limo in what seemed to her to be the direction of the airport. She sipped champagne and nibbled on some chocolate-covered strawberries that had been waiting for her when she got in. She had no idea where she was going, only that she was to have packed an overnight bag. She had dressed carefully, deciding to go with her long red coat and jeans for now. Underneath, she wore an off-the-shoulder cashmere sweater in a cream colour. Watching the sights of Boulder go by under the soft glow of the late-day sun, Megan could feel excitement building in her. It had been three weeks since she had seen Luc, and every inch of her filled with desire at the thought of being back in his arms.

As the limo neared the airport, Megan's curiosity overtook her. She sent a text to Luc.

I'm almost at the airport. Where are we going? And where am I meeting you?

All in good time. For now, enjoy the champagne and strawberries.

Come on, give me hint, at least! I'll make it worth your while . . .

No hints, Megan. That would ruin my carefully planned surprise. BTW, you look beautiful.

What? Can you see me right now?

No, but you always look beautiful. Now relax and enjoy the ride.

Minutes later, the limo pulled up to a gate at the airport. A large PRIVATE sign affixed to the chain-link slid slowly to the right as the gate opened. Megan sat up in her seat, watching for Luc, her heart beating fast in her chest as the limo stopped in front of a small jet.

There he was, standing on the tarmac in front of the plane, exuding that power and confidence that had drawn her to him in the first place. He was dressed casually in jeans and the leather jacket he had worn on their date in Paris. Megan sucked in a sharp breath at what was happening, ready to run and jump into his arms. She had never imagined anything like this would ever happen.

Luc beat the driver to the back of the car to open the door for her. "Bonjour, *mon ange*," he said in a low voice as he reached his hand in to help her out.

Megan was speechless as she took his hand. When she got out of the car and stood before him, he pulled her close and gave her a kiss that heated her entire body. It was the kiss she had been yearning for, and it was everything she remembered. His lips were warm and soft and the feel of them made her knees go weak. She caught a whiff of his cologne, which by now would forever be imprinted on her brain as his scent.

"*Mon Dieu*, you taste delicious." He rested his forehead against hers for a moment before taking her hand and turning to the jet. "I thought this would be a fun way to travel. Are you ready?" he asked, smiling at her.

"I am. But what are we . . . ?" she began, then, seeing his expression, she stopped. She could tell she wasn't going to get any closer to finding out what his plans were. "You're not going to tell me, are you?"

"Not yet. You'll see in a little over an hour." Luc's eyes shone with excitement as he spoke.

The driver handed her bag to a member of the flight crew as Luc led her over to the steps. She walked ahead of him, not sure what to expect. When she stepped into the plane, she was met by a lovely flight attendant in a blue uniform, who smiled broadly at her.

"Welcome aboard, Ms. Sullivan. I'm Sheila. I'll be looking after you and Mr. Chevalier today. Can I take your coat?"

Megan removed her coat and handed it to Sheila, thanking her as she peered around the corner to see the rest of the plane's cabin. It had four large armchairs—two facing forward and two backwards, with a table in between them, as well as a couch, all in creamy leather.

Megan selected a chair and sat down, still in shock. She pressed her palms to the cool leather, trying to determine whether this was a dream or reality. Gazing up at Luc, she bit her lip. "I hope this is really happening."

Luc nodded. "It is, I assure you," he replied as he took a seat next to her.

Sheila returned to make sure they were buckled up and to go over the safety information with them quickly before making her way to the front of the plane, leaving them alone.

"I thought we would have a light dinner now and then go for a late meal later tonight, if that's okay," Luc said.

"I'm completely in your hands. It seems like you've got the perfect evening planned. I've never been on a private jet before, obviously."

"It's not something I've done very often, either. Oh, and I've never done this with a woman before, just in case you were wondering."

Megan winced. "Thank you for telling me that. I wasn't wondering, though."

The engines started up and the plane moved toward the runway. Luc took Megan's hand in his, then held it up to his mouth. He pressed his lips to the inside of her wrist and sighed happily. "I've been waiting to be back with you."

"I've been waiting for you to come back," Megan said, turning her body toward his and lifting her knee to rest it on the arm of her chair. Luc leaned in and they kissed, drinking in the feeling of each other for a few delectable moments as the plane took off.

Sheila brought a bottle of champagne and some hot hors d'oeuvres, setting a plate in front of each of them.

"Mmm, so good," Megan moaned as she bit into a crab puff. "Luc, thank you. This is the most romantic night of my life."

"But how can you say that? You don't know where we are going yet."

"I just know," she replied.

"Well, I hope so," Luc said, taking a bite of shrimp. "You know, it's been surprisingly hard for me to keep this secret from you. The whole time I was planning it, I wanted to tell you about it. It's strange, but in a short time, you have become the person I want to call about everything—even the most irrelevant things."

Megan tilted her head to the side a little and gave him a questioning look. "Is that strange for you?"

"Yes, definitely. It's unusual for me to want to bore anyone with the details of my life."

"Uh-oh, Luc. It sounds like you might be getting attached to me . . ." Megan teased.

Luc shook his head. "Certainly not. It's just that I am only now realizing how fascinating I am for other people. I want to give them the pleasure of hearing about my every move."

Megan laughed hard, covering her mouth with her hand to prevent herself from propelling food at him. When she recovered, she swallowed and replied, "You're so full of shit, Chevalier. You like me."

Luc rolled his eyes, pretending to be uninterested. "Maybe the tiniest bit. Mostly only because I want to see you naked in those tall boots again."

"Really?" she asked, giving him a sultry look. Letting her hand roam, she rubbed his thigh, then moved up his lap. "I've missed you so much."

Leaning in, Luc let his mouth hover over hers, just shy of touching her lips. "I've missed you too. All of you."

Their lips met hungrily as urgent hands explored each other, just short of indecently. Luc pulled back, moving Megan's hair aside to kiss her neck.

She moaned a little, feeling her eyes roll back in her head as every fibre of her body responded to his touch. "Too bad there wasn't some way we could—"

The sound of a light cough from behind had them straightening up quickly. Sheila cleared their dishes and offered them more refreshments.

"No, thank you. We're fine. Actually, we were thinking of having a quick rest before we get to San Francisco. Our plans for this evening are rather involved."

"Of course." Sheila smiled. "I'll be back with pillows and blankets. If you're resting, I think I'll sit up front with the pilots. The captain, Mike, and I are getting married in a few weeks. I can use the time to pick his brain about all those little details he's been avoiding."

Megan grinned at her. "Get him while he's a captive audience. Good thinking."

Sheila gave her a little wink. "Exactly." Returning moments later, she handed them each bedding and left, turning down the lights before going into the cockpit and shutting the door behind her. If she was onto them, she had the grace to make it undetectable.

Luc fanned out one of the blankets, covering them with it as Megan hurried to lift the armrests between them before unbuckling both of their seat belts. "Can we really do this? Because I really need to do this," she murmured as he tugged at the button on her jeans.

"We can do this. We just have to be quiet," Luc warned.

"And quick. This has to be more like a sprint than a marathon."

"I can sprint. I only hope you can keep up with me," Luc answered, his voice thick with emotion.

"I was almost at the finish line when I saw you standing in front of the plane." Boots were kicked off, socks went flying, jeans were discarded and shirts were pulled over heads between frantic kisses.

Staring into each other's eyes, they both laughed for a moment, giddy with what they were about to do, knowing that they could get caught but deciding together that the pleasure was worth the risk. Megan took Luc's hand, lacing her fingers through his for a moment while they kissed and caressed each other. Her other hand dove for his boxer briefs, rubbing along the smooth fabric, reacquainting herself with what was underneath.

"You're so hard," she whispered. "And so big." She brought his hand down to her panties, letting go of his fingers and covering his hand with hers. She pressed his hand into her firmly, showing him exactly where she wanted him.

"You're so sexy, Megan. Come here." He pulled her onto his lap, gripping her hips and dragging her over him, causing soft moans of desire from both of them.

Megan wriggled out of her panties and turned so she was now facing him, straddling him. Yanking at his underwear, she freed him with one quick move as his fingers parted her, finding her wet. Gliding his hand in and out of her sex, he readied her for his thick length.

"Now, Luc. I want you right now," she whispered.

"Are you sure?"

"I've never been so sure of anything." She kissed him hard before pulling back with a gasp. "Condom?"

"Pocket of my jeans."

Reaching behind her, Megan grabbed his pants off the floor. Luc dug into his front pocket, retrieving what would allow them to put out the fire that raged between them now. Once he was ready, Megan took him in her hand, hovering over him, rubbing him along her sex before plunging herself down onto his hard cock. "Oh, that's so good. That's what I've been waiting for."

"Yes. You feel so perfect," he murmured between kisses. Lowering his mouth over her breasts, he licked and sucked and rolled his tongue over her nipples until they ached with that exquisite pain. She continued rocking herself over him, filling herself with every move, feeling his cock straining inside her tight pussy.

The weeks apart had caused their desire for each other to build. Now the relief of finally being together, blended with the thrill of possibly getting caught, had them both quickly on the edge of breaking. Megan bit down on Luc's shoulder as she felt the first of several powerful explosions inside. Luc groaned loudly as he came with her, pressing his face into the nape of her neck as his breath caught. They stayed like that, caressing, cuddling, savouring the moment as their hearts and breath slowed, their yearning satisfied, knowing it wouldn't take long to build again.

San Francisco

Two hours later, Megan found herself walking into a suite at the Mandarin Oriental. Luc carried her bag in, setting it down in the bedroom. He took her hand and led her over to the closet. "Now for the surprise!"

When he opened the door, Megan gasped. The most beautiful gown hung in the centre of the closet. It was strapless and had a sweetheart neckline, a black, beaded bodice and a metallic-tweed mermaid skirt in gold. Black strappy heels sat waiting on the floor. Megan stood for a long moment with her mouth hanging open before she allowed herself to touch the dress with one finger.

She turned to Luc. "This must have cost a fortune," she whispered.

He shrugged. "I wanted to see you in this, but only if you love it."

"I love it." Megan answered, her voice quiet. "I really, really love it."

"I'm glad. I can't take all the credit. I had a lot of help from Harper. Now, we have only a short time before we need to leave for the ballet, so if you like, I'll give you your privacy and go get ready in the bathroom."

With that, Luc gave her a lingering kiss on the neck and turned to leave the room. Megan grabbed his arm and stopped him. "Wait."

Luc turned back to her and she wrapped her arms around his neck, kissing him hard on the mouth. "Thank you," she whispered after she had pulled back a little. She stared into his dark eyes, smiling at him.

"You're welcome. If anyone deserves to be treasured, it is you."

"I don't know if *anyone* deserves to be spoiled like this, Luc. This is incredible." Her eyes were shining as she looked at him.

"So are you." He gave her a long kiss on the lips. "Mmm, I'm going to leave now, before we end up in bed and miss the ballet."

Megan slapped him on the ass as he walked out of the room. "Well, you better get going, then."

"I'm going! I'm going!" Luc waved his arms in surrender. "But hold that thought for later."

* * *

Twenty minutes later, Megan heard a gentle knock on the door just as she finished buckling her heels.

"Come in," she called.

Luc opened the door in time to see her stand up. His eyes moved over her as he leaned against the door frame. He let out a big, happy sigh. "You are a goddess."

Megan's heart fluttered at the way he pronounced *goddess*, with the emphasis on the last syllable. He was impossibly handsome in his tuxedo as he stared at her. The look on his face said that he was trying to memorize how she looked at that very moment. His hair was slightly damp and a bit messy, as usual. Megan gave a spin to give him the full effect of the dress. The skirt twirled with her as she moved.

"I have one more thing for you, to keep you warm," he said, holding up a faux-fur stole. "It's not real. I didn't know how you would feel about that."

Megan walked to him and held her hand out to feel the stole. "This is perfect. It's so soft."

Luc held it up for her. "Allow me," he said.

Megan turned her back to him and he placed it over her shoulders. She turned around. "Seeing you in that tux just makes me want to start undressing you."

"Good, that was the idea."

* * *

A little while later, the couple found themselves settling into box seats in the grand tier at the War Memorial Opera House. The lights flickered, indicating the start of the performance. Luc picked up Megan's hand and brought it over to rest on his leg, lacing his fingers through hers. Megan smiled over at him as the lights dimmed and leaned in to whisper in his ear, "I love that you planned all of this."

"I love that you are here with me."

This was as close as either of them could come to using the word *love*. Luc held Megan's hand through the entire first act of the ballet. An intense passion flowed between them as they sat, Megan utterly entranced by the graceful and vibrant performance. The music was both romantic and dramatic as the dancers leaped and spun and thrilled their audience. Everything about this moment was overwhelmingly sensuous. Luc couldn't help but think about getting Megan back to the hotel and unzipping her dress. Even just the feeling of her hand in his was completely arousing for him. Every so often, he glanced over at her and each time, he was struck by how beautiful she was. Her hair was done up, revealing her long neck, and her dress showed off her willowy arms and the feminine curve of her shoulder. He couldn't help leaning over and letting his lips graze her skin, drinking in the smell of her. When the curtain came down and the lights went up to signal the end of the first act, Megan and Luc stood and made their way with the crowd to the lobby.

"I should run to the ladies room," Megan said.

"I'll get us some champagne. Meet me back here in a few minutes?"

"Sounds great," Megan replied, following the surge of women heading to the restrooms. As she waited in line, she could feel her phone buzzing in her clutch. She picked it up, only to see that someone was calling from her house.

"Hello?"

"Mom! Mom, something's wrong with Grandma!" Elliott sobbed into the phone. He was crying so hard Megan could barely make out what he was saying. Her heart pounded as she tried to take in what he had just said.

Megan plugged her other ear with one finger and started walking to the door in hope of finding a quieter location. "Slow down, baby. Take a deep breath and then tell me what's going on."

"Grandma fell. She can't walk; she said she's really dizzy. Now she's started throwing up. I don't know what to do! Come home, Mom! Come home, because I'm really scared."

"Okay Elliott, listen to me." Megan fought the tears of panic starting to fill her eyes and focused her attention on keeping her voice steady. "Listen carefully, Elliott. You *did* know what to do. You called me. I want you to run over to Mr. Peterson's next door and get him, alright?"

"He's not home! Grandma said he's away right now!" Elliott yelled into the phone. "She just puked again, Mom! Her face looks all green."

"Okay, it's okay. You stay on the line and I'm going to find another phone to call an ambulance. We'll get help right away."

Luc walked up, holding two champagne flutes. His smile faded when he saw the look on Megan's face. Megan let out a breath of relief when she saw him.

"I need your cell right now. Call 911!" she whispered.

Luc quickly put down the drinks and dialed, then handed her the phone. He watched as she spoke calmly into the phone and explained the situation to the 911 operator. It took him a few minutes to patch her through to the emergency dispatch in Boulder. Megan spoke reassuringly to her little boy as she waited. Luc was overcome by how strong she was in this moment, handling the situation as though it were a regular event.

"Okay Elliott, the ambulance is on the way. You need to unlock the front door and let them in when they get there. The 911 operator is going to call you on the home phone, so you'll need to hang up with me, okay? I'm going to start calling your friends' parents and get someone to be with you. You call my cell back again after the ambulance gets there and the 911 lady says you can hang up with her, okay?" Megan paused for a moment, then said, "I'm going to hang up now. I love you. And tell Grandma I love her too, okay, baby?" Pause. "I'll be there as soon as I can."

Megan hung up both phones and started searching her contacts for help. Luc took back his cellphone. "I'll get our coats and be right back."

As he walked, he called Simone, who was at home in bed. "Simone, I'm sorry to wake you. This is an emergency. I need you to get a flight immediately from San Francisco to Boulder. Start with the charter service but just get us on any flight that will get us back there now. We'll be at the airport in about forty-five minutes."

"What? Where are you going?" Simone sat up in bed, turning on her light. She tried to process what her boss was saying.

He repeated himself in a firm voice. "Now, Simone. I need this right now. It is urgent that we get there as fast as possible."

"I'll call you as soon as I've found a flight."

"Thank you." Luc hung up and crossed the lobby to find Megan speaking into her cellphone, her voice breaking. He wrapped the stole around her shoulders and started walking toward the door, pressing his fingers to the small of her back to guide her along.

"Okay, thank you, Rebecca. Thank you so much. I just can't believe this is happening." Megan hung up a moment later as they stepped into a cab. Tears were now streaming down her cheeks as she stared at the phone in her hand, waiting for Elliott to call back. Her hands were shaking and she felt cold and scared.

"I shouldn't have left them. I should be there right now to handle this. This isn't something a six-year-old should have to deal with."

Luc wrapped an arm around her and pulled her close to him, kissing the side of her head. "This is not your fault. You had no way of knowing this would happen."

"But my job is to protect him! And I'm here with you when they both need me there!"

"I will get you home. Simone is getting us a plane right now. I'm so sorry this is happening, Megan."

Megan nodded, unable to speak for a moment. "It sounds like maybe a stroke or something . . . I don't know."

Two hours later, they finally boarded a jet. The tired-looking crew greeted them wearily, trying to be pleasant as they waited for permission to take off. Outside, the sky was completely black. Megan shivered, feeling cold but sweaty at the same time. Luc asked the flight attendant for a blanket and some wine for Megan to warm her and calm her nerves.

Megan got a call from Rebecca, who had picked up Elliott at the hospital and now had him tucked into bed in Jase's room for the night.

When Megan got off the phone, she looked up at Luc. "Well, at least Elliott's okay. My friend who has him said they're going out of town for the day tomorrow to visit relatives, so I'll have to pick him up by 8 a.m. She said he could go with them, but I don't want him away in case something happens . . ." Her voice broke as she trailed off.

"I'm going to stay and help you any way I can. I know it wasn't in our plan, but I could never leave you right now, even if you wanted me to." Luc wrapped an arm around Megan and pulled her to him. Megan, burying her face into his chest, allowed a sob to escape.

"I don't know what I'll do without my mom, Luc," she whispered, tears streaming down her cheeks.

"Try not to think like that. Maybe it isn't serious. From what you've told me, she's a young, healthy woman. There's every reason to believe that she'll be alright."

Megan lifted her head to face Luc. "I thought my dad was healthy and strong too. He was fine and then he just died with no warning. One day he was there and then he was just gone."

The plane was finally starting to move and the crew dimmed the lights in the cabin. The flight home would hold none of the excitement and romance of the trip earlier in the day. Megan's mind flashed to how quickly things had changed.

"Try to rest, Megan. You'll need it," Luc said, tucking the blanket around her shoulders and wrapping his arm around her again. He rubbed her arm absent-mindedly with his hand while trying to think of the best way to make himself useful. He had already arranged for a car to meet them on the tarmac, but for now, all he could do was to be there for her.

Boulder

Megan managed to find her strength again by the time they touched down. She stood, straightening her dress, as Luc placed the stole over her shoulders. She stepped out into the cold night to face what was coming. Turning to Luc, she gave him a determined nod. "I'll be okay, Luc. Thank you for being here with me."

"There is nowhere else I want to be right now. Let's go."

They climbed into the back of the waiting limo and Luc told the driver to take them to the hospital. The ride seemed to take an eternity for Megan as she sat silently watching the city lights go by. She might be on her way to find out that her mom was gone or would be left with lasting damage from whatever had taken hold of her earlier this evening.

Please be okay, Mom. Please. I need you, she begged in her mind, over and over.

When they arrived at the hospital's emergency entrance, Megan got out so quickly the driver hadn't even had a chance to unbuckle his seat belt. She rushed through the sliding doors and to the front desk, feeling ridiculous in her evening gown. Luc hurried to catch up with her.

"My mom was brought in earlier by ambulance—Helen Foster."

The nurse looked up from her paperwork. "Oh yes. She's here. I'll check if you can go see her."

"Thank you," Megan said, trying to give her an appreciative smile.

The nurse walked to the back for a few minutes and then returned. "They took her upstairs for a CT scan. They're trying to rule out a stroke right now. She was talking when she came in, but she's extremely dizzy and her balance isn't good enough to walk."

Megan nodded, biting down on her lip to stop herself from crying.

"If you could take a seat in the waiting area, we'll come get you as soon as we know anything."

Luc held her hand as they made their way over to the chairs. They sat down next to each other in the otherwise empty waiting room.

"Can I get you anything? Some tea or water?" he asked softly.

Megan shook her head. "No, thank you."

"You tell me if you need anything. Okay?"

"I will." Megan picked up his hand and placed it on her lap, holding it between both of her hands as they sat. She was grateful that she had his strong shoulder to rest her head on right now. He would see her through this—whatever was about to come and however their relationship would end. For now, she didn't have to face this moment alone and that was more than she would have expected.

An hour later, a doctor came into the waiting room and walked over to Megan. She was young and, based on the dark circles around her eyes, tired. But she gave Megan a warm smile.

"Are you Helen Foster's daughter?"

Megan nodded and stood up. Luc stood with her.

"I'm Dr. Sheppard. You can call me Bonnie. I've been looking after your mom. First, I want you to know she's going to be alright. We've been able to rule out stroke and heart attack, which were our primary concerns. I'm running a few more tests, but it looks like she has something called peripheral vertigo. It's a temporary condition of the inner ear that strikes fast and can knock someone on their butt for a few weeks. I've seen some huge men get taken down hard by this, but the good thing is that it will go away on its own."

Megan listened quietly, nodding her head and trying to blink back tears of relief.

Luc spoke up to give her a moment to recover. "That's great news. Will she need to stay in the hospital long?"

"I don't want her to go anywhere until she can at least stand and walk a little without losing her balance. I also want to make sure that the last set of tests I ordered confirm that it is, in fact, peripheral vertigo. Does she have anyone she can stay with when we release her?"

Megan replied, "She can stay with me. She'll want to get out of here as soon as possible. I don't know how much her insurance will cover."

Luc looked down in surprise at Megan. She avoided his gaze, feeling embarrassed.

Bonnie smiled at her. "Sure. You can come back and see her now." She turned and led them through the doors to the emergency treatment area. She pointed to a room on the left. "Your mom is just in here. It will be a few hours before I can pop back in to see her."

Luc stopped at the door to the room. "I'll wait in the other area."

Megan put a hand on his arm. "Okay, yeah. That makes sense. I'll come out in a bit to see you."

"I'll be here. If you need me to go pick up anything, maybe get you some clothes or something, let me know, okay?"

"I will."

Luc gave her a peck on the forehead and turned back down the hall. Megan took a deep breath and walked in to see her mom. It was close to three in the morning by now, but her relief pushed her exhaustion aside for the moment.

Helen was sleeping. She looked frail and much older than she was in the hospital gown. A machine measuring her heart rate beeped softly beside her. Megan tried to walk quietly to the bed, but the swishing sound her dress made caused her mom to stir.

"Oh no! You're here?" Helen asked. "I've ruined your special night away."

Megan pressed her hand to her mom's cheek and gave her a kiss on the forehead, tears welling up in her eyes. "You haven't ruined anything. How are you feeling?"

"I'm so dizzy, Megan. I can't believe how fast this hit me. I can't even get up without toppling over. I scared poor Elliott so badly."

"No, Mom, he's fine. Really. Don't feel bad. It's not like you did anything to cause this. We all get sick sometimes."

"I don't want to be sick. Makes me feel old and I'm not old. I'm young."

"You are young. From what the doctor said, it sounds like you're going to be back to your normal self in a couple of weeks anyway." Megan flopped down onto the chair beside her mom's bed and let her tears flow.

"I was so scared that you had had a stroke. I couldn't believe that this was happening and I couldn't get to you. It was just awful. I never should have gone." Megan slipped her hand under her mom's.

"Oh, sweet girl, don't say that. You should go and have fun. Who could have guessed that something like this would happen?"

"I know, but my job is to be here for you and Elliott, not gallivanting around the country with exotic men," Megan replied firmly.

"It was just bad timing for this to hit me now. You didn't do anything wrong. Where is your man, by the way? Did he stay in San Francisco?" Helen squeezed Megan's hand as she spoke.

"He's in the waiting room. His assistant managed to charter a jet for us to get back here."

Helen's eyes grew wide. "He came back with you? On a private jet? You might want to hang on to him, my girl. A guy like that doesn't come around every day."

"He's pretty wonderful, actually, but we're just enjoying some time together. It's not going to be a long-term thing. It wouldn't work."

Her mom's eyes closed slowly and then she reopened them, trying to stay awake.

"You get some rest, Mom. I'll be here when you wake up."

Helen spoke again without opening her eyes. "You look beautiful, Megan. Just like a princess."

Megan held her mom's hand as she slept. She suddenly wished she was dressed in a big sweater and a pair of jeans. She needed to get her car from her house and figure out how to pick up Elliott, but she didn't have her keys. Thinking about her house keys made her worry that her house might very well be sitting unlocked. She walked over to a small closet and found her mom's coat hung up on a hook and her purse on the shelf. Looking through the purse, she found her mom's keys, which included a key to Megan's house. She tiptoed out of the room and down the hall to find Luc.

Luc stood up when he saw her. "How is your mom?"

"She's good, considering. She looks really pale but at least she's asleep for now."

"Good. What can I do to help you?" Luc asked, reaching out to hold her hands in his.

Megan gave him a weak smile. "I'm not sure . . . I need to get my car and maybe some clothes from my house. I have to figure out what to do with Elliott for tomorrow." She paused, trying to think of what else needed to be done. "Oh crap, I'll have to clean out our spare room as well. She'll need to stay with us for a while, and it's full of boxes right now."

"If you're comfortable with me going to your house, I'll take a cab and bring back some clothes and your car for you. As far as Elliott goes, I know you want to keep things totally separate, but if it makes sense for you, I would be happy to spend the day with him. I don't know a lot about kids, but I think we could muddle through."

Megan stared at him for a moment before answering. She was completely exhausted from the emotional roller coaster of the evening and she had no idea what to think. Her mind was clouded with confusion and worry. If she allowed Luc into her personal life, she would be going against everything she had tried to do for so long to protect Elliott. But what harm could really come from him spending some time with Luc? She needed help and here was someone she had grown to trust offering just that.

Luc watched her, patiently waiting for an answer before he spoke up again. "I know it's a scary thought for you to let me into your family life, and I don't want to overstep any boundaries. But I'm here and I want to help however I can. We can tell Elliott that we are friends, which is true, and the rest we can figure out later. For now, let's just get through today."

"You read me like a book. I'm just so worn out right now, and I honestly don't know what to think. But you're right. I need help. The only other person I have that I can count on is lying in a hospital bed down the hall. For now, if you can go get my car and something for me to change into, I would be really grateful."

"Alright. For now, that's what I'll do, and you take your time figuring out the rest." He took his cellphone out and opened the navigation app. "Can you put your address in for me?"

Megan punched in her address and handed him his phone along with the keys to her house. "Thank you, Luc. I don't know how I'm going to repay you for all of this."

"There is no need. I'm just glad I can help," he said, giving her a kiss on the forehead. "Try to get some rest if you can. I'll come find you when I get back."

"Thank you."

Megan sat in the chair beside her mom's bed, hoping she could doze a little. She had leaned the chair against the wall and had her head propped up behind her, but it was terribly uncomfortable. Even if she had somewhere to lie down right now, she doubted she would sleep. Her stomach was twisting in knots as she thought about Luc going to her house. She was almost embarrassed for him to see where she lived. It would be his first real taste of her reality. Compared to his immaculate luxury penthouse, her slightly messy, modest home would feel cramped. Compared to his Mercedes, her little Toyota would run rough and feel junky to him. Megan suddenly felt scared that he wouldn't be interested in her anymore after this. He would see how different she was from the woman with the beautiful clothes he had met in Paris. She had tried to explain to him more than once how different their lives were, but she knew he would never fully comprehend it.

Sighing restlessly, she got up and wandered over to the window. The sky showed no sign of morning coming any time soon. The moon shone brightly on the parking lot outside the hospital. It was a cold night and she knew Luc would be chilly in his tuxedo and dress shoes, getting a cab to collect her things and then driving back here in the middle of the night. The thought of it made her heart ache.

What am I doing with this man? she thought. *We have nothing in common other than the fact neither of us wants to ever be tied down, and yet here I am, asking him to take care of me as though we were together.*

Looking back at her mom, Megan felt suddenly terrified. She had been relying on her mother since her divorce, but now she was all too aware that Helen could be taken from her in an instant. What would she do without her? How would she manage? She and Elliott would have no family left here. Megan pushed the thoughts aside. It wasn't going to happen any time soon. Her mom was going to be fine. For now, Megan just needed to get through the coming day. The rest would take care of itself in due time.

TWENTY

Luc opened the front door to Megan's house and flipped on the light to find himself standing in an entryway that led to a small living room. The house had a cozy feeling and was decorated in a way that seemed to invite guests to make themselves comfortable. Toys and children's books were strewn around the living room. He took his snow-covered shoes off and made his way slowly through the room, looking at the photos on the wall as he went. Several shots of Elliott at various stages of life adorned the walls. This was Luc's first real look at the boy. He had white-blond hair and looked a lot like Megan. Luc couldn't help but smile at a photo of Elliott laughing as he sat on a red tricycle. He appeared to be about two in the picture, and there was something about the expression on his face that reminded Luc a lot of Megan when something took her by surprise and made her laugh loudly.

He turned on the light to the stairwell and jogged up to the second floor, finding Megan's room. It was not big and he was surprised at how messy it was. Some clothes were slung over an armchair as though they had been tossed there. A pile of folded laundry sat in a basket on the floor, waiting to be put away, and stacks of books covered the nightstands on both sides of the bed. Luc reminded himself that instead of having a housekeeper as he did, Megan had a little boy as well as a business to look after. Of course she didn't have time to keep everything perfect. Feeling a little bit like an intruder, he walked over to her closet and opened it. He picked out a white long-sleeved T-shirt, a cozy-looking black V-neck sweater and some jeans. An overnight bag sat tucked into the corner. Luc grabbed it and put her things in it. Opening her dresser drawers, he found some warm socks and underwear. He went to the bathroom and grabbed a tooth-brush and toothpaste for her as well, before heading back downstairs to find her some warm boots and a coat.

Locking the front door, he carried his shoes and the bag across the kitchen to the door leading to the garage. Shutting the door behind him, he wondered if he would ever be back in Megan's home again. He hoped so.

As he drove back to the hospital, Luc struggled to keep his eyes open. It was mid-morning already back in France and he still hadn't been to bed. He thought about Megan and what she was going to have to manage in the coming weeks, looking after her mother on top of all her other responsibilities. He wanted to find a way to be useful to her during this ordeal, and he had a feeling he would have to be very persistent in getting her to allow it.

What was it about this woman that he couldn't resist? What had made him offer to watch her son? He had never wanted to look after a child in his life, but as the words had come out of his mouth, he knew that he really *did* want to meet Elliott and he really did want to spend the day with him if that was what Megan needed. He realized he would do anything for her, and he couldn't imagine ever wanting to stop being there for her. The thought both terrified him and gave him a new energy.

* * *

Luc found Megan in Helen's hospital room, staring out the window. He stood quietly in the doorway, taking in the sight of her in her gown, lit by the moon outside. She was the loveliest thing he had ever seen. His heart stirred at the sight of her. She turned and saw him, giving him a tired smile as she crossed the room.

"There you are," she whispered, giving him an appreciative smile. "How did it go?"

They walked out into the bright light of the hallway and gently closed the door behind them.

"It was fine. I just hope I brought what you wanted," Luc replied, holding the bag up to her.

Megan looked into it. "You picked just the right things; I need to be comfy right now. I just feel so bad for you. You must have been so cold, and you must be exhausted. I just remembered how late it is for you."

"I'm fine, really. Don't worry about me." Luc gave her a long hug. "How are you holding up?"

"Good. Sleepy, but I'm just so happy that she's going to be alright." Megan rested her head on Luc's shoulder for a moment as he held her.

"Me too. I'm so glad for you both," he replied, kissing the top of her head. "You know, you have a surprising amount of candy bar wrappers shoved in the door pocket of your car. Is that all you eat?"

Megan blushed a deep red. "Pretty much. Chocolate is my secret addiction."

"Maybe I could become your new secret addiction?" Luc asked, giving her a hopeful look.

"I really don't think so. I wouldn't be able to fit you into that little pocket in the car door so . . ." She shook her head, curling up her nose a little.

Luc laughed at the image. "I love your sense of humour."

There was that word again. Megan gave him a little smile. "I'm going to go find a washroom to get changed. Can you sit in the room with her in case she wakes up? I told her I'd be there. She knows you're here so I don't think she'll be startled."

"Of course."

A few minutes later, Megan folded her dress carefully, tucking it into the bag as best she could. Luc's words came into her mind. Twice that night he had used the word *love*, and this last time, it had made her heart jump. She had thought he was going to say "I love you," but he hadn't. She was surprised at her pang of disappointment. She knew it wasn't part of the deal, but she now realized it was becoming part of what her heart wanted. Walking slowly back down the hall, she let herself back into the room and found Luc fast asleep in the chair by the window. Tilting her head, she watched him with what could only be described as a look of total adoration for a few moments. She hadn't seen him asleep since their first night together, and now he looked so handsome in his tuxedo. Megan put her things down on the floor and sat back in the chair by the bed. This time, she fell immediately to sleep.

Two hours later, they were awoken by the light being turned on. A nurse stood in the doorway, startled to see two extra people in the room. "I'm here to check on our patient," she said in a singsong voice. "How are you, Helen?"

Helen lifted her head off the pillow a little and then let it flop back down. "Dizzy."

The nurse asked Megan and Luc to give them some privacy. The pair quietly got up and went into the hall.

"Did you get some rest?" Luc asked, yawning and scratching his head with his fingers sleepily.

"I did. How about you?"

"I did." He answered. "I suspect that will be it for now. Shall I see if I can find us some coffee?"

"That would be amazing. I need to leave to get Elliott in about an hour."

"Okay, I'll be right back."

Megan walked back into the room just as the nurse was leaving. "Your husband is a little overdressed for the occasion."

"Oh, he's not my husband," Megan replied.

"No? You should lock that down, honey. He's hot even at this hour in the morning."

After the door closed, Helen spoke up. "Yeah, lock that down, Megan."

"I see you got your sense of humour back, so that must be a good sign." Megan slumped down in the chair again with a sigh.

"You must be exhausted. Sorry about all of this. I feel silly about all this fuss."

"Stop it. Of course I should fuss over you."

There was a gentle knock at the door.

"Come in," Megan called.

Luc poked his head in tentatively. "Is it alright if I come in? I'm bearing coffee."

"Come in, come in," Helen said. "I want to take a look at you."

Luc walked in with a small smile as his eyes met Helen's. "Hello, Mrs. Foster. It's good to meet you, even under such circumstances."

Megan smiled up at him as he crossed the room and handed her a cup. "Mmm, you're a lifesaver, Luc. Thank you."

She looked over at her mom, trying to gage her reaction.

Helen gave him a weak smile. "I'm very dizzy right now, but I can already see what Meg likes about you. Thank you for getting her here so fast."

"No, please don't thank me. It was my responsibility. I'm the reason she was away in the first place." Luc's eyes fell back on Meg as though he had no control over them.

Megan spoke up. "Mom, I need to go pick up Elliott at Jase's in a bit. I'll bring him back here."

"Oh, I'll be fine. You go home with him and get some rest. I'm going to sleep anyway. The nurse gave me another dose of Gravol just now." Helen's eyelids moved slowly down and back up as she struggled to stay awake.

"Well, I'm not going to leave you here alone all day. I want to be here when the next set of test results come in so I can ask questions."

Helen turned her head slowly in Luc's direction. "She's very stubborn. I'm not sure if you noticed that yet."

Luc grinned from mother to daughter and nodded. "I think she said she prefers it to be called 'persistence.'"

Megan raised one eyebrow. "Ganging up on me already? I knew I shouldn't introduce you two." A hint of a smile escaped her lips.

Helen's eyes were closed now and her breathing was growing more rhythmic. Megan walked over and gently touched her mom's cheek with the back of her fingers, whispering, "We're going to go get Elliott. I'll see you in a little bit, okay?"

Helen nodded without opening her eyes. "Nice to meet you, Luc."

* * *

Megan paced back and forth a few times in the waiting room, chewing on her thumb while Luc stood patiently waiting for her to make a decision about how to proceed. Finally, she turned to him. "What do you know about kids?"

Luc looked up at the ceiling, trying to think. "Never let them play with matches. Or lighters. Or anything else that can start a fire."

Megan gave him a hard stare. "What else?"

"They are like adults, except with less life experience. You need to show them respect but guide them in matters they don't know about."

"That's pretty good," Megan responded, feeling surprised. "You're a very insightful man."

"I know."

"Shit. This is a terrible idea." Megan went back to pacing.

Luc reached out and stopped her, gently turning her to him and lifting his hands to her face. "You're scared. I understand that. This takes a lot of trust and I promise I won't let you down, Megan. But only you can decide what to do."

Megan sighed. "Okay. Let's do this. I'll go get Elliott. We'll tell him that you and I are friends."

"It's going to be alright, Megan. We're not doing anything that will hurt your little boy. I promise."

* * *

Megan gulped down her coffee as she sat in the driver's seat of her car, waiting for a light to change. She was alone, having asked Luc to wait at the hospital. The night's events would be enough for Elliott to deal with, and she wanted a chance to talk to him alone and find out how he was doing. Draining the coffee, she realized she would need several more of those to get her through what was going to be another long day.

Twenty minutes later, Megan had Elliott settled into the back seat of the now-warm car as they headed in the direction of the hospital.

"You doing okay, buddy? I bet last night was pretty rough for you."

Elliott looked at his mom in the rear-view mirror. "Yeah, it was kind of scary. I thought Grandma might die. But when the ambulance people got there, they were really nice and told me everything would be okay. That made me feel better."

"Good. Listen, Elliott, I'm so sorry I wasn't there. I should have been home to handle that, not you."

"Mom, it's not your fault. You didn't make Grandma get sick. Besides, it was kind of fun to ride in the ambulance. They let me wear a stethoscope and they gave me some Batman Band-Aids to keep! I can't wait to tell the kids at school! They're going to be so jealous."

Megan smiled back at her little boy and shook her head a little in amazement at his resilience. "You sure know how to roll with the punches, kiddo."

"I probably get that from you." He grinned.

They rode along for a moment before Megan approached the subject of Luc. Her heart was in her throat and her hands felt clammy against the wheel as she tried to think of what to say. Finally, she cleared her throat and began. "So, Elliott, you know I went to San Francisco with a friend of mine. My friend is a man, actually."

"I know. His name is Luc. Grandma told me," he replied simply.

"Okay . . ." Megan hesitated; Elliott didn't seem bothered by it. "Well, yes that's right, his name is Luc. He came back with me in case I needed any help. He's at the hospital."

Elliott's eyes lit up. "So, am I going to get to meet him?"

"Yes, if you want to."

"Yeah, I would like to. Are you are going to get married to him?" he asked.

Megan laughed. "No, no. We're just friends. He lives in France, which is very far away."

"Okay. Just wondering. You should marry someone, Mom."

"Why's that?"

"Jase's mom doesn't have to do as much as you. His dad does stuff like shovelling and taking care of their van and yelling at the kids when they fight. It would be much easier for you to have a husband."

Megan laughed a little at her son's keen observation. He was wise beyond his years, a result of spending his young life almost exclusively with adults. "Yeah, well, I'm happy the way things are. I don't mind doing all of those things myself, actually. And I never have to stop any fights since there are just the two of us."

Elliott shrugged. "I guess so. But it might be nice to have more people. You should think about it."

* * *

Megan held Elliott's hand in hers as she hurried him through the sliding doors into the hospital and out of the cold wind. Her heart pounded and she felt slightly sick to her stomach as they approached the waiting room. Luc sat, still in his tuxedo, flipping through a magazine. He looked up and smiled when he saw them. If he was nervous about meeting Elliott, no one would have been able to tell by how casual he appeared. He stood and tossed the magazine onto a table nearby.

Megan spoke up, "Elliott, this is my friend Luc. Luc, this is my son, Elliott."

Luc extended his hand. "Elliott, I'm very glad to meet you," he said with a little nod.

Elliott gave him a hearty handshake and eyed him up and down. "You talk funny and you're dressed for a fancy party." He looked up at his mom with a skeptical look on his face, then whispered to her, "*This* is the guy? He's kind of weird."

Luc burst into laughter at the boy's honest appraisal of him. Megan reluctantly joined in, trying to give Elliott a stern look at the same time but failing.

When Luc finally stopped laughing, he answered Elliott's charges. "I'm dressed this way because I don't have any other clothes, and I talk like this because I'm from France."

"You don't have any other clothes?" Elliott replied with wide eyes. "My mom can afford to buy you some new stuff. She makes a lot of money. She has hundreds, even."

Megan's face turned red as Luc began to laugh again. "No, no, kiddo, he has more than one outfit. He just doesn't have anything else with him because we were in such a rush to get back here last night."

Elliott stuck one finger in the air. "Ah! Now I get it."

Megan grinned down at her little boy. Somehow he had managed to make this introduction more amusing than awkward and she was grateful. Her cellphone rang, interrupting the moment. It was her brother, Mark, from Portland. Megan excused herself and spent a few minutes on the phone, updating Mark on their mom's condition.

When she got off the call, she walked over to find the two chatting away happily.

Elliott puffed up his chest. "Yeah, so I could probably teach you lots of new ski moves, since I'm young and all. You probably don't know all the new stuff people are doing these days."

Luc nodded in agreement. "Sure, because I am very old."

"Exactly." Elliott replied wisely.

Luc grinned over at Megan, fighting the urge to laugh.

"Can we go see Grandma now?" Elliott asked.

"Yes. She's probably sleeping, but we can peek our heads in."

"Good, because I want to make sure she's okay before we go home."

"Let's go check on her, then," Megan replied. "We'll be right back, Luc."

Luc sat back down to wait for them. Elliott turned back to him and motioned for him to come. "Let's go check on Grandma, Luc. Honestly, Mom, you can't leave him just sitting there, being bored. Have you forgotten what you taught me about being a good friend?"

"Alright, settle down, buddy," she replied, raising a stern eyebrow in his direction.

After they had gone in to see Helen, Megan checked with the

nurse. She apologetically told Megan that there was an error on one of the tests, so they would have to run it again. It would be several hours before they had confirmation of Helen's condition. They walked back into the lobby. It was clear Elliott couldn't spend the day there.

"Elliott, I really need to stay with Grandma today to make sure she's going to be okay. It's still early in the morning, so I don't want to call any of your friends yet, but I'm going to try to find someone you can spend the day with, okay?"

"I can hang out with Luc. I bet he's bored here too." Elliott shrugged, looking over at Luc.

Luc smiled kindly. "That would be up to your mother. I don't have a lot of experience looking after kids, I'm afraid."

Elliott shook his head. "I'm six, Luc. That's practically a grown-up. I really only need an adult around so the police don't take me away to an orphanage."

Megan slapped her forehead with her hand. "He's taking something I said a couple of weeks ago out of context."

Luc laughed too loudly for the surroundings, earning him a glare from a nurse who was passing by. "You told me he was funny, but I had no idea. If he wants to hang out with me, I think it might be one of the most fun days I'll have in a long time."

Megan couldn't believe she was going to agree to this. It was the last thing she had ever wanted, but at the moment, her instinct was that it would be alright. She trusted Luc and the two seemed to have such a natural rapport she figured they would probably have a good time.

"Okay. I guess if you want, you could go do something for a few hours. Maybe you could help Luc buy some clothes for himself."

Elliott grinned enthusiastically. "I know just the place! Target! They sell toys too!"

"No toys, mister. Your birthday is coming," Megan said sternly. She took out her keys, handing them to Luc.

"We'll go get some breakfast if Elliott wants, and then he can take me to Target and show me what all the cool kids are wearing these days." Try as Luc might to hide it, his face wore a slight look of horror at the thought of going to Target.

"Okay!" Elliott grinned. "And after that we can go home and play video games! I bet you don't know anything about that either."

Luc gave Megan a little wink. "It appears I have a busy day ahead of me. We'd better get started. Call me if you need anything."

Megan watched as her little boy walked outside with Luc beside him. Elliott reached up and took his hand to cross the parking lot. Something about the sight of it squeezed at Megan's heart. Any passerby would think they were father and son. A bond Elliott had never known.

A feeling of dread passed over her as she made her way back to her mom's room.

TWENTY-ONE

"Check those soldiers out! Wicked!" Elliott exclaimed. He rushed over to a low shelf holding a display of tiny green soldiers near the checkout at Target.

Luc was a good sport about shopping, letting Elliott pick out a black hoodie to go with the white T-shirts and jeans Luc had chosen for himself. He was pleasantly surprised to find he could also buy himself some hiking boots, mitts, a wool hat, socks and underwear as well as a shaving kit and other toiletries. He now felt prepared to stay as long as he was needed.

Luc crouched beside the young boy to look at the soldiers. They came in a little tin holding twenty of the tiny figures. "Very nice. That is exactly what I would have wanted when I was your age."

Elliott looked over at him. "Really?"

"Definitely. You know what? I'd like to get you a set, but only if you don't think it would bother your mom. You were quite the brave soldier yourself in taking care of your Grandma last night. I think that deserves a treat."

"Oh, she won't mind a bit! I'm sure of it. I know her better than anyone," Elliott said, carefully choosing among the identical tins.

Luc chuckled to himself as he watched Elliott pick up each tin to examine it before finally settling on one. His cellphone buzzed, indicating a message.

How's it going? Has my son said anything insulting or patronizing since you left here?

He's great. His honesty is rather refreshing, and he's helped to outfit me so I'll fit in with the cool kids. I said he could pick out a small toy for being so brave last night. I hope I haven't overstepped my boundaries.

That's alright. He has been pretty terrific about everything. I don't mind, but nothing else, please. I don't want him to start thinking he can take advantage of you.

Only his mom can do that . . .

Exactly.

We're going to your house now to play video games. He wants to teach me 'how to drive' in some car game. He thinks I can learn, although he's certain that my old-man hand-eye coordination will allow him to dominate me.

Lol. Hope you don't mind.

I'm looking forward to it!

* * *

"There's something wrong with this controller! I can't make these turns like you," Luc huffed, moving the controller erratically, causing his driver to crash into the side wall again.

Elliott was laughing hysterically as he expertly manoeuvred his car across the finish line. "It's totally you. Both controllers work."

Luc shook his head in disgust. "No, no. That's not possible. I have lightning-fast reflexes. I've even driven a race car in real life and it was easier than this."

Elliott turned to him, eyes wide as saucers, forgetting completely about the game. "You drove a real race car?"

"Yes. I have a very good friend who is a Formula One driver. I went with him one day when he was practising."

"That's amazeballs! How fast did you go?"

"Amazeballs? You think so?" Luc laughed. "I went just over two hundred kilometres per hour. Not as fast as they go in real races, but twice as fast as you're allowed to drive on the freeway."

"Wow . . . Can I do it sometime?"

"That's one of those things you can do only when you're a grown-up. I also have a feeling your mother wouldn't be as excited by that idea as you are."

"You're right." Elliott hung his head for a moment. "She never lets me do anything exciting."

"Moms are funny that way. They have this annoying habit of wanting to keep their kids alive. Mine was the same way."

"I hear ya, dude. I hear ya . . ." Elliott agreed.

"Speaking of your mom, she said she needed to clean out the spare room for your grandma. What if we did that together, you and me? Give her a bit of a break?"

"Okay, but one more game first."

"Only if you switch controllers with me."

Elliott handed him the other controller. "It won't help. I'm still going to kick your butt."

* * *

An hour later, Megan got a call from Luc. She was sitting, watching her mom pick at the unappetizing-looking hospital food. She walked over to the window and answered. "Hello?"

"Megan. I have a quick question for you. Do you have a minute?"

"Of course. How are things going there?"

"Terrific, actually. I had no idea how amusing children could be. I would have had some of my own had I known."

"Yeah, Elliott is a pretty funny little man. I'm glad you're getting along. I've been worried that it might be a bit much, or boring, for you."

"Not at all, actually. I'm very much enjoying the day. Listen, we've started a little project and I have to ask for your help."

"Okay . . ." Megan replied.

"I'm trying to figure out how to use your washing machine. There are a lot of knobs and buttons. It's not like mine at home."

"You mean the one your housekeeper uses?"

"That's the one," he admitted sheepishly.

"What are you washing?"

"The sheets for the spare room. I thought you would want to freshen them up for your mom."

"You mean you *actually* found the bed under that mess?"

"Yes. Elliott and I have been very busy getting the boxes out of there. We put most of them in the storage room downstairs. I hope that's okay."

"That's perfect! Wow! I was thinking I would have to put my mom in my bedroom for the night and spend most of the evening cleaning out the spare room. Thank you *so* much, Luc!"

"It's nothing, really. Do you know yet when you can bring her home?"

"No. She's still really dizzy. They're waiting for the Gravol to wear off so they can try another type of medication to see if that'll make a difference. The test results confirmed everything, so that's a huge relief."

"Good. I'm very glad."

"Thanks, Luc. For everything."

"You're very welcome. Now, how do I open this washing machine?"

* * *

"Elliott, what do you American boys like to eat for dinner?" Luc asked.

"Spaghetti or pizza."

"Okay, let's see what we've got for ingredients."

Luc looked through the fridge and cupboards, finding a box of spaghetti as well as everything he needed to make a tomato sauce with baby clams.

"Alright, shall we cook?"

"Yup!" Elliott grinned enthusiastically.

"If we do a good job, it will impress your mom, yes?"

"Yes, it will."

"Excellent. That's what I was hoping for," Luc replied, opening drawers until he found the pots.

"I don't think you have to impress her. She already likes you. I can tell."

"Really? How can you tell?" Luc gave Elliott a sideways glance as he filled a pot with water.

"When we saw you at the hospital, she had a funny look on her face and her cheeks turned red, like people in the movies."

"Is that so? How interesting." Luc smiled a little at Elliott's observation.

Elliott scrunched up his face at Luc. "Don't get your hopes up, though. She said you aren't getting married together."

"Did she say that?" Luc turned on the burner and poured some olive oil into the pot.

"Yes. In the car. I asked her and she said you're just friends."

"She's right. We are just friends," Luc replied, searching the drawers for a garlic press. "Would you like your mom to get married to someone?"

"Yeah, I think it would be good for her. She hates doing yard work and other jobs husbands do. She says she's happy, though, so I should stop worrying about her."

"Do you think she is happy?"

"Now that I think about it, she does seem nicer lately."

"Really? So you notice something different about her?"

"Yeah, she sings a lot more and dances around the kitchen when she cooks. She jokes with me more and she's giving me more treats than normal."

"Hmm, what do you think is making her so happy?" Luc asked.

"Probably me." Elliott shrugged. "I've been remembering to flush the toilet now that I'm almost seven."

Luc laughed out loud again as he chopped an onion into tiny pieces. The dryer buzzed, indicating the sheets were dry.

"Oh! Let's get this sauce going so we can make the bed."

An hour later, Megan walked through the door, looking completely wiped as she took off her boots. Elliott ran to greet her with a big grin. "MOM! We have a surprise for you! Lots of them, actually! Come on! Come on with me!"

"Okay, buddy. Just give me a minute to get my coat off."

Luc walked around the corner from the kitchen, wiping his hands on a dishtowel. "Hello, how's your mom?"

Megan took in the sight of him standing there in jeans and a T-shirt, looking so at home. There was something so natural about it, she was taken aback for a minute as she gazed at him. "She's okay. They said she has to stay one more night at least. She still doesn't have the balance to leave."

"That's a shame. Hopefully early tomorrow, then. Did you take a cab to get here? We would have picked you up."

"It sounded like you were so busy, I didn't want to disturb you," Megan said, hanging up her coat and shutting the closet door. "What is that heavenly smell?" she asked.

Elliott pulled her by the arm into the kitchen. "That's surprise number one! We cooked supper for you!"

"Mmm. This all looks amazing!" Megan exclaimed.

Tomato sauce was gently bubbling in a pot while next to it, water for the pasta was at a furious boil. In the oven, the light was on and carrots were roasting. A large bowl of salad sat on the table, ready to be eaten.

"It's spaghetti and clam sauce and we made carrots in the oven and Luc even put maple syrup on them! Come on upstairs! I want to show you Grandma's room!"

"Okay, Elliott! Slow down a bit. Mom's tuckered out."

He propelled himself up the stairs and turned back to frantically wave her along. When they reached the room, Megan gasped and hugged Elliott. All the boxes were gone, the bed was neatly made and a framed photo of Elliott with his grandma sat on the bedside table.

"Did you and Luc get *all* this done today?"

"Yup." He beamed proudly. "Pretty awesome, right?"

"Pretty awesome," Megan agreed, giving Elliott a big hug. "Now, how am I going to thank you both?"

"Two desserts for me?" Elliott asked hopefully.

"You're all about the sweets, aren't you?"

"Just like you." Luc spoke up from his vantage point at the bedroom door.

Megan grinned at him and shook her head a little, in shock. "This is just . . . better than the jet, frankly."

"Really? Better than a private jet? So I could have saved myself a considerable amount of money." He gave her a little wink.

"Thank you," she said, her eyes shining with sincere appreciation.

"Uh-oh! Are you guys going to kiss? Yuck!" Elliott screeched, dropping behind the other side of the bed.

Megan rolled her eyes. "Relax, Elliott, we're just friends, remember? Now, what can I do to help with dinner?"

"Come and sit down. It's all ready."

The three sat down to the delicious meal, Megan feeling overwhelmed by a sense of gratitude. If Elliott hadn't been there keeping the conversation going, she might have started to tear up. The depth of emotion she was feeling, combined with exhaustion, was catching up with her.

"Luc says all men should learn to cook but that hardly any of them bother. He says most men are not so smart, because their women do all the cooking and then they don't have energy enough for the more important things in life."

"Did he, now?" Megan raised an eyebrow at Luc.

Luc cleared his throat. "Yes, well, things like going dancing or maybe for a walk. Women like these things."

"Luc's been teaching me about romance."

"Oh, has he?" Megan tried not to laugh as she watched Luc squirm. "Does he know a lot about romance?"

"Yup. And he told me he'll give me all his best tricks for how to get the ladies." Elliott took a gulp of milk. "He said American men don't have the first clue about women, but with a few simple tricks, the girls will be like putty in my hands."

Megan broke out into a laugh, putting her forkful of noodles back down on her plate.

Luc shook his head a little, trying to look convincing. "No, I don't remember saying that. You must have me confused with some other Frenchman you know. I don't know what he was thinking, telling you that stuff. You are far too young for romance." He added some more carrots to Elliott's plate. "Here. Put lots of these in your mouth," he said with a little wink.

* * *

"Can Luc do my bedtime?" Elliott called down the stairs.

Megan glanced over at Luc with a questioning look. She was standing at the kitchen sink, rinsing the pasta pot while Luc stood beside her drying the lid with a towel.

"Do you want to read to him a bit? It's okay to say no. I can just tell him I didn't get to spend enough time with him today," she said under her breath.

"I would really enjoy reading to him," Luc answered truthfully. "Besides, if I don't go, you'll probably put me to work."

Megan laughed. "Yes. This floor needs a good scrubbing."

Elliott raced into the kitchen, wearing blue jammies that were slightly too short in the sleeves and legs. "Well? I didn't hear your answer. Can Luc do my bedtime, Mom?"

"How about if he does the reading part and I'll come up for lights out and snuggle time?" she said.

"Okay! Let's go, Luc! I want to show you these comic books my mom gave me. They're hilarious. They're about a boy named Calvin and he has a tiger that's real, except everyone else thinks he's just a stuffed animal."

Luc followed him up the stairs as Elliott talked on happily. Megan returned the pots to their place in the drawer and turned the light off above the kitchen sink. Walking slowly over to the living room, she collapsed onto the couch to rest for a few minutes. Upstairs, she could hear the distant sounds of Luc and Elliott reading and laughing together. She strained her ears, trying to catch some of what they were saying. Her cellphone rang and she answered.

"Harper, hello, my friend,"

"Hi, Meg. Just called to check on your mom."

"She has to stay at the hospital one more night, but she should be fine in a couple of weeks."

"Thank God! This must have been so scary for you. I'm just so glad she'll be okay."

"Me too. Last night, when Elliott called me, it was one of the most terrifying moments of my life."

"I believe it. Oh shit, I just realized I'm interrupting bedtime, aren't I?"

"Um, well, Luc is reading to Elliott right now."

There was a long pause from Harper before she finally replied. "What did you just say?"

"I know. I know," Megan sighed, picking at a fuzzball on her sleeve. "It goes against everything I've ever said about dating and my life and Elliott. I was desperate. I couldn't find anyone to watch him today and the two of them just seemed to like each other right off the bat. And you know what? It's turned into a shockingly good day, actually. Luc ended up spending the day with him while I was at the hospital. They had a great time. Elliott made him play video games, and Luc cleaned out the spare room and even changed the sheets so it's all ready when my mom gets out of the hospital. Then he made the most delicious meal and helped with the dishes."

"Seriously?"

"Seriously. And do you want to hear something funny? Elliott convinced him to go shopping at Target because he only had the tuxedo he was wearing. Elliott picked out a *hoodie* for him, and he actually bought it."

Harper burst into laughter at the image of Luc in a hoodie. "Oh my God, Megan. What the hell is happening out there in Colorado?"

Megan giggled quietly into the phone. "I don't know, but I'm just going with it. It sure has been wonderful to have someone to help with the load today."

"Maybe this will become a habit for you?"

"I don't think so. He's just helping me out. It doesn't mean he wants a family all of a sudden."

"But you sound like you might . . ." Harper replied.

"No, no. I don't. I like my life uncomplicated. It's just been a bit of a treat. That's all."

Harper's voice was skeptical. "I don't know, my friend. It sounds like the beginning of something that could be pretty amazing if you let it."

Megan shook her head even though Harper couldn't see her. She needed to convince herself. "It's not, Harper. Honestly. I can't afford to even let that thought seep into my brain. We're having a little fun for a while, he's helping me out and at some point he'll fly off home and I won't see him again."

"Still think you can handle that conclusion?"

"I've been through much worse, Harper. This will be nothing." Megan looked at her watch. "Listen, I have to run. I need to go relieve Luc and do snuggle time. Let's talk later this week, okay?"

"Definitely. I want you to keep me updated about Helen and whatever this is with Luc," Harper replied.

"I will. See you later."

"Bye."

Megan heaved herself off the couch and made her way slowly up the stairs to Elliott's room. Leaning against the door frame, she watched the scene for a minute before Luc noticed her. He smiled at her from his position, sitting next to Elliott on the bed, his back against a pillow.

"Is it time?" Luc asked.

"Yup, lights out, Elliott," Megan answered, walking into the room.

"Good night, Luc. I had a lot of fun with you today."

"You know what? I had a lot of fun with you as well. Especially when you weren't cheating at video games."

"Cheating?" Elliott's face wore a huge grin. "I'm just much better at it than you."

Luc stood and ruffled Elliott's hair with his hand. "In that case, I will practise so I can conquer you next time."

"Ha! Never!" Elliott gloated.

Luc extended his hand to shake Elliott's. "Good night, Elliott. Thank you for taking me shopping today and helping me impress your mom."

Elliott ignored Luc's hand and propped himself up on his knees on the bed to give Luc a hug. He pressed his little cheek into Luc's chest as he squeezed him with all his might. Luc looked temporarily uncomfortable and then smiled down at the little boy, hugging him back. He gave him a little kiss on the top of his head, then ruffled his hair again.

"Good night, Luc," Elliott said.

Megan, who had a lump in her throat, avoided eye contact with Luc as he made his way out of the room. She wasn't sure what she was feeling or what to think at that moment. She turned the light off and lay down beside Elliott for a few minutes, tracing a finger over the side of his little face absent-mindedly.

A few minutes later, Megan found Luc starting a fire in the fireplace. A bottle of red wine sat open on the coffee table with two glasses filled beside it. The scene had all the makings of a romantic evening, but Megan was too weary and too worried to have any such notions. Luc looked up at her as she came into the room, his eyes full of that devotion he reserved for her. He was so handsome, in just a white T-shirt and jeans, that her heart stirred at the sight of him, this man who had tirelessly cared for her and her son over the past long twenty-four hours.

"You must be so tired," he said as the fire caught. He shut the glass doors and stood up.

"You must be too," Megan said as she lowered herself onto the couch.

Luc joined her on the couch and picked up their glasses. "Yes. Let's relax a bit. We deserve it, I think."

Megan took her glass from him and had a sip. "Especially you. I can't believe everything you did today. I don't know how I'll ever repay you."

Luc reached out and took her hand in his, placing them both on his lap. "No need. I didn't do anything I didn't want to do. Just sit with me awhile and enjoy the fire before I go."

Megan's head turned quickly in his direction. "You're going?"

"I thought I would get a hotel room for the night. It would be too confusing for Elliott if I slept here, no?"

Megan nodded slowly. "Yeah, you're right. I think last night and today were confusing enough for him." She sighed heavily and took a gulp of wine. "I don't want you to think I'm not grateful, because I am. It's just really scary for me to have him around *any* man."

"I know it is, and now that I have met him I can understand why. He's just so little and innocent. For him, the world is still full of magic. He still believes he could find a dragon in the yard or that his dad could come back and you would all live happily ever after. It's all possible for him. That is something so precious, and I would never want to wreck that for him."

A tear slid down Megan's cheek and she quickly wiped it away with her fingers. "You do get it. He's just had more hardship than any child should have to deal with. I don't want to add to that. And you know, Ian has just fucked things up so badly. It's only a matter of time before Elliott realizes how unhealthy his dad really is and starts to become bitter toward him. It terrifies me, actually. I don't know how I'll be able to stop that."

"You won't." Luc put his arm around Megan and pulled her to him so her head was resting on his shoulder. "Only his father can do that. All you can do is be there for him when it happens and not try to deny the reality then. It will only make things worse if you defend Ian."

"You sound like you speak from experience."

"It's different but also the same. But let's not talk about that now. We're both tired. Right now, I just want to hold you in my arms before I have to leave. We should be celebrating that your mom is going to be okay."

Megan smiled a little. "That we should. I was so scared she would die. The last twenty-four hours have been an absolute roller coaster. Being at the ballet seems like weeks ago already."

She paused, watching the fire for a moment. "You took a really horrible situation and just made it so much easier for me. I can't even begin to tell you how it felt to be taken care of like that." Megan gave him a kiss on the cheek. "You just stepped in and did what needed to be done, without any complaining about how your romantic weekend was ruined."

Luc rubbed her arm with his thumb. "Why would I complain in the middle of a crisis? I would be a very selfish person to whine about missing out on some fun under such circumstances. Besides, there will always be other romantic weekends for us. I'm just glad that your mother is alright and that you let me help you. I can't believe how much I enjoyed being with Elliott. I *really* like him. He's so smart and funny and honest, and very wise for his age as well. I can tell he is going to be a good man when he grows up. You're really doing an amazing job with him."

"Thank you for saying that. When you're on your own, you don't get a lot of feedback on how you're doing as a parent." Megan smiled lovingly at Luc. She stared into his dark eyes, seeing them reflect back the need she felt for him.

"You put your heart into everything you do, Megan. That's one of the things I admire about you." He put their empty glasses back on the coffee table and sank back into the couch, reaching for her face with his hands. Kissing her lightly, he let his mouth hover over hers, tasting her and feeling the warmth of her lips. Knowing she needed rest more than romance, he pulled back and gently guided her head to his shoulder. His desire for her would have to wait.

When Megan woke up in the morning, she was in her bed, but she couldn't remember how she had gotten there. She still had her sweater on, but as she looked over to the window, she saw her jeans neatly folded on a chair next to it. In her dreamy haze, a memory of falling asleep on the couch, wrapped in Luc's strong arms, came back to her. He must have carried her to bed and taken off her jeans. A little note on her bedside table read *Call me when you get a chance. I'll come back here or to the hospital—wherever you need me most. L.*

She smiled to herself as she read it. How had she gotten so lucky, to have this man drop into her life out of nowhere exactly when she needed him most?

Megan stood at the counter of the hospital with her mouth hanging open in disbelief. "I don't understand. How could the bill have been paid if I didn't get it until now?"

The woman on the other side of the glass looked confused. "I'm not sure. Let me just ask one of the other staff."

A minute later, another woman came up to the counter, holding the bill. "This is right. I handled it myself. A fine man in a tuxedo came up and told me to put it on his credit card." She squinted down at the bill through her glasses. "Mr. Luck Chevalier."

"Luc—it's pronounced *Luke*, not *Luck*. It's French," Megan replied distractedly.

"Well, however you say it, hang on to that one. Any man who dresses like that and goes around paying a bill like this without batting an eye is a keeper."

Megan nodded. "Thanks." She slowly made her way back to collect Helen and bring her home. The bill in Megan's hand, showing a zero balance, had come as a complete surprise. When she had arrived at the hospital a few minutes earlier, she had been prepared to try to make payment arrangements on the charges. Luc had taken that worry from her shoulders without so much as a word about it.

*　*　*

That night as Megan and Luc said good night at the door, she gave him a lingering kiss.

He leaned his forehead against hers. "Mmm, you better stop that or I'll have my way with you right here in the doorway instead of going back to the hotel for the night like a decent man."

Megan giggled a little. "Have *your* way? No, no, Luc you've got it all wrong. It would be *me* having my way with *you*. I'd start by tearing your clothes off and licking that huge—"

Luc pressed his mouth over hers to get her to stop talking. He kissed her long and hard, feeling her body relax before he let up. "Stop that, you silly woman, or I'm going to take you over my knee."

"Silly woman? You know, only a man with your accent could get away with that. If it was anyone else, I'd punch him in the throat."

Luc's eyes grew wide with surprise. "I was raised by an American woman. I should know better than to mess with you."

"You should indeed."

Luc laughed and leaned down to kiss her again. "I promise not to mess with you. Only to mess around."

"Yes, let's mess around. I could show you the other uses for the washing machine."

Luc groaned at the thought of it. "I have to go. Your mom and your son are right up those stairs. Now, I'll see you first thing in the morning. I'll be here before you take Elliott to school so I can keep an eye on Helen."

"I can't wait to thank you properly for everything. I don't know how long it will take me to pay you back for the hospital bill."

"You can thank me by not mentioning the bill again. I never do anything I don't want to do. And for me, it really was nothing. I rarely have anything so important to do with my money anyway, so it would be a gift to me if you would accept it with no further discussion on the matter."

"Well that's certainly an unusual way to spin it. *I'm* doing *you* a favour by taking the money? I don't think I'll be able to wrap my head around that concept. We can agree not to talk about it, but I'm afraid I'm going to have to repay you."

"You're still talking about it . . ." Luc replied sternly.

"Sorry. I can't help myself." Megan kissed him again. She let her hands wander down his abdomen toward his pants. "I really can't help myself," she murmured.

Luc moved his hips back. "Okay. That's it." He gave her a quick peck on the lips. "I really am going back to my hotel room, except now it will be for a cold shower."

Megan grinned, loving the effect she was having on him. "See you tomorrow."

* * *

The next three days found Luc still at Megan's. He had called the hotel in San Francisco to have all of their things couriered to her house. During the day he worked on his laptop in Megan's kitchen. They chatted occasionally as she edited photos at her computer. It felt very comfortable and was fun for both of them. From time to time Megan would look up, only to see Luc staring at her.

"You're watching me again."

"I know."

"Stop it. We need to work." She grinned.

"I should point out that you were also looking at me just now."

"I could feel you staring."

"Well, it's not my fault that you're gorgeous. It's very distracting, really. It's a good thing I didn't meet you before I made my fortune. I'd be a poor man."

Megan stifled a smile. "Shut up and get to work, Chevalier."

"Yes, boss."

Helen stood at the entrance to the kitchen, watching them, "Her brother, Mark, calls her Bossy Boots. I think it suits her."

"Mom! You were supposed to call me if you wanted to come down the stairs!"

"See? Bossy Boots." Helen grinned at Luc as she shuffled slowly toward the counter. "I made it down just fine. Stop all this fussing. I just came to grab my magazine."

Luc stood up and linked his arm through Helen's, gently helping her as she made her way back to the couch. "Bossy Boots? That is very fitting. Do you think I can get away with calling her that?" he asked conspiratorially.

"Not if you don't want a throat punch!" Megan called to him. She could hardly wipe the grin off her face as she saw Luc taking care of her mom without Helen minding a bit. It had been like that since she had gotten home. He had such a way with her that she never argued with him when he helped her. When Megan tried, Helen would swat her hand away and make a comment about not wanting to be a burden.

Luc got Helen settled on the couch with a blanket on her lap and then walked over to Megan on his way back to the table. He leaned down and gave her a peck on the cheek, then lowered his voice. "Bossy Boots? Is that also your dominatrix name?"

Megan laughed softly, turning her head to his and kissing him on the lips. "I'm afraid that's a secret. Now get to work before I'm forced to go get my whips."

In the living room, Helen sat smiling to herself. She hadn't seen her daughter this happy in years, and it warmed her heart. Maybe this could work out. Luc certainly had proven to be a wonderfully thoughtful and caring man. She sat thinking about how he insisted on cooking dinner every night and had gotten the spare room prepared for her arrival, and how great he was with Elliott. She resolved to find a way to make sure he and Megan stayed together. So what if he was from France? People moved all the time.

* * *

"Mom." Elliott's voice was quiet. "Will Luc be here tomorrow?"

Megan looked down at her little sleepy boy as she snuggled him under the covers. "I think so. For part of the day, anyway."

"Good. I can see why he's your friend. I wish he could move here."

Megan sighed. "He's nice, isn't he?"

"He's fun too, and I can tell he likes you more than a friend. Maybe you two could get married?"

Megan's mind froze for a second. "Um, you know . . . Um, I don't think so, buddy. Luc lives very far away from here. He's a wonderful friend but he's going to have to go back to his home and his work soon."

"That's too bad. I would like him to live with us. It's nice to have another guy in the house to hang out with."

"It's been fun, hasn't it? Now off to sleep, kiddo. You've got school in the morning."

A feeling of dread washed over Megan, settling itself into her chest. In less than a week, Elliott had already become attached to Luc. *Shit*, she thought. *How could I have let this happen?*

Megan needed Luc to leave. Elliott was getting too attached and she was falling in love with him. She knew the longer he stayed, the harder the crash would be when he finally ended things with her.

* * *

That night Luc and Megan sat cuddled up on the couch in front of the fire talking, as they did each night before Luc went back to the hotel. Helen had gone to bed a couple of hours earlier, shortly after Elliott. Her medication made her fall asleep quickly.

Luc lifted Megan's hair out of the way and pressed his lips to her neck. Megan rewarded him with a low moan. Desire ripped through her body as he sucked on her skin. They hadn't had sex in days, and it was killing them both to be so close and not satisfy their need for each other.

Suddenly, Megan was frightened at the desperation she felt for Luc. "Luc, what are we doing? We're treading on very dangerous ground here. I'm starting to feel too much for you . . ."

Luc pulled back a bit. "I know. So am I, but I can't stop, Megan. I have to have you. I need to be with you," he whispered, running his nose along her cheek.

"But, Luc, I don't know if I can keep my promise to you. I might be falling for you . . ."

Luc took her face in both hands and looked into her beautiful green eyes. "For tonight, let's pretend that this is our home, we are here together and it's okay to need each other. Let's pretend we can wake up in each other's arms every morning." *It's all I want to do anyway*, he thought.

Luc kissed her again. Megan's eyes closed and she melted into him, resting one of her hands on his sculpted chest and reaching the other one up to his jaw. Her yearning for him was growing more intense by the second. Luc was here in her home, he had spent several days in her life and it hadn't sent him running like she had thought it would. She wanted to connect with him in the most intimate of ways, to show him what it all meant to her. She wanted to pretend that he was hers and that this was forever.

Megan pushed her tongue into his mouth, exploring him passionately. Using one hand, she pulled his T-shirt up and then ran her fingers along his abs and to the top of his jeans. Undoing the button, she let her hand slip in between his jeans and his boxer briefs, rubbing his length firmly, over the fabric. Luc moaned at the feeling of it and opened his eyes to watch her by the light of the fire.

He stopped and pulled back. "What about Elliott and your mom?"

Megan kissed his neck. "He won't wake up, and if he did, he would call to me from his room. He won't come looking for me. And that medication will have my mom sleeping for hours."

Reassured, Luc rolled himself off the couch so he was kneeling in front of her and gave her a little half smile as he undid her jeans and slid them off her legs.

Megan's skin tingled at the feeling of his fingertips on her. She leaned forward, pushing his jeans and his briefs down his thighs, freeing him of all constraints. Luc put both hands under her and pulled her body toward the edge of the couch so his cock was now pressed against her French-cut pink panties. Megan wrapped her legs around his waist, pulling him closer to her. Luc lifted her sweater over her head, leaving only her lacy pink bra to contend with. He ran his hands over her shoulders, then around to her back, making short work of her bra clasp. Gliding his fingers along the straps, he slid her bra off and tossed it behind him, taking in the sight of her naked breasts as the flickering light of the fire kissed her skin. His expression was suddenly animalistic. Her nipples were already hard, and her breathing grew heavy just from the anticipation of what was about to happen. Luc lowered his mouth over her right breast, circling her nipple with his tongue and then sucking on it urgently, rolling his tongue over it as he did.

Megan gasped at the sensation, watching him as he gave her such tender attention, every touch bringing her incredible pleasure. He moved over to her other breast, gently pushing her away so her head was resting on the back of the couch, leaving her sprawled before him. He ran one hand down the centre line of her body until he reached her panties. He rubbed his palm on the outside of the lace, feeling through the skimpy fabric how wet she already was

"Mmm, I think you must have liked what I've been doing so far," he teased. He watched her breasts rise and fall as she breathed, feeling his cock twitch with excitement.

Megan nodded, unable to speak. Her desire for him was coursing through her body now; she could think of nothing but having him inside her. She bit her bottom lip as she gazed back at him, taking in the sight of his lean muscles as they rippled with each move of his hands. Putting both hands on her hips, he pulled her panties down smoothly, letting his fingers caress her skin. Megan lowered her feet to the floor, allowing him to take her panties off all the way. He took a moment to remove his jeans and underwear completely, leaving the two of them stripped nude.

Megan reached for Luc with one hand as she wrapped her legs around him again and pulled his body toward hers. She could feel his hard length against her sex now, and the feeling of his smooth skin alone was almost enough to make her come. Reaching down for him, she used her hand to position the head of his cock at her wet opening, drenching him as he slowly slid his way inside her. Megan's breath caught, feeling each delicious inch of him where she wanted him most. This felt so right, to be with Luc, who adored her and took care of her. Megan didn't want to deny herself anymore.

Luc pushed himself inside Megan, feeling the comfort of her tight warmth around him. He was overcome by a sudden desire to come inside her, as if that would make her his forever. There was no trace of common sense left in him, only a deep need he had never felt before. He lowered his face to her shoulder, sucking along the nape of her neck and then up to her earlobe. He could feel her tighten around him as he gently held her earlobe between his teeth for a moment, rocking his hips back and forth slowly. She turned her head so that her mouth met his. She was breathing heavily and her lips were parted, waiting for his tongue to explore her mouth. Luc gave her the kiss she was searching for, thrusting his tongue to find hers.

He could feel her starting to come, and she pressed her forehead hard to his and closed her eyes as she silently came on his bare skin.

The sensation of it somehow brought Luc back to his senses, and he pulled out just before he came. Megan lifted her torso, pressing her body to his as he climaxed. She kissed him wildly, feeling his release against her stomach. Even after her own orgasm, she was still filled with an urgency to be with him that she had never felt with another man.

They kissed like this for a long moment before Luc pulled back. "Let's pretend it's okay to love each other like this."

Megan's mouth met his urgently. It was here in this moment that she knew she *did* love him and that she was powerless to stop herself. "It all feels so real, this dream of us," she whispered.

Luc held his hands to her face. "This is the dream I want. I don't want to go."

"Then stay, Luc. Stay with me here."

He responded not with words but with a kiss that held every desire he had for her. Megan could feel his passion and she desperately wished that if she could just hold him there, this moment wouldn't end. Maybe somehow, if they just stayed like this long enough, everything would be different in the morning. He wouldn't ever have to leave and they could start a life together. A life of happiness, passion and unending love.

Finally, Luc lifted himself away from her, grabbing some tissues out of a box on the coffee table to wipe both of them off. He pressed his forehead to hers and sighed, feeling filled with love and contentment.

It was late and the fire had burned out, leaving only embers glowing in the dark room as Luc pulled on his jeans. Megan pulled up her panties and watched him from the couch as he crossed to the bathroom to dispose of the tissues. She had never had the chance to fully appreciate how completely irresistible he looked from behind, especially with no shirt on. She shivered a bit as she pulled her sweater over her head and tossed him his T-shirt as he walked back into the room.

"I should be hiding that instead of giving it to you," she said with a little smile.

Luc caught the T-shirt with one hand and pulled it on. He crossed the room and wrapped his arms around her, letting his hands rest on her ass. She hadn't put her jeans on yet and he ran his fingers along the bottom edge of her panties, his body responding to the feeling of her smooth skin

"I don't want to go. I'm being selfish, but I want to wake up with you in my arms in the morning. I've been wanting to do that since I met you," he said in a low voice.

Megan nuzzled her face into his neck and closed her eyes. She could feel Luc's arms wrapped around her, and she felt so safe with him there to hold her. "I wish there was some way we could spend the night in each other's arms tonight."

"But it's not a good idea. I should call a cab."

"Not yet, Luc. Can we just hold each other for a little while longer?"

"Of course, *mon ange*, if that is what you want."

Picking up a plush blanket from the armchair, he held her hand and led her back to the couch. They sat together and Luc wrapped her in his arms, covering them in the warmth of the blanket. Megan rested her head on his chest. She could feel him running his fingers slowly up and down her arm. The feeling of it was hypnotic. Exhaustion overtook her and Megan fell promptly asleep. Luc sat awake for a long time, trying to figure out what his next move should be. Somehow their relationship had taken a turn he had never expected and had certainly never wanted.

These past few days had offered him a glimpse of a different life. Her life. And he was shocked by how much it had fulfilled him. It wasn't about money or excitement or anything else he had believed to be important. Luc had taken care of Megan in a moment of uncertainty and fear; he had eased her burden and had loved every minute of it. He had fully enjoyed spending time with her mom and her little boy, playing with Elliott and cooking for them all. He had revelled in the satisfaction of caring for Helen and helping Megan out. And it had had nothing to do with her gratitude. It had been a gift to *him* to be welcomed into their family with open arms. He hadn't been part of a family for so long, and when he had, it was just him and his mother. As hard as his mother had tried, there was always an air of loss and loneliness in their home. Here, for the first time, he felt none of that. Only the warmth and fullness of belonging in a happy home. Now that he had made these connections and had felt how rewarding they could be, he wouldn't be able to pretend he didn't know what he had been missing. *But I can't be a part of their lives. I'm not built that way*, he told himself as he finally gave in to much needed sleep.

* * *

The fire had gone out and the house was completely dark. Megan dreamed that she was sleeping in Luc's arms, warm and happy. She could feel his muscular chest pressed against her back, and she needed to feel him inside her. She reached behind her and, finding his jeans open, she put her hand inside his boxer briefs, where she found him hard and waiting for her. She could feel his hand start to move over her shirt, caressing her breasts, gently squeezing them. In her dream, Luc's hand slid down into her panties, rubbing along her sex. She was wet, her body begging for him to enter her.

Megan lowered his briefs, getting them out of the way of his cock as it strained to get to her now. She could feel him move her panties aside and she wriggled her hips to find his hard length, pushing the tip of it inside her. Luc's hand was in front of her, fingers caressing her gently and carefully. Megan arched her back as he pushed his way inside her in one quick move, causing her to moan with pleasure.

The feeling of his skin against hers was perfection. He moved slowly behind her, rubbing himself against her ass. Was this really happening or was she still dreaming? It felt so real, so passionate, that she knew it would not take her long to come.

His hand moved up her shirt and under her bra, squeezing her breasts and rubbing her nipples as he rocked forward and back. Megan reached behind her and grabbed his ass with her hand, pulling him further into her, urging him to go deeper, faster.

"*Oui, oui*, Megan," he whispered in her ear.

She could feel his cock twitch inside her as he started to come in bursts. She joined him with her own slow orgasm pulsing through her, bringing intense pleasure to her entire body. She moaned and sighed happily, still dreaming. His arm gripped her firmly as they lay there, bodies pressed together on the small space of the couch.

* * *

Megan woke with a start. The house was pitch black and she sat up and fumbled around for her cellphone to see the time. It was 5:30 a.m. *What if Elliott had woken up?* she admonished herself. *This is the last thing he needs to see.*

Realizing she didn't have her jeans on, she reached around on the floor until she found them, then quietly stood. Luc was fast asleep with his head resting on a throw pillow. She watched him for a minute, trying to decide if she should wake him or not. She couldn't bring herself to do so and instead tiptoed up the stairs to her own bed. What could be the harm in Elliott finding him asleep on the couch in his clothes? Exhausted, she collapsed onto her bed, pulling the covers up over herself and going immediately back to sleep.

* * *

Two hours later, she awoke to the smell of coffee brewing and the sound of Elliott and her mom chattering away with Luc in the kitchen. Looking at the clock, Megan jumped out of bed. "Shit!" she exclaimed. She would be late getting Elliott to school if she didn't hurry.

She brushed her teeth, threw on a bathrobe and jogged down the stairs, eyes wide and hair a mess. When she got to the kitchen, she stopped. Elliott was already dressed and eating a bowl of cereal at the table while Luc packed his lunch kit.

Luc looked rumpled in the same T-shirt and jeans, with his hair messier than normal. Megan's heart ached at the sight of him. He was so handsome and had slid so effortlessly into their lives. Here he was, making breakfast and packing Elliott's lunch as though these were things he had been doing for years. He smiled at Megan, but in his eyes was a look of concern. She could tell he was worried that she would be upset he had stayed the night.

Megan smiled back gratefully. "Good morning," she said as she walked over and gave Elliott a kiss on his forehead.

"Morning, Mom! Luc made my breakfast, and now he's packing my lunch for me. I said we should wake you up but he thought we should let you sleep a bit more."

"Thank you, Luc. That is really sweet of you," Megan replied as Luc handed her a coffee.

She held the mug in both hands, feeling the warmth of it before she took a sip. "I should run upstairs and get dressed to take Elliott to school. I might take a quick shower, if you don't mind holding down the fort for a few more minutes."

"Go ahead. We've got everything under control here. Elliott is teaching me how to get kids ready for school."

Megan gave him a big teasing grin. "Good. So you'll know what to do in case you decide to start a daycare as your next big business venture."

Helen looked up from her toast. "Megan, can you drive me over to my house after you drop Elliott off at school? I'd like some time at home to pay some bills and pick up a few things. I'll be fine on my own for a few hours."

"Okay, Mom."

She hurried up the stairs to shower. As she started to undress, memories of the night before came flooding back into her mind. She and Luc had nearly had unprotected sex.

I'm acting like a horny teenager, she thought. *Thank God Luc pulled out in time.*

She was irritated with herself, realizing that her desire for him was so overwhelming she would have risked so much so stupidly just to be with him. She had never been this irresponsible in her life, even as a college student. Her heart sank as the realization that she was completely in love with him washed over her. She stood under the hot spray of water, knowing she would have to make him leave, and soon, before this went any further. She could not under any circumstances fall in love with this man. In her panic, she completely forgot about her dream.

* * *

"So, you must be really rich, right?"

"What makes you say that?" Luc replied mildly as he took a bite of his toast. He was seated at the table beside Elliott, who was finishing his second bowl of cereal.

"You took my mom on a private jet. Only rich people do that."

"That's solid logic, Elliott. It isn't polite for me to talk about it, but I guess you could say I have enough money to do what I want."

"Good. That means you can move here then."

Luc choked on his coffee. "Why is that?"

"I can tell you like my mom, so if you can do whatever you want, that means you can move here and help her out. I'm looking for someone to help my mom out. My friend Jase's parents are married to each other and it's nice, because his mom doesn't have to do everything for herself. Even if you aren't married, you could still help my mom. She'd like that," Elliott replied.

"Oh, well," Luc stumbled to find the right words, "it's not quite as simple as that. I have a lot businesses that I have to run in different parts of the world. I can't just leave it all and move here."

"Why not? You can just pay people to look after your businesses, can't you?" Elliott looked perplexed as he tried to piece this together.

"Ah well, true, but when you own businesses like I do, you're responsible for keeping an eye on everything to make sure that things are running smoothly. You owe it to the people who work for you to have a job for them. Does that make sense to you?"

"Sort of, I guess. But if your businesses are all over the place, you could live here and then keep going to check on them, couldn't you?"

Luc didn't notice that Megan had stepped into the room a moment earlier. "Elliot, if you're done eating, you need to run upstairs and brush your teeth."

"Can Luc take me to school, Mom?" Elliott asked as he passed her on his way upstairs.

"No, buddy. He's got to get going. He has to go back home today." Megan avoided looking at Luc while she spoke.

"Aw, really?" Elliott whined. "But when will he come back?"

"Just go brush, we're going to be late!" she replied impatiently.

Luc eyed Megan uncertainly as she unzipped Elliott's lunch kit to check it. She quickly zipped it back up. "Thank you for all your help," she said without looking up.

"I've done something to upset you," he said quietly as he stood and walked toward her.

"No," she said quickly, turning away and going to the closet. "Um, it's just . . . We'll have to talk about it later. I should get Elliott to school."

Luc rubbed his cheek with his hand, feeling the stubble against his palm. There was nothing more he could say with Helen standing at the door with them.

Elliott came running down the stairs and Megan handed him his coat. He slipped it on and rushed over to Luc.

"Here," he said, placing a tiny green soldier in Luc's hand. "So you know I'm still your friend, even when you aren't here."

Luc gave him a surprised look. "Are you sure you want to give me this? You just got it."

"Yup! I'm sure I want you to have it. Besides, I have a whole box of them!"

Megan stood by the door with her coat and boots on, holding his backpack out to him. "Come on, Elliott. We really have to go."

Elliott gave Luc a big hug and then held his hand out to do a fist bump. Luc returned the gesture. "Goodbye, Elliott. I've had such fun getting to know you."

"Me too!" Elliott called back as he hurried over to Megan.

"See you in a bit," Megan said, her voice expressionless.

Luc sat, holding the small toy in his hand, not sure what had just happened. Elliott had grown so attached to him that he had just asked him to move here. Megan's demeanour had changed completely since her shower. It seemed like she couldn't get rid of him fast enough. It didn't take a genius to figure out why she was worried. She knew he would never make a good father for Elliott, and she had as much as just told him to leave. The night before, he and Megan had come dangerously close to admitting they were in love, which was the only rule they knew they couldn't break in order for this to work. He was going to break Megan's heart and her little boy's too if he stuck around much longer. Luc could never live with himself if he became that guy who showed up to get what he wanted and then abandoned them over and over again. Helen was recovering quickly, and Megan didn't need him to stay any longer to help her out.

* * *

After dropping her mom at her house, Megan pulled over on a side street. Helen had been quiet during the ride, having noticed what was going on between her daughter and Luc. Before Megan left her mom's house, Helen had given her upper arm a little squeeze. "I know this is scary. Things have maybe moved a bit fast in the last few days, but it's going to be alright if you let it happen, Megan. He's a good man. I can see it. Let him in, honey."

Megan had looked away from her mom's gaze, trying to blink back her tears. She nodded at the floor before turning to leave. "I'll be back in a couple of hours, Mom."

Now as she sat in her car, she needed to figure out what to say to Luc when she got home. Her mind was swirling with everything the week had brought. Her heart ached as she thought of the man at her house. She wished she could just rush home and spend the entire morning in bed with him. How was she going to find the strength to push away the one thing she needed most? Resting her head on her hand, she slumped down in the seat. It all felt too hard to Megan. The need to be the good mom, to be ever-vigilant of her responsibilities, had never felt like more of a burden than it did now.

Megan's ears took in the horrible cry of her fourteen-month-old Elliott as soon as she opened the front door of her house. It was an early summer evening, and she had been out for a long-overdue and well-needed night out with Harper. She hadn't been away from the baby or Ian in months, not since Ian's shoulder injury. She had cared for both of them tirelessly and finally had been able to have a few precious hours of not being responsible for anyone. She and Harper had sat on a restaurant patio, laughing until their faces hurt and lounging in the fading sun while they drank sangrias and ate appetizers for dinner. Megan was still smiling as she stepped out of the cab and practically skipped up the sidewalk to her home. It felt so nice to just be Megan, the fun-loving young woman, for a few hours.

Now, as she closed the door behind her, she realized there was something frantic about the baby's cry; it was a sound she had never heard from him before, and it made her blood run cold. Flinging off her heels, she ran across the cool tile floor of their expansive living room, her bare feet making a slapping sound with each step. She took the stairs two at a time, knowing something must be very wrong.

Bursting through the door to Elliott's room, she gasped, seeing him red-faced, sitting up in his crib, covered in vomit. His arms were outstretched, and he took no notice of her as she rushed across the room, shushing him. As she swooped him up into her arms, she gave no thought to her beautiful coral silk dress, which was quickly becoming soaked with urine and vomit.

She pressed her lips to his forehead, now feverish and drenched from crying, as he continued to scream. Her nose was assaulted by the pungent scent of his little body as she rushed to the bathroom to draw him a warm bath.

"It's okay, baby. It's okay, Elliott," she soothed with a quiet, reassuring voice, although she felt no sense of the calm she was trying to convey. Where the fuck was Ian? Why hadn't he come when Elliott began to cry? Was he okay?

She put Elliott on a towel and stripped off his light sleeper and diaper, depositing both in the Diaper Genie and slamming the lid shut. A second gasp escaped her lips as she cleaned his bottom with a wipe, revealing an angry red rash. He had been sitting in his soiled diaper for what must have been a very long time.

Tears of guilt and pity rolled down Megan's cheeks as she placed her baby in the water, which she tested first against her wrist. As he sat in the bath, finally registering that his mother's hands were washing him, his screams finally subsided into the heart-wrenching, shuddering breaths of a child who has been left to cry too long.

Megan sang his favourite song as she continued to bathe him, draining the tub once to rid it of filth and then refilling it with fresh, warm water.

"You are my sunshine . . ." she sang quietly as she lathered baby shampoo into the wisps of white-blond hair that covered his little head. Her brain was trying to register how this had happened. Had Ian left him here alone? What could possibly have happened?

She finally lifted Elliott out of the tub and pulled the stopper as she bundled him into a fluffy towel on her lap and rocked him back and forth slowly. He must be starving, she thought. Elliott's little hand touched her cheek and he smiled now. "Mom, mom, mom," he cooed.

"Come on, little man, let's get your jammies on and give you a nice bottle. Would you like a bedtime snack?" She whisked him back into his room, where she slathered his bottom with diaper cream in an attempt to combat the violent rash it bore.

Taking him to her bedroom, she quickly slipped her dress off, tossing it onto the floor and pulling on a bathrobe so she wouldn't transfer everything back to her son now that he was clean. She carried him down to the kitchen, looking for her husband. She saw no sign of him. Where could he be? Hurrying down the stairs to the basement, she finally found Ian passed out in a prone position on the couch in the basement rec room. At first her pulse raced, thinking he might be dead. As she reached him, she could see a line of drool hanging from his mouth, about to land on the floor. One arm hung off the couch, his fingers still touching a half-finished bottle of beer. Five other empties were scattered around the coffee table.

Her relief in finding him alive was fleeting, quickly being replaced by fury as she saw that the baby monitor was turned on and facing the couch. The volume was turned up, meaning he would have heard even the tiniest sound Elliott had made that evening. None of it had registered with him. Drawing a deep breath, she turned with Elliott in her arms, taking him back to the kitchen to feed him. She would deal with Ian later. An hour later, she gently placed her little boy, now with a full belly, into his crib, having changed the sheets when she had brought him back upstairs. His little hand clutched her robe tightly and he whined in protest, burying his face in her chest when he saw that they were back in his room.

"It's okay, baby. Mommy's not going anywhere. I'll stay right here with you."

She lulled him to sleep in the rocking recliner in his nursery, singing softly and tracing small circles on his temples with her fingertip. As she pressed her lips to his forehead, she could smell that wonderful, clean aroma of lavender baby shampoo. His grip finally loosened when he dropped into a deep sleep, allowing her to put him in his crib and cover him with a light blanket.

Megan sighed as she gingerly picked up the soiled sheets and tippy-toed out of his room, leaving the door open partway. Her heart pounded now with anger as she crossed the house, carrying the disgusting sheets. She tossed them into the washing machine, then washed her hands before going back to downstairs to face her husband.

He had been taking too many painkillers lately for his shoulder injury, enough that she had started to worry about it. Up to that evening, however, she had trusted him completely, believing he would never do anything to put their son in harm's way. Her pace quickened as she made her way down the stairs. Staring at her husband, her blood boiled with a rage she had never felt before. He had gotten drunk, mixing his pain meds with booze, leaving their baby crying, confused, traumatized and effectively abandoned.

Bending over him she poked him hard on the arm, yelling, "Are you awake? Wake up!"

His response was a low grunt. He slurred "Later" at her and continued to sleep.

In her first and last act of violence, Megan raised her right arm above her head so forcefully that her feet were lifted into the air, then drove her fist into Ian's back with a viciousness that shocked her. Her fist landed with a loud thump against his flesh, causing the slightest movement from his hand, waving her away.

"You fucking asshole!" she screamed in his ear as loudly as she could before she made her way up the stairs, sobbing furiously.

She spent the night in the Elliott's room, with a kitchen chair tilted under the doorknob to keep Ian out if he happened to wake up. She had put it there not out of fear, but out of concern for what she might do to him if he tried to talk to her now. She sat reclined in the armchair, watching her son sleep, getting up to pat his back gently when he stirred.

There was no sleep for Megan that night. Not even the briefest moment of rest came to her. She hadn't realized the extent of the problem Ian had been hiding from her. He should have been off the painkillers three months ago but had still been getting them from his doctor. Megan knew she couldn't risk Elliott's safety by staying with Ian. When he woke the next day, she would tell him what he had done. She would tell him that unless he got help immediately, she would take Elliott and leave. The fear of losing them would be enough for him to turn things around. She knew it would.

But then doubt crept over her as she watched Elliott sleep. What if Ian didn't get clean? She had to be prepared to leave. She had to mean it when she said it the next day, and she would have to follow through no matter how much it tore her or Ian apart. She couldn't let Elliott live with a drug addict.

As she sat watching her little boy sleep, she vowed to him that she would never again allow him to be hurt by his father, or any other man, for that matter. She would remain vigilant and keep him safe, no matter what it took.

Boulder—Present Day

Megan straightened up in her seat, starting her car again and pressing the gas pedal. Propelling herself forward, she knew she had to do whatever was necessary to protect herself and Elliott. She would find the strength to send Luc away. Elliott and her mom needed her now. She wouldn't let them down for her own selfish desires. She wouldn't allow herself to become further lost in Luc. She had proven that she couldn't control herself around him and that she was incapable of having a casual relationship with him, which was all he could offer her. If she let him stay, she would only be allowing another man to abandon her son.

Megan took a deep breath before opening the door that led from the garage to the house, preparing herself for what she was about to do. When she entered the kitchen, Luc, who was sitting at the table, looked up from his computer with a wary expression. They stared at each other for a moment, both reluctant to say anything just yet, knowing this was the end. If they didn't start talking, they might be able to fool themselves for another moment that things were going to be okay.

Luc watched as Megan slowly took her boots off and hung up her coat. She stepped silently over to the counter and poured herself another coffee.

"So, I guess we should talk about what's happening here," Luc said quietly.

Megan leaned against the counter, not wanting to come any closer to Luc. It would make it too hard to push him away. "I guess we have to. This fantasy seems to have crossed over into my real life now in a way that neither of us wanted it to."

"Yes. I would say we're at a fork in the road now. One direction takes us into the unknown and the other takes us both back to our old lives." Luc stood and crossed the room to her. He leaned against the island so he was facing her with no barrier between them. "Why don't we start by trying to imagine what would happen if we go into the unknown together?"

"We'll get hurt. All three of us will get badly hurt," Megan replied with a tight-lipped expression.

Luc folded his arms across his chest. "Maybe. Maybe not. What if there was a way to make this work?"

"I don't think there is a way, Luc. It's gone too far. Elliott has clearly decided that he wants you as a permanent fixture in his life, which just isn't going to happen. You're not going to give up everything that makes you who you are to come and live here. You wouldn't be happy. We're not going to move to France either. I can't take Elliott away from his entire life like that, away from my mom. My business is just starting to take off. I can't start over after all the time I've put in."

Megan stared at Luc, wanting him to disagree, wanting him to wrap her up in his strong arms and tell her everything would be okay and that he would love her forever. If he reached for her now, she would give in and she knew it. She would risk it all to feel the love they had shared in the past days. But she knew he wouldn't. He wasn't built that way.

"I suppose you're right," Luc agreed reluctantly. "There isn't a logical or easy solution here."

"And the risks are just too high, Luc." Megan put her coffee cup down and ran her fingers through her hair with both hands, getting it out of her face.

"If this were a business proposal, I would agree that the risks are too high and the chance of a favourable outcome is too low. I have never wanted a family. I don't think I'm meant for that, no matter how much I might want it at this moment. I'm so sorry I can't offer you both more," Luc replied.

Megan nodded, staring at her socks. She had been right. He didn't want this. "You've been honest all along, Luc. There is no one to blame here. If my mom hadn't gotten sick and we could have kept things the way they were, we could have stretched out this whole arrangement for a little while longer, but the reality is that it was always going to end this way."

Luc kept his eyes on her, looking for any sign, however small, that she might be open to allowing this to work. If she would give him even the tiniest hint she wanted him to stay, he would happily drop everything to see this through. He had never felt such a strong pull toward anything in his life, and a part of him felt as though this was exactly where he was meant to be. Here, in this little house in Boulder with Megan and Elliott, starting a life together. But he knew that his desire for this life would soon fade, just as his enthusiasm for everything else had always faded. And when it did, he would become bored and restless and start looking for ways to get out. His rejection of Megan and Elliott would just add to the lifetime of heartbreak they had already suffered, and that would make Luc no better than his own father.

"I should go back to the hotel to get my things. We both have to get on with our lives, and the longer I stay, the harder this will be." Luc's voice was thick with emotion as he spoke. He wanted nothing more than to wrap his arms around Megan and carry her up to her bed. Instead he turned and walked to the table to pack up his computer.

"Do you mind taking a cab? I don't want to drag this out."

"Of course."

Megan quietly walked up to her bedroom and shut the door. She needed a minute to get herself together before the cab came to take him away. Tears streamed down her cheeks as she leaned against the door for support. She let them fall for a few minutes before hurrying to the bathroom to splash cold water on her face. She couldn't let him see her cry, and with the years of practice she'd had hiding her tears from her son, she knew she could do a pretty convincing impression of someone who was going to be fine. Drying her face with a hand towel, she took a few deep breaths before walking out of her room and back down the stairs.

She found Luc standing at the front door, coat and shoes on, watching out the window for the cab. He turned when he heard her descending the staircase and took in the sight of her one last time. Megan managed a tight-lipped smile and a confident head nod in his direction, as if to assure him she would be fine. It nearly broke Luc's heart to see her so tough after how vulnerable she had been the night before. It was an act and he knew it.

She crossed the room and stood near him. "You've got everything?"

Luc watched her for a moment, sensing her closing off from him. "Yes, thank you," he replied with an awkward formality.

"Good."

"Megan, are you—" Luc started.

"Don't," she interrupted, shaking her head. "Don't ask me that. We're making the smartest decision. It's the only one that makes sense. We're going to have to leave it at that."

Outside, the cab pulled up and honked once, causing both of them to look outside for a moment.

Luc reached out his hand and held hers, then pulled her to him. He wrapped his arms around her tightly and gave her a kiss on her temple. Megan let herself melt into him one last time, breathing in the scent of him and feeling the warmth of his strong body against hers. She kept her face down, buried in his chest. Luc pulled back a little and lifted her chin with one hand, kissing her tenderly on the lips. He lingered there, allowing them both to have one final taste.

"Goodbye, *mon ange*," he whispered.

"Goodbye, Luc," she replied, her voice breaking ever so slightly. With that, he was gone.

TWENTY-TWO

Megan stood in the window, watching the cab take him down the street and out of her life forever. She felt broken in a way she hadn't felt before. Sobs escaped her, shaking her entire body, as she collapsed onto the couch. She was completely, madly in love with Luc, and now he was gone. She would have to pick up the pieces and move on, like she had done before.

After a few minutes, she made her way into the kitchen to find some chocolate. A note on the table caught her eye. It was for Elliott. There was a surprisingly good cartoon drawing of a boy who looked like Elliott next to a snowman in a beret. It read:

> *Elliott,*
> *Remember that you will always have a friend in an old guy with a funny accent. Thank you for the soldier. Always know you are important and are meant for great things.*
>
> *Luc*

Megan wept at the note. Luc was capable of so much more than he would allow himself to be, and it killed her. If the circumstances had been even a little bit different, they would have found true happiness with each other. Regret and pain settled over her like a horrible storm cloud.

Megan's thoughts were interrupted by the phone. It was her brother, Mark. She wiped her tears and cleared her throat before she answered.

"Just calling to see how Mom's doing."

"She's a lot better. I just dropped her off at her house for a couple of hours. She wanted to do some paperwork."

"You sure you don't want me to come get her? Lenna's home and we'd both be there to look after her until she's feeling better."

Megan took this as a subtle dig from her older, more put-together brother. "What is that supposed to mean? Just because I don't have a man, it doesn't make me incapable of taking care of our mom."

"No, of course that's not what I was thinking. What crawled up your butt? I'm just trying to help here. You've been handling everything so far, and I thought you could use a break, that's all," Mark retorted.

"Sorry, I just . . . had a rough night. I shouldn't take it out on you. Listen, we'll be fine, I'm sure."

"Okay. Well, at least send me the hospital bill. I can probably cover most of it for her and then see if I can set up a payment plan or something."

"Um, it's been taken care of, actually."

"What?"

"Long story. I have a friend with lots of cash and not enough ways to spend it."

"What? Who? We can pay our own bills."

"It's complicated and it's really nothing to worry about, okay?

"You sure? That doesn't feel right to me."

"I'm sure. We'll just have to leave it the way it is."

"I just wish I lived closer so I could do more."

"I know you do. And listen, I'm sorry about before. I know you were just trying to help."

"That's okay. Megs, you sure you're alright?"

"I'm fine. Really. I better go get Mom. I don't want to leave her alone too long." Megan dug her fingernails into her palm to keep her voice steady. She couldn't talk about this with her brother, or anyone else, for that matter. Harper had been right all along. She knew Megan wouldn't be able to handle having a no-strings-attached relationship, but Megan had fooled herself into thinking she could. Now on top of her heartache, she felt like a complete idiot.

* * *

Luc slouched in a chair in the airport lounge, waiting for his connecting flight to New York. A large plastic bag sat on the chair next to him, holding his now-crumpled tuxedo and the purchases he had made with Elliott. In the past week he had lived a different life, had fallen in love and had it yanked away from him before he could even get used to it.

He needed to put as much distance between himself and Megan as he could. A horrible empty feeling had settled over him and his stomach churned. He realized he hadn't felt this type of grief since his mom had died. He was not built for this type of emotion. He was a man in control of himself and his world, only not this time. Somehow Megan had stripped him of his self-control and made him question everything he thought he knew with just her smile, the touch of her hand, her laugh, her kiss. He had never known such fierce and complete love before, and he knew without a doubt that this was the real thing.

She made him happy and filled him up in ways he hadn't known were possible. She had stilled his restlessness where no one and nothing else ever had before. He needed her, and Luc Chevalier hadn't *needed* anything in his entire adult life.

He took the little green soldier out of his pocket and stared at it for a moment, thinking of Elliott. Elliott needed him to stay away. Luc would prove only another bitter disappointment. He shoved the toy back into his jacket pocket as the first boarding announcement was made. No matter how much he ached for Megan, he would never be what she and Elliot needed.

* * *

That night, Luc boarded the red-eye to Paris, feeling utterly drained of energy. Despite having had a couple of glasses of Scotch at the airport, he ordered one more on the plane. He nodded off, hoping that when he woke he would be home and that being home would make him feel more like himself again. He knew he was making the best choice for Megan and Elliott, no matter how much it hurt at the moment. He would get over it. He was a man who had never expected a forever anyway.

He dreamed of Megan. In his dream they were on the couch, making love. He could feel his hand under her bra, the lacy fabric pressing against the back of his hand as he caressed her breast. He could feel himself pushing further inside her as she arched her back. He woke with a start, sitting straight up. "Oh shit!" he exclaimed under his breath. The well-dressed elderly woman beside him glared in his direction. He adjusted himself, grateful he had a magazine on his lap at the moment.

"Sorry. It was a bad dream. I apologize if I have offended you."

Luc waited a minute before getting up to make his way to the bathroom to splash some cold water on his face. Had he really had unprotected sex with Megan last night? Or was it just a very vivid dream? He couldn't be sure unless he asked her, but how could he do that after leaving so suddenly? He had been so exhausted the night before, it was almost like being intoxicated. Maybe it *was* just a dream. It had to be. Megan would have woken up and stopped him. Wouldn't she?

"Oh fuck," he said to his reflection. "What have I done?"

TWENTY-THREE

Boulder—Four Days Later

"Mom! For the fiftieth time, you need to wait for help to come down the stairs!" Megan barked from the kitchen, rushing to help Helen. She had just gotten home from dropping Elliott off at school and had been about to start editing some photos.

"Don't yell at me, young lady!" Helen replied sternly. "I'm just fine. I can hold the railing and I'm feeling much better."

"Can you just let me help you a little? Honestly, you're so stubborn sometimes."

"Hmm, who else do you know that might be like that?" Helen said, raising her eyebrows at her daughter and pursing her lips.

Megan rolled her eyes and sighed. "Just call me when you want to walk down the stairs, alright?"

Her fingers gripped her mother's elbow firmly as they descended the staircase. When they got to the living room, Helen swatted her daughter's hand away. "I'm fine!" she insisted.

Walking slowly to the kitchen sink, Helen turned on the tap to let the water run cold while she reached for a glass in the cupboard.

Tilting her head back caused her to get dizzy again, and she wobbled a bit. Megan held her arm behind her mom's back to steady her and got the glass down. She gave her mom a peck on the side of her forehead and filled the glass for her.

"You've been helping me for years. Let me take care of you for a few measly days, at least."

Helen sighed. "I just hate feeling like a burden. You've got enough to deal with."

"I'm fine, Mom. Really."

"You keep saying that, but I don't believe you. Why don't you tell me what happened with that handsome man of yours? He left in quite a hurry."

Megan's shoulders slumped. "I did tell you. He had to go back home to his life and his job. It was just a casual thing anyway. It's really better that he went before we got too attached. It would never have worked for anything permanent, and neither of us wanted that anyway."

"Okay," her mom said skeptically. "If you say so." Helen made her way over to the table and eased herself into a chair. "Come and sit for a minute."

Megan did as she was told, giving her mom the same blank stare she used to give her when she was a girl and hoped to hide something she shouldn't have done.

"Listen, Megan, I want to tell you something important, something you *need* to hear. Life's short, my girl. Really fucking short."

Megan's eyes popped open at her mom's foul language.

Helen raised a finger at her daughter. "That's right. I said *fuck*. I want you to remember this moment. You young people don't understand how fast it all goes by. One minute you're thirty-five and the next you're dead. That's just the way it is. We all get only one shot at living the life we are meant to. You have to decide how you want to spend your life now, because if you think you can postpone it, you're wrong. It's *happening* while you're trying to hide from it. Your dad was here and then, in a blink, he was gone. I thought it was over for me last weekend, but I got lucky. I'm still here. And I'm going to make the most of it. I'm not going to be afraid anymore."

"Okay, Mom. Good."

"No!" Helen slapped her hand on the table for emphasis. "Don't just say 'good' as though I'm not talking about you! I don't want to watch you hiding away from love anymore! That's enough already. Ian turned out to be a bum. A horrible, fucking disappointment, but *you* are letting him ruin the rest of your life and that's your fault, my girl. That's on you. When you get to the end of the line, you'll regret not having given love a chance. Now, I hardly know Luc, but I can tell you two have something there. I saw how he looked at you, and I know everything he did for us. That's a good man, and you're a fucking idiot if you let him get away."

"When you decide to drop the F-bomb, you really let it fly," Megan interjected.

"Stop that," she ordered. "I'm not kidding. As soon as I'm feeling better, I'm going to ask Charlie to go on a trip with me for a few days. I want some romance in my life, and I'm going to get it. Being loved feels great, damn it, and I intend to spend the rest of my life being loved. And if it's not by Charlie, I'll move on to the next man and the next, until I find someone who sticks. I suggest you do the same. Now help me over to the couch, I want to watch the news."

Megan got up and helped her mom over to the living room. Helen patted her cheek a little too hard. "You're so beautiful and you're a wonderful mom to Elliott, but you can be as dumb as a rock sometimes."

* * *

That night Megan sat in bed, trying to read. Unable to concentrate, she sighed loudly and picked up her phone. There were no messages from Luc and she hadn't tried to contact him. She desperately wanted to talk to him but she didn't know what else to say. She had been waiting to feel stronger before she spoke to him, but she didn't know how long that would take.

She quickly typed a text to him and pushed Send before she could change her mind. You up?

A moment later, her cell buzzed. Yes. Just getting into bed. How is your mom?

Still dizzy but getting better each day.

Good. I'm glad she's getting better.

Can I call you? Megan's heart thumped in her chest as she pressed Send. She had to wait almost a full minute before a response came. Was he deciding if he wanted to talk to her? Was he with another woman already?

Yes, of course.

Megan felt a wave of relief rush over her as she dialed, but the sound of his voice as he answered the phone tugged at her heart. She could picture him lounging in bed with only a sheet covering his sculpted body.

"Hello, Megan." His voice was quiet.

"Hi." Megan swallowed hard, trying to find the right words. "I just wanted to thank you for everything."

"I told you that I never do anything I don't want to do," he replied, trying to brush off her gratitude.

Megan couldn't help but wonder if that included leaving her. "I know, but I just don't see how I can ever repay you for it."

"There's no need. It was nothing."

"But to me it meant everything," Megan responded.

"I'm glad I could help your mom, Megan. But I don't want you to feel bad about it. I did it because I wanted to, but if I thought it had made you feel somehow guilty, that would really bother me." Luc's voice softened.

"No, I don't want you to think that. I mean, I know you did it because you wanted to. I just want you to know I've never met anyone as generous and kind as you. You're really a remarkable man. I hope you know that."

Luc scoffed. "I'm so remarkable that you wanted me to leave."

So he didn't want to leave. "Luc, please don't say that. I didn't want you to leave—I *needed* you to. It's not the same. I couldn't keep our agreement. I thought I could do it, but I'm not as sophisticated as I hoped. I wish I could have been." Megan's voice broke as she spoke. She paused for a moment, trying to blink back her tears and force herself to find her strength.

Luc sighed audibly. Megan could picture him running his hand through his hair, and the thought of it made her body ache with longing.

"Falling in love doesn't mean you aren't sophisticated. It means you have a beautiful soul, one that won't let you hold back and keep up with the jaded lies you tell yourself. It's not a flaw to be vulnerable."

"It *is* a flaw, Luc, because it means we can't be together anymore, no matter how much either of us wants to be." Megan spoke quietly, staring out the window at the moon.

"You aren't the problem, Megan. It's me. I should have left you alone. I knew I would never be what you needed, and I selfishly pursued you anyway, thinking only of what I wanted."

"How do you know you would never be what I need? That sounds like bullshit to me, Luc. You were everything I needed when my mom got sick. You didn't just take care of me, you took care of Elliott and of her too. What if you *do* have what it takes to be with someone like me, Luc? What if you've been lying to yourself about not being capable of this, but you really are?" Megan's voice was now just short of pleading. She stopped herself before she said more. She wasn't going to beg. She had begged Ian and all it had done was rob her of her dignity.

Luc voice was sad. "You don't know everything there is to know about me, Megan. If you did, you would understand. What you do know should be enough to warn you off me, though. I am not a family man."

"Okay, Luc. I know enough about life to know that you need to trust someone when they tell you who they are," Megan answered. "You would never be happy in Boulder, shovelling snow and mowing the lawn. That would be hell for a man like you, who has spent his life in the most glamorous places in the world. I know that."

Luc pictured himself in Boulder, pushing a lawn mower in the summer heat. Immediately he could see an image of Megan smiling at him as he wiped his brow. A pang of longing hit him rather than the dread he would have expected. "I don't think either of us is willing to risk finding out if it would be heaven or hell. There's too much at stake."

Megan let out a puff of air, leaning her head against the headboard. "The fact that you seem to understand why I can't take chances makes this so much harder for me."

"Should I pretend I don't get it and that I'm angry with you? Would that help you?"

"It wouldn't work. You told me you'd be pretending."

"Listen, I need to know that you're going to be alright." Luc's voice was thick with emotion.

No! I'm not going to fucking be alright! This is going to hurt like hell! Megan did her best to sound convincing. "Of course, I'll be fine. I've been through much worse. I've got to go, okay?"

Luc paused. "I want you to promise me one thing, *mon ange*. Promise me you will call me if you ever need me. If you are in any type of trouble, ever, you let me know. I'll be there for you."

Tears rolled down Megan's cheeks as she listened to him, still wanting to care for her, even at the end. She nodded, forgetting he couldn't see her.

"Are you nodding?"

"Yes," she whispered, laughing a little at herself and at him for guessing what she was doing.

"Oh fuck, you're crying, aren't you? I'm so sorry, Megan. I wish I was there right now to hold you."

"Me too, but I'm pretty sure it would only make this much harder. Goodbye, Luc."

"Good night, Megan."

Paris—Two Weeks Later

Luc sat at his desk in the office at Cloud, looking over design boards with his decorator, René. The first club he had opened needed updating and he was in the final stages of approving designs. The phone rang and Luc pressed the hands-free button without looking up to see who was calling.

"Luc Chevalier," he answered, his voice impassive.

"Luc, you piece of shit! I hope you're ready to say goodbye to that big dick of yours! I told you'd I'd chop it off if you fucked over my best—"

He lunged for the receiver, picking it up before Harper could finish her sentence. He waved René out the door, avoiding the designer's wide-eyed, gape-mouthed expression as he exited the room and closed the door silently behind himself.

"Harper, calm down. Let me explain," he ordered.

"Oh, you can explain, can you?" Harper's voice oozed sarcasm. "Meg is sitting at home, broken-hearted, and you think you can talk your way out of this? Not fucking likely, asshole. You know what? After you pulled that bullshit cookie-cutter date in Paris, I told her she should give you the benefit of the doubt, but now I can see I was wrong. You're just another womanizing piece of shit who used her and threw her away like so much garbage."

"Harper, enough! I would have hung up by now if it were anyone other than Megan you were calling about. Now, I don't know what she told you, but she *wanted* me to go."

"*As if* she wanted you to go! She's completely in love with you. Fucking clueless male."

"Are you drunk?" Luc asked, his voice curt.

"No, I'm not drunk! I'm angry. You made her fall in love with you, got what you wanted and then you left her. Do you know how that makes *me* feel? Like a total shit friend. I'm the one who introduced her to you, I left her with you in Paris, thinking you'd take care of her, and now look what you've done to her. I can't believe how wrong I was about you. Shit, I'm stupid!"

Luc's jaw was set tightly, his eyes narrowed. If Harper could see him now, she would be a bit frightened. Simone walked into the office, took one look at him and backed out silently.

"Are you quite done?" he asked quietly.

"Are you sorry?" she retorted.

"Of course I'm fucking sorry!" he barked. "I've never felt so bad about anything in my life. I haven't slept in weeks, I've stopped going to kickboxing and I barely eat! All I do is spend every waking hour thinking about Megan, wondering what I should have done differently, trying to figure out if there's a way I can fix it, knowing she's upset, wishing I could just go there and be with her until she feels better! I don't need you to call me up threatening to cut off my dick. I have a conscience. Maybe Megan isn't the only one who was caught off guard by this, did you ever consider that?"

"What's that supposed to mean?"

"It means that I'm most likely in love with her too, but I don't know because I've never felt this way before. All I know is that I've never been this fucking miserable or pathetic in my life. I haven't enjoyed one single moment of anything since I got home, and I have no idea when or if I'll ever feel better."

Harper paused for a moment, feeling suddenly deflated by his words. "Oh. I didn't realize."

"Maybe you should get the other person's side of the story before you go on a rampage next time," Luc replied, still angry.

"Maybe." Harper's voice was petulant.

"What did she tell you, anyway?"

"Nothing. She just told me you two decided it was for the best you stop seeing each other. I sort of assumed the rest."

"You just assumed I'm a total asshole despite the years we've known each other. You've added insult to injury, Harper."

Harper sighed. When she spoke, her voice was small. "I'm sorry. I shouldn't have blamed it all on you."

"No, you shouldn't have. She wanted me to go. I was planning to stay for as long as she needed help with her mom. She realized things were getting too serious and that I shouldn't stay, so I left. I know she's right. Better now than later, when Elliott would get hurt."

"I don't get it. How are both of you so sure it couldn't work out? That doesn't make any sense."

"How could it work? Would they move to Paris and hang around my penthouse by themselves while I'm working nights and travelling? Or would I move to Colorado and start hosting barbecues for the other soccer parents?"

"You're a snob, you know that? What's wrong with Colorado?"

"You tell me. You moved away from there," he snapped.

"That's because of my work and my lifestyle," she retorted.

"So you and I are not that different, then, are we?"

"But I'm happy. You're fucking miserable, remember? Maybe you would actually love it in Boulder, hosting barbecues. How do you know if you don't give it a try?"

"It's not something you can experiment with!" His voice was harsh. "If it doesn't work, three people will be badly damaged in the process, one of them a very innocent little boy who doesn't have any say in any of it."

"Well, now I *know* you were made for each other. You're both too scared and stubborn to take a risk, so instead you're going to sentence yourselves to lives of misery and loneliness."

"We're just too different, Harper, and neither of us is naive enough to think that we'd be able to make it work."

"Wrong. You're *exactly* the same. You're a couple of idiots too scared to be in love with each other even though you'd be perfect together."

"Listen, I know you're just trying to help, but I have to go. I was in the middle of a meeting."

"Luc, don't let her get away. She could change your life. You could have it all, Luc. Everything worth having is waiting for you. You just have to go get it," Harper pleaded.

"In Boulder," he replied in a clipped tone.

"Does it matter where you find it, if it's the real thing?"

"I have to go, Harper."

"Goodbye. Sorry I threatened to cut your dick off. Call me if you need to talk, okay?"

"Don't worry about it. And no. I can't see myself doing that. Goodbye."

Boulder

Later that night, Megan sat at her computer after having calculated her projected earnings for the next few months. For the first time, she was going to have some leftover money. She smiled to herself, feeling proud of her accomplishments so far that year.

"This calls for some ice cream!" she exclaimed to herself, getting up and crossing the kitchen to the freezer.

The changes she had made to her website had helped her attract more clients. Her new, higher rates didn't seem to faze any of them, and she realized that this summer she was going to be handling four more weddings than she had during the same weeks the year before.

She thought about next winter and how she would certainly have a little extra money to put aside for Elliott's education as well as to pay someone to take on all the tasks she hated doing. No more shovelling for her!

Her first impulse was to call Luc to tell him about it, then she remembered she couldn't. They weren't together anymore and nothing was going to change that. As she heaped the cold vanilla treat into a bowl, she suddenly felt depressed. She got out a package of chocolate chips and some chocolate sauce, pouring enough of each into the bowl that the ice cream was no longer visible.

Sitting back at her computer, she looked at the numbers again as she slowly ate her snack. *Okay, Meg, get back to being happy already! You've done something amazing here. Let yourself enjoy the moment.*

Why should not having Luc in her life sully this moment for her? It didn't change what she had done in the least. And it wouldn't have been a big deal for a millionaire to find out she was going to have a few thousand extra, anyway. The more she thought about it, the more she convinced herself it actually would have been embarrassing to talk with Luc about it.

By the time she scraped the bottom of the bowl clean, she told herself it was all for the best. It was maybe the one hundredth time she had tried to assure herself of that since they had ended things. She wondered how many more times she would have to repeat that mantra before she actually believed it.

Paris

Luc finished locking up the club and decided to walk the twenty blocks to his apartment. It was well after three in the morning, but he was nowhere near ready to face going home to his empty bed. Stuffing his hands into his coat pockets, he strode down the steps of the club, seeing the full moon lending its soft light to the city. The sight brought none of its usual comfort to him. Instead, for the thousandth time since he had hung up the phone after his last conversation with Megan, his mind wandered to that talk. She had as much as admitted that she was in love with him. It was something he knew long before she had said it. He could see it when she looked at him and feel it when they touched. He thought of their last night together, at the possessiveness he had felt when they were making love. He had never in his life felt such a strong need to be inside a woman that he had lost his self-control like that. He had always been exceedingly careful, not wanting to end up tied down with a child. But with Megan that night, he had been willing to risk it. Part of him had *wanted* to make her his forever. His desire for her was so intense it terrified him.

Kicking a rock ahead of him, he followed its path along the sidewalk, then propelled it forward over and over as he made his way home. There was something soothing about this little ritual and he was desperate for some type of distraction. Anything to get Megan off his mind. Taking in a deep lungful of the chilly night air, he swore under his breath at the heartache he bore. He needed to shake this off, and soon. After all, why did he, at forty-one, suddenly think he would want to settle down?

He thought of his conversation with Harper earlier that day. Enough time had passed for him to be over his anger at how she had spoken to him, and now her words were slowly starting to sink in. *Luc, don't let her get away. She could change your life. You could have it all, Luc. Everything worth having is waiting for you. You just have to go get it.*

What if he followed his heart for once in his life? Everything about being with Megan felt more right than anything he had ever experienced before. He thought of her laugh, her smile as she looked at him with those bright green eyes. He could picture her curled up in his arms on the couch in front of the fire—her body absolute perfection, the smell of her hair, the curve of her neck. He could feel her hands skimming over his body, lovingly, greedily, longingly. He could feel her kiss. It was like none he had known before, so soft and passionate. She could tie him up in knots with that kiss. She was the one he wanted for the rest of his life and, deep down, he knew it. There would be no one else for him.

TWENTY-FOUR

Boulder—One Month Later

Megan rushed around the house the morning of Elliot's birthday party. She was a woman on a mission; she needed to get the decorations up, the food prepared and the tidying finished before the guests started arriving. She worked quickly and tried to appear happy and relaxed to Elliott and her mom, but inside she was a bundle of nerves. Her worst-case scenario would be if Ian showed up drunk or high. She hadn't told Elliott that Ian was definitely coming, even after he had emailed his flight itinerary, just in case he didn't show. Each time Elliott asked, she would say, "We'll see. I hope so."

Checking the time, she realized she had about forty-five minutes to get herself ready. She rushed up to her room to get showered and changed. A few minutes later, she stood wrapped in a towel in front of her closet, hair dripping on her shoulders, trying to decide what to wear. Why did it even matter so much to her? She selected a pair of dark jeans and a silk-blend, draped V-neck pullover with three-quarter-length sleeves in blood orange. She hurried to blow out her hair, deciding to leave it down for the day. Once her makeup was applied, she gave herself a once-over in the mirror, deciding she looked passable. Megan's heart was in her throat as she jogged down the steps to make sure Elliott had put his toys away.

The doorbell rang as the first of Elliott's friends arrived. In the next twenty minutes, Megan would greet another fifteen children from Elliott's class and send them out to the yard to play. It was a warm day and even though they needed light jackets, they all seemed to be having fun outside. The house and yard were a buzz of activity, laughter and yelling as Megan and Helen got a couple of pitchers of lemonade ready. They didn't hear the knock on the door, but Megan looked up when she heard Ian's voice.

"Hello?"

There in the doorway he stood, wearing aviator glasses, jeans and a slim-fit, dark grey military-style jacket. He wore his brown hair in a crewcut as usual, and he looked young and healthy as he smiled uncertainly at Megan. In one hand he held a large gift bag, and tucked under his arm was a bouquet of flowers. Megan walked over to the front door, not entirely sure how to greet him.

"Hi, Ian." She smiled up at him. "I'm glad you made it."

Ian stared at Megan for a minute, as if seeing her for the first time. "Meg, you look . . . terrific," he said quietly. He wanted to kiss her, but he didn't think that was proper etiquette when seeing your ex-wife.

"Thanks. You look great yourself," she replied warmly. Megan was filled with relief as he took off his sunglasses. His eyes were clear and he looked completely sober.

"These are for the hostess." He handed her the flowers.

"Oh, you didn't have to do that . . . Thank you. The kids are all out back. We were just going to bring them some lemonade."

She was interrupted by Elliott running in the back door. "DAD! You made it!" he screamed, running to his father.

Ian put the bag down beside Elliott and crouched down to scoop his son up in a hug. Elliott held on tight to his dad, burying his face in his dad's chest and wrapping his arms around his neck. Megan felt her heart twist at the sight of it. Elliott needed this.

"Come on outside! I want my friends to meet you!" He pulled his dad's hand and led him outside.

* * *

Several hours later, Megan was cleaning up the supper dishes as Ian read to Elliott in his room. She felt tired after the busy day but was relieved everything had worked out so well. This was the first special occasion in as long as she could remember that hadn't been overlaid with emptiness because of Ian's absence.

Megan plunged her hands into the hot, soapy water and started to wash the last of the glasses that wouldn't fit in the dishwasher. She suddenly felt like someone was watching her and she turned her head, seeing Ian leaning against the kitchen doorway, smiling at her. She could see the muscles in his large arms flex as he shoved his hands into his front pockets. He was still as handsome as ever.

Megan smiled back. "Is he asleep already?"

"Yeah, he was pretty tuckered out. Thank you for letting me put him to bed, Meg. It means a lot to me."

"Oh, well, it means a lot to him too."

Ian crossed the room to the counter and picked up a dishtowel to help. They stood beside each other, working quietly for a moment as though this were the most normal thing in the world for them to be doing together.

"He's an amazing kid. He's more like a little version of a grown man in some ways. Some of the things he comes out with just floor me."

Megan smiled at Ian's insight into their son. "He really is very mature for his age. I think it's from spending most of his time surrounded by grown-ups."

"I bet. It's pretty obvious you don't treat him like a baby and that's served him well."

Silence fell over them again as they worked. Megan reflected on how many years had gone by since they had done something as simple as cleaning up the kitchen together. "So, I thought maybe Georgie would come with you?"

"She had to work this weekend. She's an ER nurse."

"Oh, that must be stressful."

"She says it's hours of boredom interrupted by moments of sheer panic. How's your photography business doing?"

"Pretty good, actually. I've been keeping busy." Megan rinsed a glass, and Ian took it from her hand, letting his fingers brush against hers for a moment.

"Well, you always were so talented. It makes sense that you would be busy." There was a long pause before Ian spoke again. "I've been sober for over three months now. Been going to meetings every couple of days. Got a sponsor."

"Wow, good for you, Ian! I'm really happy for you." Megan smiled up at him, her voice sincere.

"Thanks. I feel good." Ian looked down at the glass in his hand and drew in a long breath. "Meg, I am so sorry for everything. I just wish I could go back to the time I was injured and refuse anything more than an Advil." Ian rubbed his face with his hand. "I know that words aren't ever going to be enough to fix what I've done, or how I've neglected Elliott and you . . . I just want you to know that things are going to be different from now on. I'm done disappointing you both."

Megan watched him talk, wanting to believe him.

Ian continued. "I know it's going to take a lot of time and work to rebuild the trust you had in me, but I intend to do it, starting with supporting you both more financially. I'm making more money now so I'm going to start putting more money in your account each month. I put an extra thousand in yesterday; it should be there by Monday. I know I've missed a lot of payments, so if you have a record of it, let me know, and I'll get caught up."

Megan let the water out of the sink and dried her hands on the dishtowel. "I don't have a record of it, actually. There didn't seem to be a point to it after a while."

Ian looked over at her. "You had to give up on me. I didn't leave you any choice. I failed you and I failed Elliott."

Megan swallowed hard and nodded in agreement. This was the first time he had acknowledged, out loud, any of the pain he had caused. From comments he had made from time to time, she knew he felt bad, but he had never been this honest. She leaned her back against the counter, feeling tears pool up in her eyes.

Ian sighed heavily and drew her to him, hugging her tightly. "I'm so sorry," he whispered, tears forming in his eyes as well. She let him hold her while they both let the full weight of the loss, the regret and the pain sink in.

"I fucked it all up, Megan, and I will never forgive myself for that. I have been a complete shit as a dad. I was a lousy husband too. If I could start again with you, I would do everything right this time. I would take care of you, love you like you deserve to be loved. I would be there for you and our son every day, like I should have been. You gave me everything and I just threw it all away. I missed it all. Our son turned seven today, and I missed everything. His first day of school, the first time he rode a bike, every Christmas and birthday until today. I don't even know if he still believes in Santa. And I don't know what any of this has done to him or to you. I've ruined three lives, and that's the worst of it."

Megan sobbed into Ian's chest, letting his words wash over her. It was everything she had wished he would realize and say to her. Nothing would take back all the years of neglect and distance, but at least she knew he finally understood what they had done to her.

Ian reached his hands up to her face and tilted her head back, looking into her eyes and wiping away her tears with his thumbs. "I'm so sorry, Megan. I hope you know I never stopped loving you, even when I had nothing to give. I know I hurt you so horribly, and you have never been anything but amazing to me."

Ian stared down at Megan, seeing the tears stream down her face—tears he had caused—knowing that these were just a fraction of the thousands she must have shed over the years. His heart broke at the sight of her like this. At that moment, he would have done anything to stop her from crying. He pressed his cheek to hers so she wouldn't see his eyes welling up again. Her tears were hot against his face. Her skin was so soft, the smell of her hair so familiar. Ian let his lips graze her cheek and then find their way to her mouth. He kissed her softly and slowly.

Megan allowed him to kiss her, overwhelmed by the depth of emotion they were both feeling, overcome by his tears. His kiss brought back a flood of memories. The passion, the love, the anger, the pain—all of it was there. He kissed her again, this time bringing his tongue into her mouth, exploring her passionately as he wrapped his arms around her in a tight embrace.

Megan pulled back, looking down at her feet to stop him.

"Let me stay the night, Meg," he whispered in her ear.

* * *

Outside on the sidewalk, Luc stood watching through the kitchen window, Megan in the arms of another man. As the couple walked away in the direction of the living room—or maybe Megan's bed-room—his heart felt like someone had reached into his chest and was squeezing it relentlessly. The man might have been Ian, based on a photo Luc had seen in Elliott's room, but from this distance he couldn't be sure.

In one hand Luc held a large gift bag for Elliott, containing a black hoodie like the one Elliott had picked out for him, along with the complete collection of his favourite comic, bound in hardcover. In his other hand, he had an increasingly tightening grip on a bou-quet of two dozen white roses. He had carefully tucked the real estate listing for his new house on Timber Lane into the bouquet. On the back of the listing he had written, *My life is meaningless without you. I will be right here waiting for us to start over. L.*

What had started out as the most exhilarating day of his life was now one of the most devastating. It had taken him close to sixteen hours to get to Boulder from Paris. He had gone straight from the airport to the new house to meet the realtor and the inspector. By the time the inspection and all the paperwork had been completed, it was late afternoon. He had decided to wait until Elliott was in bed before going over to Megan's.

It had been weeks since he and Megan had spoken, and he knew that what he was doing was both completely devoid of common sense and very risky. Although Luc was no stranger to risk, it was the first time he had ever wagered his heart. That didn't scare him, however; his heart didn't belong to him anymore anyway. He knew that any chance he had of getting Megan back depended on showing her how serious he was about making things work permanently.

Since making his decision, his heart had been full, his enthusi-asm nearly impossible to contain. Only a few hours earlier, his step had been lively and his smile easy as he looked around his new house, planning and dreaming of making it their home together.

This was supposed to be the day that they would start again, except this time they wouldn't lie to themselves about what they meant to each other. They were in love, and his moving to be near her would finally allow them to speak those words out loud, would allow them to be vulnerable, to take the chance that was theirs for the taking.

Luc exhaled sharply as the pain of seeing Megan in another man's arms seared through him. He had to fight every instinct that told him to kick down the door and use any means necessary to get that man away from the woman he loved. Luc clenched his fists tightly, his jaw matching them with such intensity it caused his teeth to grind together audibly. He realized in that moment that he would kill for her. She was his. And the sight of another man touching her brought out a rage so intense it was like nothing he'd known in his life.

There was no way he could create such a scene with little Elliott in the house. It would frighten and confuse him and drive Megan away from Luc. It looked like Megan was moving on anyway. He had had his chance with her, but he was too late. Using every bit of self-restraint he could muster, he tossed the flowers in the neighbour's garbage can and walked back to the car. He drove slowly down the street and away from her, his heart shattered.

If he had stayed another few minutes, he would have seen Ian leave, having been sent away by Megan.

TWENTY-FIVE

"Whoa, Megs, I don't even know what to say," Harper replied with a sigh. She had been sitting at her desk, gazing out at the Manhattan skyline for the past fifteen minutes as her best friend poured her heart out about Ian's visit the day before.

"It's really strange, you know? It was actually a good thing for me. It made me realize there really is no part of me that is in love with him anymore. Up until now, there was always a nagging question in the back of my mind. I wondered if Ian ever recovered, if we could pick up where we left off and be a family again. But now I see that could never happen. It's a relief to know that."

"Yeah, I guess. Do you think maybe that nagging question has been what's kept you from giving things with Luc a fair shot?"

"I don't know. I suppose part of me wanted to hold out in case Ian and I could make it work for Elliott's sake. Stupid, really. The eternal optimist hidden under the cloak of a jaded pessimist."

Harper smiled, thinking about how accurately her friend had just described herself. "You know, Megan, that might be the most insightful thing I've ever heard you say. I think deep down, most pessimists are really just people who are afraid of being vulnerable to life's disappointments."

Megan laughed. "Have you been hanging out with the Dalai Lama, by any chance?"

Harper laughed with her friend. "No! I'm just getting really insightful in my old age."

"Well, if you ever give up the magazine business, you should write a book of wisdoms," Megan teased.

"Yeah, yeah." Harper brushed off Meg's compliment. "Back to you. Does this change things between you and Luc?"

"No. Definitely not. There is no way anyone could make that work. That whole thing is long over."

"Hmm. Too bad. I really think you'd be perfect together. It's just a matter of logistics, you know."

Megan groaned. "Listen, it's much more than that. Luc doesn't want to be married any more than I do. He has his life, and it is far away and would never be right for me or for Elliott."

"I'm not saying it would be easy, but I think it would be worth it. I called him last month to yell at him, you know," Harper admitted.

"What?!"

Harper spoke quickly. "Don't get mad until you hear me out. I *may* have assumed he had ended things, then called and threatened to cut off his dick. He told me you sent him away, I apologized and we said goodbye."

"Ohhh, Haaarrrpppperrr . . ." Megan whined. "Seriously?"

"I'm sorry! I was only looking out for you. You're exactly right for each other and you both know it, deep down. You're also both too stubborn to admit that you need each other. You know, he told me he's in love with you."

"What?" Megan's voice was quiet.

"He told me he's in love with you. At least, he's pretty sure, but he's never felt this way before so he can't say with one-hundred-percent accuracy. If it were me, I'd be on the next flight to Paris to go get him. I'm just sayin'."

"If you were me, you'd know why you couldn't risk it." Megan shut her eyes tightly, as if that would shut out what she had just learned.

"Megan, I'm going to say something that might make you mad, but you need to hear it. And since you're already pissed at me right now, I might as well say it. I'm worried you're going to teach Elliott that he should be afraid to take chances in life, and that he'll never get married or find happiness."

Megan growled at her friend. "You're right."

"I am?" Harper's voice was hopeful.

"That made me mad."

"Oh. Damn. You're not going to stay mad at me too long, are you?" Harper sounded worried.

"I'm really pissed, but I'll get over it."

Harper gave it one last shot. "Think about it, okay? There's a reason you met. You could save each other, Meg. It could be everything you both need."

"I have to go. I need to stop at my mom's before I pick up Elliott from school. I'm looking after her orchids for a few days. I'll talk to you later, Harper." Megan sounded completely drained of all energy.

"Okay. I'm sorry. But think about it, alright?"

"I better not. I'll talk to you soon."

"Bye."

* * *

"Mom, these are beautiful!" Megan took a long whiff of the white roses displayed on her mom's kitchen table. "There must be eighteen of them!"

Helen beamed in the direction of the flowers. "Two dozen, actually. That Charlie, I don't know how to take him. Every time I try to thank him, he claims he found them in the trash outside his house." She laughed. "Honestly! That man."

"Sounds like it's going really well." Megan smiled at her mom.

"It is. I like him a lot." Helen grinned.

"I'm so glad for you, Mom. He's such a nice man. Now, show me how to keep these orchids from dying a horrible death while you're off cavorting in San Diego with my neighbour."

* * *

"Hello?" Megan cradled the phone under her chin as she finished spreading jam onto a piece of bread with a knife. It was late in the evening and she was trying to get a head start on the next day by making Elliott's lunch for school.

"Meg, it's Ian." His voice was quiet.

"Ian? Oh, hi."

"I just wanted to call to apologize for the other night. I was way out of line." His voice was full of regret yet again.

"Oh, Ian, let's forget about it, okay? It was just a really emotional moment between us. I'm fine, though, I promise." Megan's voice was soft as she spoke. She had turned and leaned against the counter to give him her full attention. The lunch could wait.

"I don't know what came over me . . ." He trailed off and paused for a moment. "Actually, I do. I just couldn't stand to see you cry like that. I didn't know what to do, so I kissed you. For some reason I thought that might stop you. I'm so stupid sometimes."

"We don't need to talk about it, Ian. I knew why you did it. We were both just caught up in the moment, I think. We've been through a lot together and we've never really had a chance to say goodbye, you know?"

"Yeah, I do. That's exactly it." His voice brightened.

"I know you're with Georgie now, and I really am happy for you. I just want you to stay clean and healthy so you can be a part of Elliott's life. A good part of his life."

"Me too. I'm really happy with her, actually. I know you and I can't ever go back to the way things were, but I really love Elliott and I want to see him a lot more. I didn't realize how much I'd really missed out on until I saw him. He's just getting so big. And he's a great kid, Meg, and that's all you. Everything good about him is from you."

"He's the best of both of us. Some of the most wonderful things about him are from you. He's such a talented athlete and he's adventurous, sometimes a little too much so, and he gets this little gleam in his eye when he's about to play a joke on someone that is pure you."

"Yeah, but I mean his values and his manners. The things you get from being raised right. That's all you. I owe you for taking that all on, Meg, and managing it on your own while I've been missing. I don't think there are enough ways I could ever thank you for that."

"Just stay clean, call Elliott every few days to talk and come and see him as often as you can. That's all I want."

"I will, Meg. I'm going to be a good dad from now on."

"I'm really happy to hear that. Now, I better go. Call back tomorrow to talk to Elliott?"

"I will."

"Excellent. Good night, Ian."

"Good night, Meg."

TWENTY-SIX

Boulder—Two Weeks Later

The late afternoon sun softened the blue sky, bringing a pink glow to the mountains in the distance. Elliott ran around the playground with his cousins while Megan stood at a picnic table with her sister-in-law, Lenna, as the two prepared supper. Charlie and Helen watched over the kids as Mark started the portable barbecue to cook hamburgers.

Mark and Lenna had come to Boulder with the kids for spring break. Megan clipped the tablecloth onto the old wooden table and was unpacking the condiments from the cooler when the first whiff of the cooking meat hit her nostrils. Her stomach churned as a wave of nausea hit her. Her face grew pale with a sickly green colour as she steadied herself, taking a slow, deep breath to try to recover.

"But I don't know. Maybe I should wait another year before going back to work full-time. I mean there's no . . ." Lenna's voice trailed off as she glanced up at Megan's face.

"Megan? Are you okay?" she asked quietly.

Megan's eyes met hers, now looking dull as another swell of

queasiness overtook her. "No," she replied softly. "It's the smell of the barbecue. It's making me sick."

"Come on, let's go for a little walk and get away from it." Lenna put a gentle arm around Megan, careful not to put any pressure on her as they moved toward the lake together.

Megan suddenly lurched forward to a nearby garbage can, emptying the contents of her stomach into it with three violent surges. Lenna hurried back to the table and grabbed a bottle of water and a napkin. She was back with Megan in seconds, pouring the liquid onto the napkin and handing it to her sister-in-law to wipe her brow and forehead.

"That was sudden, Megan. You seemed fine a few minutes ago." Lenna's voice was full of concern. "Here, have a sip of water."

Helen, seeing what was happening, hurried over to help. "What's wrong, sweetie?"

Megan was feeling a little better as she sloshed the water around in her mouth and spit it into the garbage can. "I don't know; that hit fast."

Lenna turned to her mother-in-law. "She got sick as soon as she smelled the barbecue. If I didn't know better, I'd think you were pregnant, Meg. That's how you were with Elliott."

* * *

Megan lay in bed that night staring at the ceiling for what seemed like hours. She was alone; Elliott had been invited to stay at his grandma's to be with his cousins. Megan had managed to act casual enough with Lenna and her mom, brushing her temporary illness off as something she had eaten. Helen gave her a long, questioning look when they all parted ways at the park but said nothing.

"Shit! Shit! Shit," Megan muttered as her eyes followed a beam of light created by a car passing her house. The room went black again as the sound of the car faded, leaving her utterly alone again. Tears streamed out of her eyes and down the sides of her face, falling into her hairline. A single drop managed to find her ear, bringing an itchy, wet sensation. She did nothing to stop the tears or wipe them away, but instead lay perfectly still, allowing them to pour out. Her throat held a lump so large that it had become difficult to swallow.

Panic consumed her. She was pregnant with Luc's baby. What she had thought was just a vivid dream had actually happened. On the way home from the park, she had mentally calculated when her last period had been. It was more than two months earlier. That wasn't the most unusual thing for her, however, as she had never been what she'd call regular. She had pulled into a drugstore on the way home and purchased three different brands of home pregnancy kits, all of which had confirmed her deepest fear.

Megan was already on her own with Elliot, and now, if she decided to go through with the pregnancy, she would have another mouth to feed. This time, she would have a difficult time explaining how that baby had gotten there. How would she explain it to Elliott? What would she say to the other moms at the school? What would she tell Ian? How would Luc react, finding out he was going to have a child in the world?

More and more fears and questions of how this would affect her life swirled around in her brain at a furious and unyielding pace. She cried until her eyes no longer had anything left to shed and her head pounded with the pain of it all. Sleep. She needed to sleep. Tomorrow she could figure out what to do. The answers would become clear in the morning.

* * *

The next morning found Megan sipping tea on her back deck, trying to let the warmth of the sun ease the tightly-wound ball of tension in her stomach. She was pregnant, and even though Luc lived in France, she had started to wonder if there might be a chance for them. Her mind wandered to her conversation with Harper. Luc had admitted to Harper that he had feelings for her. Megan knew without a doubt that she was completely in love with him. She hadn't been able to get her mind off him, even before she knew about the baby. But loving someone wasn't really enough. Both people had to *want* to be committed to each other.

Harper's words came back to her. *There's a reason you met . . . You could save each other . . .*

She thought of Luc, starting at the beginning of their relationship. It had only been a few months, but in that short time, she had felt more adored than she had ever thought possible. He had taken care of her and Elliott with such ease and seemed to be so genuinely happy to be with them. She could picture him laughing with Elliott and smiling at her with that look that made her feel like she was the only woman in the world. On top of all of that, he had proven that he would do whatever was necessary in order to protect not only her but Elliott as well. He had set aside his own happiness to make sure her little boy wouldn't get hurt. Surely that had to speak more for his character than his own insistence that he would never be what she needed. He *had* been exactly what she needed, time and time again. If love was proven through one's actions, he had certainly left no doubt that he was capable of real love. Maybe he could be a good father for the baby, even though he didn't want to settle down with her.

Megan stood and walked back into her house, knowing what she needed to do now. She would email him. He deserved to know that she was going to have their baby. He could decide from there on what he wanted to do about it.

TWENTY-SEVEN

Paris

Luc woke with the same empty feeling that had followed him everywhere he went for the past several weeks. He threw on some shorts and running shoes, then stepped onto the treadmill in his home office. He needed to clear his head before his meetings and running would be the best way.

As he started off at a light jog, his mind wandered to Megan and what she might be doing at that moment. It was his latest obsession and it was the most torturous one he had ever entertained. He would calculate the time in Boulder and then imagine what Megan was doing. Right now, it would be the middle of the night for her. Was she in bed with Ian right now? The image tore at his already shredded heart, causing him to pick up the pace to a full-out run, as though each powerful stride could carry him away from the pain of losing her.

Staring out the window in front of him, he took in the familiar sight of the Parisian skyline. Rain fell lightly over his city, the dark clouds looking as though they would be settling in for a long stay. They suited Luc's mood perfectly. He felt dark and empty and angry. He was angry at himself for not being more than he was, for not being capable of something as simple as love. He had had everything in the palm of his hand, and he had let it slip through his fingers because he had been too frightened to just admit the truth when he had his chance.

He glanced over to his desk, seeing the little green soldier crouched near his computer, aiming at him. Luc was overcome by a sudden pang of regret. Elliott. Luc thought of Elliott's questions the morning he had left. It was all so uncomplicated to a child. Luc was rich, he could live anywhere, so why not with them? Luc could see now that it could have been that simple, but it was too late now. Megan had moved on without him, and there was nothing he could or should do to try to win her back.

Luc heard a sound at the front door. It was Simone, letting herself in, a habit he wished he had not allowed her to get into in the first place. It definitely blurred the line for her of what she was to him. He continued to run, pretending he hadn't heard her. A moment later, she knocked on the open door of his office. He turned and gave her a little nod. He could feel her staring at him as he slowed the machine down to a stop and got off, mentally making note of the fact that he should wear a shirt on workdays.

"Here," she said, throwing a hand towel to him, her eyes shifting from his broad shoulders down to his abs. He caught it with one hand and began to mop his forehead.

"Thank you," he replied. "How are you?"

"Fine. What's wrong? You look like you've been brooding again." There was something about the way she said it that smacked of disgust. She knew he had come home from his last trip to the US upset.

"I'm fine," he replied curtly. "I'm going to have a quick shower, and then you can fill me in on today's agenda."

Simone was standing in the doorway, and he had to brush past her to exit the room. He avoided looking at her as he walked out. She plunked herself into his chair and turned on his computer, drumming her fingers on his desk restlessly as she waited for it to boot up. The image of his glistening, sculpted body, dressed only in shorts, filled her mind. He was just down the hall, naked at that very moment, showering. Simone ached to strip down, step into the shower with him and let her hands run over every magnificent inch of him. She could feel herself becoming wet with desire, which happened more often than she'd care to admit when it came to her boss.

She opened his email inbox, seeing that he had received a message from Megan. She listened for a second and could hear the shower still running. Opening the email, she could feel her heart in her throat, knowing this was both wrong and risky. She just had to know what Megan wanted to tell him.

Dear Luc,

I am writing because I have some news that will shock you, and I want to give you time to digest it before we speak. I have just discovered that I am carrying your child. I found out yesterday and am probably experiencing the same feelings that you will now that you know. I'm completely terrified.

I have wrestled with the idea of not allowing this life to grow inside me, knowing that things are over between us and that this will complicate both of our lives in ways we never wanted. I can't bring myself to end the pregnancy, however. I didn't realize until I found out about it that I very much want another child, a brother or sister for Elliott to love and who will love him and be his family when I'm gone.

*I know this will not be welcome news for you, and I want
to assure you that I don't expect anything from you. I don't
want your money. I will add your name to the birth certificate
only if you want me to. Otherwise, I will put Unknown. I am
raising one child alone; I can manage two just as well.*

*I think of you every day, of how you used to look at me like
I was the only woman in the world, of how tender you were,
how you were so good to us when we needed you. And I chased
you away, making you pay for Ian's mistakes. I have regretted
it every day since you left. I'm so sorry.*

*I won't contact you again after this email. If I don't hear
from you, I will know that you don't want to be a part of the
baby's life.*

Yours,
Megan

Simone quickly selected Mark Unread on the email and sat for a
moment, shocked at both what she had just done and what she had
read. Her fingers shook a little as she made a decision she knew
she needed to make if she was ever to have a chance with Luc. She
deleted the email, then opened his deleted items and cleared them
from his account. Her heart pounded in her chest as she looked up at
Luc as he swept through the room buttoning up the sleeve of his crisp
blue dress shirt. His hair was damp and he smelled clean and utterly
intoxicating to her as he stepped behind his desk.

"What are you working on?" Luc asked.

"Just clearing up some trash for you," she replied, smiling up at
him sweetly.

Boulder

Megan shut down her computer. It was late evening and she had been finishing up edits to some baby photos she had taken earlier in the week. She was unable to concentrate, staring at the adorable little child on the screen, so content in his father's arms. The sight of the two together tugged at her heart mercilessly. It had been twenty-four hours since she sent the email and she knew Luc would have seen it by now. It had taken her most of the previous day to draft the note—thinking about it, writing it, rewriting it over and over until she finally pressed Send.

He would have been getting up for work soon after she sent it. He should have contacted her by now. Unless he needed time to think. Every *ping* of her computer caused her heart to skip a beat; no matter how she tried, she couldn't stop thinking that maybe it was his answer. As the evening wore on, every car that drove past her house could have been him. He would have had time to get here by now, and if he *really* was in love with her and they really stood a chance, he would come to her.

Try as she might, she couldn't shake the fantasy from her head. She could picture him getting out of a cab in front of her house, rushing to the door with a bouquet of flowers in his hand to pledge his undying devotion to her. She stood at the living room window and sighed heavily. That was one fantasy that she could not afford to entertain. She was disgusted for allowing herself to daydream like that. Each passing minute she didn't hear from Luc meant it was less and less likely she would get the happy ending she hadn't really believed in in the first place.

She knew her email had said she wouldn't try to contact him, but she just had to know. Maybe he hadn't gotten the email? She decided to text him to figure it out. Megan picked up her phone and tried to think of what to write. She looked her text over several times before pressing Send, her heart thumping wildly in her chest.

Luc, it's me. I wanted to know if you've been thinking about us.

She waited a full five minutes, trying to leaf through a magazine, before allowing herself to look down at her phone again. When she did, she saw the message light flashing. She held her breath as she swiped the screen on her phone and read his message.

What's to think about? I'm afraid I have absolutely no interest in getting involved in that type of mess. Three is always a crowd and never fails to disappoint.

Megan gasped at his response. "What the fuck does that mean?!" she exclaimed to herself. "He has absolutely no interest in that type of mess?"

She paced around the living room furiously, working herself up into a full-on rage. "What happened to 'call me if you need anything ever, I will come'? That *fucking* liar!"

She furiously pounded on the screen of her phone.

What. The. Fuck. Is that what you're really made of, Luc? Here I thought you actually gave a shit about me, and it turns out you're just a coward who runs as soon as things aren't perfect.

*   *   *

Luc sat up in bed staring at his screen in disbelief. It was seven in the morning, and he had been woken up by the buzzing of his cellphone when Megan's first message had come through. He was tired from being out late at Cloud the night before and was in no mood for drama, especially from a woman who had moved on. Now she was accusing *him* of being the bad guy? And a coward, no less?

"She must be fucking crazy," he murmured to himself. "Why the fuck would I want to be in the middle of that?" He texted back without thinking.

I don't know what your problem is right now, but you should just move on with your life. You've decided what kind of family you want, and I don't want any part of that. What sane man would?

* * *

Megan actually growled when she read his last message. *How dare he? How fucking dare he treat me that way! He gets me pregnant and then asks me what* my *fucking problem is?*

She dialed his number four times, ready to let him have it, and then hung up four times. She knew calling him would be a mistake. She was a ball of fury right now and would only end up screaming at him.

Oh God, I wish I could have a glass of wine right now! I bet he's having a drink. He'll just go on drinking wine and port and Scotch with his perfectly ripped abs as I sit here unable to drink, getting fatter and fatter until I can't see my own fucking feet! That son of a bitch! Three's a crowd. Fuck him.

She stomped to the kitchen, opening the pantry cupboard and digging around until she found a bag of potato chips. "Perfect. Salt!" she exclaimed angrily.

Tearing the bag open, she shoved a handful of chips into her mouth, spilling crumbs onto her shirt as she chomped down furiously. As fast as she could, she crammed in another mouthful and another, until the bag was empty. Now she felt sick as well as angry. The chips had not calmed her the way she had hoped they would. Apparently they were not powerful enough to turn Luc into a decent human being. She stared down at her cellphone. He was still an asshole.

In a surge of hormones and desperation, Megan began to weep. She plunked herself into a chair and sobbed until snot ran down her face. Until that moment, Megan hadn't realized how attached she had become to her new dream of her and Luc making a family. In the past twenty-four hours she had let herself believe that everything was going to be alright. Luc would come back as soon as he knew about the baby, and they would get married and live happily ever after. Instead, he had decided that three was a crowd.

Paris

The next morning Simone sat alone in a café along the Seine, picking at her breakfast. It was her day off, and she had decided that getting some fresh air might make her feel better. She hadn't slept more than two hours the night before and had gotten out of bed with a horrible sense of dread. She had no appetite after having crossed a line that, until the day before, she had never considered herself capable of crossing. For some time she had pushed Luc's women out of her way, but never like this. It had always been the one-night-stand or the overly ambitious waitress who had set her sights on Luc's money. Simone had always considered it an act of love toward him. She was making Luc's life easier, less complicated.

But yesterday she had let her love for Luc deal a death blow to her sense of morality. She had done something so cruel she didn't know if she could live with herself. She had deleted Megan's email, knowing that Megan was not likely to attempt to contact Luc again, and that he might never know he had a child. As she sipped her coffee, she tried to tell herself that she was saving him. He had never wanted children. If Megan had been stupid enough to get herself pregnant then it was her own problem, and she didn't need to ruin Luc's life along with her own. Deciding there was nothing she could do about it at this point anyway, Simone pushed away her breakfast and left, leaving a small tip on the table.

Outside, it was a sunny and warm day. Her favourite time in Paris, late spring. The streets were crowded with tourists and cars rushing around, but she loved it. It normally made her feel alive to be part of the romance and the glamour that was Paris. She loved to see the look of awe the tourists wore. It always gave her a smug sense of satisfaction to know she had grown up in this beautiful city and knew all the secrets they would never know. But today was different. Her heart was heavy with the burden of betrayal. She had done something unforgivable. If Luc found out, it would be the end for them. He would hate her.

She walked along the Left Bank with her coat folded over her arm, barely noticing the heat of the sun on her body or the beautiful surroundings. Walking past a newspaper stand, she turned her head, and what she saw stopped her dead in her tracks: *Style* magazine.

"Oh shit."

She had completely forgotten Harper would find out Megan was having Luc's baby. It would be only a matter of time before Harper would come after Luc, and it wouldn't take him long to question whether Simone had deleted the email from Megan. He would remember how she had run Megan off when she was in Paris and would certainly start to suspect her. She somehow needed to make sure he would never know what she had done. She could deny it, but she would need to find a way to make her denial believable.

A smile spread across Simone's face as she continued to walk. She had the answer. She could delete a few other emails in the coming days. She would make sure none of them were vital, but they would all be messages their senders would follow up with him on. When Luc was questioned about them, she could blame it on their server. A glitch she could offer to take care of for him.

She hurried along now, her heart pounding. She had gone too far to go back now. She could never admit what she had done, but she could cover her tracks.

TWENTY-EIGHT

Boulder—Two Months Later

"You're getting married?! Oh, Mom, I'm so happy for you!" Megan hugged her mom tightly.

"You don't think I'm crazy? It's been only a few months since we started dating." Helen pulled away from her daughter's hug so she could see her face.

"I don't think that at all! I've known Charlie for a long time and I know you'll be really happy together. He's kind and funny and I know you'll take good care of each other." Megan gave her mom a wide smile.

"Oh, I'm so relieved. I thought you were going to give me a hard time about it," Helen replied, giving her daughter a kiss on the cheek.

"I'm the one who's relieved," Meg answered with a wry expression. "Now I'll have you off *my* hands."

Helen shook her head. "You little brat. And here I was just about to ask you to be my maid of honor."

"Really? Thanks, Mom!" Megan wrapped her arms around her mom again.

"I was going to, but now I'm thinking I should ask Charlie's daughter," Helen teased.

"Wow! It didn't take long for you to replace me with a new daughter." Megan laughed.

"It was only a matter of time, really. You're a bit of a pain in the butt," Helen replied. "Now, should we have the wedding before or after the baby is born? I was thinking before so you won't have so much on your plate."

Megan's eyes were wide and her mouth hung open.

"Of course I know. I knew when we were at the barbecue. I've been waiting for you to be ready to tell me about it, but you seem to be intent on keeping it a secret. Don't worry, I'm not going to lecture you about it or ask you any questions. You already know I'm here if you need to talk, so there's not really anything else for me to say."

Tears of relief sprung to Megan's eyes. She had felt very alone with her secret for weeks now. Helen wrapped her arms around her daughter and kissed the top of Megan's head as she cried onto Helen's shoulder.

"It's all going to work out, sweetie. I have a feeling that things will be okay. I'm going to sell my house and move in with Charlie, so we'll be right next door. Between all of us, we'll manage nicely."

Megan pulled back and nodded her head as her mom wiped the tears off her cheeks with her fingers.

"Thanks, Mom," she whispered.

"Thank you! When this year started I thought things would just stay how they were. Because of you, I'm getting married to a wonderful man, *and* I'm going to have another grandchild to spoil."

Paris

Luc sat at his desk at Cloud, rubbing his temples with the pads of his fingers as he stared down at a copy of the listing for his new house in Boulder. His head ached as much as his heart just looking at it. He hadn't been able to bring himself to call his realtor and admit that the house needed to go back up on the market. It had sat empty for weeks now waiting for an owner who would never come.

He knew he needed to get rid of the house but he hadn't been ready to face doing so yet. It would be the final nail in the coffin for his relationship with Megan, and the humiliation of calling the realtor was something he had been avoiding. The despair that had fallen over him the night he stood in front of Meg's house watching her with Ian still had a hold on him in spite of the time that had passed. Even after their angry exchange of texts, Luc still had feelings for Megan. She had been trying to reach out to him, and his pride and mistrust had turned her away. It didn't sound to him like Ian was still in the picture, but Luc could never feel confident that he wouldn't be back again. Not after what he had seen.

Today he realized he needed to get on with it. Once the house was sold he would finally be able to move on with his life. Texting the realtor, Luc told him they would have to meet in two days. He felt a need to go back in person to see the house one last time and take care of all of the paperwork in person. Somehow he felt that the trip would allow him time to grieve the end of his relationship with Megan, and hopefully that would put an end to this horrible yearning.

The house had sat on the market for several months before he bought it, and he knew it would be a long process to sell it now. There were few people who could pay over two million for a home these days. Luc hoped that by the time the house did have a new owner, the memory of Megan would be faint.

He looked up to see Simone standing in the doorway watching him. Her eyes glanced over the page. "What are you looking at?"

"A ridiculous lapse in judgement," he replied, putting the paper into the top drawer of his desk.

He looked back up at her, his face impassive. "I need you to cancel my appointments for the next few days and book me a flight to Boulder for tomorrow. There's something I need to take care of." Luc hadn't told Simone about the house, wanting Megan to be the first one to know. He could see her stiffen at his request.

"Boulder? I thought things were over between you and the American." There was fear in her eyes as she tried to steady her voice.

"They are. This isn't about her. Why does that concern you?"

She waved her hand nonchalantly. "It doesn't. It just seems like you came back from there in a bad temper. I'm thinking maybe I should take a vacation when you get back so I won't have to be on the receiving end of it."

Luc fixed her with a cold stare. "Just book the flights. I'll only be there for one night, and then I need to go to Aspen for two days, then New York for a week. If you choose to take a vacation when I get back, that's entirely up to you. You have time owed to you, and I will manage without your attitude quite nicely."

Simone turned on her heel and walked away without answering. Luc felt a pang of guilt at his response to her. He *had* been excessively harsh lately with everyone, especially her. His restlessness and anger were never far from the surface. Rubbing his face with one hand, he stood and went to find her.

She was standing outside on the balcony of the club, having a cigarette. Her arm was folded across her chest protectively and she avoided his gaze as he approached her.

"I'm sorry, Simone. I've been in a foul mood for the past few weeks, and it's not your fault. I'm going through something and have been taking it out on everyone around me." He lifted her chin slightly with his fingers as he spoke.

Simone's eyes were brimming with tears. She gave him a little nod but said nothing as he let his hand drop down to his side.

"I apologize. When I get this trip over with, I'll feel better. And even if I don't, I promise to be kinder to you."

"I hope so, Luc." She touched his arm with her hand as she spoke. "I'm here for you. I've always been here for you."

"I know you have. You're a good friend and an excellent assistant. I need to show you more appreciation." Luc's voice was tender now.

"I hope that I'm much more than just an assistant to you. I've been part of your life for over six years now and yet you've never let me in. I thought I would have earned your trust by now."

"You have, Simone. I tell you more than I tell anyone else."

"And yet you have a secret from me now. Something has been upsetting you for months, and you refuse to speak of it."

Luc leaned against the railing and folded his arms. "I haven't wanted to talk about it. I'm embarrassed to say that I've broken all my rules when it comes to women. I let myself get drawn in much deeper than I ever intended with Megan, and I've been having trouble getting over it. I need to go to Boulder to sell a house I bought."

Simone's mind was racing, but she managed to appear calm. She dropped her cigarette onto the floor, pivoting her red stiletto over it to extinguish it before speaking again. "You bought her a house? Is that the lapse of judgement you were referring to?"

Luc kept his eyes trained on the wall of the nightclub to avoid her gaze. "I bought it for myself with the intention of moving there. I thought it would convince her that I was serious about making things work with her. When I got to her house to tell her, I saw her with another man. I think it was her ex-husband, but I'm not sure. I left before I found out." He stared at a little scuff mark on his shoe, feeling thoroughly humiliated to admit this to anyone, least of all Simone.

Simone reached out for him, wrapped her arms around his waist and leaned her head against his chest. Although her heart ached to see him so unhappy, she was relieved to find out that he thought Megan had moved on already. She had been right to delete the email. Obviously Megan had never loved Luc if she could throw him over so quickly.

She tilted her head up to face him. "I'm so sorry she hurt you like that, Luc. You must have really loved her to consider leaving everything for her."

Luc held his arms at his sides, wishing Simone would let go of him but not wanting to hurt her feelings after how he had been acting. "I did. I have never felt that way about anyone before, never been so happy. It didn't even feel like it would be a sacrifice for me. It felt like it would be a privilege to give it all up so I could be with her. I was going to start a life with her and her son. When you love someone like that, you would do anything for them."

"I know, Luc. I know from experience." Simone's voice broke as she unwrapped her arms from his waist and placed her hands on his chest. "Love can make you do things you never thought yourself capable of, things that make it hard to look in the mirror. Love will force you to accept someone taking you for granted but refuses to let you give up."

Luc watched Simone's face as she spoke. He realized for the first time that she was in love with him. Suddenly it all became clear. He had thought she just didn't like other women in general, but she had been chasing them away from him all these years. He immediately felt caged by her hands on him, and something deep in his gut told him he needed to get away from her. He stood rigid as he stared at her.

"It's over now, Luc. If you want, I'll take care of selling the house for you. There's no need for you to think about it anymore." Simone took a step back, smiling lovingly at him.

"No." He shook his head. "Thank you for the offer, but it's something I must do for myself so that I can finally put this behind me."

"You go on your trip, Luc, and when you get back I want you to think about who has been here for you, always waiting for you to return, caring for you, expecting nothing from you but always hoping. Always hoping, Luc."

Simone turned and walked back into the club, hoping that she had given him something to think about.

* * *

Simone had just gotten out of the shower when she heard her buzzer ring. Looking at the clock, she realized it was after 10 p.m. Who could be wanting to come up at this late hour?

She threw on her bathrobe and rushed across her apartment. "Alright, I'm coming!" she snapped at the buzzer.

She hit the receiver button. "Yes?" Her voice did little to hide how annoyed she was by the interruption.

"It's Luc. I need to come up."

"Oh, Luc, of course. I just got out of the shower," she purred as she pushed the button to let him through the front door of her building.

Simone's heart pounded as she took the towel off her head and quickly combed out her jet-black hair. She covered her lips with gloss and applied some perfume. As she waited, she straightened her robe, making sure the front opened to reveal a little cleavage. Maybe her words had struck a chord with him and he had finally realized how perfect they were for each other. A light knock at the door caused her to draw a deep breath.

Simone swung the door open and leaned against it, giving him her best version of bedroom eyes. "Hey, boss, what brings you here at this late hour?"

Luc's brows were knit together as he rushed in past her. She closed the door behind him, her heart in her throat. He didn't look like a man who had romance on his mind. He looked like a man on a mission. And the thought of what his mission might be made her freeze with fear.

He didn't bother with greetings. "You said you've done things you never would have thought you were capable of. What did you mean?"

Simone's mouth gaped open for a second before she recovered. "I wasn't referring to anything specific . . . I just meant people in general."

"No, you said you knew from experience, you'd done things that make it hard for you to look in the mirror. I want to know what you've done, Simone." His tone was harsh and his dark eyes bored into hers. He could see fear, confirming his suspicions.

She shook her head, trying to move away from him. Luc caught her by the arms and held her in place. Simone tried to avoid looking at him but said nothing.

"What things, Simone?!" He was yelling now, gripping her arms tightly.

"Nothing! You're hurting me!" she cried.

Luc loosened his grip but didn't let go. His voice was dead calm and his jaw was set as he spoke. "Answer me."

Simone shook her head. "I haven't done anything but take care of you. I've gotten rid of so much trash for you over the years, you have no idea. Women who wanted nothing but your money, who would have hurt you. I follow behind you and clean up all your mistakes! And instead of thanking me, you come in here to hurt me and yell at me! How dare you!"

Remembering himself, he looked down at his hands, releasing her with a sense of shame. His desperation to be back with Megan had him completely out of control. "I'm sorry. I don't know what I'm doing. Please forgive me."

He turned and started for the door. As his hand turned the knob, the word *trash* popped into his head. He could picture her sitting at his desk smiling up at him. *Just clearing up some trash for you . . .*

He took a deep breath before slowly turning back to her. *Megan, she was talking about Megan.* His eyes were ice cold and his voice dead calm. "Tell me about the trash, Simone. What trash did you clear up for me on my computer that morning when I was in the shower?"

Simone opened her mouth, then clamped it shut, pursing her lips. Her eyes darted up to the ceiling, then down to the floor.

Luc's voice was quiet now. He was using every ounce of effort to restrain himself. "If you really love me, you'll tell me."

Simone could feel the breath leave her. Her shoulders slumped as she stared down at her feet to avoid his glare. It was over. He would hate her now forever, but she had to do what was right for once.

"I deleted an email from her." Her voice was tiny, almost inaudible.

Luc stood perfectly still, blinking slowly. "What did it say?"

"It said she was pregnant. She claims it is your child."

Luc felt his knees go weak for a second as he tried to digest what he had just heard. Pregnant. Megan was going to have his baby. And she had heard nothing from him for these past long weeks since she reached out to him. He stared at Simone, rage surging through him, his mind racing.

She crossed the room to her kitchen table. Her hands shook now as she tried repeatedly to light a cigarette. His silence was deafening. Simone couldn't bring herself to look at him, but she knew he was simmering with a violent anger, and it terrified her. She heard the door open and glanced up to see his back as he walked out the door. Collapsing onto a chair, she sobbed pitifully.

Luc peeled out of the spot he had parked his car in a few minutes earlier, driving with such speed it was as though he were trying to outrace his own mind. Megan had emailed to tell him he was about to be a father. And she would have thought he had ignored her all this time.

"*Merde!* The text!" Luc shouted as he slammed on the brakes and veered off to the side of the road. He quickly searched his phone, finding their conversation.

"Oh shit, shit, shit!" he groaned when he read his first response.

What's to think about? I'm afraid I have absolutely no interest in get-ting involved in that type of mess. Three is always a crowd and never fails to disappoint.

Leaning his head on the steering wheel, he let out a huge puff of air. "Fucking Simone!" he shouted as he sat up and slammed his hand into the wheel. He suddenly wished Simone were a man so he could justify going back over there to beat her senseless. He had never felt this level of rage at a woman before. She had tried to hide the fact that he was going to have a baby from him. She had tried to fuck up his entire life. He would never forgive her. Never.

He called the office manager of Cloud, Lisette. She picked up on the third ring.

"Lisette, it's Luc. I'm sorry to call you at home at this late hour. I have something of an emergency. Simone is no longer working with us, and I have to leave town for a situation overseas that requires my immediate attention. First thing tomorrow morning, I need you to have two of the bouncers go to Simone's to pick up the computer and any files she has at her apartment. I want you to go with them. You'll know what to look for. Get her keys back. She has keys to my apartment and all of the clubs. There will be a letter on my desk when you get to work in the morning informing her that she has been let go. Take that with you. She won't be surprised. She knows this is coming. Did you catch all of that? I know I went over it fast."

Lisette sounded positively thrilled when she answered. "I did. I caught every word, Luc. Let me know if there's anything else I can do for you."

"I will. Thank you."

TWENTY-NINE

Megan drove with her window down on her way to the photo shoot. It was a sunny, beautiful morning, and she glanced out at the mountains on her way to Timber Lane. Having just dropped Elliott off at school, she smiled to herself as she took in the sights of her hometown. Boulder was a beautiful place this time of year, nestled in the majesty of the Rocky Mountains under the Colorado sun.

She wore black dress pants with a pin holding them together at her expanding waistline. She was at that awkward stage where her real clothes were too small but she wasn't big enough for maternity clothes yet. She had covered her little fashion faux pas with a white button-up dress shirt, untucked. Until now, she had managed to keep her pregnancy a secret from everyone except her mom. Soon it would be visible to everyone and she would have to face the barrage of questions, other people's worries and disapproving looks.

For now, it felt good to have the chance to fall in love with this little person inside her, even though the circumstances were far less than ideal. A feeling of utter loss came over her whenever she thought of Luc. He wanted no part of her life or their baby's life either. She fluctuated between feeling angry on behalf of their child and relieved to know now what his true limitations were. It would be easier to start out this way rather than have an unwelcome surprise later on. She could grieve this, adjust to it and be over it before she had two mouths to feed.

As much as she wished that Luc had been able to rise up to be more than he thought he was, it wasn't going to happen. She would be on her own, like she had been for so long before, and she could handle it.

At night, she dreamed of Luc. In her dreams, he was kneeling in front of the bathtub, bathing a little baby and speaking in French while the baby cooed and smiled up at him. Megan would walk in and watch them for a moment and then leave the room to put Elliott to bed. Each time she returned, the baby was alone in the water, screaming for her, and Luc was gone. She would wake with a start each time and have trouble getting back to sleep.

In last night's dream, however, Luc had stayed and finished the bath. When she had finished getting Elliott to bed, she found Luc sitting in the tiny nursery, rocking the baby and giving her a bottle. He smiled up at her, his eyes full of that adoration she felt from him.

"You look so beautiful this evening, *mon ange*."

Megan had woken that morning with a feeling of contentment, although she wasn't entirely sure why, as she stretched her body across the mattress and sighed happily. Somehow she had a feeling of optimism as she got up, and that feeling was still with her now as she pulled up in front of a large house with a beautifully landscaped garden. She sighed appreciatively as she took in the sight of the house. It had that timeless log-cabin feel, with grey stone and stained wood accents.

She had gotten a call earlier that morning from a realtor named

Walter Harris, who wanted professional photos of the home taken as soon as possible. Walter had told her he was in a rush to get the photos done for his new client. The house had been on the market for some time without any luck, so Walter had just been hired to take over the listing.

Taking her camera out of its bag, Megan stepped away from her car and onto the grass to take a few shots of the exterior. Then the front door of the house opened and Megan's heart jumped into her throat. There in the doorway stood Luc.

"Hello, Megan." He smiled warily down at her from the covered porch.

Megan stood rooted to the ground, staring up at him. Her mouth hung open for a second before she turned away and hurried across the lawn to her car.

"Megan, please wait!" Luc called, running after her.

"Nope. No. You are *not* here," she called back as she quickened her step. She opened the car door and scrambled into the driver's seat, slamming the door behind her. Luc was standing beside the car. She glanced up at him quickly before starting the engine.

"No," she said firmly, as if her words would cause him to vanish. Throwing the car into reverse, she pulled out of the driveway and onto the road. She took the first curve fast as she sped away, trying to get as much distance from Luc as possible.

A couple of moments later she glanced in the rear-view mirror only to see him catching up in a black car.

"Shit!" she exclaimed. She heard her cell, lying on the passenger seat, begin to ring. Luc's name was across the screen. She pressed Ignore and kept driving.

Megan stopped at a red light and Luc pulled up next to her, motioning for her to pull over. Megan's heart raced at the sight of him. Hurt and fear clouded her thinking. Her only concern was that she needed to get away from him immediately. His horrible texts came into her mind. His face was panicked, angry even, as he pulled up next to her.

The light turned green and Megan took off, her tires squealing as she slammed her foot on the gas pedal. She took a right toward the freeway, weaving her way through traffic. She didn't know where she was going, but she felt an overwhelming need to get away from Luc. Did he really think they could just start over after what he had done? Just because there was a new child coming into the world didn't mean he would suddenly be father material. Those texts, followed by two months of dead silence, meant it was too little too late for them to make their relationship work.

Luc easily kept up with her, weaving around the cars that separated them now, growing increasingly irritated. She was going to get herself killed if she didn't calm down. He pursued her through two sets of yellow lights and out onto the freeway that led north toward the mountains. Stepping on the gas, he pulled up beside her, trying to get her to look over.

"Slow down!" he yelled, knowing she couldn't hear him. They were travelling over ninety miles per hour now.

Megan refused to look at him as she continued. She stared straight ahead in a stubborn show of will. As they neared a sharp curve in the road, her higher-level thinking kicked in, causing her to slow down. She pulled over onto a dirt road off the freeway and stopped, watching in the rear-view mirror as Luc rolled to a stop behind her.

"Asshole," she muttered to herself, getting out of her car.

Luc had his seat belt off and the car door open before he had even come to a full stop. He slammed the door as he stormed up to her, gesturing furiously.

"What the fuck is wrong with you, driving like that? You're going to get yourself killed!"

Megan puffed up her chest to meet rage with rage. "Isn't it obvious? I was *trying* to get away from you, you asshole!"

Luc folded his arms, regaining control of himself. He shouldn't be yelling at an angry pregnant woman. "Did you forget that I know where you live? Even if you could have outdriven me, I would know where to find you, you silly woman."

His words did nothing but fuel the flames of her anger. "Silly woman?" Megan shrieked. "Fuck you, you arrogant prick! Don't you think I realized that on my own?"

"Yes, I suppose that's why you stopped."

"Yeah, well, maybe!" Megan's tone was petulant.

His mouth twitched a little, dangerously close to expressing his amusement, but quickly recovering before he did anything to infuriate her more. He stared at her for a moment, seeing that something was different about her. Her cheeks were fuller, not as defined as they normally were, and she had a lovely glow, even though she was glaring at him. She had never looked more beautiful to him. It was all he could do to stop himself from wrapping his arms around her and raining kisses all over her. The thought of her driving erratically flashed into his mind again.

"You were driving far too fast. You scared me." His voice was much too reasonable for Megan's liking. What he hoped would come across as calm struck her as condescending.

"If you were so worried about it, why didn't you just stop chasing me?" Drawing a quick breath, she continued before he could get a word in. "And you know what? I don't care if I scared you! It's none of your fucking business. Now leave me alone!" She spun on her heel to go back to her car.

Luc grabbed her wrist with one hand, holding her in place. "Of course it's my business. You had my baby in the car with you."

"What do you care?" she spat out. "You made it really fucking clear that you don't want anything to do with us! Three's a crowd and never fails to disappoint, remember?!"

"Let me explain," he said quietly, as he let go of her wrist and held his palm up in resignation.

Her rage drained out of her body as she stared up into his eyes. Her voice grew quiet as disappointment took over, an all too familiar feeling for her. "I can't do this, Luc. You've proven that you don't want to have a family, and I've finally managed to accept it. Now go away. Just leave us alone so we can get on with our lives without you."

"No."

"No?"

"No. I will not. I didn't know about the baby until three days ago."

Megan said nothing but rolled her eyes in disbelief.

"Simone deleted your email. I had no idea."

"Oh, really? Then what was all that three's a crowd bullshit?" she shouted.

"I was talking about Ian!" He yelled so she would hear him. Then, taking a deep breath, he lowered his voice. "I saw you with Ian; at least, I assume it was him. I came to your house to try to start over but you were with him. I saw you kissing each other by the kitchen window."

"What? You saw us? Oh God! Nothing happened. He came for Elliott's birthday and we talked. He was apologizing and things got very emotional. I think he just kissed me to get me to stop crying. I can't believe you were there."

"Well, I was. I wanted to break down the door and kill him with my bare hands, but I just walked away. I thought you must have wanted to start over with him. Ian was the third person I was referring to. Not the baby. I would never be disappointed to find out you were having my baby."

"You wouldn't?"

He wrapped his arms around her. "Surprisingly enough, I'm fucking thrilled, actually. Since I left here, I have thought only of you and Elliott. I've missed you every day. I have been an absolute nightmare to be around. I just wanted to get back to you. If Simone hadn't interfered, I would have been here two months ago."

"That fucking harpy," Megan muttered under her breath.

"Yes, she is a fucking harpy. And now she's an unemployed one as well. As soon as she admitted she had deleted your email, I started making plans to get here. I would never have ignored you like that. You know that, right?"

Megan's voice broke. "Do I?"

"In your heart, you do. And I would never have written those horrible things about our baby. You know I am not so heartless, yes?"

Megan nodded.

Luc broke into a wide grin as a wave of relief rushed over him. She believed him. It was going to be okay. "I'm here now, Megan, and I want you to know that I'm not going anywhere."

He pulled her to him, hugging her tightly. He could feel her slightly protruding tummy against him and, for the first time, knew the thrill of an expectant father. It took a second for him to realize that her body was stiff. She was completely unresponsive. Pulling back, he looked down at her with concern. "What's wrong? Isn't this what you wanted?"

"No, Luc. If you want to be part of the baby's life, we can work it out, but you and I are over. We aren't in love with each other."

"What are you talking about? I bought a house. I'm moving here so I can be with you and Elliott and the baby. I can't imagine what else you would possibly need me to do to prove that I *want* to be here, because as far as I'm concerned, giving up my entire life should be enough."

Megan stared up at him, her eyes wide. The thought of him giving up his entire life for her was terrifying. If she let him do it, he would grow to resent her someday. Better to send him away now than to try to build something on the shaky foundation of bringing a child into the world, only to have their relationship fail in a few years. Marriage was hard enough if both people wanted it badly, if both people were madly in love. This would never work and she knew it deep down. If they were meant to be together, they would have found their way back to each other *before* they learned about the baby.

Taking a deep breath, Megan prepared herself to do the very last thing she wanted to do. She had to send him away. Her face was expressionless as she spoke. "I never asked you to give up anything, Luc. I never asked you to love me. I don't want your love and I don't want you. You're not in love with me. You're only here because of the baby. If I hadn't gotten pregnant, we would never have seen each other again."

"I'm here because I'm in love with *you*, Megan. I've been in love with you since you fell into my arms at the club, and every moment since. The baby is going to be a wonderful adventure for us, but I'm here for you." He reached his hands up to gently cradle her face. His voice was all but pleading, his eyes full of longing and love.

Megan stared into his dark eyes, wishing she could accept his love but knowing she couldn't. "It's a great offer, Luc. Really. You moving here, wanting to take care of us. A lot of women would jump at that in a heartbeat. But I can't. It would be wrong because I'm just not in love with you. I never have been. It was just sex for me. I'm sorry if you got the impression that it was more."

Luc shook his head as if to shut out her words; the pain on his face was visible, and his hands gripped her cheeks more tightly than he meant to. "No. No. Don't say that to me. That's a lie. You're just scared. I know you're in love with me."

Megan felt a tear streaming down her cheek and onto his finger. "I'm not. I'm sorry, Luc. You were just a warm body. I can't let you go on believing it was more than it was. We'll find some way for you to be part of the baby's life if you really want to, but you and I are never going to happen."

Reaching up, she pulled his hands off her face. This is what she had to do to protect herself, to protect Elliott and their baby from the trauma of Luc leaving them sometime in the future. It shattered her heart to turn away from him but somehow she willed her feet to move to the car.

Opening the car door, she paused for a second. "I'll email you the ultrasound pictures. We'll figure out the rest later. Goodbye, Luc."

With that she got into her car and made a U-turn back to the freeway.

Luc stood on the dusty road in shock, the pain she had just inflicted on him squeezing his heart with a viselike grip. He had been so sure it would work out this time. He would explain why it had taken him so long to get to Colorado, and she would rush into his arms. He had imagined it over and over in his mind during the last two days and nights. He had planned exactly what he would say and how he would say it. Once she heard him out she would know he had always loved her. They would vow to never let each other go again. He would pick her up and carry her inside to show her their new home. They would spend the afternoon making love and making plans, then go together to pick up Elliott and give him the news. Today they were supposed to become a family, and it would be every ridiculous fairy tale he had laughed at in his entire life.

He slowly walked back to his car, unsure of what to do next. How had his desperation for her become all-consuming? A life with her was everything he had never wanted, but now, as it was slipping through his fingers, he knew it was the only thing he had ever needed. Only Megan could still his restlessness and fill his very soul with all the love and contentment that had been missing in his life.

Her words raced through his mind. *I'm just not in love with you. I never have been. It was just sex for me . . . You were just a warm body.*

He drove slowly back to his new house, stopping on the way for some wine and a corkscrew. When he got to the house, he remembered he had no glasses. He had gotten Walter to convince the previous owners to leave a large sectional in the living room and some lounge chairs next to the pool in the yard. Luc's footsteps were heavy as he dragged himself across the main floor and out the back door. He uncorked the wine and tipped the bottle up, filling his mouth with huge gulps of the warm red liquid.

"Women," he said to himself, settling into a lounger. The day had grown hot and the world around him seemed still. Luc took in the view of the mountains, watching a hawk swoop in the distance. It was a beautiful place. This should have been a perfect day.

For the first time in his adult life, he had no plan. He had a baby coming into the world in a few short months. He was alone in Boulder, Colorado, and the woman he loved was across town insisting that she didn't love him.

Three hours later, Luc woke up, sweating and dizzy from the heat and the wine. He had been sleeping in the sun, in a black T-shirt and jeans, for hours. His stomach lurched as he stood up. Looking down at his arm, he noticed the redness before he felt it. He had the worst sunburn of his life. Making his way down to the master bedroom, his mouth fell open when he saw his reflection in the bathroom mirror. His face, neck and arms were already the colour of the inside of a ripe watermelon. He winced, thinking of how he was going to feel in a few hours.

"Of course," he said to the bright red man staring back at him.

THIRTY

Boulder—Four Days Later

"Elliott, can you get that? It's probably Grandma." Megan called from the kitchen. It was Elliott's first day of summer vacation, and she was getting a picnic ready for them to take down to the beach.

The doorbell rang again.

"Elliott! Where are you?" Megan called, wiping her hands on a dishtowel and walking briskly to the door. She swung it open and came face to face with Luc, who had a dark tan. Her eyes grew wide as she took in the sight of him.

"Luc? You've been tanning?"

"I may have fallen asleep in the sun. But I'm not here to talk to you. I'm here to talk to my baby."

Megan folded her arms across her chest. "What?"

"I've been doing some reading and found out that a baby will recognize her parents' voices when she is born *if* she hears them talking enough. So I am here to talk to the baby. You go on about your day. I won't disturb you."

Megan sighed heavily, ushering him out onto the front steps. She followed him and closed the door. "I don't want Elliott to know you're here. I haven't told him about the baby yet. I'm trying to figure out how to explain it."

"Oh. I see," Luc said. He paused for a moment. Her stare was ice cold as she looked up at him. "Okay. Well, I want you to call me as soon as Elliott knows, so I can come talk to my baby. Or maybe I can come after he's in bed, if that makes it easier for you."

Megan shook her head. "I know what you're trying to do. You think you can say all sorts of wonderfully romantic things and I'll change my mind, right?"

Luc pretended to be offended. "I would never do that. I know you've made up your mind. This is between me and my child. For now, I just want to tell her that I love her and that she doesn't need to be scared of love like her mom is. I'm not going anywhere, and I'm never going to turn into a drug addict, and I'll always be here for her. I'll have to go on business trips from time to time, but I'll always come back as quickly as I can because this is my home."

"Her?" she asked quietly.

"I'm hoping it's a girl. Then we'll have one of each." He gave her a sincere look.

Megan fought back tears but said nothing. It took every ounce of willpower for her not to wrap her arms around his neck and kiss him.

Luc stared at her. "I'm going to go now, but I'll be back. I'll come every day, again and again, until the baby knows she can trust me completely."

He turned and jogged down the steps, then turned back to her. "You look absolutely beautiful, by the way. Just fucking gorgeous."

Megan could feel herself melt as she watched him get into his car and take off. He was driving a Mercedes SUV now, which meant he must have gone car shopping in the past few days and, in true Luc style, picked something sleek and luxurious but also practical.

The next day, Megan found herself working in Charlie's garage alongside him, her mom and Elliott. They were preparing for Helen to move in and needed to clear out a lot of clutter.

"Maybe the easiest thing to do would be to start with all this recycling?" Megan wore a doubtful expression as she surveyed the mess. It was worse than her basement.

Charlie gave her a little nod. "Good thinking. Elliott, help me carry this stuff out to my truck. We can go hit the recycling depot and maybe grab an ice cream on the way back."

"Oh no, you don't," Helen called to him with a big grin. "You are not going to hightail it out of here and leave us to clean up this disaster."

Charlie just smiled. "She's on to me, hey, Elliott?"

"Yup."

The two started moving bundles of newspapers, old envelopes and other papers that were stacked in the corner. After the pile had been cleared, Megan noticed a paper poking out from under an empty gas can. She crouched down and picked it up.

"You missed this . . ." she started to say before looking at it more closely. It was a neatly folded paper with Luc's handwriting on the back.

My life is meaningless without you. I will be right here waiting for us to start over. L

Her hand started to shake as she unfolded the paper. It was the real estate listing for his house. It showed SOLD across the photo of the front of the house.

"Charlie, how did this get here?" she asked, feeling panic.

Charlie walked over to her. "What's that, Megan?" He peered at it for a second. "Oh yeah, this is that paper that was in those roses I gave you, Helen. Remember how you wouldn't believe that I found them in my garbage can? Ha! Here's proof."

Megan let out a sob. "Oh shit!" she muttered, tears springing to her eyes. He had bought the house months ago. Before either of them knew about the baby. He really *was* in love with her.

"What's wrong, dear?" Helen looked over at her daughter with concern.

"Nothing." She smiled through her tears. "For the first time in years, everything is going to be fine." Megan swiped her hand across both cheeks. "I have to go for a bit. There's something I have to do. Okay? Elliott, stay here with Grandma and Charlie."

"Can I come, Mom?"

"No, baby, you go get ice cream with Charlie and Grandma. I'll be back soon."

She rushed down the driveway and into her house to get her car keys.

*　*　*

Luc sat on an Adirondack chair under an umbrella in his back-yard. He was reading a book for expectant parents. Beside him on a table was a copy of *Home Maintenance for Dummies*. He didn't hear Megan's car pull up. He didn't hear the click of the latch on the gate. He didn't hear the doorbell from where he sat. He did hear Megan call his name.

"Luc." It was the sweetest sound he'd ever heard and it made his pulse race, just like it did every time.

He turned to see her standing across the patio. Her hair was messy and she wore dusty-looking jean shorts and a grey T-shirt that was a bit snug around her growing belly. She looked lovely to him as he stood up and watched her rush toward him, her flip-flops slapping against the lawn. She stopped in front of him with a paper in her hand. He recognized it immediately.

"Why didn't you tell me you bought this house months ago?" she said, her voice shaking.

"Because you kept insisting that you didn't love me. I have my pride, you know."

Megan grinned and started to tear up. "Sorry. These fucking hormones make me cry at everything. Last night I wept for an hour over a Dairy Queen ad."

Luc smiled down sympathetically, "I know. I read about it in the book." He wiped her tears away with his thumbs.

Megan reached up and wrapped her fingers around his wrists, keeping them in place on her cheeks. "Oh, Luc, I'm so sorry I said those horrible things to you. None of them were true. I was just *so* scared that if we tried to build something together *because* of the baby, it would never work out. I was scared that if you gave up everything for us, you would start to resent us and then you'd leave. I couldn't go through that again.

"And now I can finally see the truth, that if I don't give us a chance, I'm just going to ruin all of our lives: mine, yours and the kids'. I'm going to end up teaching them both to never allow themselves to love anyone. And that would be a horrible, terrible thing to do, because loving someone is the best part of life. So, I'm finally ready to take a leap of faith and tell you the truth. I fell in love with you when we were on top of the Eiffel Tower watching the sunset. You had your arms wrapped around me and I wanted to kiss you so bad, but I wouldn't let myself. And I knew right then that I loved you, but I've been too stubborn and scared to admit it, even to myself. I love you. I am so completely and sickeningly in love with you, Luc Chevalier, that it frightens me when I think about it. I need you, Luc. Even if there were no baby, I would need you and . . . and I hope you believe me. Everything I said the other day was a huge lie and I'm—"

A devilish grin spread across his face as he kissed her hard on the mouth to get her to stop talking. "I know. I knew you were lying. The book says that pregnant women tend to lie as much as drunk women."

Relief swept over Megan, causing her to laugh out loud at his joke. She reached up, wrapping her arms around his neck, kissing him back. "God, you're arrogant."

"You love that about me." He smirked as he pulled her close and rested his forehead against hers.

"Yes, I actually do. There must be something seriously wrong with me. This is the one and only time you will hear me admit to it, but there is something about your cocky attitude that just turns me on. I will go to my grave denying it."

"I don't care. I'll always know it's true." He kissed her tenderly on the lips. "So, can we finally start our life together?"

"If you still want me after everything I've put you through."

"I do, because I am sickeningly and completely in love with you too. There must be something seriously wrong with me as well." Luc smiled, kissing her on the lips.

Tears welled up in Megan's eyes again. "Then we must be meant for each other."

"We are. You know, it's just like I've always said—everyone finds their happily-ever-after," Luc replied.

Megan pursed her lips. "You have never said that in your life."

Luc gave her confused look. "You must have mistaken me for someone else. I've always believed in true love."

Megan shook her head. "Shut up and kiss me again."

"Yes, Bossy Boots."

They held each other for a long time, their mouths moving in perfect unison, their hands exploring each other again. Their embrace embodied the pure and infinite love they had for each other. It was full of tender passion and honesty. Luc ran his hand ever so gently across her tummy, feeling the firm and warm home his baby was growing in. A surge of unbridled happiness moved through his body at the thought. They were going to be a family. The four of them. And he had never felt so content or at peace with anything in his life. As he looked into Megan's eyes, he knew that his life of restlessness and loneliness was forever over. Everything he needed was right here, just like Harper had told him it was. In Boulder.

He picked her up and carried her across the lawn and up the steps to the back door of the house. Opening the door with one hand, he kissed her hard on the mouth.

"Welcome home, Megan."

Announcing the "I Want More Luc" Giveaway

Need more Luc?

Here's your chance . . .

I have put together a booklet including 3 Steamy Scenes that didn't end up in the novel. They are hot, and coming from me, that's saying something. ;) Anyone who posts an honest review of the book will get a copy of the booklet – for free, of course!

Here's how to get it:

1) Post a review on the online store where you purchased *Breaking Love* and/or Goodreads.

2) Go to http://tinyurl.com/mjsummersreview to redeem your booklet!

Happy Reading Everyone!!!

MJ

COMING APRIL 2015 . . .

Breaking Clear

Book 3 of the Full Hearts Series
Clever. Steamy. Inspiring.

Harper Young is a talented, feisty art director at *Style* magazine. Sitting at her desk one Tuesday morning, she answers a call that will forever change her life. Her father has had an accident and needs Harper to leave Manhattan and come home to Boulder, Colorado, to care for him. Given an ultimatum by her heartless boss, Harper chooses family, leaving her career behind. She drives across the country to find that the only man who has ever made her heart ache with desire will be her new neighbour.

Evan Donovan is a contractor who's been dealt a rough hand when it comes to love. His wife, Lisa, left him just as the recession forced him to shut down his contracting company. Now after three years of rebuilding, he is finally getting back on his feet again. When Harper drops back into his life, he does his best to keep things on a 'just friends' level. Her older brother, Evan's best friend, won't take kindly to Evan dating Harper.

Proving that old flames are easily relit, Harper and Evan quickly find themselves in each other's arms. But will Harper's career call her back to New York when her father has recovered? Will a man whose heart has been snapped in pieces learn to trust again?

Lose yourself in Harper and Evan's romantic journey as they fight for their forever.